The Boy in the Woods

Katherine A. Ganzel

The Boy in the Woods

Copyright © 2018 Katherine A. Ganzel

Cover Design: Artemis Jang

Edited by: Monica Kuebler

ISBN: 978-0-692-19570-3

All rights reserved.

This book or any portion thereof may not be reproduced or used in any manner whatsoever without the express written permission of the publisher except for the use of brief quotations in a book review.

This is a work of fiction. Names, characters, businesses, places, events and incidents are either the products of the author's imagination or used in a fictitious manner. Any resemblance to actual persons, living or dead, or actual events is purely coincidental.

The Boy in the Woods

To all of you who supported me during the process of writing this book, I thank you from the bottom of my heart.

The Boy in the Woods

Chapter One
Earth Angel

May 1958

"SIT UP STRAIGHT, Jessica! For goodness' sake, this is the Russian Tea Room."

Jess straightened her back, but she didn't take her eyes off her Shirley Temple.

"You're not a child anymore," her uncle continued, his words sharp. "You're thirteen years old and I expect you to act your age."

"Yes, Uncle Jonathon." She lifted the deep red drink to take a sip so she wasn't expected to say more. It was too sweet, tasting like cough syrup, but she still swallowed it down.

She hadn't wanted it. She'd ordered a Coca Cola, but Uncle Jonathon had spoken up, instructing the waiter to bring her a Shirley Temple instead. Arriving with a paper parasol speared through two maraschino cherries, it was an over-the-top drink, matching the over-the-top, ornate red-and-gold restaurant where they were eating lunch.

The waiter appeared at Uncle Jonathon's left and set

another martini in front of him with a trembling hand. Jess gave him a sympathetic smile, but he had his head down as he bowed and stepped back.

Her uncle's eyes flashed. "Excuse me!"

"Yes, sir?" The waiter stepped forward, bowing his head lower.

"Did you repeat my instructions to the bartender before he made this?"

The waiter bobbed his head. "Yes, sir. I did."

"Very well." Uncle Jonathon waved his hand to dismiss him.

The waiter made a final bow and escaped. Jess watched him, wishing she could leave too.

The crunching sound of Uncle Jonathon chewing the pearl onion from his first martini got her attention. He was handsome for an older man, with his tall, lean frame and his impeccably tailored dark brown suit. A maroon silk tie with its centered dimple stood out against his starched white shirt. His hair was the same shade of brown as hers, but graying at the temples and combed in place with hair cream that made it gleam. He sat ramrod straight, his bearing exuding power and wealth. Over the last week, it had shocked Jess to see how he treated people, making a point of letting them know he thought they were beneath him.

Jess's dad, Uncle Jonathon's younger brother, had been just as wealthy. Their family owned a profitable hundred-year-old iron ore mining business. But unlike her uncle, he'd never shown off his wealth or behaved as if he was better than anyone else.

Her dad had worn suits for his job on Wall Street, but as soon as he came home he'd changed into comfortable clothes. When they ate out, instead of eating in fancy establishments, her parents preferred homey diners or family-run restaurants, places where the owners greeted them by name and told jokes on the way to the table. This was the first time Jess had ever been in the Russian Tea Room even though she'd lived in Manhattan her whole life. *But then, everything is different now*, she thought with a sigh.

"Don't sigh, Jessica," her uncle said through his teeth. "It's unladylike, and *straighten* your spine."

"Yes, Uncle Jonathon." She lifted her Shirley Temple for another sip.

The waiter appeared with their lunches, setting down the baked sea bass Uncle Jonathon had ordered for her. In front of her uncle, he placed a steak so rare it was resting in a pool of its own blood. Uncle Jonathon made a show of inspecting their meals to make sure they were prepared to his exact specifications. Jess squirmed in her seat while her uncle belittled the poor man, the stiff petticoats under her mint green dress scratching her bare legs.

"We have an hour before we're due at the lawyer's," Uncle Jonathon said, after the waiter left. "I would rather you not have to attend, but he insisted on your presence. I don't know how he thinks you'll understand what's being discussed. I'm sure it will all be over your head. As soon as we're finished, we'll go back to the apartment to pick up our luggage. The train doesn't leave until eight p.m., so we'll have time for dinner. Are you listening to me?"

She automatically straightened again. "Yes."

"Yes, *sir*?" he said, raising an eyebrow.

"Yes, sir," she repeated. Uncle Jonathon had the same brown eyes as her dad, but instead of the warmth she'd always been used to, they were hard and disapproving.

He looked around the crowded room and sneered. "We'll be home by tomorrow afternoon, thank God."

Not my home, she thought.

"How my brother could stand all this, I'll never know." He waved his hand in a vague way at the other diners. "There are far too many people in this city, crowded together like rats in a cage, too many cars, too much noise. Our home is in the country. Fresh air, green grass, lots of trees, life is slower, more peaceful." He sawed into his steak. "You'll like living there much better, Jessica."

"Yes, sir." The ache in her chest became sharper at the thought of leaving.

By 'our,' he meant him and his son, Douglas. Jess had never met her cousin, but he was two years older than her. Uncle Jonathon's wife had died giving birth to Douglas's little brother, and the baby had died too. Jess knew how sad Douglas must have been to lose his mom and brother at such a young age.

As soon as they'd finished their meal, Uncle Jonathon snapped his fingers to signal the waiter. While he chastised him for not having the bill ready, Jess kept her eyes on her plate, not wanting to witness the man's embarrassment. Once the bill was paid, she followed her uncle to the coat-check, glad to be leaving.

Uncle Jonathon was all smiles when he handed the pretty brunette their ticket. She returned with their coats and his fedora, and he showered her with compliments while she giggled. When she saw the large bill he held out to her as a tip, her eyes grew wide. She tried to take it, but he didn't let go, leaning in close to whisper something in her ear. She giggled more, her face turning a deep crimson, and he released the money with a wink.

Jess turned her back to them, yanking on her white cotton gloves. How could anyone be so easily fooled by her uncle? Then she was tugged from behind as he put on her coat. She knew he was only doing it because the coat-check girl was watching.

They stepped out into the cool May air and a door man in a long red coat and black top hat hailed them a taxi. He opened the door and stood at attention while Jess climbed in. Once seated, she faced the window so she wouldn't have to look at her uncle. As the taxi wound its way through the congested New York City streets, she listened to the honking horns and occasional sirens.

In a few hours, she'd be leaving her city forever, but she didn't *want* to go. She didn't want to see the lawyer. She just wanted to go home to her family's apartment and find everything the way it used to be.

The law firm was located in one of the city's many skyscrapers. An older woman in a dark blue dress and cat-eye glasses sat behind a reception desk. She greeted her uncle by name as they stepped off the elevator. After taking their coats. she led them down a long hallway. Jess heard typewriters as they passed open office doors but she kept her eyes on the floor, despair rising with each step.

The woman walked through a door and announced, "Mr. and Miss Blackwell are here to see Mr. Levin."

A young woman in a pale pink shirt and black pencil skirt stopped typing and stood to greet them. She opened yet another door, saying, "Mr. Levin," and then stepped aside so they could enter.

The corner office was large and impressive in a city where real estate was at a premium. Windows on two walls filled the room with weak light from the overcast sky. A short, balding man much older than Uncle Jonathon walked around an enormous desk, welcoming her uncle. After they shook hands, he turned his attention to Jess and his expression became somber.

She lowered her eyes, dreading what was coming.

He took her hand in both of his and held it rather than shaking it. The heat from his hands seeped through her glove. It felt oppressive. "I'm very sorry for the loss of your parents, Jessica."

"Thank you," she mumbled, and pulled her hand to let him know she wanted it back.

"We're all sorry about the accident."

The pain in her chest was making it difficult to breathe, and she needed him to stop.

"It's times like these that make us consider how fragile life is."

"Excuse me," she said louder than she'd intended, and wrenched her hand free. "Where's the powder room?"

He eyed her with worry. "I'll, uh, have my girl show you." He opened the office door and stuck his head out. "Edith, will you show Miss Blackwell to the powder room?"

"Yes, sir." The secretary rose from her chair. "Come along, dear."

She put her hand on Jess's back to guide her. Jess resisted the urge to shrug it off. Thankfully, the bathroom wasn't far.

Once she'd closed the door and locked it, she took several deep breaths while gathering toilet paper from the roll near the single toilet. She pressed the wad so hard against her eyes, she saw stars. "I will not cry, I will not cry, I will *not* cry," she whispered over and over. She didn't dare. If she started crying, she'd never be able to stop.

After a few minutes, the worst of the pain had passed, and she checked herself in the mirror. To her dismay, her face was pale, making the freckles across her nose stand out more than they usually did. Even worse, her brown eyes were red-rimmed as if she had been crying. She considered washing her face, but dismissed the idea. It wouldn't help her look any better. She patted her short brown hair in place to prolong the time before she had to face the lawyer, feeling helpless. She was trapped in a nightmare with no one to save her.

When the secretary saw her enter the office, she stood. "Are you alright, dear?"

Jess kept her eyes lowered so the secretary wouldn't see how red they were. "Yes, ma'am."

In the lawyer's office, the men sat on either side of the desk, shrouded in a cloud of cigar smoke and holding tumblers of brown liquor. They rose as Jess entered and she slid into a large leather chair next to Uncle Jonathon without looking at either of them.

"Are you ready, Jessica?" Mr. Levin said.

"Yes, sir." She ran her gloved hands over her cotton skirt, concentrating on smoothing it out.

"I'm going to read your father's will now."

"Yes, sir." She clasped her hands on her lap.

He picked up a stack of papers and adjusted his reading glasses.

Taking in a slow, deep breath, she held it while squeezing her fingers so tightly they hurt.

"I, William Joseph Blackwell, residing at 533 East 11th Street, New York City, New York, being of sound mind, declare this to be my last will and testament."

As Mr. Levin's voice droned on, Jess let out the air in her lungs. He was no longer speaking her dad's name or the address of her home, but legal words that had little meaning and held no pain. A pigeon sat on the ledge of one of the windows, grooming itself. She watched it while his voice receded further into the background.

"Jessica!" Uncle Jonathon's brown eyes had that hard, disapproving look again.

"Yes?"

"Did you understand what Mr. Levin said?"

"Yes, sir. I did."

"Then why didn't you answer him?" he said, his voice rising.

"I'm sorry, Mr. Levin. I understood what you said."

"And the trust? It's clear to you how it will work?" Mr. Levin said.

"Yes, sir. Very clear."

"I think that settles it." Mr. Levin and Uncle Jonathon stood. "I'll have my girl prepare the paperwork and mail it to your lawyer."

Uncle Jonathon shook his hand. "Very good."

Mr. Levin walked around the desk and took Jess's hand again, repeating his condolences while she muttered a 'thank you.'

When they stepped out onto the pavement, Jess filled her lungs with the crisp spring air, grateful this part was over.

It was a silent ride to her apartment building and up the elevator. The whole time Jess kept her mind blank, trying not to think about how she was leaving soon. But when they walked into her apartment's small living room, it was no longer possible to pretend, and a lump formed in her throat.

The furniture was still in place, but the knickknacks, books, and framed photographs were packed into the cardboard box that sat taped shut on the coffee table. The hanging pictures that had been taken off the walls were leaned against the couch.

Cora stepped out of the kitchen in her gray uniform. She was a welcome sight, and Jess fought the urge to run into her arms. Cora hadn't been cleaning or cooking like she normally would, but had been busy packing up the last of her family's belongings.

"Good afternoon, Mr. Blackwell, Miss Jessie," she said. She approached to take their coats.

Uncle Jonathon waved her off. "We'll be leaving soon."

"Yes, sir, Mr. Blackwell." Cora kept her tone formal.

"I'll be making a few phone calls in the master bedroom and I do *not* want to be disturbed."

"Yes, sir," she said as he brushed past her.

Jess ground her teeth as she watched his rigid back disappear down the hallway. It was one thing to see him order around strangers, but the way he'd treated Cora over the last week had disgusted her. Cora *wasn't* a servant. She'd been with the family for as long as Jess could remember and helped raise her. Warm and caring, Cora had been a constant presence in Jess's life. Now it felt like she was the only family Jess had left.

The bedroom door closed, and Cora turned to Jess with a look of deep concern. "How are you doing, Jessie?"

Tears pricked Jess's eyes. Her throat had closed, making it impossible to speak, so she shrugged.

Cora opened her arms. "Come here, baby."

Jess buried her face in Cora's uniform, sobbing while Cora rubbed her back and shushed her. When Jess had cried the last of her tears, Cora ran her soft brown hands over Jess's face to wipe them away. "I've got a special surprise for you," she said with a smile, but she was fighting back her own tears.

She took Jess's hand and led her into the kitchen. Jess took a seat at the kitchen table where a pile of newspapers lay. An open cardboard box was on top of the stove, the sight tearing open the wound in Jess's heart. Cora placed a small plate of iced lemon cookies and a tall glass of milk in front of her. Jess wasn't hungry, but she ate the cookies, savoring them. It would be the last time she'd get to taste Cora's cooking.

While she wrapped plates in newspaper and packed them in the cardboard box, Cora talked about her family. Her twin grandsons were graduating high school in a few months and had been accepted to the same school in the South. They were the first of Cora's grandchildren to attend college and she was filled with pride. Jess was happy for her. Helping them prepare for the move would keep her busy so she wouldn't be too lonely after Jess left.

Uncle Jonathon appeared in the doorway. He pressed his lips together, looking between them, and Cora quieted. "How much packing is left?" he asked.

"This is the last room, sir."

"I've arranged for the movers to be here at eight a.m. sharp tomorrow. You'll need to be here to let them in. Once my brother's things arrive safely, I'll mail your last paycheck."

"Yes, sir, Mr. Blackwell," she said, tightness in her words.

Why does he have to be so mean to her? Jess wondered, anger flaring inside her again. Cora wouldn't steal their things.

"It's time to leave, Jessica. Get your suitcase."

"Yes, sir." She kept her eyes on Cora as she got off the chair. Sorrow was etched on Cora's face.

Walking down the short hallway, she tried to not let her grief overwhelm her. But when she entered her small bedroom, she had to choke back a sob.

Cora had been busy since Jess and Uncle Jonathon had left for lunch. The mattress of her single bed was stripped of bedding and the brown leather suitcase Cora had packed for her was laying on it. Her dresser no longer held her collection of porcelain animals and figurines and the pale blue walls were empty, except for the outlines where pictures of ballerinas had hung. The stack of cardboard boxes in the empty closet contained the contents of her room.

She approached the window and looked at the brick wall of the building next door. It was the only thing in her life that hadn't changed.

"Jessica!" Her uncle's voice boomed in the small space, making her jump. "What's taking so long?"

"Nothing." She reached for the suitcase handle and dragged it off the bed.

He took in the bedroom, shaking his head before stepping out. During the week he'd been with her, he'd commented often that their two bedroom Manhattan apartment was too small, as if her parents hadn't provided her with a good home. But how much room did a family of three need?

She pulled on her coat by the door, managing to keep the tears back. Even though her uncle watched with narrowed eyes, Cora dared to give her a hug goodbye.

"You be a good girl, Jessie," Cora whispered, as she folded her arms around her. "Make your momma and daddy proud of you."

Jess buried her face in her uniform, taking in the sweet scent of her Shalimar perfume.

"Maybe you'll write to your old Cora once in a while." She'd tried to keep her tone light. "Let me know how you're doing."

"I will, Cora. I promise," Jess choked out.

Cora lifted her chin and kissed her forehead. "And I promise I'll write back, baby," she said, her voice rough as tears appeared in her eyes.

Her uncle opened the door. "It's time to leave."

Cora glared at him as she wiped her eyes.

Jess reluctantly turned and walked out of her home for the last time, feeling like her heart was being ripped out.

Chapter Two
On the Street Where You Live

"JESSICA, WAKE UP."

A firm hand shook Jess's shoulder, bringing her out of a sound sleep. She opened her eyes to find Uncle Jonathon standing over her. Their train had stopped outside a one-story brick station where people waited on the platform under an overcast sky. Beyond them, an empty two-lane road ran alongside a thick forest. It was a marked difference from the crowded Grand Central Station where they'd boarded the train in New York City the day before.

"Gather your things, and mind you don't forget anything," Uncle Jonathon said.

"Yes, sir." She covered her mouth, unable to suppress a yawn. Fortunately, he was too busy buttoning his coat to notice.

As Uncle Jonathon retrieved his suitcase from the overhead net, Jess hurried to pull on her white gloves and coat before wrestling her own suitcase down. He put on his fedora and left the compartment. Jess followed, carrying her suitcase with both hands.

The Boy in the Woods

A porter came forward to take their luggage. Uncle Jonathon handed his over without a word, but when the porter took Jess's, she thanked him and he gave her a kind smile.

"James," her uncle barked as he climbed off the train.

A stocky man with thinning hair and a black uniform approached and then passed them on his way to the porter. He handed the porter a dollar bill, and took their suitcases. Uncomfortable she wasn't introduced, Jess glanced over her shoulder at the man, but he kept his eyes on the pavement as he trudged behind them to a large black car parked at the curb. Her uncle waited while James set their suitcases on the pavement and opened the rear door for them. Jess hesitated, thinking her uncle would want to do introductions.

"Get *in*," Uncle Jonathon said through gritted teeth, and she rushed to climb inside. "We'll go home," he said to the driver. "But I'll be leaving for the office soon after."

"Yes, sir." James shut the door.

There was a stack of mail on the seat between them. Uncle Jonathon sorted through it while James started the car. They encountered little traffic on the two-lane road, and as they passed patches of woods separated by farms with black-and-white cows, Jess swallowed against the lump in her throat.

This was as far from Manhattan as she could be, but whether or not she liked it, this was her home now. She had a new family: Uncle Jonathon and his son, Douglas. Thinking of her cousin, her spirits lifted. She'd always wished she had a brother or sister. Perhaps he'd felt the same, especially since he'd lost his baby brother. With Uncle Jonathon for a father, his life couldn't have been easy. Surely he would appreciate having her in the family. No longer noticing the passing countryside, she imagined being welcomed by her cousin.

They turned off the two-lane highway onto a deserted dirt road. A high iron fence topped with spikes ran alongside it, enclosing dense pine trees. After a few minutes, they pulled into a short drive and stopped in front of a wrought iron gate, ornamented with bronze ivy and padlocked with a heavy chain. James got out of the car and pulled a bundle of keys from his pocket.

Once the gate was open, he drove through and then stopped the car again. Jess was surprised when he got out and turned to watch him go back and lock the gate. She wondered if Uncle Jonathon would say anything, but he was absorbed with his mail. She wanted to ask him why he lived behind a locked gate, then thought better of it. In the week she'd spent with him, she'd learned he didn't like being questioned.

Continuing down a winding lane, they were soon enveloped by the forest, and a sense of foreboding came over Jess. She'd never been this deep in the country before, and peering into the dark foliage, she worried what wild animals lurked out of sight. What if they'd been trapped behind the locked iron gate for a long time and were hungry?

The car emerged from the forest and an expansive yard stretched out ahead of them. Dotted with several large oak trees and ringed by woods, it was much bigger than her neighborhood park back in Manhattan. James parked next to a barn-like two-story garage across from an enormous house. Jess leaned close to her window to get a better look. The house had a hipped roof topped with a cupola. A covered porch held up by pairs of Greek pillars sheltered the double-wide front door. Despite all the carved details, Jess thought it looked creepy, the kind of gloomy mansion that would be in a horror movie.

After James opened the rear door, she climbed out of the car and walked behind Uncle Jonathon as he strode up the walkway. The front door swung open and when she stepped inside, her stomach sank. The woman who'd opened it wasn't tall, but she was still intimidating in a black maid's uniform that buttoned up to her neck and hung on her thin body. Her dark hair, threaded with wisps of gray, was pulled back in a tight bun at the nape of her neck. Fine lines framed her hazel eyes, and dark eyebrows stood out against her pale skin. She was the exact opposite of Cora.

She studied Jess, then dropped her eyes. "Welcome home, Mr. Blackwell, Miss Blackwell," she said as James set their suitcases in the hallway.

"Where's Douglas?" Uncle Jonathon said. "I instructed him to be here."

Hearing her cousin's name, Jess glanced around for him. The hallway had doorways leading to other rooms, and along the left side was an elaborate carved staircase that led to the second floor, but there was no sign of him.

The maid took Uncle Jonathon's coat and fedora. "He's in his bedroom. Would you like me to get him?"

"Yes, and make coffee. I'll have a cup before I leave for the office."

"Yes, sir."

She gazed at Jess, and Jess waited for her uncle to introduce them, but after a moment of silence, she realized the maid was waiting for her coat. She slipped it off before Uncle Jonathon became impatient with her. As soon as she handed it over, the woman turned to the open coat closet.

"Come, Jessica." Uncle Jonathon went through the nearest doorway.

The room they entered was long, with two large fireplaces spaced far apart. Woven Oriental rugs anchored a pair of seating areas comprised of antique chairs, couches, and delicate tables. Detailed plasterwork rimmed the high ceiling, and circular medallions anchored by two imposing light fixtures hung over the seating areas. The space had an air of stiff formality and smelled of wood and furniture polish.

"This is the grand parlor," Uncle Jonathon said.

An appropriate name, she thought.

"Follow me." They crossed the hall to another room half the size of the first one with a closed set of pocket doors at one end. Chairs and a couch were placed at the large front window. It was as uninviting and cold as the grand parlor. "This is the living room."

Wasn't that what the grand parlor was? she wondered, but didn't dare say it out loud. Above a fireplace hung a portrait of an attractive young woman with bobbed brown hair and wearing a 1920s-style dress. Jess crossed the room to examine it.

"That's my mother, your grandmother," Uncle Jonathon said. "Ah, Douglas."

Jess turned around, and her mouth dropped open. Douglas was almost as tall as his father but lanky, as if he'd recently grown. He wore his wavy brown hair swept off his face, but one curl had escaped the hair cream and fell above a pair of striking blue eyes. His straight nose and square jaw were softened by his full lips. He was the most handsome boy she'd ever seen, even more handsome than Elvis Presley.

But as he came closer to her, his beautiful features changed into an incredulous scowl. Standing over her, he gaped as if he couldn't believe what he was seeing, and then he turned to his father. "She's just a kid!"

Jess worked hard to hide how hurt she was while Uncle Jonathon chuckled. "Now, now, Douglas. That's no way to greet your cousin. You don't want her to think you're rude."

Douglas turned to face her, his shoulders drooping. He stuck out his hand. "Hello, Jessica," he said to the floor.

"Hello, Douglas." She put her gloved hand in his, but he let go without shaking it, hurting her further. She knew she looked young for her age even though she was thirteen. Why would that matter so much to him? She was only two years younger.

"How was your week?" Uncle Jonathon asked Douglas.

For the first time since she'd been with him, Jess heard warmth in her uncle's voice.

Douglas shrugged, shoving his hands in the pockets of his wool trousers. "It was okay, I guess. Kind of boring."

She admired the easy way Douglas spoke to his father. Would she ever be that comfortable around him?

"I hope Annie took good care of you," Uncle Jonathon said.

"Yeah, she took good care of me. You know she always does."

Who was Annie?

"I was showing Jessica around the house. Perhaps you'd like to give her the rest of the tour?"

Douglas's face fell as his hands came out of his pockets. "I've been stuck at home all day waiting for you. Can't I go see the fellows for a while?"

"Douglas, I don't think–"

"Please, Dad?" he said, his blue eyes pleading.

Her uncle raised his hand in defeat. "Alright."

Jess couldn't believe it. She didn't think her uncle ever gave in on anything.

"I don't want James to be gone long," Uncle Jonathon continued. "I'm leaving for the office soon."

"He won't. I'm just going to Jeff's."

"And you'll be back by dinner? It's a school night."

"I will." Douglas pivoted away from his father with a triumphant grin, but when his eyes fell on Jess, it turned into a grimace.

Why did he dislike her so much?

"Jessica," her uncle said, getting her attention. He slid the pocket doors open for them to pass through. "This is the library."

Book shelves containing leather-bound books lined all four walls except where a writing desk stood. Yet another fireplace had two high-back leather chairs in front of it.

"You are allowed to read these, but you will wash your hands first."

"Yes, sir." She pretended to examine the books while shame and anger seared through her. She *wasn't* dirty. When she focused on the titles, she knew she wouldn't find anything interesting. She preferred mysteries like *Nancy Drew*, *Trixie Belden*, and *Cherry Ames, Student Nurse* but all she found were boring adult books. Disheartened, she followed him further down the hallway. She already hated this massive house and she hadn't even seen all of it yet.

They entered a formal dining room where a large, dark, polished table was surrounded by ten chairs. Jess's footsteps echoed around the wood-paneled space where, unlike the other rooms, there was no rug to muffle the noise. The only part of the room she felt drawn to was the beautiful bay window with its panes of diamond-shaped glass.

The maid appeared out of nowhere like a ghost. "Your coffee is ready in your office, sir." Jess didn't know how she could make no noise when every step Jess took reverberated through the room.

"Very well. Show Jessica the rest of the house."

"Yes, sir."

Alone with the strange woman, Jess felt shy. She faced the bay window, looking out across the gravel drive at the garage with the woods behind it.

"Do you want to see the kitchen?" the maid asked.

"Okay."

Jess followed her through a swinging door into a butler's pantry and then entered the kitchen. Colorful rag rugs were scattered throughout the white room, making it seem cheery. Much warmer than the rest of the house, the air was filled with the delicious smell of a cake baking in the white enamel stove. It reminded her of Cora's baking, and a sudden longing to be home with Cora swept through her.

Beyond the stove was a modern icebox with it's motor humming on top, and a set of stairs leading to the second floor. A kitchen table in the middle of the room was covered with ingredients as if someone had been interrupted while making a meal. Next to a window that faced the driveway was a cozy eating area with a smaller table and two chairs.

"Uh, where's the cook?" Jess asked.

"I do the cooking for the family."

"Oh." Jess tried to hide her disappointment. She'd hoped it would be someone as warm and comforting as Cora.

The maid pointed to a closed door next to the eating area. "I sleep through there. Let's go upstairs. I can't wait for you to see your room."

The maid was smiling. It was the first time someone had smiled at Jess since she'd left the train station. Perhaps this woman might be a little like Cora after all.

Jess followed her back through the dining room and down the hall to the staircase. At the top of the stairs, the maid pointed to the left side of the hall where there were two closed doors. "Those are Mr. Blackwell's bedroom and office. They're connected with a bathroom in between." She pointed to the opposite side where there were two more doors. "Over here, Doug has the front bedroom and through that other door is another bedroom. Would you like to see it?"

Jess nodded, thinking it must be hers. The door opened to reveal a large room, much larger than her parents' bedroom in Manhattan, with a big bed, dresser, and wardrobe, all made of heavy dark wood. A desk was placed in front of a window and the walls were covered with cream striped wallpaper.

"This was your father's bedroom," the maid said.

Jess looked at her with surprise. Until that moment, she'd forgotten her father had grown up in this house.

She examined the cold, barren room, but there were no signs of her father. Her parents didn't discuss why they'd moved away to New York, or much about their lives before she was born. Reflecting on her parents' terse answers whenever she'd asked questions, Jess had the impression her father must have left on bad terms with Uncle Jonathon. There were no toys in the bedroom. No books of a growing boy, or pictures of cars or sports heroes. She wished there was some trace of him. She missed him so much.

"You look very much like your father, you know," the maid said, her voice softer.

"You knew my dad?"

"Yes, I knew him, and your mom too. I watched him grow up since we all went to the same schools. Billy was a good boy, always so kind. He was sweet on your mom for a long time before they got married. They were a cute couple." Her expression became sad.

Jess turned her back to the maid, knowing what was coming. She pointed to a closed door. "Where does that go?"

"That's the bathroom, and Doug's bedroom is on the other side. We can go to your room now."

"This isn't my bedroom?"

"Your uncle didn't think it would be suitable for you and Doug to share a bathroom."

Jess was disappointed, but also relieved. It would have been nice to sleep in her dad's old room, but she didn't want to share a bathroom with Douglas either.

They continued down the hallway to another closed door at the end. On Jess's right was a steep narrow staircase. "That goes up to the attic," the maid said, opening the door in front of them.

Jess peered up the stairs, but it was too dark to see the top.

The maid stepped back. "I hope you like your bedroom."

Jess crossed the threshold, and tried not to let her dismay show. Dark wood floors polished to a high sheen ran the length of the room with no rugs or carpeting to give it warmth. The ceiling was high and peaked in the middle, matching the peak of the roof. There wasn't just one queen-sized bed, there were two. *Two.* Was she expected to sleep in both of them? A night table sat between them, and against the other walls were a dresser and a wardrobe. This room could be as big as her apartment back home.

"I wasn't sure what you liked, but I picked out furniture I thought would make it look pretty," the maid said.

The Boy in the Woods

Jess stood behind an oak desk tucked in the niche formed by a bay window, the only inviting part of the room. The window was identical to the one in the dining room. Then it hit her. They'd stuck her in the back of the house, away from the rest of the family. Tears stung her eyes.

"Your bathroom is this way."

Jess blinked them away before following her.

"You have the biggest bathroom in the house," the maid declared, as if this was something Jess would find enviable.

It was indeed big, the size of her old living room with a white tiled floor, claw-foot tub, sink, and toilet. The maid walked across the bathroom to yet another door. She motioned for Jess to come forward. "This door leads to the kitchen."

She opened it, and the smell of cake rose up the stairs to surround Jess.

"When you get up in the morning, you can come right down for breakfast. Isn't that swell?"

The maid's hazel eyes were warm, reminding Jess of her father, and it gave her hope. "Yes, ma'am."

"Oh, I forgot," the maid said. "You can call me Annie. That's what everyone calls me."

"Okay... Annie."

Annie returned to the bedroom, and Jess trailed behind her. "Well? What do you think of your new room?"

"It's... nice," Jess lied while Annie placed her suitcase on the bed closest to the desk. She didn't want to make Annie feel bad when she'd tried to make it pretty for her.

Annie pressed the snaps on the suitcase and opened it. "Oh." She lifted out a framed photograph, her features filled with pain.

Jess recognized the frame and spun around. Cora had packed her parents' wedding picture in her suitcase. She wiped her eyes, fighting to keep more tears from coming. Annie's shoes made a soft sound as she walked across the hard floor, and Jess dared to turn around.

Annie placed the photograph on the table between the two beds, moving an alarm clock out of the way to make room. "It'll be nice having someone young in the house again," she said with forced cheeriness as she returned to the suitcase and took out Jess's clothes. "Doug is too big to want me to fuss over him anymore."

Jess was grateful that Annie didn't make her talk about her parents. "Have you worked here a long time?"

"It's been over sixteen years. I started when your father was still in high school and before Mr. Blackwell married Doug's mother. After she was gone, I raised him. He was only five years old."

Jess crossed to the windows on the opposite side of the room. She didn't want to talk about people dying. Annie didn't seem to either because she remained quiet while she put away the rest of Jess's clothes.

Jess looked out at the large yard ringed by trees. She'd never seen such a large piece of land empty of people. It was a stark reminder of how different her life was going to be now.

Annie closed the suitcase and took it by the handle. "I should finish making dinner. Before I go, do you need anything, Jessica?"

Jess shook her head, fighting to stay in control of her emotions. What she needed, Annie could never give her.

"You know where to find me if you do." She headed

for the door.

"Annie?"

Annie stopped, her hand on the door knob. "Yes?"

"Can you call me Jess?"

Annie smiled. "Of course I can, Jess."

Jess tried to return her smile, but her throat hurt too much. Once the latch on the door clicked into place, she listened to the silence while gazing around the huge room. Her eyes settled on the picture of her mom and dad, and she went to it. Taking it off the night table, she sat on a bed. Her parents' faces were young, their eyes filled with happiness and hope as they smiled at her.

They're gone forever. Grief ripped through Jess, and she fell over onto the bed, hugging the picture. She didn't want to be in this house. She wanted to be back in her tiny bedroom with its single bed, the comforting smell of Cora's cooking filling the apartment, her mom playing bridge in the living room with her friends, her daddy's deep voice announcing he was home after a day at work.

Drawing her knees up, she sobbed for everything that had been taken from her, burying her face in the pillow so no one would hear her.

Chapter Three

Tears on My Pillow

———⋙○⋘———

JESS WAS WOKEN by a hand stroking her hair. She lifted her head and rubbed the dried remains of tears from her eyes.

Annie was lit by the lamp on the bedside table. "It's time for dinner." She took the wedding picture off the bed and set it back on the table.

"It is?" Jess sat up. It was already dark outside. How long had she been asleep?

"Why don't you wash your face and comb your hair before you come downstairs."

"Okay."

Annie left, closing the door behind her.

In the bathroom, Jess examined herself in the mirror with dismay. Her bangs stuck straight up, but worse, her blotchy face and red-rimmed eyes made it obvious she'd been crying. Rubbing her skin with a wet washcloth, she tried to scrub away the blotchiness, then smoothed down her hair. When she was as presentable as she was going to be, she headed out of her room.

The overhead light in the hallway made the window at the far end black. In Manhattan, the city lights kept it from ever being completely dark at night. On the way down the stairs, she couldn't help thinking someone, or something might be watching her from the other side.

Uncle Jonathon and Douglas were already seated when she entered the dining room. Steaming dishes filled with ham slices, mashed potatoes, lima beans, and bread rolls were set between them, but their plates were empty.

From the expression on her uncle's face, she knew she was in trouble. "We were waiting for you," he said, his voice echoing in the paneled room.

"I'm sorry," she murmured, and slid into a chair opposite Douglas.

"It's rude to keep people waiting. I don't want this to become a habit, do you hear me?"

"Yes, sir." She bowed her head while she placed her napkin in her lap, her face burning with embarrassment.

Douglas handed his plate to his father, and Jess peeked up at him. He ignored her, watching Uncle Jonathon fill it with food, and she dropped her eyes to her own plate.

"Jessica!" Uncle Jonathon had his hand out and she handed him her plate. She was disheartened to see the number of lima beans he put on it. She hated lima beans. Back home her mom let her serve herself, and as long as she took a small amount of something she didn't like, she didn't insist Jess have more. She knew Uncle Jonathon would expect her to eat all of them. There was no use even asking.

Picking up her fork, she looked at the seven empty chairs.

"I spoke with Quincy about the steam shovels that

were giving us trouble last fall," Uncle Jonathon said. "He thinks the repairs worked. They're holding up fine so far."

"That's good," Douglas said as he dug into his food. "Maybe we can get another year out of them before we have to replace them."

They continued their conversation about mining machinery while Jess made sure each nasty lima bean had a bite of ham or mashed potatoes to help it go down. While she chewed, she stole glances at Douglas. He never looked in her direction, or even acted as if she was there. Instead, he seemed engrossed in the discussion with his dad. She didn't know why he wasn't bored to death talking about the details of iron ore mining, but it was a good thing he enjoyed it. He'd need to know everything about it if he was going to take over the family business.

As time passed, it was clear they weren't going to talk about anything else, and with nothing to say on the subject, she remained silent, feeling lonelier by the minute.

When Annie brought out a pineapple upside down cake and a dish of whipped cream, signifying the end of the meal was near, Jess was grateful. Uncle Jonathon began slicing a piece of cake for her, and she dared to speak up. "A small slice, please."

He shot her a withering look, but gave her a smaller portion than Douglas.

By the time they finished eating, she was anxious to escape to her bedroom. Douglas excused himself, mentioning homework, and she took his cue. "May I please be excused?" She began to stand.

"Not yet," her uncle said, and she sat back in the chair. "There's something I want to discuss with you."

Her heart rate increased. Had she done something else wrong?

The Boy in the Woods

"There are only a few weeks left of school and as far as I'm concerned, it's not worth having you enroll. By the time you get caught up, the school year will be over."

He eyed her challengingly, as if daring her to disagree, but she was relieved. Starting a new school and meeting new people wasn't something she wanted to do. There would be a lot of questions about why she was there and what had happened to her parents. She didn't think she could bear to talk about it. "Okay."

"You may leave the table now."

"Thank you," she said, not knowing if it was the correct response.

Luckily Annie walked into the room with a tray to clear the dishes, and his attention shifted away from her.

Walking down the hallway back to the stairs, her footsteps echoed through the dark rooms on either side. A chill ran down her spine as she peered into the shadows, and she hurried to the staircase.

From the upper landing, she could see Douglas's bedroom door was open. The light from inside spilled onto the hallway floor. After considering it for a moment, she approached his doorway. Maybe he'd be more willing to talk if they were alone.

He sat at his desk, reading from a textbook, while he fiddled with a pencil. The bedroom was the same as her father's with identical furniture and wallpaper, but his was more lived in. There were clothes on his bed, a letterman jacket on the back of his chair, and sports trophies on his dresser. A bulletin board hung over his bed with photos, postcards, and buttons pinned to it.

He glanced over, noticing her. "What?"

"Nothing," she said, failing to make her voice casual

despite her best efforts. He glared at her while she tried to think of something to say, but no words would come.

"Do you mind? I'm busy."

"Sorry." She backed away. *Why doesn't he like me?* she wondered again on the way to her room. It didn't make any sense. She hadn't done anything to him.

Back in her bedroom, she changed into a nightgown and brushed her teeth in the bathroom, the cold tiles under her feet chilling her. After, she scurried to her bed and slid between the frigid sheets. While she shivered under the bedding, a blast of wind hit the windows, making them rattle. She opened her eyes with alarm. Shadows waved on the wall, looking like monster arms, and she sat up, heart racing.

Outside her windows, a bright light mounted on the garage illuminated tree branches swaying in the wind. She noticed lit windows on the second story, then James, the driver, walked past one in a white undershirt. He must live above the garage.

Another blast of air hit the house harder than the previous one, and it groaned. The windows rattled louder and fearing the glass would shatter, Jess pulled the covers over her head. Tears spilled from her eyes, soaking into her pillow. She wanted desperately to be home in her little bed with only a brick wall outside her window and the comforting noises of the city to lull her to sleep.

Jess awoke to sunshine streaming onto her bed. The howling wind she'd fallen asleep to had died down. She threw off her blankets and climbed out of bed. When her feet touched the wood floor, she sucked in her breath from the cold. She hurried to the wardrobe and found her slippers and robe. After putting them on, she went through her bathroom to the door that led down to the kitchen. Opening it a few inches, warm air wafted in along with the delicious aroma of bacon and the tune of a country song playing from a radio.

Annie looked up from a sizzling frying pan when Jess came down the stairs. "Good morning."

"Good morning, Annie."

"I bet you're hungry." Annie indicated the small table in front of the window. "Go ahead and take a seat and I'll bring your breakfast."

When Jess sat, the morning sun bathed her in its heat.

Annie set a glass of orange juice in front of her. "Doug and your uncle left a while ago."

"Where did Douglas go?" Jess asked, guessing her uncle was at work.

"He's at school."

"Oh, right." How could she have forgotten it was a school day?

"Do you like scrambled eggs and bacon?"

Jess grinned and nodded.

"Good." Annie returned to the stove. "Did you sleep well?"

"Yes," Jess lied, looking out the window at the garage and the woods behind it.

"That's good. Sometimes I have a hard time–"

"Jessica!" Her uncle's loud voice made her startle. He was in the doorway of the butler's pantry dressed in a dark suit with a folded newspaper under his arm. From the look on his face, she knew he was angry with her.

What now?

"We take our meals in the dining room, *not* the

kitchen," he said.

"Yes, sir." She stood, taking her glass of juice.

"It was my fault," Annie said. "I thought you'd left with Doug."

"Don't assume things, Annie," he said through his teeth.

She lowered her head. "Yes, sir."

Jess reclaimed the dining room chair she'd sat in during dinner, noticing how much cooler the room was than the kitchen. Even with her robe and slippers, she was chilled.

Uncle Jonathon opened his napkin with a snap. "You're entirely too familiar with the staff."

She bowed her head. "Yes, sir."

"Things may be different in the city, but here you need to be aware of the boundaries. Annie is *not* your friend."

Annie appeared from the butler's pantry, carrying a tray with their breakfast plates, and Jess dropped her eyes. She had to have heard him.

"She'll be working for you some day," he continued, as if Annie wasn't placing his breakfast in front of him, "and it's going to be impossible to give her orders if you carry on like this."

Annie gave Jess her breakfast, and then left through the swinging door.

"Do you *hear* me?"

"Yes, sir," Jess mumbled.

"From now on, I expect you to be dressed when you come down to eat. You shouldn't be walking around the house like that."

"Yes, sir."

He opened his newspaper, and she pulled the front of her robe tighter to cover herself, shame burning through her. While her stomach twisted itself into knots, she choked down her breakfast. Uncle Jonathon read his paper, and in the empty silence, Jess wished Douglas was there to relieve the pressure.

As soon as she finished, she excused herself and fled to her room. Flinging herself on her bed, she clutched her knees to her chest and waited for her stomach ache to go away. How could her uncle speak in front of Annie in such a terrible way? Then she remembered how he'd treated Cora, and all the other people he'd considered beneath him while they were in New York. She sat up, a firm resolve taking hold. No matter what he said, she would never treat Annie or anyone else as if they were less worthy than her.

Jess took a hot bath and put on one of her everyday dresses, grateful she didn't have to wear a scratchy petticoat under it for the first time in a week. Still chilled, she pulled on a sweater and finished with ankle socks and her Mary Jane shoes. Now that she was dressed, she wondered what she should do.

She went to the desk in front of the bay window. Out the window, the woods behind the garage were so dense it was impossible to see beyond the thick growth of trees. The desk had drawers, and she pulled one open. There were pens and a box of flowered stationery. She'd promised to write to Cora. Jess sat in the chair and took out a sheet printed with peach blossoms. After unscrewing the pen cap, she began.

Dear Cora,

I hope you are doing well. It's nice here. My new home is very big. I think our apartment could fit in my bedroom. I even have my own bathroom.

The housekeeper is named Annie. She is kind and I

like her a lot. She is taking good care of me. She is a good cook.

Realizing how that might sound, she added, *but not as good as you.*

We have a big yard and there are so many trees. It looks like Central Park. We are in the country. I saw cows and farms when we drove to the house from the train station.

Jess chewed the end of the pen, wondering what else to write. Cora would want to know about Douglas, but what could she say?

My cousin is named Douglas. He is tall like Uncle Jonathon. I haven't had a chance to talk to him very much.

She tried to think of what else to say, but none of it was good. Douglas hated her, being in the country scared her, and she wished with all her heart she could go back to Manhattan. Cora was already concerned about her living with Uncle Jonathon. She didn't want to worry her more.

I have to go now, she continued, *but I hope you'll write to me and let me know how you're doing.*

Love, Jess

Reading over the letter, she was dissatisfied it was so short, but it would have to do. After folding the paper, she slid it into an envelope and licked the flap to seal it. Then she realized she didn't have Cora's address. Uncle Jonathon had it, she remembered. He was going to mail her last paycheck. She'd get it from him at dinner.

Then she wrote letters to her best friends, Margaret, Nancy, and Linda. They all shared her old address, except for the different apartment numbers. With the letters finished and stacked on her desk, Jess put the pen back in the drawer.

Unsure of what to do next, she left her room. As she descended the carved staircase, her footsteps echoed through

The Boy in the Woods

the quiet house. In the grand parlor, she found a high-fidelity stereo cabinet, but when she looked through the record collection, she was disappointed there wasn't any rock and roll. Uncle Jonathon didn't own a TV either. She would miss her favorite shows.

In the library, she searched the shelves for something that might appeal to her, perhaps books bought for Douglas, but she had no luck. His books must be in his bedroom and he'd probably never let her borrow them. Back in the hallway, she thought of seeking out Annie, but remembering how her uncle had behaved at breakfast, she couldn't face her.

With nowhere else in the house left to explore, she approached the front door. The metal knob was cool to the touch, and she hesitated. It felt strange to walk outside without telling Annie where she was going. What if Annie wondered what happened to her?

That's stupid, she decided, and turned the knob. Where else would she be if she wasn't in the house? There was no way to get off the property when it was surrounded by an iron fence with a locked gate. Cool air engulfed her as soon as she opened the door, and she stepped out and closed it. The outdoors smelled different than the city, like damp soil mixed with pine needles. Instead of honking horns and sirens, birds chirped in the trees. The edge of the forest was so close to the front of the house, she could hear leaves rustling. Still uneasy about the wild animals that might be hidden in the woods, she headed towards the back of the house.

The sun warmed her against the cool breeze, and near the kitchen, white sheets hung on clotheslines stretched between two metal poles. She walked past them, watching them billow like sails, before spying a swing hanging from a large tree. Unlike in Manhattan where there was a park at the end of her block filled with playground equipment, this was the only thing in the yard to play on.

The Boy in the Woods

When she sat on the wooden seat, it rose and fell as the branch moved in the wind. She missed hearing children playing. Back home, she could step outside her building at any time and find a stickball game to join, or her friends playing hop scotch, jump rope, or jacks. With so many kids in her neighborhood, she always had someone to play with, but here she was all by herself. She began to swing, going higher and higher. Closing her eyes, she pretended she was flying, and for a little while, she could forget.

Her stomach began rumbling too much to ignore, and she got off the swing. She wasn't sure what kind of mood Annie would be in after the way Uncle Jonathon had talked about her, but she was too hungry to stay away any longer. As she entered the kitchen, she smelled baking bread.

"Hello, Jess," Annie said.

"Can I please have lunch? I'm hungry."

Annie laughed and wiped her hands on her apron. "I'm surprised you weren't here earlier, it's been hours since breakfast. Would you like a sandwich, or something else?"

"Sandwich, please."

Annie got a package wrapped in white butcher paper from the icebox.

When she opened it, Jess's stomach sank. "Um, Annie?"

"Yes?"

"Can I have peanut butter and jelly instead?"

"You don't like bologna?"

Jess shook her head.

"We don't have peanut butter. Your uncle doesn't like it, but I can make a ham sandwich with last night's leftovers. Would you like that?"

Jess smiled and nodded, but then her smile fell. "Can I eat in here? I don't want to eat alone."

Annie's expression became softer. "Of course you can. When your uncle's here, he likes the family to eat in the dining room." She took the package of bologna back to the icebox. "I know he can be gruff and difficult to be around sometimes, but he wasn't always like that. Losing his wife and baby was hard on him. If he hadn't had Doug…" She shook her head.

Seeing sorrow in Annie's eyes, grief for her parents engulfed Jess.

"He hasn't been the same since, but no matter what, I *know* he's a good man."

Jess sat down at the small table by the window to hide her face, and Annie went to the bread box. Jess could understand how her uncle might be changed by what had happened to him, but it was still hard not to blame him. Losing his wife and son didn't give him the right to treat other people badly. After all, she'd lost her parents, but it hadn't made her mean.

Outside, tires crunched on gravel, and Jess saw the black car park in front of the garage. James climbed out and opened the rear door for Douglas.

"Doug is home," Annie said, noticing him out the window. She returned to the icebox and got out the package of bologna again.

A minute later, Douglas appeared from the butler's pantry carrying a stack of books. When he saw Jess, he scowled, then turned his attention to Annie. Jess kept her face composed, not wanting him to know he'd hurt her.

"Hello, Doug." Annie didn't seem to notice his reaction to Jess.

"Hi, Annie."

"How was your day?"

He shrugged. "It was okay."

"How did you do on your math test?"

"Alright. I think I aced it."

"That's good. Take a seat and I'll get your sandwich made."

Jess straightened.

Doug seemed to have been caught off guard too. "Uh, I'm going to eat in my room."

"Oh?"

"Yeah, I've got a paper I have to write for English." His eyes shifted away from Annie when he said it, and Jess was certain he was lying.

"I'll bring it up to you then."

He headed out. "Thanks, Annie," he said over his shoulder.

Annie returned to making sandwiches.

Watching her back, Jess couldn't stop thinking about how her cousin was treating her. Would he refuse to have anything to do with her for as long as she lived there? "Douglas hates me," she blurted out, unable to hold back her emotions.

Annie turned to her, taken aback. "What?"

"He hates me."

"That's not true, Jess."

"He went upstairs because he doesn't want to be around me."

Annie gave her a sympathetic smile. "I'm sure he doesn't hate you. He's just not used to having you here. He's a boy. He needs time to warm up, that's all."

"I...guess so," Jess said, her hurt easing.

"You'll see." Annie placed a sandwich and a glass of milk in front of her. "He'll come around once he's had time to get used to you."

She left with Douglas's plate and Jess took a bite of her sandwich. Maybe Annie was right. After all, he'd been an only child his whole life like her. If their positions were reversed, if he'd come to live in Manhattan with her family, she'd need time to adjust too.

That evening, Jess slid the letters for Cora and her friends into her pocket before going downstairs for dinner. Uncle Jonathon and Douglas were seated when she entered the dining room, but Annie was still setting food on the table, much to her relief.

Jess took her seat. "Uncle Jonathon, I've written some letters. One is to Cora, and I need her address and stamps so I can mail them."

"Why would you want to write to that maid?"

"I – I..." she stumbled, startled by the question. She looked at Douglas, but his attention was on his father. "I promised her I'd write. I wanted to tell her about my new home and—"

"Very well." Uncle Jonathon held his hand out. "Give me the letters and I'll have my girl mail them."

Jess hesitated. *What if he decides not to send the one to Cora?*

"There isn't a post box anywhere near here, Jessica," he said, his voice rising with exasperation. "If you want them mailed, they have to be taken into town."

Reaching into her pocket, she pulled out the envelopes. She watched him tuck them into the inside pocket of his suit jacket with despair. Cora would never get that letter.

As soon as their plates were filled with food, he and Douglas talked about business matters like they had the previous night. She noted again how differently her uncle dealt with his son. He patiently corrected Douglas when he was wrong and encouraged him to come up with ideas for the mine. Meanwhile, Douglas basked in his father's approval. Why couldn't Uncle Jonathon be as gentle and kind with her?

Absorbed in their discussion, they never once acknowledged Jess's presence. Climbing the stairs after dinner with a heavy heart, she wondered if she would ever be accepted as a part of their family.

Chapter Four
Lonesome Town

June 1958

"WHAT?"

Uncle Jonathon's loud voice cut through Jess's thoughts, and she looked up from her dinner plate. After living in her new home for almost a month, she was used to her uncle and Douglas talking about business through the entire meal. She found the time passed faster if she made up stories in her head while she ate. It also helped ease her loneliness.

From the expression on Uncle Jonathon's face, Douglas must have said something he didn't like.

"Jeff's family invited me to go with them to France," Douglas said. He seemed unconcerned by his father's reaction.

"But you said they'll be gone for the whole summer."

"Yeah. Jeff's mom has family in Paris, but they're going to travel around the country too. They're even going to see the World's Fair in Brussels."

"I'm surprised his father can afford to be away from the office that long," Uncle Jonathon said, a muscle in his jaw twitching. "He is my lawyer after all. Perhaps I need to have a talk with him."

"Aw, gee, Dad. Don't get mad at Mr. White. He's only going for the first week."

"We were planning for you to work at the office this summer."

"But, Dad–"

"You need to start taking on more responsibilities, Douglas. You can go to Europe another time."

"But there might not *be* another time. I promise I'll work in the office next summer. Please let me go?"

"But it's the *whole summer*, Douglas," Uncle Jonathon said, trying to reason with him.

Jess rolled her eyes at her plate. She already knew who would win this argument.

"Please don't say no." Douglas's eyes crinkled as if he was about to cry, but Jess knew it was just for show. "Once I take over the mine, you know I won't be able to travel like this."

Uncle Jonathon slumped.

Douglas held still, waiting, but Jess knew it was over.

"Alright, you can go."

Douglas's face brightened. "Really? Gee, thanks, Dad. You're the best. I can't wait to tell Jeff. May I please leave the table to make the call? I won't take long."

Uncle Jonathon waved his hand and Douglas leapt out of his chair. Jess resumed eating, but she noticed her uncle wasn't moving. She peeked up at him, and was struck by the

The Boy in the Woods

sadness in his expression while he stared at his plate.

Douglas's happy voice echoed from the hallway and Uncle Jonathon's eyes turned steely before meeting Jess's. Dropping her gaze, her heart hammered in her chest while he glowered at her. Had she done something to make him angry again? Or was he upset that he'd given in to Douglas?

"You may leave the table now, Jessica."

His low voice scared her more, and she didn't dare look at him. "Yes, sir." She placed her fork on her half-finished plate and got up.

In the hallway, she passed Douglas. He was leaning against the door frame, facing the living room, his back to her. While he talked to his friend, an intense jealousy flared in Jess, replacing the fear she'd felt a moment earlier.

Why did he get everything he wanted while she was treated like an unwelcome guest? It wasn't fair he had a parent who loved him when she'd lost both of hers. Then a wave of guilt came over her. She wouldn't wish losing both parents on anyone, not even Douglas.

Laying on her bed, she wished once again she could just go home.

During the next week, there was a flurry of activity, leaving Jess feeling lonelier than ever. She usually spent a large part of her day with Annie, the two of them talking for hours while Jess pitched in with the cooking or cleaning. But preparing for Douglas's two-month trip meant Annie was busy shopping for a new wardrobe and luggage for him. Apparently, he wasn't allowed to travel to Europe wearing the clothes he already owned.

Annie spent long hours in town or with Douglas as he tried on the things she'd bought, making sure they fit and he liked them. She seemed as excited about the trip as he did, which made Jess feel worse. She knew it was wrong to be jealous, but she couldn't help it. She'd give anything to spend the summer somewhere other than her uncle's home.

At first, Uncle Jonathon's decision to have her skip the end of the school year had seemed like a good idea, but now she wished she'd tried to convince him to let her go. If she had, she'd have friends by now. She'd considered asking him if she could invite someone from her old neighborhood to come for a visit, but gave up the idea. He'd never agree to it. The long summer months loomed ahead of her, and with only Annie and Uncle Jonathon at home, she wondered how she was going to survive.

On the morning of Douglas's departure, Jess followed Annie outside to say goodbye.

"Have a wonderful time," Annie said in a tremulous voice. She'd been struggling to keep her emotions in check ever since she'd served him breakfast earlier. Jess was sad for her, knowing how much Annie would miss him.

"I will."

Douglas began to get in the car, but Uncle Jonathon put his hand on his arm. "Don't forget to say goodbye to Jessica."

"Bye, Jessica," Douglas said to the ground in front of her feet.

"Bye, Douglas," she said, but he was already climbing into the back seat.

Uncle Jonathon followed him, and Jess and Annie waited while James turned on the engine. As the car rolled down the driveway, Annie pulled a handkerchief from her apron pocket and covered her mouth to stifle a sob.

Jess took her hand. "It'll go fast, you'll see," she said,

trying to convince herself as much as Annie. "He'll be back before you know it."

Annie attempted a smile and wiped her eyes. "Sure he will, pumpkin."

Leading Jess by the hand, they went to the front door. Inside, the house seemed quieter than usual.

That evening, when Jess entered the dining room, she was dismayed by the newspaper and stack of mail next to her uncle's plate. Was he planning to read through the meal? After she sat, she tried to hide her despair, smoothing her napkin over her lap. Even though they didn't get along, she'd thought he might talk to her a little.

Annie came in through the swinging door with a basket of sliced bread and a butter dish.

"Annie," Uncle Jonathon said, stopping her before she left. "Since it's summer and Douglas is gone, there's no need for you to be here every day. Every other day should be sufficient."

Annie exchanged a surprised glance with Jess. "Wouldn't it be better if I'm here?"

"There's no reason for it."

"But that means Jess would–"

"So?" Uncle Jonathon said, cutting her off. "She's not an infant." He shifted his focus to Jess. "You don't need constant care, do you?"

Jess dropped her eyes. "No, sir."

"Does that mean tomorrow–" Annie started.

"*Yes*, it means tomorrow. You were here today, weren't you?"

"Yes, sir." Annie looked sad when she turned towards

the swinging door.

"Leave something for Jessica to heat up for dinner tomorrow," Uncle Jonathon said, his attention already on his mail.

"Yes, sir."

Jess picked up her fork, the ache of loneliness worsening. She would spend the entire day alone, and then it was almost certain she'd have a silent dinner while her uncle read. Tears threatened, but she blinked them back. She would *not* cry in front of him. She'd just have to figure out how to fill the time while Annie was away.

At the end of dessert, Jess excused herself, and Uncle Jonathon lifted his head from his newspaper. "I forgot. You received a letter." He reached into the pocket of his suit jacket. "I still don't know why you insist on writing to servants."

Jess took the pale blue envelope, her spirits soaring. *Cora had written to her.* "Thank you," she said, but he was back to reading his newspaper.

On the way to her room, she traced her name written in Cora's delicate handwriting with her finger. Settling on her bed, she took her time prying the flap open, not wanting to tear the envelope, and unfolded the cream stationery. A hint of Cora's Shalimar perfume rose up, and she brought it closer to breathe it in.

My dear sweet Jessie,

What a happy day it was when I got your letter. I was glad to hear about your new home, the housemaid, and your cousin. I thanked God that things are going well for you. A big house is quite a change from your old apartment. You must be having fun exploring all those rooms.

I have been busy since you left. The day the movers

were here to take your things, a mother from two floors down came to the door and asked if I wanted to work for her. I said yes and started the very next day. She has two sweet baby girls. Two-year-old twins, and they look exactly alike. They remind me of you at that age.

I hope you are enjoying your summer. Be glad you're in the country and not here. The city is already so hot, you can fry an egg on the sidewalk. Write me again soon and tell me what you're doing.

Sincerely,

Cora

Jess lay on her bed, tears soaking into her bedspread. She was happy Cora had a new job, but the letter reminded her of everything she'd lost. The people she knew back home were moving on without her, even Cora. She had a new family with new little girls to take care of. Meanwhile, Jess was barely tolerated in her new home. She knew it wasn't Cora's intention, but she felt abandoned.

She wiped away her tears and stood. After putting the letter back in its envelope, she took it to her desk drawer. Placing it inside, she imagined tucking the memories of her old life beside it, along with all the grief and pain it caused her, and then she closed it tight. When she walked away, she tried to ignore the ache in her heart.

The next morning, Jess walked down to the quiet kitchen, missing Annie's cheerful greeting and the smell of her breakfast cooking. She found a box of cornflakes in the pantry and retrieved a bottle of milk from the icebox. While she ate her cereal, she looked out the window at the woods beyond the garage and wondered what she would do with a whole day to fill.

Once she'd finished washing and putting away her dishes, she went outside. The garage door was open and she

The Boy in the Woods

saw James. He was bent over the engine compartment of the black car in a denim workman's outfit instead of his usual black uniform. Jess approached him, grateful she wasn't alone.

Not wanting to startle him, she stopped close by and waited for him to notice her, but his head was buried too far under the hood of the car. She cleared her throat. "Hello, James."

He didn't move.

"Hello, James," she said, louder.

He lifted his head, gave her a curt nod, and returned to his work.

"What are you doing?" she said, hoping to start a conversation.

His annoyed glance let her know he thought it was a stupid question.

Sighing, she tried again. "I guess you're working on the car."

That got no response at all. While she watched him, it occurred to her that whenever Douglas wanted to go somewhere, he'd tell James to take him. If she asked him to take her to the town, she could walk around and explore for hours. "Can you take me into town, please?"

James straightened and picked up a dirty cloth, wiping his blackened hands.

A thrill of excitement went through Jess. Why hadn't she thought to ask him sooner? But when he turned towards her with hard eyes, her excitement vanished.

"Did ya ask yer uncle if ya could go ta town?" he said, his words clipped and heavily accented.

"Uh, no. I didn't."

"Then I'm not going ta be takin' ya then, am I?"

She tried to think of a response, but he bent over the engine again without waiting for one. Face flaming and ego bruised, she walked in the direction of the swing. She'd ask Uncle Jonathon that evening, she decided, and plopped onto the swing. It would be so satisfying to tell James tomorrow he had to take her to town. But as she pumped her legs, doubt crept in that her uncle would agree to let her go.

That night, while sitting at the table eating a beef stew she'd reheated, she tried to pluck up the courage to ask him. It wasn't made any easier by the fact he was reading a folded newspaper next to his bowl as if she wasn't there.

"Uncle Jonathon?"

"Mhm?" he said, not taking his attention off the paper.

"Can I go into town tomorrow?"

He leaned back in his chair. While he eyed her, she allowed herself a small amount of hope; he didn't seem angry by the request. "Why do you want to go?"

"I wanted to see what it's like."

He leaned over his paper. "It's a small town. No different from any other."

"I'd still like to see it."

"I already answered your question, Jessica." His rising voice echoed off the wood-paneled walls.

"Please?" She knew it wasn't a good idea to press him, but she was desperate. She didn't want to be stuck on the property all summer.

His eyes narrowed. "Why do you want to go so badly?"

"There's nothing to do here and–" Anger flashed in

The Boy in the Woods

his eyes, but she dared to continue anyway. "I thought it would give me something to do."

"I'm sorry living in this beautiful home on all this land isn't enough for you," he said, his voice laced with sarcasm.

"That's not what I meant. It's that there isn't anyone here–"

"When Douglas returns, you'll have him to keep you company."

"But he won't be home for the whole summer."

Uncle Jonathon's fist slammed on the table, making the dishes rattle, and Jess jumped. "That's enough! I'm not discussing this further with you, do you understand me?"

She leaned over her bowl, heart banging in her chest. "Yes, sir." Scooping up stew with a shaking hand, she put it in her mouth. To her relief, he returned to his paper.

I hate him, she thought, blinking back tears. I hate him for being so mean. Then she imagined her parents looking down at her, seeing the person she was turning into. They didn't raise her to be a hateful person. Swallowing her bitterness with her stew, she resolved to never become as mean as he was.

Jess smiled when she woke the next morning. She kicked off her covers and jumped out of bed, hurrying to pull on a dress.

"Good morning, Annie," she said, dashing down the backstairs.

"Good morning, pumpkin." Annie let out a huff when Jess ran into her, giving her a tight hug. She chuckled. "That's a very nice 'good morning.'"

Jess let go and took her place at the table. She downed a long drink of orange juice. "How was your day off?"

"It was nice. I got to relax with my mom and visit my kitties. How was your day?"

Jess opened her mouth, about to answer, then closed it. She didn't want Annie to worry about her being lonely when there wasn't anything she could do about it. "I had a swell time too."

"Good." Annie scooped scrambled eggs and bacon onto a plate.

After Jess finished eating, she brought her empty plate and glass to the sink, prepared to help Annie with the dishes.

Annie took them from her. "Being back in my neighborhood reminded me, it's summer now and you should be playing outside instead of cooped up in the house."

Jess's mouth dropped open. "But it's boring out there. There's nothing to do."

Annie put her hands on her hips. "Jessica Blackwell, are you telling me that on this whole property you can't find anything to do? You've spent too much time in this house already. There's a whole world out there to explore. Now scoot." She made a sweeping motion with her hands.

"Annie…"

"Go out and get some fresh air, and don't let me see you back here until lunch time." She opened the door that led to the back porch.

"Okay, okay," Jess grumbled, knowing it was useless to protest.

She stomped around the outside of the house to the gravel drive. *How am I supposed to have fun all by myself?*

Spotting James in the garage, washing the windows of

The Boy in the Woods

the black car, Jess reversed course to the swing. But when she reached it, she didn't feel like swinging and kept going across the large yard. At the edge of the forest, she peered into the dense growth. Animals rustled through the leaves, but she couldn't see them. She walked along the edge, counting each step while watching her feet.

On step 317, she stopped. There was an opening in the foliage almost large enough for a person to pass through. She pushed aside a branch to reveal a narrow path in the woods. It curved and then disappeared behind the trees. How had she not noticed it before? She glanced over her shoulder and discovered she was behind the garage. It had been hidden from view. Looking at the path, her curiosity proved stronger than her fear of the animals that might live there. She had to know where it led.

She stepped into the woods and cool air surrounded her, encouraging her to move forward. Her eyes and ears scanned for danger, but the only thing she saw were squirrels scampering away from her crunching footsteps. All around her, birds sang, and sunlight streamed through the gaps in the branches overhead, illuminating patches of ground where ferns grew. The longer she meandered down the path, the more beautiful the woods seemed.

After another curve, the path ended and she blinked with amazement. The trees opened into a grassy clearing filled with bright sunshine. In the center was a small cabin with a chimney made of river stones. Mesmerized, she approached its door and reached for the handle. *What if someone lives here?* No, she decided, shaking her head. It was impossible. No one else could get on the property with the gate locked all the time.

The latch lifted with ease and the door swung open, revealing a tiny living room, and Jess stepped over the single stone stoop to enter. The smell of the pine floorboards mingled with stuffy air. Two wooden chairs sat in front of the stone fireplace, a small table between them, covered with magazines.

On the rough-hewn mantel rested a row of carved wooden animals. Examining each one, she marveled at their lifelike features. Squirrels, rabbits, deer, turtles, and even dogs and cats, posed as if the person who'd carved them had used live models. The hunting and fishing magazines on the small table were decades old, giving her a clue about how long it had been since the cabin was last used.

Opposite the fireplace, a closed door led to a single bedroom with a dresser and an iron bed and springs, but no mattress. Across the living room, Jess went into a galley kitchen where another door led outside. She opened it to let in more air and light.

A ceramic sink with an old-fashioned water pump had been installed beneath the room's sole window. When she lifted the pump handle and pushed it down, no water came out. In the kitchen cabinets and drawers, she found a box of dish soap, a coffee mug, mismatched cutlery, and an ancient tea tin with bags of tea. There was a cast iron cookstove set in the corner next to a small table with two stools. It had a battered tea kettle on top. She lifted the lid, but of course, it was empty.

Back in the living room, she ran her hand along the back of one of the wooden chairs. Even though the cabin was spare and the furnishings simple, it was charming, like a play house, and there was something about it that tugged at her. After living in her uncle's mansion for a month, she'd forgotten how comforting small spaces could be. It felt like home.

She explored the rooms further, but the only new thing she discovered was a fishing pole tucked behind the open front door. When she grew too hungry to stay any longer, she closed the cabin doors and set off across the clearing. Before she walked down the path, she turned back for one last look. *It's the most beautiful cabin in the world*, she thought, and since no one else was using it, she would claim it as her own. It would be her secret place. The whole way back to the house, she imagined how much fun she would have in *her* cabin.

That evening at the dinner table, Uncle Jonathon was once again absorbed in a stack of documents, but for the first time it didn't bother Jess. Instead, her head was filled with plans. Picturing the cabin's small rooms, she tried to think of all the things she could do. She could take her stationery and write to Cora. Wouldn't Cora be excited to learn about it? And if she had permission to take a few books, she could read.

"Uncle Jonathon?"

He grunted without looking up.

"Do you think–"

As his brown eyes met hers, she remembered his refusal to let her go into town.

"Well? What is it?"

Her pulse raced. What if she brought up the cabin, and he told her she wasn't allowed to go back? This was the first fun thing she'd found to do on the property.

"I don't like being kept waiting, Jessica."

"I – I wondered if it's okay," she stammered, "if I take a few books from the library to keep in my room?"

His eyes narrowed and she worried he'd seen through her lie. "Why?"

She forced herself to meet his gaze. "I like to read in bed before I go to sleep."

"You'll be careful with them?"

"Yes, sir."

"And you won't stay up all night reading?"

"No, sir, I won't."

"I'll allow it," he said grudgingly, and returned to his papers.

"Thank you."

While her heart slowed to its normal rate, she knew it was a close call. He was sure to forbid her from visiting the cabin for one stupid reason or another, and she couldn't let that happen. There was a whole summer of solitude ahead of her, and if she couldn't escape to the cabin, she'd die of boredom.

The next morning on the way to the cabin, Jess encountered two squirrels. She laughed as they chased each other, jumping from branch to branch. They reached the clearing before she did, sprinting through the unkempt grass to a nearby oak tree. She continued walking while they climbed the trunk, circling each other until Jess lost sight of them in the leafy branches. When she focused on the cabin, she stopped short, her heart leaping into her throat. The front door was wide open.

James must be inside, she thought, her breathing becoming shallow. She was already so close, he could spot her from inside. He'd be sure to tell Uncle Jonathon, and then she'd be forbidden to come back. She needed to get away fast or she would lose the cabin forever.

She'd taken a step to turn away when a teenage boy leapt through the front door, missing the front stoop. He landed a few feet from her, throwing his arms out as he skidded to a stop in the grass.

"Oh!" she said, while he stared at her with wide

The Boy in the Woods

brown eyes.

Chapter Five
Lonely Boy

THE BOY WAS still, as if he was frozen. Jess stared at him, trying to make sense of what she was seeing.

This must be James's boy. After all, the gate was locked at all times. But as she studied him further, something didn't add up.

He was smaller and younger than Douglas, but still taller than her. He had to have spent a lot of time outdoors, judging from his tanned skin. And he hadn't been to a barber in a while because his golden brown hair was long and falling over his eyes. There was a hole in his striped T-shirt where the neck had separated from the body, and his jeans were well worn and smudged with dirt. The legs were too short, exposing the tops of his lace-up boots, the brown leather ancient and scuffed. Surely James wouldn't let his son go out in this state.

"Who are you?" she asked.

His face contorted. "I'm nobody," he snarled.

"Where did you come from?"

"It doesn't matter." He pivoted and headed across the clearing in the opposite direction of the path.

"Wait!" She hurried to catch up to him, but he turned, stalking towards her. His menacing expression reminded her of the tough kids who would sometimes come into her old neighborhood, looking for trouble. She took a few steps back, afraid of what he was going to do.

He loomed over her. "Listen, kid. Forget you ever saw me, get it?" His brown eyes were clouded with anger and suspicion, but there was something else she recognized – fear.

"I'm not going to tell anyone I saw you."

He snorted with disbelief, but remained where he was. While he studied her, she kept her eyes on his, hoping he would see she was telling the truth. After a moment, his face relaxed, but then his expression became guarded again. "Just make sure you don't." He turned and walked away.

"Don't go."

This time, he didn't stop.

"Wait." She ran to him, and when she reached him, he rounded on her.

"Why? What's your deal anyway?"

"I thought we could talk a little." She cringed, knowing how dumb it sounded.

"Maybe I don't want to talk to *you*," he sneered.

An image came into her head of Douglas's rejection, and her throat constricted, making it impossible to reply. She couldn't take this boy rejecting her too.

He straightened, keeping his eyes on her, then he took a deep breath and blew it out. "Listen, kid. I'm busy, okay?" His eyes weren't as guarded now. "So why don't you–"

The Boy in the Woods

"What are you doing?"

"What do you mean?"

"You said you were busy. What are you busy with?"

He waved his arms with exasperation. "I don't know!"

"I can help you."

He made a face, letting her know what he thought of the idea.

"I mean, whatever it is, wouldn't it be easier if–"

His expression became suspicious again. "Why would you want to help me?"

"I like helping people, and besides, there isn't anyone else here to talk to."

"You're lying! You think I don't know other people live here?"

"My uncle works all day." By the look of alarm on his face, she knew she'd said the wrong thing. "And my cousin is gone for the summer," she added, hoping to contain the damage. "The housekeeper is–"

"Okay, okay, I get it," he said, but he still seemed wary.

She didn't blame him for his reaction. Uncle Jonathon must have a terrible reputation in town. "I promise I won't tell anyone I saw you," she repeated.

"How do I know you're telling the truth?"

The seconds ticked by, and while she tried to think of something that would convince him, she knew his distrust was growing. Desperate he was about to leave, she blurted out the first thing that came into her head. "Because I swear it. I swear on my parents' graves I won't tell."

Surprise crossed the boy's face at her declaration, but

then he hid it. "Just see that you don't."

He'd tried to sound as menacing as before, but Jess detected a shift in his tone. Deciding to take advantage of it, she stuck out her hand. "I'm Jessica, but everyone calls me Jess."

He considered her hand for a moment, then put his hand in hers. The darkness of his tanned skin contrasted with her paleness. "Marty," he mumbled.

She smiled. He'd told her his name. "It's nice to meet you, Marty." She tried to shake his hand, but he yanked it out. "So? What are you doing?"

He gazed at the ground, then lifted his head, his lip curling. "You'll see."

He made a sharp turn towards the woods. Watching his back, it occurred to Jess that it might not be a good idea to follow him. She didn't know anything about this boy. But when he pushed through the brush and disappeared from view, she ran to the place where he'd vanished. Once she worked her way through the thick growth, the woods opened up and she spotted him a short distance away.

The forest floor was littered with fallen trees and branches and her Mary Jane shoes were no help at all as she scrambled over them. Sticks grabbed at her skirt and scratched her bare legs, and before long, her ankle socks were covered in burrs. While she struggled to keep up with him, she noticed he didn't seem to have any trouble with the terrain. His jeans and boots were much more suited to walking in the woods.

She was soon breathing hard and sweat ran down her neck, but Marty kept marching forward. She didn't dare stop for fear of losing sight of him. If she did, he might run off and they were now so deep in the woods, she worried about finding her way back.

The Boy in the Woods

Eventually, Marty glanced over his shoulder, saw her still scrambling behind him, and stopped. Grateful for the chance to catch her breath, she wiped the sweat off her forehead. While she recovered from the hike, he picked up a fallen tree branch and snapped it in half. Throwing the two pieces on the ground, he picked up another, smaller branch and added it to the first two. As he continued picking up and stacking fallen branches, snapping the larger ones into more manageable pieces, she figured out he was gathering firewood.

Eager to help, she looked around and found a branch. He watched her place it on his pile, then turned his back to her, snapping a large branch into several pieces with his foot. While the two of them worked in silence, a million questions ran through her mind. Who was this boy? Where did he come from? She was almost certain he wasn't living in the cabin. The lack of a bed and food meant he must stay somewhere else, but where? Could there be another cabin on the property? Or was there a way to get through the fence? She thought about asking him, but he was already so suspicious of her. If she pressed him for information, it could cause him to run away.

"Not the green ones!" He snatched the branch she was holding, green leaves still attached to it. "Don't you know they don't burn?" He threw it away with disgust.

"Oh."

"Find the old dead ones," he muttered without meeting her eyes.

"Okay," she said to his back as he walked away, but a thrill of happiness went through her. He was talking to her.

When they had a sizable pile of branches, he gathered them in his arms.

She stepped forward. "I can help carry."

The Boy in the Woods

He scoffed as he straightened with the bundle. "Yeah, right. You can barely walk not carrying nothing."

"I guess you're right," she said with a light laugh, trying to hide her embarrassment, but he'd already started off in the direction they'd come from.

With the pile of branches in his arms, he was slower, making it easier for Jess to keep up. He pushed through a thicket of brush and when Jess followed, she found herself back in the clearing. He tossed the bundle of branches on the ground near the back door of the cabin, then broke them into smaller pieces and threw them into a wood crate inside the kitchen door. Jess joined him at the work, but he ignored her.

When they finished, he went to the sink and pushed on the pump handle repeatedly until water poured out. While he washed the dirt off his hands and arms, Jess looked down at her own dirty hands. It must be late afternoon by now. She needed to get back to the house so she'd have time to clean up and get dinner on the table, but she was reluctant to leave. What if Marty decided he couldn't trust her and she never saw him again?

"I have to go now," she said. "I hope you believe I won't tell anyone I saw you and – I hope I can see you again, if it's okay with you."

He wiped his hands on his T-shirt. "It's a free country, ain't it?"

She wished he'd said yes, but at least it didn't sound like he would never return. She forced a smile and held her hand out. "Well, goodbye."

He crossed his arms over his chest and leaned against the counter. She dropped her hand and turned towards the front door, sadness overwhelming her. She didn't want to leave now that she'd found a someone to play with. At the threshold, she looked over her shoulder. He was watching her,

The Boy in the Woods

still in the same position. She gave him a small wave before stepping out.

The whole way back to the garage, she couldn't shake her sorrow. Before she stepped out of the woods, she stopped to collect herself. Whether or not Marty came back was out of her hands. What she had to worry about now was making sure her uncle didn't notice her emotions. If he did, he might demand to know what was wrong, or even guess something had happened. She'd made a promise to Marty and even if she never saw him again, she wouldn't break it.

Pushing aside the last few branches, she left the path and crept to the front of the garage. After checking that the doors were closed, she hurried to the kitchen. When she saw the clock on the wall, she was stunned at how late it was. There wasn't much time before she needed to get dinner ready and she was filthy. She ran up the stairs to her bathroom and turned on the water for a bath.

Dressed in clean clothes, Jess returned to the kitchen and pulled the casserole Annie had left for their dinner out of the icebox. She put it in the oven and then set the dining room table. With nothing left to do, she took a seat at the table in the kitchen and waited for her uncle.

Listening to the ticking of the clock on the wall, she wondered what Marty was doing at that moment. With his unkempt appearance, old clothes and long hair, it was clear he had a hard life. If Uncle Jonathon found out he was on the property, he'd make his life worse than it already was, and Marty didn't deserve that.

She was taking the casserole out of the oven when the black car passed the kitchen window, and her stomach twisted. She backed through the swinging door and set the dish on the dining room table.

Uncle Jonathon appeared in the doorway with a stack

of mail and a newspaper. "Jessica."

"Hello, Uncle Jonathon." As she sat, her anxiety rose.

He held his hand out for her plate. Without another word he filled it, and then filled his own plate. They ate in their usual silence, much to her relief. When they finished, Jess took their dishes to the kitchen sink. While she washed them, she looked at the woods through the window.

Tomorrow morning she'd go back to the cabin and she hoped Marty would be there. If he was, he'd know she'd kept his secret. She grinned, imagining spending more time with him. She'd always enjoyed playing with the boys in her old neighborhood as much as the girls. It might take a while, but if he'd give her the chance, she knew they could be great friends.

Chapter Six

Maybe

THE NEXT MORNING, Jess burst through the brush onto the path, and ran until she was out of breath and had to slow down. When she reached the clearing, she stopped. The front door of the cabin was closed, but maybe Marty was inside anyway. She went to the door and knocked, but heard nothing. She opened it part way. "Hello? Marty." Heart sinking, she stepped inside.

Even though it was futile, she checked the bedroom, but she was alone. Returning to the front stoop, she listened, hoping to hear him walking through the woods, but the only sounds were the familiar rustling of small animals and birds singing in the trees.

She plopped down on the narrow stoop, deciding to wait. *What if he doesn't come back?* a small voice inside her said. She pushed the thought away. He wouldn't have been gathering firewood if he didn't use the cabin regularly. He wouldn't be willing to give up the cabin just because she found him, would he? She wouldn't if she were him.

The sun moved overhead and her stomach growled.

After a while, the hunger pains became too strong and she reluctantly closed the cabin door. Heading for the path, she tried to be hopeful. Perhaps he was busy elsewhere and that's why he hadn't shown up. He'd come back tomorrow, she decided. He had to.

While she ate a late lunch, Annie mixed cake batter for that night's dessert. When Annie offered the bowl and mixing spoon to Jess, she took them, forcing excitement. Later, she went to her room to read, trying to distract herself from thinking about Marty. She read the same paragraph over and over, while his face kept popping into her mind, but with one last attempt, she escaped into her story.

Dinner was a somber meal, and when she finished, all she wanted to do was go back to bed. The sooner she was asleep, the sooner tomorrow would come, and the sooner she could see Marty.

After eating breakfast alone, she left the house through the front door. The black car was parked outside the garage and James was polishing it. He glanced at her before turning his attention back to his work. Jess hesitated, wondering what she should do. When he glanced at her a second time, she went around to the other side of the house, not wanting him to guess where she'd intended to go.

She waited a bit and then peeked around the corner. He was still polishing the car. *Come on, James*, she thought, her desperation rising. How long was he going to take? Marty could be at the cabin, and she was stuck with James between her and the path. What if Marty left before she could get there? She looked at the woods across the large yard. She could enter at a different spot where James wouldn't see her. But if she stayed close to the edge to find the path, he would hear her since every step she took would crunch on the dried branches and leaves that littered the ground.

She took one last look. James set down his cloth and disappeared into the garage. Taking her chance, she ran to the corner of the building and pressed herself against the side. When there was no sign he was coming, she continued to the path. She half ran, half walked, eager not to waste another moment, but when she got to the clearing, she slumped. The front door was closed.

The hot stuffy air inside the cabin confirmed Marty wasn't there. Maybe he was elsewhere on the property. If she searched for him, she might be able to find him. *Or you might get lost*, a voice inside her said. She shook her head. How could she get lost when the property was surrounded by a fence? She had to try to find him.

At the spot where he'd led her into the woods, she pushed her way through the brush. Trying her best to remember the way they'd gone, she wove her way around fallen tree trunks and large rocks. But the deeper she traveled into the forest, the more uneasy she became. She could find her way to the fence and follow it to the gate, but how long would that take? It seemed as though she'd walked forever without reaching the fence when she'd collected wood with Marty. She couldn't have Annie or James deciding to search for her. The first place they'd check would be the cabin.

The longer she walked, the more certain she became that she wouldn't find him. The property was just too large. Turning around in defeat, she stumbled back to the clearing. She looked inside the cabin once more, but it was still empty. Back at the front door, surrounded by the wall of trees, the intense loneliness she'd kept at bay came back all at once, crushing her. She collapsed on the front stoop and buried her head in her arms, wishing bitterly she was back in New York where friends were around whenever she wanted to play with someone. She wiped her face and stood, leaving the cabin without looking back.

The Boy in the Woods

The next morning, Jess went to Annie at the kitchen stove for a much-needed hug. When she let go, Annie's hazel eyes studied her with concern. "Do you feel okay?"

"Not really." Jess swallowed against the lump in her throat.

"Are you sick?"

"No... I'm tired."

"This early in the morning?" She put a hand on Jess's forehead. "You don't have a fever. Are you achy? How does your neck feel?"

Jess shrugged. "Okay, I guess."

"Oh, Jess, does it hurt? I hope you haven't caught polio!"

From the alarm in her voice, Jess knew she'd made a mistake. "It's not that. I didn't sleep well. I was reading a scary book, and it kept me awake, that's all."

"Which one?"

Jess thought fast. "Uh, *War of the Worlds*?" She hoped it sounded believable. She'd seen the book in her uncle's library but hadn't wanted to read it. Her dad had taken her to the movie when she was younger and she'd had nightmares for months after.

Annie put her hand over her heart. "No wonder! I heard that terrible radio show when I was around your age. Scared us half to death. My mother thought the aliens were coming to kill us all." She gave Jess another hug. "Don't read that book anymore, okay?"

"Okay," Jess said into her chest.

After breakfast, she was sent outside with a warning that if she felt tired, she should come back so Annie could give her a mustard plaster to keep her from coming down with

The Boy in the Woods

a cold. Not knowing what a mustard plaster was and not wanting to find out, Jess knew she was doomed to spend the entire day outside.

She wandered over to the swing and sat on it. A breeze reached the tree, and she closed her eyes to enjoy it, but Marty's face appeared in her mind, and the terrible ache of loneliness returned.

He wasn't coming back, and she had to accept it. He must have decided he couldn't trust her, and with the threat of Uncle Jonathon catching him, he'd chosen to stay away. She'd already prepared herself to spend the whole summer alone, so why should it be such a big deal now? She should go to the cabin anyway. Even though it was sad knowing she wouldn't have a friend, she could still have fun there.

Walking down the path, she took the time to notice the beauty of the woods surrounding her. It really was a magical place. She should spend the summer exploring it.

Stepping into the clearing, she stopped, her mouth dropping open. Marty was sitting on the narrow front stoop of the cabin with his head down.

"Marty?" she said, hardly believing what she was seeing.

He looked up at her through the long bangs that obscured his face, then scowled and dropped his head. He was whittling a piece of wood with a penknife, shavings flying off with each cut as she approached. When she reached him, she waited, but he ignored her while he worked his penknife.

"Can I sit with you?"

He shrugged.

It was the closest thing to a yes she would get, and she took a seat on the far edge of the stoop, not wanting to make him uncomfortable.

He shifted away from her anyway, putting more space between them. He continued whittling, and she stayed silent while she watched him work.

When she peeked up at his face, she gasped. There was a scrape on his upper cheek, under his eye, and the area surrounding it was puffy and purple. "What happened to you?"

"I fell," he muttered.

"Are you okay?" She reached out to touch his cheek.

"Yeah, I'm okay," he said, jerking his head away, and she dropped her hand.

"Does it hurt?"

He made a face. "What do you think?"

"Did you fall in the woods or–"

"Will you shut up about it?" he said, glaring at her.

"Okay."

He hunched over his whittling.

"I didn't mean to – sorry." She stopped short when he shot her another dark look out of the corner of his bruised eye.

"Jeez," he said under his breath, making quick, deep cuts in the wood. Not wanting to upset him further, she bit back the rest of her questions. After a while, his movements slowed and became more purposeful.

"What are you making?"

"What does it look like I'm making?" he said, sounding annoyed again.

She examined the wood while he continued to

carve. It was still rudimentary, but she realized it was an animal. Then a thought came to her. "You're the one who carved the animals on the fireplace mantle."

"So?"

She stood and went inside the cabin to look at them again. Their poses were so natural it was as if they were real. "These are really good, Marty." When she returned to the stoop, she noticed a slingshot poking out of his back pocket. "You're really talented."

He scoffed, but his expression lightened. He liked the compliment.

"Which animal is that?"

"A beaver."

"I've only seen those at the zoo."

He didn't reply.

She pointed to his back pocket. "What's that for?"

"It's a slingshot. Don't tell me you don't know what that is either."

"I know it's a slingshot," she said, hurt by his accusation. "I just wondered what you use it for."

He gave her an incredulous look. "What do you think I use it for? To shoot things."

She stayed quiet so she wouldn't irritate him further, but after a few minutes, her curiosity became too strong. "Can you hit anything with it?"

Without a word he set down his knife and wood, and pulled the slingshot out of his pocket. He examined the ground around them before choosing a rock, then took aim and let it go. There was a sharp crack as it hit a tree trunk, causing the squirrel that had paused there to scramble away.

The Boy in the Woods

"That's swell, Marty. You hit it."

He looked at her like she was stupid again. "No, I didn't. I missed."

"You hit the tree."

He picked up his penknife and wood. "I was aiming for the squirrel."

"Why would you want to hit the squirrel?"

"To kill it."

"Why are you trying to kill a squirrel?" she said with horror.

"Why do you think? To eat it! *Jeez*."

Jess was shocked into silence. Who would want to eat a squirrel? It sounded disgusting, like eating the pigeons or rats in New York City. *No one* did that. And then a thought came to her. If someone was hungry enough, they'd eat a squirrel.

She studied Marty out of the corner of her eye. His filthy, ragged clothes hung on him as if they'd been passed down from a larger boy, but underneath, his body was thin. Did Marty get so hungry that a squirrel looked like a meal? Her heart ached for him. Then she remembered all the people who'd told her how sorry they were her parents had died. She'd hated seeing the pity in their eyes. Squaring her shoulders, she pushed her emotions away. She wouldn't do that to him.

He continued to work on his piece of wood, and she watched with fascination as the beaver took shape. As time passed, she sensed Marty's hostility easing as he concentrated on what he was doing. With the tip of his knife, he made small cuts, putting the finishing touches on the beaver's face, then set the knife down. Turning the animal over, he examined it.

Jess extended her hand. "Can I see?" She expected him to refuse or make a wisecrack, but he gave it to her. Small enough to fit in her palm, the beaver was sitting, its rounded back ending in a thick flat tail. Its front paws were clasped under its chin and it looked like it was sniffing the air with its two front teeth peeking out from under its top lip. She grinned at Marty. "It's so cute."

He snatched it from her and stood. She followed him into the cabin and watched as he approached the fireplace. He moved the other animals around to make a space for it, and stepped back to admire them.

Her stomach growled, and she wrapped her arms around it, not wanting Marty to hear. It growled again, and he turned towards her, raising an eyebrow.

"Hungry?"

Heat rose in her cheeks. "Uh, yes." Her stomach grumbled a third time, broadcasting her hunger. It had been hours since breakfast. "I guess I should go. Will I see you again?"

He shrugged. "Maybe."

It took every ounce of strength she had not to beg him. "Well, I'll see you around." When he didn't reply, she turned to leave, even though she didn't want to.

At the edge of the clearing, she stopped and looked over her shoulder. Marty was leaning against the door frame. Out of habit, she raised her hand to wave. He didn't wave back, but as she continued down the path, she was more hopeful. If he was interested enough to watch her, that alone was a big improvement. He would come back again. She was certain of it.

Chapter Seven
Just a Matter of Time

"WHAT ON EARTH?"

Jess looked up from her breakfast plate, and nearly dropped her fork. Annie was holding up her dirty dress, the one she'd worn the day she'd gathered firewood with Marty.

"What were you doing that got your dress so dirty?"

While Annie waited, Jess's mind raced. What should she say?

Annie's face softened. "I'm not mad, pumpkin. I was wondering, that's all."

It didn't make Jess feel any better. She took a deep breath. "I was in the woods, and I was gathering wood – *big* pieces of wood. I was going to build a fort." She hoped by sticking close to the truth, this new lie wouldn't be as bad.

"I used to do that all the time in the woods behind my house with my sister and–" Annie's face fell, and she turned her back to Jess. "I'm glad to see you're out playing like other kids," she said, returning to sort laundry. "But I wish you had different clothes to do it in. I'll ask your uncle about buying you play clothes so you don't ruin your dresses."

Jess was relieved Annie hadn't asked for details, but she still felt guilty. She didn't want to lie to Annie, but she couldn't break her promise to Marty. Then she remembered she kept having to cut her visits with him short because she got too hungry. "Uh, Annie. Do you think I could take a lunch when I go out today? Sometimes I get so busy I forget about eating."

"Of course, pumpkin."

"Could I have two sandwiches?" she said, watching Annie's expression. "I get really hungry." She hoped the request hadn't sounded as lame to Annie as it did to her. To her relief, Annie didn't seem to notice.

"I bet you do. You don't get enough to eat when you're gone most of the day with no food. I'll pack you a good lunch, but you have to help me hang the sheets. Deal?"

Jess grinned. "Deal." Now she had to figure out how to offer the extra sandwich to Marty without letting him know she'd brought it so he wouldn't go hungry.

After the sheets were on the clothesline, Annie gave Jess a basket with her lunch. Jess was delighted to find the garage doors closed, and headed for the path. There was a possibility Marty might not show up, but she was ecstatic when she saw the cabin door wide open.

At the entrance, she stopped. Marty was in the kitchen washing a mug in the sink with his head down. He was in the same striped T-shirt he'd been wearing the day she'd met him, the grime from the wood they'd gathered still on it.

"Hi, Marty."

He staggered backwards and almost dropped the soapy mug in his hands.

The Boy in the Woods

She felt bad for frightening him, and kept her smile going, pretending she hadn't noticed. "Is it okay if I come in?"

His face tightened, but he shrugged with resignation and turned back to the sink.

On the kitchen counter was a battered brown paper bag with the top twisted so it resembled a Hershey's Kiss. She wondered what was in it as she set her basket next to it. Marty eyed the basket, but said nothing. His bruised eye looked like it was healing. The swelling had gone down, and the purple parts were turning yellow.

"How are you?" she asked.

"Peachy." He shook the excess water out of his mug. When he stepped towards her and reached for the cupboard door behind her, she moved out of his way.

"I'm doing good too." She tried to mask the awkwardness with a cheery tone. "It's nice today, not too hot."

He didn't reply, but instead reached under the sink to pull out a rusting metal pail. He stepped out the back door, and Jess followed him. Pushing past the brush behind the cabin, he was soon out of sight in the woods. Not wanting to be left behind, Jess ran to catch up with him. On the other side of the shrubs, Marty was kneeling on the ground. Pulling his pen knife out of his pocket, he opened it and used it to turn up the loamy layer of leaves. He sorted through the dirt before dropping handfuls of it into the pail.

"What are you doing?" she asked.

"What does it look like? I'm getting worms." He stood and wiped his knife on his jeans before closing it and putting it back in his pocket.

"Why do you need worms?" She leaned over to look

in the pail, but he headed in the direction of the cabin.

"If you must know, I'm going fishing."

"Really? You fish?" She fell in step behind him. "I've never seen anyone fish before. Can I come?"

He whirled around. "Absolutely not."

"Why not?"

"You talk too much. You'll scare the fish away."

"I'll stay quiet. I promise."

"For *hours?*" he sneered. "I don't think it's possible for you to be quiet for five minutes."

From his eyes, she knew he wasn't going to let her join him, and her desperation increased. She didn't want to be left at the cabin, sitting alone for hours while she waited for him. Not knowing what else to do, she motioned like she was zipping her lips closed, then clasped her hands in front of her chest to silently plead.

"No," he repeated, turning for the cabin, and she ran to get in front of him.

Walking backwards, she shook her clasped hands, beseeching him.

He tried to step around her, but when she wouldn't let him, his shoulders sagged. "Okay, already."

She dropped her hands and smiled.

"But you better not do anything to scare the fish."

"I won't, Marty, I promise. You won't regret it."

He retrieved the fishing pole from its resting place behind the door, and then set off across the clearing, heading in a direction Jess hadn't gone before. She was delighted when Marty led her to another path that had been hidden from view by the thick growth at the edge of the clearing.

The Boy in the Woods

Excitement coursed through her. They were on a grand adventure, and she couldn't wait to see where Marty was taking her.

Watching his back, she noticed how at ease he seemed. He walked with a casual stride, the fishing pole laid against his shoulder. She tried to match the way he moved, wanting to seem at ease as well.

The tops of the trees thinned out and Marty pushed through another patch of growth. When Jess stepped through to the other side, she gasped with wonder. A field almost as large as the yard surrounding Uncle Jonathon's house spread out before her. Marty continued along a narrow path and she followed, running her hands over the tall grass that was almost as high as her waist. Ahead of them were willow trees, and as they got closer, she spied cattails and the sparkling water of a large pond.

When she reached the pond's edge, a breeze made the surface of the water ripple while the cattails rustled. She grinned at Marty, wanting him to know how beautiful she thought it was, but he turned his back to her. He set his bucket down and rummaged through the dirt for a worm. Jess leaned in close and with a mixture of revulsion and fascination, she watched him pierce it on the hook. Then he motioned for her to give him space.

Drawing his right arm back, he cast out the line with a fast, fluid motion, sending the hook to the center of the pond where it landed with a plop. He went to a large tree trunk that had fallen near the water and sat on it. Jess joined him on the trunk and the two of them watched the red bobber floating on the rippling water. Jess didn't mind not talking. It was peaceful sitting next to Marty in silence and sharing the beauty of the surroundings with him.

After a while, there was a tug on the line, and Marty stood. Jess knew it must be a fish. He approached the water's edge, all the while reeling in the fishing line, and she joined him. Then the line went taut. Marty pulled on the rod, but he couldn't reel in more line. From the concern in his face, she knew something was wrong. He kept trying to turn the reel and tugged the pole, but it made no difference. He lowered the pole, letting the line go slack. "Darn it!"

"What happened?" Jess said, forgetting all about her promise to remain silent.

"The fish must have dropped the hook, and now it's caught on something."

"Oh."

"Here." He surprised her by thrusting the fishing pole at her. When she took it, he unlaced his boots.

"What are you doing?"

"I got to see if I can get it free." He kicked off his boots, exposing dirty gray socks. His big toe stuck through a hole in one of them. "I need you to let the line stay slack, but not too slack."

"Sure thing, Marty." She tried not to smile too hard, but her heart was bursting that he'd asked for her help.

Then he pulled his T-shirt off with no warning at all. She stared at his exposed skin with shock. She'd seen boys with their shirts off before, but never one as old as Marty, at least not this close. Her eyes traveled up from the waistband of his jeans, which hung shockingly low, well below his belly button, over the tanned muscles of his stomach, to his chest, and nipples. She didn't think it was possible for someone so slim to be so muscular at the same time.

"Turn around."

His fingers were at the button of his jeans. She spun away from him and put her free hand over her eyes while her face burned red-hot. *He wouldn't get all the way naked,*

The Boy in the Woods

would he? she wondered with horror, and then she heard water splashing. She couldn't help peeking through her fingers and was relieved to see Marty wading into the water in his underpants. She closed her eyes, knowing it was wrong to look, but when she heard a splash, she peeked again. He had done a belly flop and was dog-paddling out to where the fishing line disappeared into the water.

This was when he needed her help, and she let the fishing line go slack. He took an audible gulp of air, and held his nose before he went under. There was a tremendous amount of splashing as he kicked his legs, but he came up right away. He shook water and hair out of his eyes, then took another deep breath and held his nose. Going under again, his legs splashed as he disappeared, but he could only stay down for a few seconds. He tread water for a minute, then dog-paddled back to Jess with a grim expression before joining her on shore. He looked at the center of the pond as water dripped out of his hair.

"Couldn't you get to the hook?"

"It's too deep."

"Do you have another hook?"

"No," he snarled.

He must not have money to buy hooks. That meant he could never fish again. She couldn't let that happen. Not when she could do something about it. "Here." She handed him the rod, then bent down and unbuckled her Mary Janes. When she had them off, along with her ankle socks, she straightened and undid the top button of her dress.

Marty's mouth dropped open.

"Turn around," she commanded, and he did, his neck turning a bright red. She slipped her dress over her head, leaving her in an undershirt and panties.

The Boy in the Woods

When she stepped into the water, she grimaced. It was disgusting to feel mud squishing between her toes, but she ignored it. That couldn't stop her from helping Marty. She did a shallow dive and swam to the center of the pond. Grasping the fishing line, she took in a lungful of air and dove down. The water was clearer than she expected, and as she swam down, she could see where the line ended in the branches of a fallen tree.

A flash of movement caught her eye, and when she focused on it, she almost gagged. A small fish with the hook piercing its mouth wriggled, trying to free itself from where the line was tangled. She kicked to the surface and when she broke through, she gasped, trying to come to terms with what she'd seen.

"What happened? Are you okay?" Marty said, taking a step forward.

"I'm okay. The hook is in a fish's mouth. The line is caught on branches at the bottom of the pond and the fish is trapped. I don't know if I can get it loose."

Marty's body seemed to deflate.

She had to get that hook. Taking another deep breath, she dove and swam to the fish. She tried to grab it, but it was moving too fast. Then she took hold of the branch the line was wrapped around, intending to untangle it. It snapped off in her hand, and she kicked hard to the surface.

She thrust her arm out of the water with triumph. "I got it!" As soon as the fish was exposed to the air, it whipped its tail, hitting her arm and splashing water on her face. With a shriek, she dropped it. Marty lifted the pole and reeled in the fish. She followed it to the shore, grinning like mad.

When the fish was close enough, Marty took hold of the line and lifted it out. Jess ran out of the water and stood beside him. He worked the hook out of the fish's mouth while it wiggled its tail. Then Marty picked up the bucket and dumped the remaining worms on the ground. After filling it with water, he dropped the fish in and they watched it swim in quick circles.

"It's too small. I should let it go," he said.

Even though he sounded disappointed, Jess was glad. She didn't want the fish to die.

He took the bucket to the water and tipped it until the fish swam out. Watching it disappear in the depths, Jess imagined it returning to its family.

"Are you going to try for another one, Marty?"

"Nah, all the fish are scared away by now. Aw, jeez." He turned away from her, his neck flushing with color again.

She looked down and was horrified. Her wet undershirt was see-through as it clung to her body. To hide herself from his eyes, she raced into the water and dove. She swam under the surface for as long as she had air, then came up, laughing with embarrassment. Turning around, she saw Marty standing on the shore. The extra layers of cloth of his underwear provided him with a barrier from her eyes, but Marty's expression changed as he realized he was exposed. He covered himself with his hands, making her laugh again.

"Come on in, Marty. Come swim with me." She beckoned, but he didn't move. She swam back and forth. "The water is nice. It's so warm."

He hesitated a moment longer, then shrugged and came into the water, still keeping himself covered. As soon as he was deep enough, he jumped forward and dog-paddled towards her. She swam to meet him and when she was close enough, she pushed her hands across the surface of the water to splash his face.

He blinked the water out of his eyes, but then he had a

wily grin. Sweeping his arms, he threw wave after wave of water at her.

She screamed and swam away from him while he chased her, continuously splashing. When he stopped, she turned and chased him back to shore while he dog-paddled away from her. When she could touch the bottom, she leaped forward, landing on his back. He rolled, pulling her with him until she was underneath him in the water. She let go and tried to swim away, but he wrapped his arms around her waist. Picking her up as he stood, she came out of the water, shrieking. He tossed her, and she landed with a huge splash. As soon as her head broke the surface, she yelled, "Do that again."

This time, he scooped her up under her back and knees, propelling himself with his legs so he could toss her even further. After a few more times, he complained he was too tired to lift her anymore. They circled each other in the shallow water, while catching their breaths.

"You swim good," Marty said with grudging respect.

"Thanks. I took lessons at the 'Y.'"

"What's a 'Y?'"

"The Y.M.C.A." A memory came to Jess. Her mother's large hand holding her small one as they walked up the front steps of the old brick building where she took her swimming lessons. Blinking hard, she tried to gain control of her emotions. "You know, I should teach you how to swim."

"I already know how to swim." From the scowl on his face, she knew she'd hurt his pride.

"I know you can swim. You swim real good. I meant I could teach you a *different* way to swim."

"I don't think so." He dog-paddled away from her, but not before she saw the uneasy look in his eyes.

"Come on, Marty." She caught up to him with a few strokes and circled around to confront him. "It'll be fun. Please?"

"Okay," he groused.

"Great." She swam to where the water was shoulder deep.

Marty took his time following her, refusing to meet her eyes.

"We'll start with the movements. First, you need to be on your stomach with your legs out behind you."

"I'll drown if I do that."

"No you won't. I won't let you." He scoffed, but she continued. "Now listen. You need to straighten your legs out and kick them like this." She held her arms out in front of her and mimicked the motion of kicking legs. "Put your hands on my shoulders."

He complied, but he was still frowning. "Now straighten your body out and when you're flat, kick your legs." She was elated when he did what she'd asked. "Good job, Marty."

As he got used to the motions, his movements sped up, and she had to brace herself so she wouldn't be pushed over.

"Okay, that's good."

He stopped.

"While you're kicking your legs, put your face in the water and—"

"I can't," he said.

"What?"

"I can't put my face in the water. Water will go up my

nose."

"It does?"

"Yeah. Doesn't it go up your nose?"

"No."

"How do you keep it from doing that?"

"I don't know. It just never happens."

"I can't do it."

Sensing he was about to give up, she changed tactics. "Okay, you can do it with your head out of the water too." She bent over so her chest was in the water. "While you kick your legs, move your arms like this." She made the motions, turning her head with each stroke. "Try it, Marty."

He complied, putting his chest in the water and mimicking her movements.

"I think you're ready to do them together. Watch me." She pushed off and swam like she'd showed him, slowing her movements so he could study them. Then she heard splashing. Marty was swimming towards her. His movements were jerky and awkward, and he was splashing much more than he needed to, but he was swimming the way she'd showed him. "You're doing it, Marty."

He flashed a grin as he passed her, and she followed to swim alongside him. When he went back towards the shore, she turned with him. They swam back and forth across the pond until they were tired, and headed to the warm shallows to relax.

"I wish I'd kept that fish." Marty lifted his hand out of the water to examine his puckered fingers. "I'm hungry."

Jess thought of her basket with the extra sandwich. "I brought a lunch. It's at the cabin. I can share it with you... if you want," she said, stumbling when his eyes became suspicious.

"I have a lunch too. I just didn't bring it."

"I can get it, I don't mind. We can have a picnic."

He sneered. "You sure you remember the way?"

"Of course I do." She stood and splashed out of the pond. He stayed in the water and while she watched to make sure he kept his back to her, she peeled off her wet underwear and put on her dress and shoes. "I'll be right back, Marty."

She turned and ran down the grassy path. Maybe while they were eating, he'd be comfortable enough to answer some of the questions she had about him.

Chapter Eight
Hearts Made of Stone

JESS WAS BREATHLESS by the time she reached the cabin, but she rushed to the kitchen, grabbed the handle of the basket and Marty's battered brown paper bag, and then sprinted back to the path. She had an extra sandwich for Marty, but how was she going to convince him to take it? By the time she'd made it back to the pond, she still had no idea.

Marty was sitting on the fallen tree trunk wearing his jeans but no shirt. He stood as she approached. She averted her eyes to avoid looking at his bare chest, and spotted his underpants draped across a bush.

He's naked under his jeans. Embarrassed, she turned her head the other way only to see her own underwear lying in a wet heap on the ground near the tree trunk. She was mortified. How could she have left them lying where he would see them?

"Here." She pushed his paper bag at him. He took it and she scooped up her underwear, hoping he didn't notice her flaming face. Hiding behind a large shrub, she spread them out on the branches to dry like Marty had, making sure

The Boy in the Woods

they would be hidden from his view.

When she came out, Marty was under a willow tree next to the pond. She stepped through the veil of willow branches and sat near him, careful to tuck her skirt around her bare legs. He was untwisting the top of his paper bag with his head down, hair covering his face. She opened the dish towel Annie had used to line her basket. Marty pulled out a thin sandwich crudely wrapped in wax paper and unwrapped it. Wishing she knew how to get him to take a sandwich, Jess took one of hers out, noticing how thick it was compared to his. Then she saw his unwrapped sandwich as he was about to take a bite. "Is that peanut butter and jelly?"

His hand froze halfway to his mouth. "Yeah," he said, his eyes wary. "What about it?"

Not wanting him to guess her true intentions, she smiled, hoping to reassure him. "I haven't had one in forever. My uncle doesn't like peanut butter so we don't have it in the house."

He shrugged and brought the sandwich to his mouth.

"Marty?"

"What?" he said with annoyance, lowering the sandwich.

"Would you mind – I mean, would you like to trade with me?" She offered her sandwich to him. "It's ham and Swiss, but maybe you don't like Swiss cheese," she added, remembering how she used to hate it when she was little.

"I like it okay," he said, but he seemed reluctant.

"Do you want to swap? I really miss peanut butter and jelly."

He studied her, and she waited. He held out his sandwich. "I reckon."

After they traded sandwiches, he unwrapped the wax paper around her sandwich, and Jess took a bite of his. As soon as she tasted the sweet jelly mixed with the salty peanut butter, she closed her eyes with pleasure. "It's so good."

He didn't reply, taking an enormous bite out of the ham sandwich instead.

She rummaged through the basket to find the homemade dill pickles Annie had packed. Once she'd unwrapped them, she laid them on the grass between them. "Help yourself to a pickle."

This time, he didn't hesitate to take one and bit into it with a loud crunch. She took one and made just as loud a crunch when she took a bite. While they ate, she looked out at the pond. The breeze made the cattails sway while willow branches trailed back and forth in the water. The pond glittered, and dragonflies skimmed across its surface. Being in this beautiful place and eating lunch with Marty made her feel lighter than she had in a long time.

Hunched over as he ate, Marty was concentrating on his food more than the surroundings, but he seemed relaxed too. She wondered if now might be a good time to ask him questions. "How old are you, Marty?" She hoped starting with a small one wouldn't seem too intrusive.

"Fourteen," he said, his mouth full of ham.

"I'm thirteen."

He didn't respond, still intent on his sandwich.

"You don't live here on the property, do you?"

He stopped chewing and lifted his head, looking at her through his hair. His eyes were guarded, but she met his steady gaze, hoping he'd know he could trust her. He looked away. "Of course not, don't be stupid," he said before taking another bite.

"But how do you get through the fence? Is there a hole in it or something?" If there was, he could show her the way out.

"I climb it."

"How can you climb the bars? They must be slippery."

"I just do."

"But there are spikes on the top."

"It's not that hard if you know what you're doing."

With his muscles he might not have trouble climbing a high iron fence, but she could never do it. She took a deep breath against the heaviness that descended on her. "So, uh, where do you live?"

He stiffened. "What's with all the questions?"

"I just wondered." She tried to sound casual, but his eyes didn't change. They were full of suspicion, and there was a hint of anger. It reminded her of how he'd looked the day he met her. "You know I won't tell anyone. I swore I wouldn't and I meant it."

After a moment, his shoulders curved inward. "I live in a house, like everyone else."

"With your parents?"

"Do you think I was hatched?" he said, the words biting.

She waited, thinking he might offer more details, but he didn't. "Do you have any brothers or sisters?"

He looked out at the pond, his face stormy. "Not anymore."

What did that mean? She watched him as he stared at the water, anger radiating off his body. Whatever was going on at his home, he didn't want to talk about it. She didn't want to ruin the good time they'd been having, so reaching into her basket, she pulled out the chocolate chip cookies Annie had packed for dessert. The rustling of the wax paper got Marty's attention, and she set it on the grass between them, a peace offering. He looked at the cookies, but didn't move.

"Go ahead. You can have some if you want."

He tentatively reached out and chose one. Bringing it to his nose, he inhaled with his eyes closed. After he took a bite, he examined the cookie while he chewed. As he continued to eat it, his anger melted away. Jess chose a cookie, and made a mental note – Marty liked sweets.

With all the food eaten, he stretched and yawned. "I'm bushed." He lay in the grass and put his arm over his eyes. She was tired too, and joined him. Once settled, she turned her head so she could see the pond past the willow branches. The sound of the birds in the trees and the cattails rustling soon lulled her to sleep.

When she opened her eyes, she was looking at Marty. He was still lying on his back with his eyes closed and his arms up. His head rested on them like a pillow, his face turned towards her. She marveled that his shaggy golden brown hair was long enough it fell over his arms. His chest rose and fell as he slept. His tanned skin looked smooth, the muscles and ribs easy to see on his slim body. Her eyes traveled down to the waistband of his jeans and his exposed hip bones.

When her gaze returned to his face, his brown eyes were open, looking right at her. Her face flamed, mortified he'd caught her examining him, but his expression remained neutral. She turned her head to the other side, hoping he didn't notice her embarrassment. While she waited for her face to cool, she felt a fluttering in her stomach. She didn't know if it was caused by him catching her, or what she'd seen, but she hoped it would go away soon.

After a while, her eyes drifted closed, and she realized she was about to fall asleep again. Worried about how late it was getting, she sat up. She glanced over at Marty. He was on his side, facing away from her. "Marty," she said. When he didn't move, she put her hand on his arm and jiggled him.

He jerked away from her touch, eyes wide and blinking under his long hair.

She picked up their wax paper wrappers as if nothing had happened. "I have to go soon."

He got on his knees, running his fingers through his hair to get it out of his eyes, then located his empty paper sack. After smoothing it flat on his leg, he folded it and slid it into his back pocket. Jess hid behind the shrub and plucked off her underwear. They were still damp, but she put them on anyway, not having any other choice. When she finished, she called out, "Are you dressed?"

"Yeah."

Marty had already collected his fishing pole and pail, and he headed down the path. The wind had picked up and while they made their way across the field, the tall grasses around them undulated like a green-gold sea. Watching the seed heads sway under the afternoon sun, Jess felt happy. It was the first time since her parents had died that she'd felt that good, and she knew it was because she'd spent the day with Marty.

At the cabin, Marty went to the kitchen sink and pumped the handle. He drank from the spigot and then stepped away, wiping his mouth with the back of his hand. Jess took his place at the pump to do the same. The water tasted delicious, cold and refreshing, and when she finished, she wiped her mouth with the back of her hand like Marty had.

"I have to go," she said.

He crossed his arms over his chest as if he was afraid she would try to shake his hand again.

"Thanks for taking me fishing."

He snorted. "I didn't catch anything."

"I know, but it was still fun."

"I reckon." He shrugged and looked away, but she saw the corners of his mouth twitching.

She grinned. "See you later."

Before she stepped onto the path to go back to her house, she looked back. Marty was watching her, and she waved at him. As usual, he didn't wave back, but she didn't mind. She was awash with joy.

When she let herself into the kitchen, Annie stopped stirring a pot on the stove and came towards her, wiping her hands on her apron. "Have a good time?"

"Yep."

"Be sure to wash up. You must be dirty after being in the woods all day, although you look clean as a whistle," she said, examining Jess more closely.

Jess's heart beat faster, and she turned to leave, but Annie put her hand on Jess's shoulder.

"Why, you're wet." Jess turned towards her and Annie ran her hands over Jess's shoulders, feeling the dampness from her undershirt coming through her dress. "What on Earth have you been doing?"

Jess didn't want to admit she'd been at the pond, but what other explanation could she give?

"Jessica Blackwell, you tell me this instant," Annie

said, her voice rising.

Jess knew she had no other choice. "Swimming."

Annie raised her eyebrow. "In a *pond*?"

"Yes, ma'am," she said, unable to meet her eyes.

"Jess, I *know* that pond. That water is *deep*. It's *way* over your head."

"I know how to swim. I've been taking lessons practically my whole life."

"And you ate lunch while you were out there," Annie continued as if she hadn't heard her. "Don't you know you could've gotten a cramp and drowned? You were all alone!"

"Nothing happened."

She shook her head. "You can't go back there again."

"What? No, please, Annie."

"It's far too dangerous."

"What if I promise never to go in over my head?" Jess said. Annie opened her mouth to argue with her, but Jess spoke up. "I promise, I won't ever go in that deep."

Annie closed her mouth and let out a sigh. "You promise to wait a while after you eat so you don't get a cramp in the water?"

"I swear it."

"Okay, but I'm *trusting* you're telling me the truth."

"I promise." Jess hugged her, not wanting Annie to see her guilty expression. She'd told so many lies already. "Thank you."

"It's okay," Annie said. "You know I'm only saying this because I'm worried about you, pumpkin. I don't want anything to happen to you." There was a sudden roughness in her voice and Jess squeezed her tighter.

"I know. I won't let anything happen to me."

When she let go, Annie turned back to the stove, but Jess saw her wipe her eyes with her apron before she stirred the stew. "I don't suppose you have a bathing suit to wear," she said, her tone stern. "Even though you're alone, I don't want you swimming in your underwear. It's not proper."

"I have a bathing suit, remember? You put it away when you helped me unpack my boxes."

"If you're going to insist on swimming, you should wear it." She still sounded unhappy that she'd given in. "I suppose I can find you an old towel."

"Thank you, Annie." Then Jess thought of something else. "You won't tell Uncle Jonathon I'm swimming, will you?" She had no doubt if her uncle knew she was going to the pond, he'd forbid it. Not because it was dangerous, but because it was fun.

Annie seemed to struggle with herself. "I won't mention it to him, but don't make me regret my decision."

"I won't."

"You better go change before he gets home."

Grateful the conversation was over, Jess ran up the backstairs. Once her bathroom door was closed, she leaned against it. That was a close call, but at least something good came out of it. Now she wouldn't have to lie to Annie about swimming, or at least she wouldn't lie *too* much. And from now on, she'd get to wear her bathing suit. That would be a lot less awkward than swimming with Marty in her underwear. She pulled away from the door and unbuttoned her dress to change for dinner.

That evening, she had almost reached the dining room when she heard Annie's voice and stopped in the hallway.

Was Annie telling Uncle Jonathon about the pond?

"I don't understand," Uncle Jonathon said. "She already *has* clothes."

"But they're not meant for playing in the woods. Her dresses will get ruined."

Jess had forgotten Annie was going to ask Uncle Jonathon about getting her new clothes.

"What does it matter what her dresses look like. It's not like anyone sees them."

"But if she had play clothes–"

There was a loud bang and the sound of cutlery rattling. "I know it may look like I'm made of money," Uncle Jonathon shouted. "But I can assure you, I'm not."

Jess shrank back even though she wasn't on the receiving end of his temper.

"I won't waste money on clothes when she already has clothes she can wear outside. Do I make myself clear?"

"Yes, sir."

Annie was so quiet Jess almost didn't hear her, but her humiliation came through loud and clear. White hot anger flooded through Jess. Douglas had gone to Europe with an entire wardrobe of brand new clothes. Uncle Jonathon hadn't had any trouble paying for *those*.

"I suppose when she outgrows the clothes she has," Uncle Jonathon grumbled, "you could get her some outdoor things."

"That's grand. Thank you, sir."

Jess was more angry knowing Annie had just forgiven him for yelling at her.

"Why isn't she at the table yet?"

Jess tensed.

"I don't like how she's always late for dinner."

"I can pop into her room and see what's taking so long," Annie offered.

Jess hurried into the dining room, her stomach churning. What if he figured out she'd been listening in?

"There you are," Annie said with evident relief.

Uncle Jonathon's harsh gaze stayed on Jess while she crossed the room. "Excuse me for being late."

"Don't make this a habit, Jessica. I don't like it."

"Yes, sir." She slid into her seat.

Annie was already going through the door to the butler's pantry and Jess watched it swing closed, wishing she hadn't left. She didn't like being alone with her uncle when he was angry.

He held his hand out for her bowl, and she gave it to him, keeping her attention on the food in front of her. Soon the only sound was their spoons scraping against porcelain and paper tearing as her uncle went through his mail. In the silence, she let her mind drift, imagining she was eating her meal with Marty.

The sun setting behind the trees made the shadows in the clearing deepen and the crickets awakened. Marty stood from the front stoop of the cabin, listening to their chirping. He stretched until his back made a satisfying crack and returned to the kitchen. As he walked, he noticed stiffness in his legs. *Must be from all the swimming.*

He closed the back door and shook his head with bemusement, thinking of the kid. Being with Jess today had been… fun. More fun than he'd had in a while. Knowing her, she'd likely come back the next day. It was strange, but the thought didn't bother him. After all this time, he didn't think he'd ever like being around anyone, but after only two days, he didn't mind if she showed up again, even if she could be annoying sometimes.

He closed the front door and set out across the clearing. In the woods, the quickening darkness did nothing to slow his pace. After years of walking the same route to the fence, he knew the way so well, he could walk it with his eyes closed.

It was dark when he stepped out into a cleared area next to the iron fence. He pressed his face against the bars, listening as he looked up and down the two-lane highway that ran alongside it. There were no headlights and all he heard were crickets. Glancing up to make sure he was in the right spot, he wiped his hands on his jeans then grasped the bars. He pulled himself up while using the grips of his boots to keep from sliding, and bit by bit, made it to the top. He held onto the top railing with one hand and grabbed onto a tree branch that hung over the fence with his other. Lifting his body, he navigated over the spikes until he was on the other side. Within seconds, he'd slid down to the ground. After a quick check in either direction, he crossed the highway.

Heading down a dirt road, he walked with his head down and his hands balled into fists, all thoughts of Jess gone.

Chapter Nine

Don't Be Cruel

August 1958

COVERED IN FLOUR, Jess used the back of her hand to push stray hair off her face. Douglas was due home after his summer-long trip to France, and Annie was teaching her how to make an apple pie for the celebratory dinner. She'd tried her best to roll the pie dough into a circle, but it kept resembling a kidney-shape no matter how much she worked at it. It didn't help that she couldn't stop thinking about Marty. He had to be waiting at the cabin for her, wondering why she wasn't there.

Today was hot, a perfect day to go swimming. And that's what they'd be doing if Annie hadn't made her stay home to greet Douglas. Having Douglas home was going to complicate things. She hoped he wouldn't be hanging around, asking what she was doing in the woods all day. Would he treat her any differently than he had before he left? She didn't hold out a lot of hope.

"Oh, my goodness," Annie said.

Jess looked up from her pie dough to see the black car coming down the driveway.

"They're here. Hurry, Jess, take off your apron."

Jess suppressed a sigh as she removed it, and while she walked behind Annie, she resigned herself to Douglas rejecting her again. Before Annie could open the front door, Uncle Jonathon walked in followed by Douglas and then James, laden with suitcases.

Despite the heat, Douglas was wearing a beret and scarf as if a few months abroad had turned him into a Frenchman. Jess had to work hard not to laugh. Instead of sophisticated, he looked ridiculous.

"Welcome home, Doug," Annie said.

"Hi, Annie," Douglas said. His smile fell away as his eyes swept over Jess.

"Did you have a good trip?"

"*Oui, très bon.* That means 'yes, very good,'" Douglas said, puffing out his chest.

Jess knew it was best not to roll her eyes, but she really wanted to.

Annie clasped her hands to her chest. "Listen to you speak French."

"I learned a little so I could speak to the natives."

Uncle Jonathon put his hand on Douglas's shoulder. "I hate to go, son, but I have a meeting at the office."

"Wait, Dad. I got you a present." He opened a suitcase and rummaged through it, pulling out a slim black box. "I got this at one of those fancy shops in Paris." He handed it to Uncle Jonathon.

Uncle Jonathon lifted the lid and pulled out a navy

blue tie scattered with small polka dots.

"It's real silk, I hope you like it."

Uncle Jonathon beamed. "It's a fine tie, son. Very fine, indeed. I'll wear it today."

"I got something for you too, Annie." Douglas reached back into the suitcase and pulled out another slim box, this one larger and a pale gray.

"You didn't have to get me anything," Annie said, her voice hushed.

Douglas gave her a kind smile. "I couldn't go to Paris and not get you something."

She opened the box and pulled out a scarf.

"It's got the Eiffel Tower on it, see?" Douglas took it from her so he could unfold it. Large single-stemmed roses were scattered over it, with the city of Paris below.

"It's beautiful," Annie said, her face glowing.

Jess smiled, knowing how much the gift meant to her. Even Uncle Jonathon seemed to approve.

"Thank you, Doug."

"You're welcome. I, uh, got something for you too, Jessica," he said in a quieter voice. He reached into his suitcase for a box identical to Annie's.

When he held it out, he had his eyes on the box instead of her. She stared at it, unable to believe he'd bought her a present. Then she noticed the silence as everyone waited.

"Uh, thanks, Douglas." The gray lid said 'Christian Dior' and when she lifted it she wasn't surprised to see a scarf similar to Annie's. She took it out of the box and the silky fabric unfurled, revealing pink and yellow flowers on a pale gray background. "It's – pretty," she said, surprised. "Thanks."

He bent to close his suitcase. "You're welcome."

When he stood, Uncle Jonathon grasped his upper arm. "It's good to have you back, son. It's been too quiet here without you. We've missed you."

Douglas's face lit up. "I'm glad to be home."

Jess felt as if she'd been punched in the stomach. The way her uncle had spoken, it was as if she hadn't been there at all.

"I'll see you at dinner," Uncle Jonathon said.

"Let me take your suitcases up to your room, Doug," Annie said after Uncle Jonathon had closed the door behind him.

"I'll do it. I'm sure you're busy."

"Jess and I are making your favorite dinner, aren't we, Jess?"

Jess managed a weak smile, but Douglas was already gathering his suitcases.

"Roast chicken, mashed potatoes and gravy, corn on the cob, and apple pie for dessert."

"That sounds swell, Annie." He headed up the stairs.

"Come along, Jess. We've got a lot more to do."

On the way to the kitchen, Jess examined her scarf. She couldn't believe how beautiful it was, and the label said it was silk. It had to have cost a lot of money. Did Douglas decide to buy her a present on his own? Or did someone tell him to do it? Perhaps his friend's mother purchased the gifts, and he pretended he'd chosen them. After all, what teenage boy goes shopping for women's scarves?

But he seemed excited when he gave the gifts to his father and Annie, like he was proud of what he'd picked out for them. She sighed, setting her scarf on the backstairs so she wouldn't get flour on it. It was a mystery. She put her apron back on, ready to attack the pie dough again.

That night, Douglas spent the entire dinner talking about his trip. Listening to his stories, Jess was jealous he'd had such an adventurous vacation. Then she thought of what her summer had been like, and the jealousy melted away. She would never have met Marty if she'd been in Europe. Maybe she hadn't experienced all the excitement Douglas had, but she'd still had a lot of fun. Marty hadn't just become her friend, he was her *best* friend, and she wouldn't trade that for any trip.

Jess arrived at the cabin earlier than usual the next morning and was surprised the door was already open. She quickened her steps. It had been two days since she'd last seen Marty, and the time had dragged. Over the summer, she'd come to rely on Marty's company. He'd become everything to her. Everything that Uncle Jonathon and his big, cold house was not.

She found him in the kitchen, going through the wood in the crate by the back door, looking for a new piece of wood to whittle.

"Good morning," she said.

When he saw her, his eyes lit up before he hid it. "Hi." He examined the wood in his hand, turning it around. He liked to keep up the facade he didn't care whether or not she came to see him, but she could see through it. Not that she'd ever let him know. There wasn't any need to.

She set the basket on the counter next to his paper sack. "Are we going fishing today?"

He shrugged, and put the wood in his jeans' pocket. "I reckon."

"Then I'll go change."

They'd gone to the pond almost every day under the pretense of fishing, but they'd ended up swimming instead. She kept her bathing suit and towel in the bedroom where she went to change. It was a simple one-piece suit made of yellow-green cotton. It didn't bother her to wear it in front of Marty now, but she'd been self-conscious the first time, knowing it made her look like a little kid. She hoped she wasn't doomed to be skinny forever.

When they arrived at the pond, Marty laid his fishing pole on the fallen tree trunk and unlaced his boots while Jess pulled off her dress. Within seconds she was in the cool water, and Marty followed, splashing her.

Hours later, they were lying on the grass under the willow tree, propped up on their elbows so they could look out at the pond.

"I didn't come yesterday because my cousin came home from France." Jess lifted her hair off her neck to cool it. She was growing it out so she could wear it in a ponytail and it had reached that annoying middle stage; too short for the ponytail but long enough to make her neck hot. "His name is Douglas."

Marty barked out a laugh. "I know who your cousin is, Jess."

She sat up. "You know Douglas?"

"I don't *know* him, but I know who he is. We go to the same school."

Jess found that more unbelievable. She'd never imagined Marty attended school. But it was dumb for her not to have figured it out. Just because she'd only seen him on her property didn't mean he wasn't like any other ordinary boy his age. "I can't wait for school to start. It's going to be so much fun."

Marty snorted.

"What was that for?"

He tried to catch a fly that had landed on his leg, but missed. "School is never fun."

"Sure it is."

"Not for me. I hate school."

"Why do you hate school?"

"There's no point to it."

"But, you learn stuff."

He scoffed. "Useless stuff."

"It's not useless. You need to know those things if you want to go to college."

He gave her a pointed look.

"Even if you don't go to college, it's still better if you know those things," she said in a quieter voice.

"I don't think so," he muttered.

"What about seeing all your friends? I always miss my school friends during the summer."

"I don't have—"

"Hey." She faced him as a brilliant idea came to her. "We're going to the same school. We can be friends."

Marty kept his eyes on the water.

"We'll have to be careful, of course, but we can *pretend* to meet, and then we can be real friends, right out in the open. We'll be able to have lunch together, and we can study together." She leaned back on her elbows. "Now I *really* can't wait for school to start."

Marty jumped up. "I'm done here."

"What?"

He walked to his clothes.

"What about lunch?"

He tugged his jeans up over his wet underwear. "I'm going back to the cabin. You can stay if you want."

"I guess I'll go too."

By the time she reached her dress, he was pulling on his boots. She threw it on over her suit and slipped on her socks. He got the fishing pole and headed down the path while she was putting on her shoes. "Wait, Marty." She rushed to do up the buckles.

He'd forgotten his paper bag and she grabbed it when she retrieved her basket and towel from under the willow tree. She ran to catch up and then fell in step behind him. As they wove their way through the field of tall grass, she thought about how wonderful it was that they'd be in school together.

"I wish we could be in some of the same classes," she said. "But we probably won't since I'm going into the ninth grade and you're going into tenth. Or maybe you're going into eleventh like Douglas."

Marty spun around, and she almost ran into him. "Would you shut up about it?" he shouted.

"Marty," she said, shocked by his sudden anger. "What's wrong?"

"I'm going into *ninth* grade. Are you happy now?" He waved his arms as he lost control. "That's right, they made me repeat a grade. But you know what?" He stepped close enough he was looming over her. *"I don't care!"* he said, making her wince with each word. He pivoted and stalked off into the woods.

She watched his back disappear, tears pricking her eyes. How could he have turned on her and been so mean? Continuing down the path, she wiped her eyes while her pain turned to anger. He'd better apologize to her when she got to the cabin.

When she walked into the kitchen, he was already sitting at the little table with his shoulders hunched. She set his paper bag in front of him, but he didn't move. She waited for him to apologize, but instead, he opened his sack and took out his peanut butter and jelly sandwich. Slowly reaching across the table, he placed it at her spot, then pulled his arm back and set his hand in his lap.

She considered leaving, walking out the door and never coming back. It's what he deserved after yelling at her. But when she thought about never seeing him again, a tremendous sadness overwhelmed her.

She collapsed on her stool and opened the dishcloth covering her basket. She took out a sandwich, thick with slices of roast chicken and held it out to him. He didn't move. She waited, refusing to set it down for him, and he reached out and took it. She felt a wave of disappointment he still wouldn't say anything.

They ate in silence, and as soon as Jess finished, she went to the bedroom to change out of her suit. When she finished, Marty was sitting in a wooden chair in front of the dark fireplace reading an old fishing magazine. She stood where he would see her, but he kept reading as if she wasn't there. She spun away and stomped into the kitchen.

With her hand on the basket handle, she tried to decide what to do. It was clear he had no intention of saying he was sorry, or even explaining why he'd become so angry. She wasn't going to bring it up when he was the one in the wrong. Deciding she was done with him for the day, she left through the back door.

She'd been walking down the path for less than a minute when she heard him running behind her.

"Jess, wait up."

She didn't stop.

"I'll walk with you," he said when he reached her.

She continued without acknowledging him. If he wasn't intending to say anything, neither was she.

When the curve before the garage came into view, he put his hand on her arm, stopping her. He dropped his head, and dug the toe of his boot into the dirt. "I shouldn't have yelled at you."

Relief washed through her. "It's okay, Marty. I didn't know you'd been held back a grade. I'm sorry I brought it up."

He lifted his head, his brown eyes troubled. "This whole being friends at school thing, it's not going to work, see? So forget it."

"What do you mean?"

"Your *cousin* won't like it," he said, his lip curling when he said the word 'cousin.'

"I don't care what he thinks, or anyone else. I'm not going to let anyone tell me I can't be friends with you, Marty."

"Listen to me," he said, then looked over his shoulder in the direction of the garage. He stepped closer and lowered his voice. "Your kind doesn't hang out with people like me." She opened her mouth to protest, but he continued. "You're going to cause *problems* – for *both* of us."

She wanted to argue with him, but then she thought about how her uncle treated everyone he considered beneath him. The people in town must fear him, she realized, and with good reason. She knew the iron mine was a big company. Everyone in town probably relied on it for their income. Her uncle was powerful enough he could ruin people's lives if he wanted to, including the family of a poor boy he considered too low to be friends with his niece.

"Okay," she said. "But just you remember one thing."

He looked up, startled by her change in tone.

"When you see me pretending not to know you, don't you dare think I'm not your friend."

His brow furrowed, and then a playful smile spread across his face. "Sure thing, kid."

She stamped her foot. "I told you not to call me that."

"I don't remember that."

"Don't lie. You do too."

"I think you must have dreamt it."

"I did not."

She lunged to grab onto his arm, determined to shake him until he admitted the truth, but he jumped out of her reach with a laugh. He ran down the path still laughing, and she chased after him.

Chapter Ten

One Summer Night

A WEEK LATER, Jess sat at the table waiting for Douglas and Uncle Jonathon to join her for dinner. Her stomach rumbled while she looked at the dishes of food before her, and she rubbed it, trying to ease her hunger.

Dinner had been delayed since the two of them were late getting home. With Douglas back from his trip, he and Uncle Jonathon were working every day at the mine, but that was fine with Jess. She was glad Douglas wasn't around so she could spend time with Marty without him wondering where she was.

They walked into the dining room, and took their places. Jess put her napkin in her lap, anxious to eat, but looked up when she heard a clinking noise. A set of keys on a key ring had fallen out of Douglas's napkin and were lying on the table next to his plate.

Douglas picked them up. "What's this?"

"What do they look like?" Uncle Jonathon said with a knowing smile.

"Wait. No. You didn't," Douglas sputtered, his eyes widening.

"Why don't you go outside and take a look?" Uncle Jonathon said.

Douglas jumped out of his chair and ran through the swinging door to the kitchen.

Uncle Jonathon slid his chair back. "Come, Jessica. You should see this too."

Jess put her napkin on the table and stood even though she didn't want to. By the time she was outside, Annie and Uncle Jonathon were watching Douglas examine a teal and white car she'd never seen before, confirming what she'd suspected. Uncle Jonathon had bought Douglas a brand new car.

Douglas got behind the wheel and turned on the ignition. When the engine roared to life, he grinned at them, and the now familiar jealousy swelled inside Jess. Uncle Jonathon had balked at spending money on outdoor clothes for her a month ago, yet it seemed money was no object when it came to his son.

Douglas got out of the car and approached Uncle Jonathon. "Thanks, Dad," he said, throwing his arms around him.

Uncle Jonathon seemed taken by surprise. He patted his back with one hand, appearing uncomfortable. "It's alright, son. Now that you have your driver's license, I thought you'd find it useful."

"It's a beautiful car, Doug," Annie said, as he returned to the car and stroked the hood.

"I love it."

Jess leaned close to Annie. "Doesn't Douglas have to be sixteen to get a driver's license?"

"The state allows fifteen-year-olds who've lost a parent to get a license."

"Oh."

"We'd better go back in the house," Uncle Jonathan said. "Dinner will get cold."

Douglas gave his car a last longing look before following his father and Annie. Jess trailed behind, no longer hungry.

Back at the table, Uncle Jonathon listed the features of the car while Jess pushed her food around her plate. It no longer surprised her that her uncle would be so obvious in favoring Douglas over her, but it still stung even though she'd long given up hope he'd treat her better. This was how it would be for the rest of the time she lived in her uncle's home and she might as well get used to it. At least she had Annie and Marty to make life bearable.

Hearing Uncle Jonathon say her name, she lifted her head.

Douglas seemed startled as well. "What did you say?" he asked.

"Now that you have a car, I want you to take Jessica into town on Friday night. Show her around a little. Perhaps take her to a picture show."

Jess saw her shock mirrored in Douglas's eyes.

"But I already have plans," Douglas said.

"You'll have to change them. Jessica said she wanted to spend more time with you."

"I did?" Jess said, wondering what he meant.

Douglas glared at her as if she'd betrayed him.

"Yes, you did. When Douglas was in France."

"That wasn't what—"

"It's the last weekend before school starts!" Douglas said.

"You can visit with your friends another night," Uncle Jonathon said, his voice rising.

"But Dad—"

Uncle Jonathon slammed his fist on the table. "I've made my decision, and that's it!"

Jess stared at him. Uncle Jonathon had never lost his temper with Douglas in front of her before.

"I don't approve of how the two of you are behaving towards each other," Uncle Jonathon continued. "You need to spend more time together, do I make myself clear?"

Douglas opened and closed his mouth without making a sound. Why wasn't he arguing? He could easily win this fight. Then his shoulders dropped. "Yes, sir," he mumbled, head bowed.

Jess was stunned. How could he have given up?

"I'm sure you two will have a good time," Uncle Jonathon said in a softer tone.

"Yes, sir," Douglas repeated to his plate.

Uncle Jonathon reached over to put his hand on Douglas's shoulder. "You know what you should do? After dinner, you should take your car out for a spin. Show it off to your friends. Since you've been able to get your license a year before them, I bet they'll be impressed."

Douglas managed an unconvincing smile. "I'll do that."

"Good."

Uncle Jonathon returned to his meal with a satisfied

expression while Douglas and Jess hunched over their plates. Choking down her dinner, Jess tried to make sense of what had happened. It was as if the world had turned on its axis. Uncle Jonathon losing his temper with Douglas, Douglas caving in on an argument, and now she'd have to go into town with him – alone. She didn't want to go out with Douglas any more than he wanted to take her. She already knew it would be horrible.

For the next two days, both she and Douglas pretended their upcoming night out wasn't happening. He ignored her like he'd always done, and she did the same. The only one who seemed excited about it was Annie, who brought it up all the time, much to Jess's chagrin. She'd even insisted on helping Jess get ready.

"I think you should wear this dress," she said, while Jess lay on her bed, hugging a pillow. She had a stomach ache even though she'd eaten little of her dinner.

When she saw the dress Annie was holding, she sat up, shaking her head. "No." It was the mint green dress she'd worn the day she'd gone to the lawyer's office to hear her father's will being read.

"Are you sure? It's so pretty."

Jess lay back on the bed, her stomach hurting more. "I'm sure."

Annie rummaged through the wardrobe. "Okay, but you don't have that many dresses to choose from."

Maybe if Uncle Jonathon would buy me clothes I'd have something to wear, Jess thought sourly.

"What about this one." Annie held up a pale blue plaid dress with a white Peter Pan collar.

"Fine." At least that one didn't have any sad memories attached to it. Taking it from Annie, she turned towards her bathroom to change.

"Wait, Jess." Annie slid hangers back and forth in the wardrobe. "Let me find your petticoat."

"I don't *want* to wear a petticoat."

Annie put her hands on her hips. "Jessica Blackwell, if you think I'm going to let you go into town without your petticoat, you've got another think coming. I don't want people to see you looking like you don't know how to dress like a lady."

Jess didn't care what they thought, but she knew there was no use arguing. "Okay, okay."

Once she'd put on the scratchy petticoat and plaid dress, she looked in the mirror with disgust. It wasn't just that the dress was made for a ten-year-old, but her nose was covered with freckles from her summer spent in the sun. She opened the door and walked out, her shoulders hunched.

"You look so cute."

The comment didn't make her feel any better, but she held her tongue, not wanting to get into another argument.

"We need to do something about your hair." Annie tapped her chin with her finger. "Perhaps a headband. What do you think?"

"Sure." It couldn't make her look any worse than she already did.

After fixing her hair, Annie located a pair of white gloves and a cotton sweater in case it got cool later. Jess balked at wearing her black patent leather Mary Janes, but Annie wouldn't back down. Her everyday shoes were scuffed from being worn outside.

They were leaving the bedroom when Annie stopped. "You know what? You should wear the scarf Doug bought you in Paris."

"No." How could Annie think that was a good idea?

"Why not? It'll go perfectly with your dress."

Jess crossed her arms over her chest. "If I have to wear it, I'm not going." Wearing the scarf would be like saying she was happy Douglas was taking her out. He was only doing it because he was forced to, and there was no way she was going to pretend otherwise.

"I don't understand why you're so dead against it, but if you insist…" Annie opened the bedroom door, and Jess followed her, still angry. The night hadn't even started yet, and she was already having a terrible time.

Douglas and Uncle Jonathon appeared from the living room as they came down the stairs. Douglas looked grim, still wearing the trousers and button-down shirt he'd worn to the office, but he'd removed his tie.

"Here she is," Annie said with a smile.

Douglas didn't look up, but Uncle Jonathon eyed her with approval. Jess was surprised he seemed in a good mood, but perhaps it was the drink in his hand that accounted for it.

She joined Douglas and the two of them stood by the front door, gazing at the floor while the adults examined them.

"I hope you have a good time," Annie said.

Neither of them said anything.

"Get a jacket, son. The nights are already getting cooler."

"Uh, yeah," Douglas said to the floor while Annie opened the coat closet to get him one. "Let's go," Douglas said without meeting Jess's eyes.

Douglas opened the door and she walked out, grateful to escape their scrutiny, but Annie and Uncle Jonathon followed them out. Even worse, James was outside as well. She could feel everyone's eyes on her as she walked to Douglas's car. She reached for the door handle at the same time Douglas put his hand on it to open it for her, making her more embarrassed. Once she was seated, he closed the door and walked around to the driver's side. When he turned on the ignition, James got in the black car and pulled away. Douglas drove behind him.

At the gate, they waited in silence for James to unlock it, and after he opened it, Douglas drove through. Jess turned to see him closing it behind them. When she faced forward again, she took in a deep breath. It was the first time she'd left the property since she'd arrived three months ago.

Douglas steered the vehicle down the dirt road that ran along the high iron fence. She leaned forward to see the spikes at the top. It was so high. She didn't see how it could be possible for Marty to climb over it. Was he still at the cabin? She wished she was with him instead of Douglas right now.

They reached the two-lane highway, and Douglas stopped the car. She thought he'd pull out, but he turned towards her. "Look, Jessica, I'm not taking you to the movies. I already made plans for tonight and I'm not changing them."

"Don't flatter yourself, *Douglas*," she said, emphasizing his name with a sneer. "I didn't want to go to the movies with you anyway."

His face flushed. "My name's Doug, not Douglas."

"I'll call you *Doug*, when you call me *Jess*."

He glared at her, flustered she'd talked back to him. Then he pulled out onto the highway, his hands gripping the steering wheel so tight his knuckles were white. Jess faced the passenger window, hating him more with each passing second.

By the time they reached the town, the sun was setting. Closed shops and two-story homes with their lights on lined the road. It was as different as it could be from Manhattan. Douglas turned into a neighborhood filled with houses almost as large as theirs. This must be the part of town where rich people lived.

Pulling up to the curb in front of a Victorian home, Douglas stopped and honked the horn twice. Within seconds, the front door opened and a thin teenage boy with short blond hair and a letterman jacket came out. When he opened the passenger door and saw Jess, his eyes widened for a moment and then he laughed. Jess crossed her arms over her chest, seething. That's when she noticed Douglas was also staring straight ahead, still clenching the steering wheel.

"Get in, Whitey," he said through his teeth.

As much as she didn't want to, Jess slid closer to Douglas on the bench seat to make room for the boy.

"Are we babysitting tonight?" he said, when he plopped down next to her.

She glared at him while Doug pulled away from the curb.

Then his eyes widened. "Hey. You're the cousin."

"Yes, I am."

He seemed chastened. "I'm sorry about the babysitting joke." He stuck his hand out. "I'm Whitey. Well, Jeff, but everybody calls me Whitey."

Jess hesitated to shake his hand, but his smile was genuine and his eyes were friendly. "I'm Jess." She put her gloved hand in his. "You're the one Douglas went to France with."

"That's me. I'm glad I got to meet you. Doug hasn't wanted to talk about you."

"Put a lid on it, Whitey," Douglas warned.

"I bet he hasn't," Jess said, smiling tightly.

Whitey winked at her as Douglas pulled up in front of another large home and honked the horn. A shorter teen boy with curly hair came out, and climbed into the back seat.

"Kenny, this is Jess, Doug's cousin," Whitey said. "Jess, Kenny."

"Oh, hi." Kenny looked between all of them with confusion, then offered his hand over the back of the seat.

They stopped at two more houses, and with Whitey making the introductions, Jess met Jerry, a wiry boy with glasses, and Chuck, a stocky kid whose unfortunate choice of a crew cut emphasized his square-shaped head.

He grinned when he shook her hand and then pulled a paper bag out from under his letterman jacket. "Looky here." He took a bottle of whiskey from it and waved it in the air. All the boys shouted while Jess faced forward, her breathing becoming shallow.

"Where did you get that?" someone said.

"My brother got it for me," Chuck said.

"Swell!"

"Open it now," Douglas yelled, and Jess looked at him. He ignored her.

She heard the bottle being passed around in the back seat and squeezed her hands together in her lap. Her body went cold every time she heard a whoop of laughter or a cough as they took turns taking swigs.

It was handed up to Whitey, who didn't hesitate to

The Boy in the Woods

take a drink. He coughed a few times. "That is *strong*," he said, and the boys roared with laughter. He held it out to Jess.

Douglas grabbed the bottle out of his hand. "Don't be stupid."

"Aw, gee, Doug," Chuck said from the back seat. "Let her have a drink. Kids are cute when they get drunk."

"Shut up, Chuck," Douglas said. To Jess's horror, he lifted the bottle to take a drink.

She wanted to grab it out of his hands, but she knew it wouldn't do any good. What was already a bad night was turning into a nightmare, and she was powerless to stop what was happening. The boys continued to pass the bottle around as they drove, and Douglas took two more drinks while her terror intensified. Eventually, he stopped the car in a wooded area. She was relieved he was no longer driving, but she worried how much more he could drink now that they'd parked. If he did, the drive home could be catastrophic.

The car's headlights illuminated a fire pit ringed with rocks and large logs for seats. Chilled by more than the cool air when she got out of the car, she pulled on her sweater and hugged herself while the boys gathered wood and piled it in the center of the pit. Kenny produced a book of matches from his pocket and he and Whitey worked on trying to get the fire lit. Chuck and Jerry sat on a log and passed the bottle back and forth.

Douglas walked over to his car and leaned against the hood. Seizing the opportunity to talk to him alone, Jess went to him. He looked over her head when he noticed her approaching.

"Douglas – Doug? Can I please ask you something?"

"What?" he said, jaw clenching.

"Doug, *please* don't drink anymore" she said, keeping

her voice low so the others wouldn't hear.

"Leave me alone. I'll drink if I want to."

"But you're *driving*."

"So?" His eyes met hers. "I know when I've had too much. I've done it before, you know. I can handle it."

He began to walk away, but Jess stepped in front of him. "Doug, please listen to me." He tried to dodge around her, but she anticipated his move. "The boy who killed my mom and dad was drunk." She could feel tears welling up. "He was seventeen and he died too."

Doug's eyes registered shock. "I didn't know that's how they died."

"I'm sure he thought he could handle his drinking. I know he didn't mean for it to happen, but it did, and now they're all dead." A tear slid down her cheek, and she wiped it away. "Please don't drink, okay? I don't want what happened to them to happen to you, or to anyone else."

There was cheering as the boys got the wood to catch fire. Doug's face was lit by the growing flames, and Jess saw sorrow in his eyes.

"Okay, I won't drink anymore tonight," he said.

"Thank you, Doug."

"It's okay – Jess."

The headlights of two more cars appeared and pulled off the road. Watching them coming towards the fire pit, Jess had an ominous feeling. It was clear the night was just beginning, and after what had happened already, she feared it would only get worse.

Chapter Eleven
Problems

———◦———

THE TWO CARS parked near the fire pit opposite from where Jess and Doug were standing. Doors opened and there were shouts and greetings mixed with rock and roll music coming from the car radios. Four teenage girls got out of one car and two couples emerged from the other. Jess noticed both of the boys were carrying six packs of beer. Doug stepped away to greet them, leaving her alone.

As Jess examined the older girls, she felt self-conscious. They were all in jeans or circle skirts with sweatshirts and saddle shoes. Not one of them was wearing a dress or a petticoat. Doug walked up to a blonde-haired girl and pulled her close. She circled her arms around his neck and the two of them kissed while the other teens walked around them, seeming not to notice.

Jess spun away, hoping what she'd seen wouldn't be burned into her brain. She escaped to the fire pit and sat on a log, keeping her back to them so she wouldn't see their make-out session. Staring into the fire while the teens laughed and joked around her, she wished that she was at home in bed with a book. To distract herself, she concentrated on the flames, following the sparks of yellow and orange as they shot upwards, catching on the breeze before they disappeared.

"Hey." Chuck sat down next to her with two bottles of beer. He offered one of them to her. "Want one?"

"No, thank you."

"Aw, go on." He thrust the bottle close enough she could smell it. "I won't tell Doug."

She pushed it away, giving him a stern look. "I don't drink."

"Suit yourself." He took a sip out of the one he'd offered her.

Uneasy about him drinking next to her, she pretended to ignore him. Gazing at the flames, she hoped he'd take the hint and leave.

He pointed his beer bottle towards Doug and the girl he'd been kissing. "That's Donna."

Donna had her arms around Doug's waist while he talked to Whitey and another boy. Even in the dim firelight, Jess could see how pretty she was, with loose blonde curls that fell to her shoulders and bright red lipstick. They made an attractive couple. Noticing her looking, Donna scrutinized her, and Jess dropped her eyes to the fire.

"She's not his girlfriend, but they've been together since last year," Chuck said.

"How can she not be his girlfriend if they're together?" Jess glanced at Donna again, but the teen girl was still watching her. Jess turned to Chuck, embarrassed to be caught looking a second time.

"He broke up with her last spring. His dad made him do it."

"Why?"

"I guess he didn't approve, maybe because she's not rich. Her dad owns the grocery store in town."

Jess was horrified, but it sounded like something her uncle would do. It seemed his strict ideas about social status weren't just an excuse to belittle people; he'd forced Doug to break up with a girl he loved. Jess had never considered that being Uncle Jonathon's son would be hard since he had everything handed to him. But now she realized it might not be that easy.

Then she thought of Marty. If a grocer's daughter wasn't good enough to date his son, it was likely a boy as poor as Marty wouldn't be good enough to be her friend.

"You know," Chuck said, interrupting her thoughts, "you're real pretty. I bet you had a lot of boyfriends back wherever it is you came from."

He had to be joking. She leaned back to study him, but he appeared to be sincere. "You should stop." She pointed to the second bottle he'd been drinking from. "You're already drunk."

He scooted closer to her. "What's the matter? Don't you like compliments?"

She jumped off the log to get away from him. "Excuse me. I, uh, have to go talk to Doug."

"Okey dokey. Catch you later."

Feeling Chuck's eyes on her back, she walked towards Doug and Donna. She didn't want to approach him after the looks Donna had been shooting at her, but she didn't have anywhere else to go. When Donna noticed her drawing near, she tightened her arms around Doug and lifted her chin. It made Jess more ill at ease. Then Doug spotted her and made a face.

She stopped in front of them and waited for Doug to introduce her. Now that she was closer, Jess thought Donna was even prettier than she'd appeared from a distance. She had the delicate fine-boned features of a magazine model, and blue eyes that were a shade lighter than Doug's. Standing next to her, Jess felt ugly and gawky.

Doug kept looking over her head as if she wasn't there, and she gave up on him, sticking her hand out. "Hi. I'm Jess, Doug's cousin."

Donna hesitated and then seemed to make a decision. She let go of Doug long enough to shake Jess's hand. "Donna. I wasn't sure if Doug was telling me the truth about you, but you're exactly how he described."

In her head, Jess heard Doug's voice when he'd met her for the first time, *'She's just a kid!'* and her face flushed with heat. "Uh, that's nice." Her cheeks became even hotter, mortified she'd said something so dumb.

While Donna continued to examine her and Doug pretended she wasn't there, the silence stretched, making the awkwardness of the moment more acute. Finally, Doug took Donna's hand. "Let's go sit by the fire. Later, Jess."

"Yeah, later," she said to their backs while they walked away. Watching them, she let out a sigh. Could she have acted more like a stupid kid?

Hours later, Jess kept yawning as she sat in front of the dying embers, trying to stay warm.

Kenny and Jerry kicked dirt over the fire, while the two couples who came together got in their car and drove away. Jess stood, grateful there were signs she'd be going home. Doug was far from the rest of the group, huddled with Donna. The two of them were lit by the headlights of the other car and it looked like they were having an intense discussion.

She went to Doug's car, her teeth chattering from the cold night air. Chuck, Jerry, and Kenny were already in the back seat, and she decided to get in too since it would be warmer than standing outside. Whitey joined her on the front bench, and while she rubbed her upper arms, she continued to watch Doug and Donna. Donna was waving her arms and it was clear she was upset.

"What's taking him so long?" Jerry whined from the back seat.

Kenny laughed. "Doug's getting chewed out."

"Someone must be on the rag," Chuck said.

"Hey," Whitey said, turning around. He jerked his head in Jess's direction. "Watch the language."

Hurry up, Doug, she thought. She'd had enough of teen boys for one night.

Doug took Donna's hand and walked to the car with his head down. "I'm giving Donna a ride home," he said, after opening the driver's side door.

"Aw, jeez. That's going to take *forever*," Kenny grumbled under his breath, but Doug didn't hear because Chuck had snickered loudly at the same time.

"Whitey, get in the back seat," Doug said.

"What? There's no room!"

"How about Jess?" Chuck said. "She's smaller."

"Yeah, she's little," Jerry said.

He gave her an apologetic expression. "Jess, do you mind?"

She wanted to say she minded, but she knew it was no use. She slid across the bench seat and got out.

The Boy in the Woods

"Thanks, Jess," Donna said cheerily, climbing in to take her place.

Doug opened the rear door, and Jess's heart sank. She had to sit next to Chuck. When the door was shut, it was a snug fit, but at least she was warmer than she'd been all night. She leaned her forehead against the glass, hoping Chuck wouldn't talk to her, but he seemed engrossed in a discussion with the other two boys about a girl. Doug drove away, and the movement of the darkened car combined with the hum of the engine made her drowsy. She closed her eyes.

The next thing she was aware of was the sound of boys talking and a hand rubbing her knee. When she lifted her head off the glass, she noticed Chuck had moved closer. She was now wedged tight against the door.

She pushed Chuck's hand off her knee. *"Stop,"* she whispered. Donna was gone from the front seat. They must have dropped her off while Jess was asleep.

"Relax," Chuck said in her ear. The sour smell of alcohol on his breath made her turn her head away. "I'm not doing anything."

He placed his hand on her knee again, and she pushed it away. He put it back, this time sliding it under her skirt. When she tried to push it off, he held his arm rigid, keeping his hand in place. She pushed as hard as she could, but she wasn't strong enough to remove it.

"Calm down, will ya?" he said.

His hand inched up her bare leg even though she was straining to stop him. The boys next to them carried on their conversation, not noticing the two of them struggling. But she didn't want to call attention to what was happening. It was too mortifying.

"You're so pretty." Chuck's hot, sour breath was in her ear as he pressed against her. "Don't worry. I'm not going to hurt you."

She was finding it difficult to breathe as she understood what he was about to do, and her mind went blank with terror. *"Stop!"* she screamed, thrashing her body in a desperate attempt to get away from him. *"Leave me alone!"*

She broke free and, in a panic, launched herself over the front seat. Doug slammed on the brakes and she landed head first on the floor while the boys swore, having been thrown forward. Buried under her petticoat's nylon netting, she struggled blindly to get up. *"Doug,"* she sobbed as someone grabbed her arms and pulled. It was Whitey. She wrestled out of his grip and lunged towards Doug, clutching onto him for protection while her tears came in a flood.

"What happened, Jess?" he said, but she was crying so hard, she couldn't breathe. Opening the car door, he got out, pulling her with him. "What's wrong?"

She clung to him, sobbing. Doors closed as the rest of the boys got out of the car.

"What happened to her?" Doug shouted at them.

"I don't know, she just started screaming," someone said.

She heard Chuck's voice say, "I think she fell asleep and had a nightmare or something."

"No," she cried into Doug's chest.

Doug bent lower. "What happened, Jess? Tell me."

"He – he had – he had," she hiccuped, trying to catch her breath.

"He had what?"

"He had – his hand – under my skirt."

Doug's body stiffened. "What did he do?"

"He tried to, he tried to," she whispered over and over, but she couldn't say the rest. It was too horrible.

Doug straightened. It seemed he'd heard enough to understand.

"She's lying," Chuck said.

Doug's face was a mask of rage as he pushed Jess aside. "What did you do to her?" he roared, stalking towards Chuck.

Chuck's eyes widened and he raised his hands. "I didn't do anything. I swear."

Before anyone could react, Doug punched him twice in the face, the second punch throwing him to the ground. The other boys rushed forward to grab Doug and dragged him backwards.

"*You broke my nothe,*" Chuck howled as he struggled to his feet.

Jess covered her mouth in horror. Chuck's nose gushed blood. He covered it with both hands, trying to stop it, but it ran through his fingers and soaked into his T-shirt.

"How dare you touch her," Doug roared, trying to shake off the boys who were holding him. "I'll kill you if you ever go near her again."

"Stop, Doug," Whitey pleaded.

Doug finally stilled, and the boys let go of him one by one until he was standing alone. He breathed heavily, staring down Chuck. "I better not see you so much as *look* at her again. Do you hear me?"

"I di'n do nothin'," Chuck said through his bloody hands.

Doug made a move towards him.

The Boy in the Woods

"Okay, I won'," he cried, backing up.

"It's time to go," Doug said, not taking his eyes off Chuck. "Everyone in the car, except you." He pointed a finger at Chuck who'd taken a small step forward. "Find your own way home."

"B-b-bu' we're mileth from town."

"Doug," Whitey said. "He needs to go home. He needs to go home so his dad can fix his nose."

"He should have thought about that before he tried something with her." Doug turned towards Jess. His blue eyes were like ice, but when he saw her, his face softened. "Come on." He put his hand on her back and led her to the car. He joined Jess on the front seat. "Anyone who wants a ride better get in now." With that, he slammed the door shut.

The boys looked at each other as if they weren't sure what to do, then they climbed back in the car, leaving Chuck, standing at the side of the road. He still had his hands over his bleeding nose. When the last door closed, Doug hit the gas, squealing the tires as they pulled away.

"He needs medical attention," Whitey said. "He needs–"

"Forget it, Whitey," Doug said, "unless you want to walk home too."

Whitey turned his face to the window.

In the strained silence that followed, Jess was sick with humiliation. She could still feel Chuck's hand creeping up her bare leg and had to resist the urge to rub her skin to get the traces of him off. Doug and Whitey would notice, and the last thing she wanted to do was draw more attention to herself.

Why had Chuck done that to her? Had she said or done something to make him think she wanted it? How could

The Boy in the Woods

he be attracted to her anyway? It didn't make any sense. All those other girls were older and prettier than she was.

When they reached town, Doug dropped off the boys at their houses, stopping at Whitey's last. "Call James and tell him I'm on my way," he said, staring straight ahead.

"Sure thing, Doug," Whitey said, and got out.

With the two of them left in the car, Jess slid across the bench seat and leaned her head against the window. All she wanted to do was climb into her bed, pull the covers over her head, and forget the night had ever happened.

When they reached the gate at the end of the drive, it was already unlocked and the black car was parked nearby with its headlights on. Doug drove through and when he reached the garage, Jess got out and headed for the house before he'd turned off the car. All the lights were off inside except the one in the stairwell. Anxious to be alone, she ran up the stairs to her room. She couldn't get her dress and petticoat off fast enough, throwing them on the floor of her wardrobe. Then she put on a nightgown and headed to bed, not bothering to brush her teeth.

As she was pulling her bedding up, there was a quiet knock on her door. Her heart sped up. *Was it Uncle Jonathon?*

There was another knock. "Jess, it's Doug."

She sighed, and put on her robe.

When she opened the door, Doug's face was full of remorse. "Can I come in?" he whispered.

"I'm really tired, Doug." She didn't want to talk to him either.

"Please?"

She considered saying no, but she knew he wouldn't

The Boy in the Woods

give up. She stepped aside to let him in, then closed the door.

He hung his head. "I'm sorry, Jess, about everything."

"It's okay."

"I wanted you to know that you don't have to worry about Chuck." He met her gaze with a determined look. "I'm not going to have anything more to do with him. He won't bother you again."

She was grateful Doug was willing to stand up for her, but she didn't want to be the reason he lost a friend, especially when she knew his dad had made him break up with his girlfriend. "It's okay, Doug. If you still want to see–"

"It's not like that. We weren't really friends." He dropped his eyes, but not before Jess saw shame in them. "I only did stuff with him because his dad is the head surgeon at the hospital. I've never liked him."

"Oh." Was this another example of what it was like to be Uncle Jonathon's son? Pretending to be friends with people you didn't like because they had money and status?

"I've decided I'm not going to drink if I'm driving."

"That's good, Doug. I'm glad."

"You won't tell Dad, will you?" He looked at her through his lashes, his beautiful blue eyes pleading with her. "You know, about not going to the movies – and the drinking – and Donna."

As he waited for her answer, it occurred to Jess what was going on. How many times had she seen him use these same tactics on his father? He hadn't come to her room because he was worried about *her*. He was there to make sure she kept quiet, not just about how he'd disobeyed his dad by not taking her to the movies, but about all the things he was doing behind his back.

135

Had he been truthful about anything he'd said? Perhaps he wasn't lying about Chuck, but the rest? She felt like a fool for believing him. But how could she tell Uncle Jonathon what happened? If she did, he was certain to find out about Chuck, and she couldn't bear to discuss the humiliating details with him.

"I won't say anything, Doug."

Doug's expression brightened.

She held up a finger. "*But* I will if I find out you've been drinking while you're driving. I mean it."

"Yeah, I mean no," he said with a relieved smile. "I won't ever do it again, you can be sure. Thanks, Jess. You're the best." He'd said the same thing to his dad when he'd allowed Doug to go to France.

She went to the door. "I need to go to bed."

"If anyone asks, say we saw that Elvis Presley movie, *King Creole*," he said behind her.

Disappointment overwhelmed her. She would have loved to see the Elvis movie.

"Good night," he whispered as she closed the door, but she didn't reply.

She climbed into her bed and burrowed under her blankets, trying to push away the memory of Chuck in the car.

Chapter Twelve
Twilight Time

THE NEXT MORNING, Jess laid in the semi-darkness under her covers. She hugged herself as the agonizing events from the night before ran through her mind. Almost all of it had been awful, but what had happened with Chuck was the worst part.

Not wanting to relive it a moment longer, she kicked off her covers, intending to go down to breakfast. Then she remembered how excited Annie had been about her and Doug going to the movies. She was bound to ask questions about it. How was Jess going to convince her she'd had a good time when she was still shaken by what had happened? *But what other choice do I have?* She'd just have to do her best.

"Good morning, pumpkin," Annie said when she came down the backstairs, and Jess went to her for a hug. When she let go, Annie's brow furrowed. "Are you okay?"

Jess forced a smile. "Yes, I'm fine."

"What movie did you see?"

"We saw the Elvis Presley one."

"Good. I told Doug he should take you to see it."

"You did?" Jess struggled to keep her smile from fading.

Annie waved her hand. "Boys can be so clueless about these things, and I know how much you love Elvis. Was it good?"

"Yeah, it was." Jess had tried to sound cheerful, and turned towards the table to hide her face. Why hadn't Doug taken her to the movies like he was supposed to? If he had, she wouldn't have all these terrible feelings swirling inside her.

Annie set a plate of fried eggs, bacon, and toast on the table in front of Jess. "It's the last Saturday before school starts. Are you going out to play like usual? I can pack a lunch."

"Yes, thank you." Spending the day with Marty was just what she needed.

The birds chirped in the trees on her way to the cabin, and she already felt lighter. But when she entered the clearing, her heart sank. The cabin door was closed. She crossed the open space to the cabin, fighting against the emotions that threatened to overwhelm her. He'd arrived late before, but today she really needed him.

She opened both doors wide to air out the cabin and left her basket on the kitchen counter. At the front door, she listened for signs he was walking through the woods, but there was nothing except the usual sounds of forest creatures scampering through the underbrush. With nothing to do but wait, she sat on the front stoop.

As the minutes dragged on, her thoughts alternated between nagging doubts that Marty wouldn't come and the

The Boy in the Woods

image of Chuck's hand creeping up her bare leg. Unable to stand it any longer, she entered the cabin to change into her bathing suit. She'd swim to distract herself until Marty showed up.

She was about to leave when she realized she didn't have a way to let Marty know where she'd gone. Looking around, she wished she had a pencil and paper to write a note. Then she spied the fishing pole propped in a corner. She laid it against a wooden chair, hoping Marty would recognize it as a sign.

Taking her time on the way to the pond, she focused on the beauty around her. In the open field, the tall grass had turned a golden yellow after the month of hot summer weather. As a breeze swept through the open space, they made a dried rustling noise that seemed to be whispering to her, telling her that her carefree summer was ending.

When she reached the water's edge, she listened to the birds in the trees. It was the first time she'd been to the pond alone. It seemed empty without Marty. Deciding she didn't want to swim after all, she went under the willow tree and sat. Leaned against the trunk, she watched the glittering ripples of water through the willow branches.

In two days, school would start. Along with all her normal worries about attending a new school, foremost in her mind was that Chuck would be there. He was too old to be in any of her classes, but she might see him in the hallways. What if he tried to talk to her? She'd tell Doug, she decided. He'd protect her, and Marty would be there. Even though they couldn't talk, it would still be a comfort to have him nearby. She was lucky to have a best friend like Marty. He wasn't like the friends Doug had. What she shared with Marty was real.

"Jess."

Marty's familiar voice came from behind, and she leapt up to greet him. But when she saw him, the words died in her throat. "Marty," she moaned. "Your *hair*."

The shaggy golden brown mop that was always falling over his eyes was gone, or almost all gone. It had been shaved so close to the sides of his head she could see his scalp, and all that was left on top were short dark spikes. As she stared at his crew cut, all she could think was he didn't look like Marty anymore.

The sadness she'd been fighting all day rose inside her, and she choked out a sob before she could clamp her mouth shut.

He rubbed the fuzz on top of his head "That bad, huh?" he said with a rueful smile.

She wiped her eyes, embarrassed she'd cried in front of him. "No. It's not bad."

He raised an eyebrow. "You sure?"

There was no use pretending. "I don't like it. It was better longer."

He barked out a laugh. "Holy smokes. I don't reckon anyone ever said that about my hair before. Usually people give me a hard time."

"Why did you cut it?"

His smile vanished. "Why do you think?" he said, his words icy.

"School," she said as the answer came to her. She didn't know why she didn't think of it sooner. Of course they would have strict rules about the length of boys' hair.

"Thanks to *them*, I got to waste money on haircuts." He stalked out from under the tree, knocking the willow branches out of his way with his arm.

The Boy in the Woods

Jess joined him at the edge of the pond where he stood. He stared at the water, his hands clenching and unclenching. She struggled to find something to say to make him feel better, but what? If he couldn't afford to buy fish hooks, it must be hard for him to find the money for a haircut. Then a worse thought came to her. Did he have to spend the money he used to buy food?

"Marty?"

He looked at her, still twitching.

"Do you want to swim?"

He took a deep breath, and when he let it out, his anger dissipated. "I reckon."

When he waded in, she got an idea. "Race you," she yelled, sprinting past him. He splashed behind her, and she leapt forward, doing a shallow dive to gain speed, but Marty's hand grasped her ankle. She kicked to get loose, but his grip was too strong. As he dragged her backwards, she came out of the water laughing. "You're cheating!"

"You didn't say I couldn't." He let go so he could rush past her.

She tried to catch up, but he doused her with a wave of water and that started a splashing war. Playing like they always had, she no longer noticed how different he looked. He was simply Marty.

Jess was on her way to the dining room, still reliving the fun she'd had that afternoon when Uncle Jonathon's loud voice rang through the hallway. "What about it?"

She stopped. What on Earth was wrong now?

"I'm concerned about what she's going to wear to school," Annie said. "She doesn't have that many clothes."

"What are you *talking* about? I see her wearing different clothes every day."

"Jess, what are you doing?"

She jerked sideways, Doug's sudden appearance scaring her. He passed her on the way to the dining room, and she waved frantically, trying to stop him.

"What's the matter?" he said, clueless to her signals. "Aren't you coming to dinner?"

From the silence in the dining room, Uncle Jonathon had heard him. She followed Doug into the room, sick with fear. The ferocity of Uncle Jonathon's gaze confirmed he knew she'd been eavesdropping.

"We'll discuss this another time." He dismissed Annie with a wave of his hand, his eyes not leaving Jess.

"Yes, sir," Annie murmured, and left.

Jess slid into her seat with Uncle Jonathon's eyes boring into her. She kept her head down, pretending everything was normal, but her palms were slick with sweat. She wiped them on her napkin.

Doug didn't seem to notice the way his dad was staring at Jess, and held his plate out. After a hesitation, Uncle Jonathon took it. "Jessica!" he said as soon as he'd handed it back to Doug, not giving her the chance to reach for her plate.

She didn't dare meet his eyes when she gave it to him. When he'd finished filling it, she tried to take it from him, but he kept his hold on it for a second before releasing his grip. Setting the plate down, she looked at it as if she was studying her pork chop and roasted potatoes. How was she going to eat them when she felt as if she might throw up? Instead of filling his own plate, Uncle Jonathon continued to glare at her.

"What's wrong, Dad?" Doug said, catching on as he

looked between the two of them.

"I have something to say to Jessica."

Jess's heart was pounding so hard, she was sure both of them must hear it.

"What is it?" Doug asked.

"Jessica," Uncle Jonathon said.

She met his eyes. "Yes, sir?"

"After giving it a lot of thought over the last several weeks, I've come to a decision. I'm hiring a tutor for you."

"W-what?" she stammered, unsure if she'd heard right. "Oh," she said as she understood. "I don't need a tutor, Uncle Jonathon, I always get good grades in school."

"You *will* have a tutor. The tutor will give you your lessons at home."

She searched his eyes trying to understand what he meant, and then it was as if the floor dropped out from under her. "I *want* to go to school," Jess said, panic taking hold.

"I've had a lot of time to observe your behavior, and I've decided it's best if you learn your lessons here."

"I don't understand. I've never had a problem at school."

"I know it means nothing to *you*, Jessica, but the Blackwell name means something to the people in this town. The children at that school are our future employees and the way we conduct ourselves in public has consequences. I've warned you in the past about your behavior, and I'm not about to let you jeopardize what this family has built over the last hundred years."

"*No*," she wailed, unable to stop her tears.

He jabbed a finger in her direction. "*That's* what I'm

talking about. You've never been taught your place."

"Please, Uncle Jonathon. I *have* to go."

"That's enough," he shouted, banging his fist on the table.

Jess covered her face with her hands, unable to stop sobbing. He was going to keep her trapped behind the locked gate forever.

"Dad, wait," Doug said.

"I've made my decision, Douglas."

"I think you should let her go to school."

"Don't involve yourself in this," Uncle Jonathon warned.

"But I *am* involved," Doug shouted.

There was a shocked silence in the room, and Jess took her hands off her face. Was Doug standing up for her?

"She's my, I mean she's–" Doug stuttered, before pausing for a brief second. He tried a third time. "What I mean is–"

"Now, Douglas–"

"She needs to learn how to be a Blackwell, doesn't she?" Doug said, lifting his chin, "and with me at school, I can help her."

Uncle Jonathon opened his mouth, but closed it. No one said anything while he seemed to be considering what Doug had said. "Very well."

Jess slumped.

"But if you behave in a way that jeopardizes this family's reputation," Uncle Jonathon said, returning his harsh gaze to Jess. "I'm pulling you from school. Do I make myself clear?"

The Boy in the Woods

"Yes, sir."

There was no talk of the mine that night, only a strained, uneasy silence. Jess pushed her food around her plate, no longer hungry. She was grateful Uncle Jonathon had changed his mind, but this would complicate things.

She'd held onto the hope that she could figure out a way to be friends with Marty out in the open once school began. After all, she could be sociable with the other kids. But now it would be impossible. There was no way her uncle would approve of her being friends with someone like him, and if he ever found out, he might keep her home for the rest of high school.

Jess stole a glance at Doug, who was hunched over his own plate with a grim expression. Who could have guessed that the boy who'd acted like he hated her from the moment she'd arrived, would rescue her twice in the last twenty-four hours?

Outside the diamond-paned bay window, the sky was darkening. Her nerves about the beginning of school were now far worse. With Doug having promised to keep an eye on her, it would be even more important she hide her feelings about Marty.

Marty sat on the front stoop of the cabin, sharpening his penknife on a rock while he tried to ignore the gnawing pain in his stomach. He'd been making a habit of saving his extra sandwich for dinner since Jess always shared one of hers with him. But since he'd had to go into town early that morning to scrounge up odd jobs to pay for his trip to the barber, he hadn't brought a lunch. Looking up at the stars that were emerging, he knew it wasn't late enough, but his stomach wouldn't stop telling him to go home. *Maybe it'll be okay.*

He stood and went inside to close the back door. Twenty minutes later, he was over the iron fence and walking down the dirt road to his home. When he reached his weed-filled yard, he stopped. Light was coming through the dirty windows of the front room. While he weighed his options, his stomach rumbled, knowing food was close.

He crept past a rusting pickup truck, and ducked below an open window. The crackling sound of a baseball announcer on the radio drifted out, but there were no signs of movement. With the pain in his stomach urging him forward, he made his way to the kitchen door at the back of the house.

He turned the knob and eased it open, cursing under his breath when the rusty hinges squeaked. He held still, but there was only the roar of a crowd. There must have been a home run. Stepping into the semi-darkness, he closed the door before the crowd quieted.

In a cupboard, he located the peanut butter and jelly jars, then turned to the bread bin. It was open and empty. He swore under his breath. The bread couldn't have been eaten already. There was almost a whole loaf yesterday. Then he spotted the white plastic bread bag lying on the stove. As he reached for it, relief mixed with anger that it was left out for the mice to find. He froze as his hand closed around the loaf. Behind it on the stove was a tin pie plate mounded with fried chicken. More fried chicken than he'd seen in a long time. Big pieces too. His mouth watered. *Where had it come from?*

Swallowing hard, he picked up the bag of bread. He turned his back to the chicken while he opened it, pulling out a handful of slices.

"Is that you, boy?"

The Boy in the Woods

His chest constricted, hearing the growl from the front room. *Darn it.* He should have waited until the noise from the radio covered the rustling of the plastic. "Yeah," he said. There was a grunt and the squeaking of the sofa springs, and a knot formed in his stomach. He opened the peanut butter while the floorboards creaked.

"You better not be eating my chicken, boy," his old man snarled, appearing in the doorway. The smell of alcohol filled the small kitchen.

Marty opened a drawer to get a knife, but it was empty of cutlery. "I ain't." He reached into the sink to get a dirty knife. Not wanting to take the time to wash it, he stuck it in the peanut butter.

"Better not be." He stepped behind Marty.

Marty tensed, but didn't dare turn around.

Then his old man came into view with a drumstick in his hand. Leaning against the door frame, he tore a large chunk out of it and smacked his lips as he chewed. Marty spread peanut butter on the bread slices while his old man scratched his large belly under his dirty undershirt.

"Finally got your rat's nest cut off, I see," he said with his mouth full of chicken.

Marty stayed silent and tried to open the jelly jar, but his hands were too sweaty.

"I reckon school's starting, but I don't know why they bother lettin' *you* in."

Marty gritted his teeth and wiped his hand on his jeans, wishing the old man would shut up and eat his chicken.

"Waste of taxpayer's money to try to teach you anything."

Marty tried to spread the jelly on the bread, but he was

having a hard time because his hands were shaking.

"I knew you were a worthless piece of crap the minute you came out of your mother."

The old man was baiting him now. He worked hard to keep his breathing under control while he smoothed out the lumps of jelly.

"Like your lousy good for nothing brothers. Run off, didn't they?"

With his sandwiches assembled, Marty fumbled to screw the lids back on the jars.

"Bunch of no account punks. Never amounted to nothing, just like you."

Marty put the bread in the bread bin and stacked his sandwiches.

"Listen to me when I'm talking to you, boy!"

Pain exploded in Marty's shoulder as he was punched, the force of the blow pushing his head into the cabinet door. He spun around and leapt back, keeping himself out of the old man's reach.

The old man looked him up and down, while Marty's shoulder throbbed and the pain in his forehead made his eyes water. Then his old man grinned. "You going to cut me with that, boy?"

Marty realized he was holding the butter knife in his trembling hand like a weapon. "No." He lowered it.

"Didn't think so." He threw the chicken bone and Marty flinched as it almost hit him, landing in the sink. The old man shuffled back to the sofa. "Worthless piece of–" he muttered under his breath.

Marty stayed where he was, still holding the knife, his body shaking with rage. The floorboards creaked under his old man's weight, and it took everything Marty had not to go after him. He'd seen what would happen if he fought back, and it wasn't good.

When he heard the squeak of the sofa springs, it was safe to move. He scooped up his sandwiches and went to his bedroom, keeping an eye on the back of his old man's head. Once the door was shut, he felt around in the dark for a nearby chair and shoved its back under the door knob. Stepping over the clothes on his floor, he reached his unmade bed and sat, balancing the stack of sandwiches on his knee.

His forehead stung and he prodded it with his fingers, relieved no lump was forming. He took a bite out of a sandwich and while he chewed, he rubbed his shoulder with his other hand, trying to ease the pain. Through his door, he heard the muffled sound of the crowd roaring while the announcer called out another home run.

Chapter Thirteen
I Got a Feeling

JESS WALKED BEHIND Marty on the way to the pond, but instead of the usual comfortable silence between them, the air was heavy. She wanted to tell him how her uncle had almost kept her from going to school the night before, but she suspected he wouldn't be sympathetic. Knowing how much he hated school, she wasn't sure he'd understand how horrible it would be for her. He'd probably be happy if someone told him he wasn't going back.

But that wasn't the only thing weighing on her. Ever since she'd woken up that morning, there had been a nervous fluttering in her stomach. Tomorrow was the first day of school. Worries mounted even though she'd tried to push them away. Would she be able to find her way around? Would her classes be hard? What would her teachers be like? And most importantly, would the other kids like her? If that wasn't enough, she had the added burden of knowing if her uncle found fault in anything she did, he'd force her to stay home.

The biggest issue would be who she chose as friends. Judging from the kinds of friends Doug had, her choices were

The Boy in the Woods

limited to the daughters of the wealthy and powerful. Would she like them enough to want to be friends with them? She hoped there would at least be one.

And then there was Marty. As she watched him striding through the tall grass, fishing pole propped against his shoulder, she felt terrible. How hard would it be to pass him in the hallway, or be in the same class with him, and act as though she didn't know him? He was her best friend, and she'd have to treat him as though he didn't exist. It wasn't right, but even he'd said she had to ignore him.

When they reached the pond, Jess put their lunches and her towel under the willow tree while Marty unlaced his boots. Eager to leave her troubled thoughts behind, she was soon splashing into the cool water. She did a shallow dive, swimming under the surface until she had to get a breath of air. Marty was swimming towards her with a grin, and she turned, shrieking with laughter as she tried to escape the deluge of water he threw at her.

That afternoon, with the sun hanging low in the sky, Jess looked over at Marty who was dozing on his back, his arm over his eyes. "Marty, I have to go," she said loud enough to wake him, and he stirred.

She stood and stretched before wrapping her towel around her waist. She reached for her basket, and as Marty passed her on the way to his clothes, she glanced up. "Marty?" she said, straightening with surprise. There was an ugly purple bruise on his shoulder.

He stiffened but continued through the willow branches without stopping.

She followed him. "What happened to your back?"

"I fell," he said, scooping up his T-shirt.

She walked behind him so she could examine the bruise, but he pulled down his shirt, covering it.

"How did it–"

He spun around. "Will you give it a rest already?"

She stared open-mouthed, shocked by his sudden anger.

A look of regret crossed his face, and he turned to retrieve his jeans. "It just happened, okay?"

She watched him yank his pants up, certain he was lying. She opened her mouth to demand he tell her what happened, then closed it. Something was terribly wrong, but pressing him about it would only upset him more. She got her shoes while he took the fishing pole and bucket and headed to the path. She hurried to close the buckles, then snatched the rest of her things and ran to catch up to him.

Walking behind him, she allowed herself to contemplate the truth. Someone had hit him. When she considered the possibilities of who could've done it, she realized it had to be someone in his home: his father, or maybe his mother. *Why would they do that to their own son?* she wondered, thinking of how much her own parents had loved her. They would never have hurt her on purpose. They never even spanked her.

Then she remembered the other time she'd seen Marty with a bruise. After she'd first met him, he'd stayed away from the cabin for two days, then shown up with a black eye. He'd said he'd fallen then too. As the pieces came together, tears stung her eyes. He'd been trespassing on her uncle's property to escape whoever was hurting him at home. Wiping her eyes as they entered the forest, she tried to gain control over her emotions. Marty would hate it if he saw her crying for him.

In the cabin, Marty stashed the fishing pole in the corner, his features grim. She decided to give him a moment alone, and headed for the bedroom to change out of her swimsuit. After she was dressed, she found him in the kitchen, leaning against the cookstove, his eyes on the floor.

"I'm nervous about school tomorrow," she said, deciding to change the subject away from his bruise.

"I don't know why," he muttered. "You'll do fine."

"I hope so." She waited, but he didn't volunteer anything else. It was clear he didn't want to talk. "I guess I'll go," she said, disappointed.

He didn't move, and she turned towards the door.

"I'll walk with you."

Relief flooded through her. She hadn't wanted their last day of summer to end with ill feelings and awkwardness, and she was glad he didn't either.

He walked beside her, his eyes on the dusty path and his hands clenched into fists. She tried not to read too much into his silence, determined to enjoy their last minutes together.

At the curve before the garage, she stopped. She waited, but he remained quiet, digging his toe into the dirt. "I guess I'll see you at–"

"Bye, Jess." He pivoted in the direction of the cabin without a backward glance.

She sighed as she watched him leave. He was smart enough to know she'd seen through his lie, and now it was sitting there, driving a wedge between them.

Heading to the garage, she tried to console herself. The next time she saw him, they would have had their first day of school. That would give them something else to talk about while she pretended she didn't know someone in his family was beating him.

Chapter Fourteen
School Day (Ring, Ring Goes the Bell)

THE LOUD RINGING of her alarm clock pierced Jess's consciousness. She blinked her eyes open, but the room was too bright, and she squeezed them shut again. The alarm was still ringing, the jarring sound boring into her brain. She sat up to turn it off.

With her stomach doing nervous flips, Jess looked through the dresses in her wardrobe and settled on a pale blue one she hoped didn't look too faded from repeated washing. After putting on ankle socks, she reached for her everyday Mary Janes. Even though they were scuffed from spending the summer in the woods, they seemed more appropriate than her black patent leather shoes.

In the bathroom, she contemplated herself in the mirror. At least her nerves weren't showing in her face. Her hair was now shoulder-length, and she brushed it back, gathering it into a high ponytail, but it looked dumb since it was still too short. With another sigh, she took out the hair elastic and put on a headband before heading down the stairs to the kitchen.

"Good morning," Annie said when she saw her. "You're eating breakfast in the dining room this morning."

"The dining room?" That wasn't where she normally ate breakfast.

"On school days, you and Doug eat breakfast with your uncle," Annie said.

"Okay," Jess said, trying not to sound disappointed, and walked through the butler's pantry.

Uncle Jonathon was seated at the table drinking coffee when she entered the dining room but Doug hadn't come downstairs yet. She was relieved, but then she noticed her uncle's disapproving gaze while she walked to the chair. *What have I done now?* She slid into her seat, keeping her head down to avoid his eyes.

"Good morning." Doug appeared, stifling a yawn. He looked nice in khaki trousers and a plaid button-down shirt.

Annie backed into the room through the swinging door with a tray holding their breakfast plates.

"Annie," Uncle Jonathon said as she placed fried eggs and bacon in front of him. "I'll tell James to take you into town this afternoon. You can pick Jessica up after school and take her shopping for clothes."

Jess and Annie exchanged a surprised glance.

"Alright." Annie tried to hide a smile while placing a plate in front of Doug.

Jess tried to keep her face neutral as well, but she was excited. Finally, she would get new clothes.

"I called the superintendent of schools to have you enrolled last night," Uncle Jonathon said to Jess, opening his napkin. "Douglas will take you to the school office to pick up

The Boy in the Woods

your schedule. If there are any problems, Douglas, you call me right away so I can deal with it. Principal Petersen wouldn't know where his head was if you handed it to him."

From the stern way he'd said it, Jess hoped there wouldn't be any problems for the sake of the principal.

Uncle Jonathon looked at his watch. "Hurry up and eat, Jessica! If you make Douglas late, he won't have enough time to get your schedule before the bell rings."

"Yes, sir." She bowed her head and scooped up as much egg as would fit on her fork.

When it was time to go, she had a stomach ache from a combination of eating too fast and nerves. She followed Doug through the butler's pantry and Annie handed them each a paper sack with their lunches inside.

"Have a good day," she said.

At the gate, they waited in Doug's car for James to unlock the padlock.

"Why does Uncle Jonathon always keep the gate locked?" Jess asked.

Doug shrugged and turned on the car radio. "I don't know. It's always been locked, I guess because we're rich." He dialed through the stations.

Jess was about to point out that being rich didn't mean they had to live behind locked gates, but decided it wasn't worth it. If this was how Doug had been brought up, it would seem normal to him.

They reached town, and Doug turned off the main two-lane highway. They wove through neighborhood streets with modest one and two-story homes, passing groups of teens, all walking in the same direction. Jess examined what the girls were wearing. None of them had on simple cotton dresses like hers. At least tomorrow she'd have the right clothes, but today she was going to stick out like a sore thumb.

They pulled into the parking lot of a large two-story brick high school, and Jess's breakfast roiled in her stomach. Hoping she didn't throw up, she got out of the car and followed Doug, who was striding towards the school's entrance.

They were there early enough that there were only a few people milling around, but all of them stared at her. A few of the older teens shouted greetings to Doug, and he waved, climbing the front steps.

A double set of glass doors led to a hushed, empty hallway. One door had a sign above it, labeling it as the office, and they crossed the threshold. An older woman with short gray hair peered up at them over her reading glasses. "Hello, Mr. Blackwell," she said with a broad smile, standing from behind her typewriter.

Doug and Jess walked up to the high wooden counter. "I came to get my cousin's class schedule," Doug said.

"I'll let Principal Petersen know you're here. He's been expecting you."

Doug drummed his fingers on the counter, appearing bored, while the secretary went to a rear door and opened it.

"Mr. Petersen, Mr. Blackwell is here with his cousin." She stepped back from the door and a stout man with thick Coke-bottle glasses and a thin mustache burst through.

"Mr. Blackwell!" He waddled to Doug with his hand extended. "Welcome back, welcome back. Ready for another year?" His thick glasses made his eyes appear larger than normal. Combined with his thin mustache, he looked like a cat with whiskers.

Doug shook his hand. "Yes, sir."

Principal Petersen's attention shifted to Jess and he appeared startled. "This is your cousin, uh, Jessica?"

"Yes, sir," Jess said, speaking up for herself. "But everyone calls me Jess."

"Er, that's fine, Jessica, just fine." He pulled an index card out of his inside jacket pocket and examined it with concern. "What was your birthday again?"

It dawned on Jess what he was worried about. "December 22, 1944."

His body relaxed. "Splendid. Splendid." He must be relieved he didn't have to face her uncle and explain why she was too young to attend high school.

"I think we have everything in order. Here is your schedule." He handed over the index card to her with a small bow. "If you have any questions about anything, *anything at all*, you come to me. Alright, Jessica?"

"Thank you, sir," Jess said.

"Come on, Jess," Doug said. "Class is starting soon."

Mr. Petersen clapped his hands together. "That's right. I mustn't make you late." He stuck his hand out. "Mr. Blackwell. Jessic– uh, Miss Blackwell." He shook both their hands in turn.

As soon as Principal Petersen released Doug's hand, he turned to leave and Jess hurried to follow.

"Have a good first day of school," Principal Petersen called out, but Doug kept walking, leading her back through the double doors. Outside the building, he scanned the now larger crowd of students.

"Do they always talk to you like that?" Jess asked.

"Like what?" Doug said, still examining the crowd.

The Boy in the Woods

"Never mind." Having adults fawn all over him was obviously something else Doug thought was normal.

Doug headed down the steps. "Follow me."

Walking behind him, Jess felt every pair of eyes on her. Students talked in hushed whispers behind their hands as she passed.

"Janet," Doug shouted, and a young girl turned around.

She gaped as Doug approached, and another girl standing next to her appeared just as shocked.

"You're in ninth grade, right?" Doug said to Janet when he'd reached her.

She didn't answer until her friend nudged her with her elbow. "Uh, yeah – yeah – yes, Doug," she sputtered, blinking her wide eyes.

"I'm in ninth grade too, Doug," her friend said, breathless.

Doug ignored the second girl and pointed to Jess with his thumb. "This is my cousin, Jess. She's starting ninth."

Both girls' eyes traveled over her, taking in her plain cotton dress and scuffed Mary Jane shoes before they gave each other meaningful looks. Jess wanted to disappear under the concrete.

Doug held his hand out to Jess. "Where's your schedule?"

She handed him the index card and he thrust it at Janet. "Make sure she gets to all her classes."

"Sure thing, Doug."

"I will too," the other one piped in.

Janet frowned at her friend. "We *both* will."

Doug turned to leave and Jess panicked. Was he going to leave her alone with these strangers? She opened her mouth to call him back when he spun around and returned. She relaxed, grateful that he wasn't going to abandon her.

"This is Janet," he said pointing to the first girl. "She's Whitey's little sister. And this is, uh ..." He snapped his fingers, trying to remember.

"Patty," she prompted.

"Right, Patty. She's Jerry's little sister. See you around, Jess."

Before she could say anything, he was gone. She watched the place where he'd vanished into the crowd, feeling desperate.

"Oh! My! Gosh!" the two girls chanted, and then collapsed against each other with high-pitched squeals.

"He's so *dreamy*," Patty moaned.

"I can't believe he *talked* to us," Janet said.

Patty swatted Janet's arm. "What do you mean?" she said with a pout. "You got to spend the entire summer with him. Lucky."

"You mean he spent the summer with my stupid brother. He didn't say one word to me the entire time."

"But you got to see him in a bathing suit."

Janet's eyes had a dazed look. "Yeah, I did." She stared at nothing with a smile.

Then Patty nudged Janet, and they turned their attention to Jess. She burned with humiliation while the two of them looked her over again, mentally cursing her uncle for refusing to buy her decent clothes before school started. Unlike the simple dress Jess wore, Janet and Patty

The Boy in the Woods

had identical circle skirts, short-sleeved sweaters, and penny loafers. They even had the same short permed hairstyle. The only difference between them was Janet had cat-eye glasses.

Jess was tired of their staring. "So? Am I in any of your classes?" If it wasn't for the fact that Janet was holding her class schedule, she would have taken her chances on finding her way around on her own.

"Let me see." Janet held Jess's index card next to her own. Patty added hers and Jess came around to see the cards.

"Same homeroom, English, and social studies as me," Janet said.

"Gym and math with me," Patty said.

"It looks like all three of us have home economics, science, and, of course, lunch," Janet finished.

"Oh, that's good," Jess said with a weak voice. She wished Doug had left her to fend for herself. She wasn't sure if she liked these girls yet, and now she had to spend the entire day with them. A bell rang through the school yard.

"Stick with me," Janet said.

Jess followed behind her and Patty, as teens crowded together, making their way to the front stairs.

Once inside, they walked down the packed hallway. Patty waved and went into one doorway, and Jess followed Janet into another. Janet took a desk in the middle of the room and Jess sat in the desk beside her.

While Janet talked to the girl in front of her, Jess looked around the classroom. Portraits of various presidents and posters about government and laws covered the walls. She noticed a dark-haired girl sitting next to her studying her out of the corner of her eye. She was wearing a cotton dress similar to Jess's and lace-up leather shoes. Jess felt an instant connection to her. This was someone who could be a friend. She smiled and was about to introduce herself when her heart leapt in her throat.

Marty had just stepped through the doorway.

Chapter Fifteen

All Shook Up

JESS WATCHED MARTY turn towards the back of the classroom, willing him to see her, but his head was down. The dark-haired girl caught Jess's eye as Marty walked past her. She gave Jess a small smile, perhaps thinking Jess was looking at her. Jess returned the smile, and faced forward.

She had an overwhelming urge to look behind her. She wanted Marty to know she was there, but she didn't dare take the chance. Maybe he'd spot her after he was seated.

A man in a black suit walked in and peered around the room. Students who were talking quieted when they noticed him staring at them. He took a seat at his desk and a crackling noise came from a round speaker set high in the wall. There was fumbling and then Principal Petersen's voice welcomed the students to another school year. While he read through a list of announcements, Jess looked over her shoulder, but all she saw were other students staring at her.

The office secretary stepped into the classroom and handed the teacher papers. "New class lists, Mr. Miller."

"Oh?" He squinted back and forth between two sheets she'd handed him.

"We had a late enrollee."

"Alright." He laid them on the desk.

When Principal Petersen finished, the teacher cleared his throat and everyone straightened in their chairs. "I'm Mr. Miller, your homeroom teacher. Some of you may also have me for social studies. As I read your names, please answer."

Jess sat up straighter, realizing that if Marty didn't know they were in the same homeroom yet, he would when the teacher read her name.

"Sharon Allen."

"Here," said the dark-haired girl sitting next to her.

Jess exchanged a smile with her.

"Robert Baker."

"Here," said a boy in the front row.

"Jessica – Blackwell?" Mr. Miller looked up with shock. It had been quiet in the room already, but it seemed much quieter now.

"Here." Jess raised her hand, and then let it drop as every single student except Janet turned to stare at her. Even Sharon was scrutinizing her with confusion. Jess gave her a reassuring smile.

"I wasn't aware there was more than one Blackwell attending this school," Mr. Miller said. "Are you related to Doug Blackwell?"

"Yes, sir. He's my cousin."

There was a tightening in his expression. "I see." His eyes dropped to the other class list lying on his desk, and then focused on the one in his hand.

Jess's stomach sank. She now knew she was in his social studies class, and he wasn't happy about it.

"Louise Brooks," he continued.

Jess looked at Sharon, hoping to connect with someone sympathetic, but Sharon faced forward, her mouth set in a firm line.

"Martin Cappellini."

"Here."

Jess's heart skipped a beat, hearing Marty's familiar voice behind her.

Martin *Cappellini. He's Italian.* She'd never known that about him. While the teacher read through the rest of the class list, she repeated his full name in her mind, rolling over this new bit of information about him. By the time Janet White's name was called and she said, "Here," the bell rang. Jess stood, hoping to see Marty.

"Come on, Jess. We've got English next," Janet said.

All the students had risen by now and Jess was too short to see over them. Disappointed, she followed Janet out of the room and down the hallway.

When they entered the next room, a short middle-aged woman in a dark blue dress was writing on the blackboard. Jess kept her eyes glued on the doorway. She prayed Marty would walk through, but when the bell rang, the teacher closed the door. "Quiet everyone," she said.

The students stopped talking and faced forward.

"I'm Mrs. Landers and this is English literature. We'll start with attendance and then I'll discuss my expectations for this class." She picked up a sheet of paper and adjusted her reading glasses.

"Sharon Allen."

"Here."

Jess didn't bother to find her.

"Jessica *Blackwell*."

"Here," she said.

Mrs. Landers had a look of horror on her face, and Jess sank lower in her seat. A good number of students turned to stare at her. The only ones that didn't were those who were in her homeroom.

"Are you one of the Blackwells of Blackwell Iron and Mining?" Mrs. Landers said, her voice shaky.

"Yes, ma'am. My uncle owns the company."

She staggered back against her desk as if she needed help staying upright. "Oh." She focused on the sheet of paper, her hand trembling, and cleared her throat before continuing to read names. She seemed so rattled, Jess wondered if she'd had a run in with Uncle Jonathon while Doug was in her class. Did all the teachers in this school hate or fear him?

Jess concentrated on her clasped hands on her desk and wondered if staying home with a tutor would have been better after all. She'd thought once she'd gotten beyond the property's gates, she'd have some freedom, but it was clear there was no escaping her uncle's looming shadow. When the bell rang, her nerves increased, dreading what her next teacher's reaction would be.

"Back to homeroom for social studies," Janet said.

Jess was relieved. At least Mr. Miller already knew she was in his class. After collecting her English textbook and a battered copy of *Romeo and Juliet*, she and Janet returned to their homeroom.

They sat in the same seats as before and she watched the door hoping against hope she'd see Marty – and then he was there.

This time Marty's brown eyes came up and held hers for one breathless moment before he headed to the back of the room. She watched him for as long as she dared. He'd washed his battered jeans, but they still showed smudges of grime. She'd never seen his striped T-shirt before. It was too big on him, but at least it wasn't as tattered as the ones he'd worn over the summer. He had it tucked into his jeans, which were cinched tight with an ancient leather belt.

The bell rang and Mr. Miller took attendance. Jess's name came first without a reaction from him. None of the students appeared surprised either. Word seemed to have spread that Doug's cousin was now attending school. When he said Marty's name, Jess had to hide her smile, hearing his familiar voice again. Class was over far too soon. When she stood, she tried to find Marty, but again, she wasn't fast enough to beat the taller students who stood between them.

"We've got to find Patty so she can take you to P.E.," Janet said.

"Okay," Jess said, dispirited.

They located Patty in the crowded hallway, and she led Jess down another hall to the gymnasium. Seated on bleachers with twenty other girls, she waited nervously while the teacher stood in front of them holding a clipboard. She was tall and athletic, dressed in a no-nonsense skirt, top, and white tennis shoes. Next to her was an open canvas bin on wheels.

"Quiet ladies," she ordered when the bell rang, her loud rich voice echoing through the gym. "I'm Miss Gillis. Welcome to your physical education class."

Jess straightened, recognizing the woman's accent.

"You'll be learning how to stay healthy in this class. Not only through physical exercise, but also healthy eating

The Boy in the Woods

and how to take care of your body."

She was from the East Coast, Jess was sure of it. Maybe New Jersey or even New York City.

"While you're in this class, you'll be wearing these." Miss Gillis reached into the bin and pulled out a white short-sleeved button-down shirt. After holding it up, she pulled out a pair of white cotton shorts, and the girls groaned. They were hideous, looking like old-fashioned bloomers.

"Do we really have to wear those?" Patty whined.

Miss Gillis shot her a stern look. "Yes, you do. Please be quiet while I read your names."

"I hope no boys see us," Patty said under her breath. Jess was thinking the same thing, and then she heard her name being called.

"Here," she said.

Miss Gillis's eyes widened, but at least she didn't seem angry. "Are you related to–"

"Doug Blackwell is my cousin," Jess said, wanting to hurry the conversation.

"That's wonderful."

Jess was relieved to finally have a teacher who wasn't unhappy to have her in a class.

"Are you planning on playing any sports?"

"I'm – not sure." Jess wondered why Miss Gillis would want her. She was so much smaller than the other girls, she'd be terrible at just about anything.

"Doug is *such* a good athlete, and his father is a terrific supporter. Whenever the team needs something, he makes sure they have it."

Jess's face flushed with heat while Miss Gillis waited.

The Boy in the Woods

"I, uh, haven't decided yet."

"I hope you'll consider it. We'd love to have you."

Jess slouched on the bleacher. "Yes, ma'am."

Miss Gillis resumed calling out names and after attendance, she had the girls paw through the bin to choose their uniforms. Jess let the other girls fight over the clothes and when someone cast off something as too small, she took it in the hopes it would be small enough for her. By the end of class she had a too-large gym outfit and a headache. Grateful it was time for lunch, she followed Patty to a smaller gym set up as a lunchroom.

They found Janet at a long table and were soon joined by other girls, all friends of Janet and Patty. Janet introduced her to everyone, but there were too many names to remember. Hoping her headache would go away soon, she pulled a sandwich out of her lunch bag and unwrapped the wax paper.

She was about to take a bite when she spotted Marty. Watching him walk along the wall under a line of high multi-paned windows, she wished she could ditch the girls and go with him. After the rocky first half of the day, all she wanted was to sit somewhere quiet with him. Then she noticed his hands were in his pockets. Where was his paper sack? Did he not have a lunch today?

"Jess, why are you looking at that boy?" Patty asked.

"What boy?" Janet said, and looked over as Marty pushed open a door and left the building. "Eww. No, Jess. Stay away from him. There's something wrong with him."

"What do you mean there's something wrong with him?" Jess said, her voice loud.

"For one thing, he doesn't bathe," Patty said, waving her hand in front of her nose. "And he doesn't talk."

"He does too."

All the girls at the table stopped what they were doing and stared at Jess.

"When did you hear him talk?" Janet said, not realizing Jess had replied to both statements.

"Uh, when the teacher took attendance." Jess hoped it would contain the damage.

Patty snorted. "That's all you'll hear him say. He's not even supposed to be in our grade. They made him repeat second grade."

"He's bad news, Jess," said another girl. Was she Cheryl? Or maybe Carol? Jess couldn't remember. "He's dangerous."

Jess opened her mouth to tell her to stop saying such terrible things about Marty, but Janet interrupted her.

"He gets in fights all the time. Last year he beat up Bobby Baker so bad he had to get stitches."

Jess closed her mouth. Had Marty really hurt someone that badly?

Patty nodded in solemn agreement. "That's right. He got kicked out of school six weeks early for that."

"I say Bobby had it coming to him," said a girl with red curls. Wasn't she the one named Louise? Jess remembered her from a few of her classes.

"How can you say Bobby deserved it?" Patty said.

The red-haired girl lifted her chin. "Because I saw the whole thing. Bobby shot spitballs at him all through Mr. Granger's class. You know Mr. Granger always made that boy, Marty, sit in the front row. Anyway, when class was over, Marty told Bobby not to do it again. Bobby said, 'Why don't you make me?' and then he called him a bad word that I can't repeat." She blushed from the memory.

"That still doesn't make it okay, Louise," another girl said.

Louise shrugged without replying.

Jess fought the urge to go hug her for defending Marty.

"Let's not talk about *him* anymore," Patty said to Jess, her face brightening. "Tell us what it's like living with Doug."

Jess wondered why she would ask such a question. "It's okay, I guess."

"Only okay? Are you *kidding?* Look at him."

All of them turned to find Doug seated across the room, surrounded by older teens. The table was crowded and those who couldn't fit had pulled over folding chairs from the other tables so they could be closer. Donna was sitting beside him, gazing at him with adoration as he talked. Whatever he was saying must have been funny because there were gales of laughter every so often.

"I can't believe living with him could ever be just okay," sighed the Cheryl-Carol girl.

"Doug's a nice guy, and everything," Jess said. "But he's my *cousin*."

Most of the girls reacted as if Jess had grown a second head.

"I wish he was *my* cousin," Patty moaned, still watching Doug.

"Me too," echoed several other girls.

Jess met Louise's gaze across the table. Louise shook her head then rolled her eyes dramatically, making Jess laugh.

"What?" Patty said.

"Nothing," Jess said, while she tried to suppress her smile.

"Look at Chuck," someone said.

Jess's breath left her when she spotted him.

Chuck crossed the lunchroom, his face puffy and bruised with medical tape crisscrossed over his swollen nose. He went to a table occupied by three freshman boys. Looming over them, he snarled something, and they gathered their things and vacated the table, leaving him to sit alone.

"Is it true Doug punched him because he tried to make out with you?"

Jess stared at the girl who'd said it with horror as a hush fell over the table. *How did she know that?* She studied the other girls, and from the looks in their eyes, they'd all heard something about the incident. While shame burned through her, her mind whirled. She didn't want to talk about what he'd tried to do to her, and she worried about how much of the details they already knew.

"Leave her alone," Janet snapped, and much to Jess's relief, everyone turned their attention to her. "Chuck's always been a stupid jerk. He needed someone to knock some sense into him."

At that moment, a group of boys passed the table, making the girls forget all about Chuck. They huddled together and debated which one was the most handsome.

"Thanks," Jess whispered to Janet.

"It's okay."

Jess's heart lurched, seeing the shame she was feeling was reflected in Janet's eyes. Chuck had tried to do something to her too. "Janet–" The bell rang, cutting Jess off.

Janet took her empty wrappers and shoved them in her paper bag. "Time to go."

Janet wasn't interested in talking about it anymore than she was, and she didn't blame her. As she collected her textbooks and gym uniform, she hoped the rest of the day wouldn't be as horrible as the first half.

The next class was science with both girls, but no Marty. Jess waited with dread while Mr. Schaffer took attendance. When he read her name, his eyes flickered to her before he went on to the next student's name, and she let out a breath. Perhaps word had spread to the rest of the teachers that a new Blackwell was attending school.

Once attendance was over, he walked up and down the aisles between the desks, passing out textbooks. "While you are in my class, there will be no *monkey business*. At times, we will be doing dangerous experiments, working with open flames, handling poisonous chemicals. I expect you to follow the rules and carry out my instructions *to the letter*. All assignments will be completed and turned in on time. There will be *no* exceptions. I don't care who your family is."

Mr. Schaffer was looking right at Jess, and she dropped her eyes. With her stomach twisting in knots, she kept her head down while he continued his lecture, not wanting to know if any more of his offhand comments were directed at her. When the bell rang, she jumped out of her seat, not wanting to be there a moment longer.

Patty took her to their math class, and when she walked in, Marty was already seated at the back of the room. Their eyes met, and he leaned forward and opened a book as if he was going to read. She wished she could sit next to him, but chose a desk next to Patty instead. She faced forward and studied the male teacher, wondering what she could expect from him. Would *any* of her teachers ever see her as herself and not the niece of Jonathon Blackwell?

Mr. Taylor didn't react to her name during attendance. Nor did he make stern comments about not making exceptions for late assignments. In fact, he seemed like a quiet, mild-mannered man, and Jess relaxed. She'd always loved math. And Marty was there. That meant they'd get to do math homework together.

This time when the bell rang, she took her time gathering her growing number of textbooks, hoping to time her exit so she could walk out with Marty. As soon as he passed her desk, she stood to follow.

"Miss Blackwell," Mr. Taylor said.

She turned back towards his desk, sad to let Marty go. "Yes, sir?"

"If you need any help with your assignments, you'll come to me, won't you?"

She was dismayed by the concern in his eyes. "Mr. Taylor, you don't need to–"

"If you don't understand something, I'll explain it to you."

"But I never have any trouble with–"

"I'll take all the time you need!"

"Yes, sir," Jess said, giving up. It was clear he wasn't going to listen to her.

"Good. You'd better go. I don't want to make you late for your next class."

Both girls were waiting for her in the hall, and Marty was long gone. "Home Ec. is next," said Janet, and Patty laughed.

"Hello, easy 'A.'"

Jess was glad the day was almost over. She sat with

The Boy in the Woods

Patty and Janet in a large room, surrounded by kitchen stations and waited while the petite Mrs. O'Reilly took attendance. After she'd called Jess's name, she said, "It's nice to have you in the class." Even though it was a more mild response, it still made Jess uncomfortable to be singled out.

When the final bell of the day rang, Jess was more than ready to leave. Following Janet and Patty into the hallway, she made a decision. "Janet," she said, stopping her. "I'll take my schedule back. I know my way around now."

"Oh, uh, okay." Janet retrieved the index card from inside one of her textbooks. "But you know if you need any help–"

"Yeah, I know." Jess walked away from them with a satisfied smile. From now on, she'd figure things out on her own.

When she stepped outside, the black car was parked at the curb with Annie standing next to it. She was a welcome sight after the day Jess had had, and she rushed to greet her. But as Jess drew closer, she took her in with astonishment. "Annie, you look *beautiful*."

Annie beamed at the compliment. "Why, thank you. I guess you've never seen me in my normal clothes."

Jess was astounded by the transformation. Instead of her usual plain black maid's uniform, she was wearing a fitted forest green suit, the color bringing out the green flecks in her hazel eyes. Her hair was swept up in a French twist and a matching hat was pinned on her head. She was even wearing lipstick. She looked so smart, Jess could easily imagine her strolling on the sidewalks of Manhattan.

"Did you have a good first day?" Annie said.

"Yes," Jess lied, and gave her a tight one-armed hug while holding the stack of textbooks and gym uniform.

"Are you hungry for a snack? We can eat before we shop for school clothes."

"Yes, ma'am."

They climbed in the back, and Jess threw her things on the bench seat between them. Annie picked up the two-piece gym uniform, wrinkling her nose. "Oh, my. Are they still making you girls wear these things? I wore the same uniform when I went to that school. My mother had a terrible time keeping it white." She sighed. "I suppose I'll have to ask her what she did. I hope she still remembers."

"They're too big for me," Jess groused.

She patted Jess's hand with her gloved one. "Don't you worry about that. A few tucks here and there and they'll fit just fine."

James took them to the edge of town to a train car that had been converted into a diner. While Jess ate a hamburger and sipped on a chocolate malted milkshake, Annie peppered her with questions about her classes and the girls she'd met. Jess kept the reactions of her teachers to herself.

At the town's department store, Annie helped Jess choose skirts, sweater sets, dresses, and shoes. When they got home, she and Annie put them all away. After Annie left to get dinner ready, Jess stood in front of her open wardrobe, admiring her new clothes.

Even though it had been a rough day, the worst was over. She'd always done well in school and she hoped her teachers would recognize that once she'd handed in an assignment or two. She wanted them to know her for who she was rather than being Jonathon Blackwell's niece.

An hour later, Uncle Jonathon was filling Doug's plate with food. "How was school today?"

"Fine," Doug said.

"And how about Jessica? How did she do?"

Jess watched Doug, wondering what he was going to tell his father. Except for first thing in the morning, he hadn't seen her at all.

Doug took his plate from his father. "She did well. She's already made some friends."

"Oh?" Uncle Jonathon turned his attention to Jess. "Who are they?"

She glanced at Doug and he gave her slight nod, encouraging her. "Uh, well, Janet White."

"Jeff's little sister," Doug said.

"And Patty Melleville."

"She's Jerry Melleville's little sister," Doug said.

Uncle Jonathon nodded with approval. "The mayor's daughter. You've done well. I hope this is a sign of what I can expect from you for the rest of the year, Jessica."

She picked up her fork. "Yes, sir."

She'd passed her uncle's first test. Now she had to make sure she passed the rest of them.

Chapter Sixteen

Why

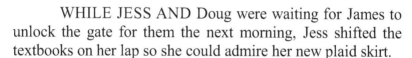

WHILE JESS AND Doug were waiting for James to unlock the gate for them the next morning, Jess shifted the textbooks on her lap so she could admire her new plaid skirt.

"Why'd you bring all those books home?" Doug asked. "Did your teachers assign homework?"

"No, I had to bring them home. I don't have a locker yet."

"Where's your schedule?"

She opened her new purse and handed the index card to him.

He pointed to a series of numbers at the bottom. "There's your locker number, and the numbers after that are your combination."

"Oh."

He shook his head as he drove through the open gate. "That Janet."

When they reached the school, Doug gave her a curt,

The Boy in the Woods

"See you later."

He strode towards a cluster of older students, and Jess wandered towards the entrance. She looked around for Marty, but didn't see him. Then she spotted Janet and Patty with a group of girls. Louise, the girl with red curly hair who had defended Marty was with them, and she walked towards them. Louise waved when she saw Jess.

While the two of them chatted, Jess discovered they were in five of the same classes together. After the bell rang, Louise helped her locate her locker and figure out the combination. Rid of most of her books and lunch bag, Jess went to homeroom with Louise, excited about seeing Marty. She looked to the back of the room when she walked in, but he wasn't there yet. She and Louise sat next to each other, and she tried to carry on a conversation while sneaking glances at the door.

And then he was there. Their eyes met, and Jess beamed with happiness. Instead of smiling back, he scowled and headed for the rear of the classroom. She faced forward, shocked by his reaction.

Was he angry at her? Then she realized what a terrible mistake she'd made. She shouldn't have smiled at him. If anyone noticed, they might figure out they knew each other. She peeked at the other students, but no one seemed to pay any attention. Taking a deep breath, she leaned back in her seat. She'd have to be careful from now on.

The next class they had together was social studies, and she looked for him at the back of the room. He was already seated, but didn't raise his head before she had to sit and face forward. In math, he came after she was at her desk, but he wouldn't look at her. Even though she understood why he was ignoring her, it still hurt. By the end of the day, she was struggling to keep her composure. If this was what she could expect for the rest of the school year, she didn't know if she could take it. Pretending they didn't know each other hurt far more than she'd expected.

When she and Doug walked into the kitchen that afternoon, Annie greeted them. Jess noticed the kitchen table was set for two, with a large plate of sandwiches in the middle, and her heart sank. Doug sat and helped himself to a sandwich.

"Uh, Annie. I was really hoping I could take some food outside to do my homework," Jess said.

"Oh?" Annie said.

"It's so nice out, and I've been cooped up all day." She hoped it sounded believable.

"I was going to sew your gym uniform today. Don't you need it soon?"

"Yes, ma'am. Tomorrow." She'd been so eager to see Marty, she'd forgotten.

"I need to pin it before I sew it, and you have to be wearing it when I do."

"Can't we do it after dinner tonight?"

Annie shook her head. "That's too late. I don't want to be up all night sewing."

Jess tried to think of something. The minutes were ticking by, and she was losing precious time she could spend with Marty.

"How about this?" Annie said. "Go in my room and change into the uniform while I pack you a basket of food. As soon as we're done, you can go do your homework."

"Okay," Jess said, knowing this was the best she was going to get.

Looking for the uniform in Annie's bedroom, Jess

realized this was the first time she'd been in there. It was small, but not cramped, and the antique furniture was simpler than the furniture in the rest of the house. A brightly colored quilt covered her bed and flowered wallpaper adorned the walls. It suited Annie's warm, feminine nature. She spotted the gym uniform on a table next to a sewing machine, and yanked off her clothes.

She was glad Doug was gone when she came back into the kitchen. She didn't need to see Annie's sour expression to tell her she looked awful in the too-large top and giant bloomers. Annie worked fast, pinning the cloth in different places, then sent Jess back to her room with strict instructions not to let any of the pins fall out when she took it off. Jess couldn't change back into her skirt and sweater fast enough. Once dressed, she hurried to the door with her school books and basket.

After a quick check to make sure James wasn't in sight, she was soon on the path. When she saw the door to the cabin open, she sprinted to it and bounded into the living room. Marty was at the table in the kitchen, drinking a mug of tea.

"Hi, Marty," she said, breathless. She put her basket and books on the counter while he stood to wash his mug.

"What are you doing here?" he asked, pumping the handle at the sink.

"What?" She was surprised by the question. "I came to see you."

"Shouldn't you be with your new friends?"

She was shocked by the anger in his eyes. "What do you mean?"

He gave her clothes a disgusted once over. "You even look like one of them now."

"Why are you mad at me?" she said, trying but failing to keep the hurt out of her voice.

"Who says I'm mad?" He shook water out of his mug with hard, sharp motions.

Watching him put his mug in the cupboard, Jess thought about how difficult the last two days had been, and her emotions boiled over. "You *told* me to pretend not to know you," she shouted, stamping her foot.

He flinched at the sound, and then faced her while keeping his attention on the floor. She waited for him to explain himself, but after a minute she knew he wasn't going to say anything.

"Why are you mad at me for doing what you told me to do? Do you know how hard it is for me to see you and not say anything?" Her voice cracked, and she swallowed. She would *not* cry. "I don't even like most of those girls. The ones I want to be friends with won't talk to me. The teachers either hate me or treat me like a princess because of my name, and now my best friend is mad at me. I *hate* school," she said with another foot stamp.

"Join the club," Marty said, but the anger had left his face. The tension in the room eased along with his expression.

"Are you really mad at me?"

"Maybe." He shrugged, but the corners of his mouth were twitching.

She gave him a small push. "Stop it, Marty."

"Ow." He laughed as he rubbed the spot where she'd touched him, as if he'd been injured.

She grinned. The familiar Marty was back. "Do you want to eat?"

"Let's go to the pond. We can go fishing."

"I thought we'd do homework."

"Homework."

"Yeah. We have stuff that's due tomorrow, you know?"

"I don't do homework," he said, lifting his chin.

"Why not?"

"There's no point to it."

"What about your grades?"

"What about them?"

"How do you pass your classes?"

He shrugged again. "I don't know. I just do."

"I have to do my homework."

His mouth dropped open. "Come on, Jess. That's no fun. Let's go to the pond."

"Nope, I'm doing homework."

"Well, I'm going fishing."

She scooped up her books and basket. "Well, I hope you have fun."

"Don't worry, I will."

He pivoted and stomped into the living room, and she placed her books on the table. When she sat, she noticed Marty standing in the center of the living room. He was holding the fishing pole and watching her, waiting to see if she would change her mind. She arranged her books in front of her and then opened the dishcloth lining the basket. As she reached inside it, he walked out the front door.

Sighing, she dropped her hand. She didn't want to be at the cabin while he was at the pond. She'd missed him so much over the last two days. But when she considered joining him, she remembered the reactions of her teachers. She had to do well in her classes. Not only did she want to prove to her teachers she was a good student, she needed to make sure Uncle Jonathon didn't intervene. She could only imagine what he would do if he wasn't happy with her report card.

She emptied the basket of food, still thinking of Marty, when he appeared. He walked to the kitchen without looking at her.

"What are you doing?" she asked, hoping he'd changed his mind.

He made his way to the sink. "Need worms."

"Oh." She got an idea. Unwrapping the wax paper, she had Annie's chocolate chip cookies in full view by the time Marty stood. She saw his eyes linger on them before he headed out the back door. She paged through her social studies book to find the assigned chapter, and waited. It wasn't long before she heard his footsteps and as he stepped in, she picked up a cookie.

"What are you doing now?" He stopped, and when she had his full attention, she took a bite.

"I'm getting my fishing pole." He watched her chew for a moment, then continued to the living room where he snatched the pole and stalked out.

She set the cookie down, disheartened. It hadn't worked. She leaned over her open book, determined to read, but instead of the words, she saw Marty on the path to the pond without her.

There were footsteps in the living room again. She held her breath with her head still down while Marty approached. She could hear his breathing in the quiet kitchen, but she kept pretending to read.

"Aw, heck Jess. Won't you come?"

The Boy in the Woods

"No," she said without looking up, and he collapsed on his stool with a huff. She pushed the wax paper closer to him. "Have a cookie."

After a hesitation, he took one. Now able to relax, she picked up her cookie and ate it while she read. He finished his cookie and she could feel him watching her, but she ignored him.

"Are you just going to sit there and read?" he said.

"I can share my book with you." She pushed it towards him. "We can read together."

"Never mind," he grumbled. "Got my own book."

He went to the living room and retrieved his stack of textbooks. With a loud thud, he dropped them on the kitchen table and plopped on his stool. He found his social studies book and smacked it down in front of him. While he flipped loudly through pages, she kept her head down. He soon settled, and it was quiet while the two of them read. When she was ready to answer the questions at the end of the chapter, she got out pencils and paper, and without saying anything, pushed a pencil and sheet of paper towards him. After a few minutes, he took them and began writing.

They'd been working for a while when she paged back and forth through the chapter, trying to find an answer.

"What number you on?" he asked.

"Fifteen." She continued to flip through the pages.

"Ha. I'm ahead of you."

"If you're so smart, where'd you find the answer to number fifteen?"

He turned to a page and held up the book. "Page twenty-three," he said, tapping the paragraph with his finger.

They moved on to math, and she was working through

the assigned problems, when Marty threw his pencil on the table. "This is stupid." He shoved his math book away from him.

Afraid he was about to stomp out of the cabin, she spoke. "Wait, Marty. My old teacher explained it a different way. I can show you. It's easier than the way Mr. Taylor did it."

"Mr. Taylor is dumb."

She showed him how to solve the algebraic equation, making sure he understood each step before moving on to the next one. He growled and grouched at first, but when they'd reached the solution, he was in a much better mood and worked on the next one on his own. She returned to her own homework, but kept an eye on him to make sure he wasn't getting frustrated. By the time they'd completed their assignments, the sun was dipping close to the tops of the trees.

"I better go."

While she gathered her books and papers, Marty stood and stretched. "I'll walk with you."

"Oh, okay." He'd been so odd the last time he'd walked her home, and then got angry with her at school. She didn't want the same thing to happen again.

When the garage was almost in sight, she stopped. "You're not going to get mad at me again tomorrow, are you?"

He kicked loose gravel on the path. "No."

"Do you *want* me to talk to you at school?"

"No. Look, forget I said that stuff, okay? It was stupid."

From the look in his brown eyes, she knew he meant

it, and she smiled. "Okay, Marty. I'll see you at school tomorrow."

His face lit up with a rare, genuine smile. "Yeah, I'll see you."

He turned towards the cabin, and she watched him until he disappeared behind the curve. Heading for home, her heart was bursting.

Chapter Seventeen
Alone With You

"DOUG, DO YOU know Louise Brooks?" Jess asked on the way to school the next day.

Even though she'd only known Louise for a few days, Jess had grown to like her a lot. Not only did the girl with red curls make her laugh, Louise wasn't afraid to be herself. It would be fun to have a female best friend to do things with, but there was one huge obstacle – her uncle.

"Brooks, Brooks, Brooks," Doug repeated to himself. "No, I don't know anyone named Brooks. Why?"

"She's a girl I met at school. She's really nice."

"What's her dad do?" Doug turned off the two-lane road onto the street that led to the high school.

Jess's shoulders drooped. "I don't know." If this was the first question he asked, Jess now knew more than ever how important the answer was. Her suspicion was confirmed by the wary look in his eyes as he glanced over at her.

"You weren't going to mention her to Dad before you

found out, were you?"

"No. I know better than that," she said, looking at the groups of teens they were passing.

"Good, because I don't need the hassle. Find out, and I'll tell you if it's okay or not."

Jess sighed. Life was so much simpler when her parents were alive. It never mattered to them what friends she brought home, or what their fathers did for a living. It made her sad to realize she'd never have that kind of freedom again. "Doesn't it bother you to live like this?"

"Like what?" He drove the car into the high school parking lot.

"Not being able to be friends with whoever you want."

He frowned while he parked the car and turned off the ignition. "I'm lucky to be living this life, and so are you," he said, surprising Jess with his forceful tone. "We aren't like the rest of the kids in this school. We have responsibilities that go along with all of – this." He moved his hand to indicate his new car. "Maybe not all of it's fun or easy, but I'm grateful to be in this family, and you should be too!" Without waiting for a reply, he got out of the car and slammed the door before stalking off.

Gathering her books and purse, Jess felt wounded. She wasn't ungrateful, she just wanted to be allowed to choose her own friends. What was wrong with that?

Among a group of girls that included Patty and Janet, she spotted Louise's red curls and walked towards them. Doug was the one who didn't understand, she decided. He didn't know he could live a life that was different from the one his father had made. The other girls chatted, but she remained quiet while a realization hit her. This must be why her dad and mom had moved so far away. They didn't want this kind of life, and she didn't either, she decided. As soon as she was old enough, she'd move far away too.

In Social Studies class later that day, Jess and Louise laid their homework assignments on Mr. Miller's desk before taking their seats. Jess pulled out paper and a pencil to take notes when Marty walked in. He gave her a warm glance before heading towards the back of the room. Then he stopped and went to Mr. Miller's desk, pulling a folded sheet of paper from his back pocket. After tossing it on the pile of homework, he turned and walked toward his desk.

"Mr. Cappellini!"

Marty stopped mid-stride and everyone in the room stilled.

"Mr. Cappellini, come here."

Marty's shoulders curved inward and his head dropped as if he was trying to make himself smaller. Jess held her breath while he approached the teacher's desk.

"What is this?" Mr. Miller demanded, picking up Marty's folded paper by the corner with two fingers. The room had become silent, everyone in the class focused on the two of them.

"Homework," Marty said. He was so quiet, Jess could barely hear him.

Mr. Miller's eyes narrowed, and then he unfolded the paper. Scanning it, his expression changed from skepticism to shock. He opened and closed his mouth as if the ability to speak had left him. "Thank you, Mr. Cappellini," he said finally. "You may go to your seat now."

Marty's head snapped up. He gawked at Mr. Miller before pivoting. As he passed Jess, he seemed to be in a daze, and she felt a fierce pride for him. It might be the first time he'd done something that impressed a teacher. During the rest of the class, she couldn't concentrate on Mr. Miller's lecture on the Constitution. Instead, she relived that glorious moment in her mind.

The bell rang, and she slowly gathered her notebook and papers, wanting to leave at the same time as Marty.

"Jess, come on," Louise said. "We have to get our gym uniforms from our lockers before class."

Jess gave up, scooping up her books. "Okay."

When they entered the girls' locker room, Jess noticed everyone undressing, and she was immediately uncomfortable. She didn't want to undress in front of them. She tried not to look at anyone while unbuttoning her shirt and then accidentally caught sight of Louise's bra.

Turning to face the wall, she was mortified. Unlike the other girls, she was still wearing undershirts. She kept her eyes on the wall the rest of the time she changed, not wanting to see if the other girls noticed she still dressed like a little kid.

"Are you ready?" Louise said as Jess finished tying the laces on her second gym shoe, and she straightened. "Oh, my gosh. Look at you." Louise gaped at Jess while the other girls turned their attention to her. They gazed at her gym uniform with a mixture of astonishment and envy, including Patty, whose mouth was hanging open. "How did you get your uniform to look like that?"

Jess looked down and then at the surrounding girls. Unlike the rest of them with their ill-fitting tops and enormous bloomers, Annie had tailored her shirt, and sewn tucks in the bloomers, hiding most of the extra fabric so they looked more like shorts.

"Annie fixed them for me."

"Who's Annie?" Louise asked while they walked out of the locker room.

"She's the person who…" Jess stumbled for the right words to describe her, "who takes care of our house."

"You mean she's the maid?"

It occurred to Jess that Louise's family might not have someone like Annie working for them, but to her relief, there were no signs of jealousy in Louise's expression. She was about to agree, then stopped. Annie was so much more than a maid or housekeeper. "She's more like a mom to me and Doug. She takes care of us. I love her like a mom," Jess declared with a smile.

"That's swell," Louise said, smiling back at her, then it dropped as she looked over Jess's head.

Miss Gillis was eyeing Jess's uniform and from her stern expression, it was clear she disapproved of Annie's sewing job. Jess was afraid she'd tell her she had to take the uniform back home and have the stitching removed, but instead, Miss Gillis turned her attention to the girls taking seats on the bleachers.

"Ladies! Pair up and get a basketball from the storage room."

Jess and Louise grinned at each other, and took off running towards the storage room, starting a race with the other girls.

Later, Jess was opening her lunch sack when she saw Marty heading through the small gym. Relieved to see he had a sack in his hand, she couldn't help smiling while unwrapping her sandwich.

"What's so funny, Jess?" Patty said cattily.

"She's remembering how you looked in gym class today," Louise said just as cattily.

The Boy in the Woods

Patty huffed and turned to face Janet on her other side. Jess and Louise shared a smirk.

While she chewed her sandwich, Jess thought about her conversation with Louise in the locker room. Was Louise's lack of reaction to finding out Jess had a housekeeper because her family had one too? If she did, it would make Jess's life a lot easier. Uncle Jonathon wouldn't stop her from being friends with a girl whose family could afford a housekeeper. But how to bring it up? She didn't want to ask because if Louise didn't have one, it would be awkward. And she didn't want Louise to think things like that mattered to her. Anger boiled through her. She shouldn't have to ask if her friend was rich. It wasn't right.

"Do you have any brothers or sisters?" she said, hoping to ease into the conversation.

"Yep, I have two brothers and a sister."

Jess couldn't imagine what it must be like to live with so many siblings. Until moving in with Uncle Jonathon, she'd always been an only child. "I bet it's really busy at your house," she said, thinking of how quiet her own home was.

"You don't know the half of it," Louise said with a wave of her hand. "Jack is four. I swear he thinks he's Tarzan." She laughed, shaking her head which made her curls bounce. "Joyce is easier to deal with. She's seven and Gary is nine. He's not as crazy as Jack, thank goodness."

"That does sound busy." How different things would have been if Jess had had brothers and sisters? She wouldn't have been all alone when she'd lost her parents.

"After school is the worst. My mom has to go help my dad and Jack is running around like a wild man while I'm trying to make snacks for all of them. But then they usually settle down and I can do my homework before I have to make dinner."

"Oh?" Jess said, with a sinking feeling. "What does your mom help your dad with?"

"My family owns The Golden Skillet."

"The what?"

Louise gave her an odd look. "Haven't you seen it? It's a restaurant. There are only three in town."

Jess pretended to look for cookies inside her paper sack. "I've been too busy to get into town much."

"Anyway, my mom helps get ready for the dinner rush and stays until they close. On the weekends I get to work there." Louise sat up straighter with obvious pride. "They even pay me."

"That's great." She imagined Louise's brothers and sister, all with red curls like Louise, sitting around a kitchen table. But when she imagined Louise's mom and dad, it was her own parents she pictured, and the familiar sadness came over her. A bell rang through the gym, signaling the end of lunch. While she gathered her trash, she thought about how much her parents would have loved to meet Louise.

Walking to her next class, she spotted Marty approaching the door. The corners of his mouth twitched as he dropped his eyes. She quickened her steps, walking in behind him. He approached Mr. Taylor's desk and laid his math homework on top of the other students' pages. Mr. Taylor watched him from his place at the blackboard with bewilderment. Jess grinned at Mr. Taylor while laying her own homework on top of Marty's.

"Did you find out where your friend's dad works?" Doug said on the way home that afternoon.

Jess leaned her head against the bench seat, her happiness vanishing. "He owns The Golden Skillet," she muttered to the window.

"Oh, that family. Don't mention her to Dad."

She crossed her arms over her chest. "Don't worry. I wasn't planning on it."

Doug stayed silent for the rest of the trip, perhaps sensing Jess's anger. When they walked into the kitchen, she went to Annie and gave her a tight hug. "Thank you."

Annie laughed. "You're welcome, but for what?"

"My uniform."

"How did it fit?"

"It was perfect."

Annie beamed. "I'm glad. I thought you'd want to go outside to do your homework, so I packed your basket. It's over on the counter."

Jess took the basket and headed out. When she walked into the cabin, Marty was in the kitchen, his textbooks already on the table in front of him. "Hi, Marty."

"What took you so long?"

She opened her mouth to reply that she wasn't late, and then saw him trying to hide a smirk. "Stop being such a smart aleck." She gave him a push.

He laughed and rubbed his shoulder. "You don't have to push people around all the time, you know? You could hurt a person."

"And you don't have to tease people all the time. Now get your social studies book." She set the food from her basket on the table. "We've got a lot of reading to do."

"Yes, ma'am." He gave her a mock salute before he

searched through his stack of books.

On the way home, that afternoon, Marty joined her. Crossing the clearing, Jess looked up at the darkening sky. The days were already getting shorter. It wouldn't be long before it would cut into her time with Marty, since she couldn't pretend to be doing homework in the dark. A cool breeze swept through the trees, and she shivered.

"Cold?" Marty asked.

"A little." She clutched her books tighter to her chest and eyed his T-shirt. Did he have other clothes, or even a coat? "Are you cold?"

"Naw."

"It won't be long before it's winter." She studied his reaction to see if he was worried about it.

"I reckon."

They'd reached the curve before the garage, and she stopped. While his brown eyes held hers, she wished she could ask him if he had warmer clothes, but it wasn't a good idea to put him on the spot. "I'll see you tomorrow."

He smirked. "Yeah, see you, kid."

"Don't call me that," she said, but couldn't help smiling. "You know I don't like it."

"But you're so easy to rile up."

"Time to go, you."

"Okay," he said, putting his hands up.

He walked down the path while she watched him. Before the curve, he turned and waved, then stepped out of sight. She gazed at the empty spot, and then turned towards the garage, her heart lighter. It was the first time he'd waved at her.

Chapter Eighteen
Who's Sorry Now

November 1958

ANNIE SET JESS'S breakfast plate in front of her on a Saturday morning. "Doug's Birthday is coming up in a week. He's going to be sixteen."

Jess smiled up at Annie's glowing face.

"I can't believe it. I remember the day he was born like it was yesterday."

In the six months that Jess had lived in her new home, Annie had become as much a mother to her as she was to Doug.

"Would you like to go shopping so you can get him a birthday present? We can buy you a winter coat and boots while we're at it."

"That would be nice," Jess said. Over the last few weeks, the weather had become cooler. But when the temperature dropped below freezing, Jess found she'd grown since last winter and her old coat no longer fit.

"We'll go Monday, right after school, okay?" Annie said, going to the sink.

"Uh, okay." That meant Jess wouldn't see Marty after school. She ate her scrambled eggs, gazing at the barren trees beyond the garage. At least she could tell him so he wouldn't be wondering where she was. They could even do extra homework over the weekend so he wouldn't get behind.

Marty would never admit it, but homework had become important to him. Now that he'd seen how his teachers reacted, he was no longer willing to put it off. Yesterday, he'd insisted on doing homework even though they'd had the whole weekend to get it done.

Or perhaps it was because it was too cold to be outside. Even with both fires lit, the cabin took forever to warm up. Marty kept on his heavy cloth coat while they'd done their homework, and Jess shivered even though she had on jeans and a sweater. Uncle Jonathon's house was too close to the forest for the smoke from their fires to be spotted, thank goodness, but it would be much better if they had something else to help keep them warm.

"Annie, do you have any old blankets I can take outside today?" Jess asked as the idea occurred to her. "I still want to do homework, but it's getting so cold."

"I don't think it's a good idea." Annie dried the frying pan with a dishcloth. "I know you're doing your homework in the woods. They'll get too dirty."

"I promise I'll keep them clean."

Annie stopped drying the pan and studied Jess with a frown. Then her eyes widened with alarm.

Jess knew she was in trouble.

"You're going to the cabin," Annie said in a hushed voice.

Jess jumped out of her chair. "Please don't tell Uncle Jonathon."

"You're right I shouldn't tell him, Jess. *No one* is allowed to go to the cabin. You have to stop going there," she said,shaking her head. "You can't go back ever again."

"*No,*" Jess cried. This couldn't happen. "Please, Annie."

"Do you know what your uncle would do to you if he finds out?"

"I *need* to go there. I *have* to." Annie gave her a quizzical look, and she realized she was about to make things worse. She couldn't let her guess any more of her secrets. "You don't understand, it's been really hard for me since I moved here. Everything is so different from–" Her throat closed up as emotions overwhelmed her. She swallowed until she could speak again. "I found the cabin a long time ago, and it helped me a lot. I can't explain why, but it did. Please don't take that away from me. I won't let Uncle Jonathon find out, I promise."

"If he catches you – Jess, if he finds out I knew and let you go anyway, he'll fire me. I'll never get to see you again."

Jess hugged her as the enormity of what Annie had said sank in. She never imagined she might lose Annie, but she believed her uncle would be that vindictive. She thought of never going to the cabin again, of never speaking to Marty again, and an unbearable pain constricted her chest. She couldn't lose him. "I *swear* I'll be careful," she pleaded into Annie's uniform. "I can keep secrets real good."

"You sure had me fooled, at least until now."

"Please don't take this away from me," she whispered. "Please, Annie."

"Okay."

Jess sagged against her.

"I can see how much this means to you, but I'm doing this against my better judgment. Don't make me regret this."

"I promise I won't."

When Jess let go, Annie turned away from her. "I guess I better go find some blankets in the attic," she grumbled. "The last thing I need is your uncle asking questions because you've come down with pneumonia."

She hated that she'd put Annie in this position. "Thank you."

"I know, I know." Annie left through the butler's pantry.

Jess walked back to the kitchen table. Pushing her plate away, she put her head in her hands, now sick to her stomach. How could she have been so stupid to ask for blankets? Of course, Annie would figure out something was fishy the minute she mentioned them. And now Annie's job was at risk.

Still, she couldn't bear the thought of losing Marty's friendship. It would be torture to only see him at school and know she could never speak to him again.

It was all because of her uncle and his strict rules about class, she thought bitterly. Because of him, everyone she cared about would be hurt if she made a mistake: Marty, Annie, and even Doug. If Annie was banished from their home, Doug would lose the only mom he'd had since his real mom died. He didn't deserve that.

With the weight of all the secrets she was carrying pressing on her, she took her plate to the trashcan to scrape off the breakfast she was no longer interested in eating.

Annie appeared with two wool blankets, still looking sober. "I suppose you'll want to take a lunch?"

"Yes, ma'am," Jess said, unable to meet her eyes.

"When you go out, use the back door, and go around the back of the garage in case Doug is looking out his bedroom window."

"I will."

"We can't have him asking questions either."

"I know," Jess whispered, ashamed she'd forced Annie to be sneaky too.

When she was ready to leave, she checked to make sure the garage door was closed and James was nowhere in sight. Carrying the blankets, school books, and basket, she slipped behind the garage. It was only when she'd reached the clearing that she felt a bit better. Smoke was rising from the chimney, and Jess hurried to the door.

It was difficult to manage the latch with her arms so full, but she got it open. Marty was in his cloth coat, putting wood in the firebox of the cookstove. She pushed the door closed with her back as he entered the living room. Even though there was a roaring fire in the fireplace, it was still chilly in the room. She laid the blankets on the back of a chair.

"What are those for?" Marty said.

"Since it's getting so cold, I thought we could use these to keep warm." She forced her voice to stay light.

"Didn't they ask questions when you took them?"

"No."

There was a wariness in his eyes. Was he seeing right through her lies like Annie had?

"I had to promise I wouldn't get them dirty," she added.

"Oh."

She kept her eyes on his, willing him to trust her. He returned to the cookstove and she let out a breath. Following him to the kitchen with her basket and books, a heaviness came over her. It didn't make her feel good that she was lying to Marty now too.

"Do you want to do homework?" she said, intent on filling her mind with studies so she wouldn't have to think about it.

"I reckon," he said with a shrug, pretending not to care.

"What should we start with?"

After giving the fire in the cookstove a final prod, he went to his stool. "I don't know. What do you want to do?"

"I have a lot of reading to do for English."

He grimaced.

"What?"

"I don't like those Greek stories. Let's do math."

Jess laughed. "Don't you like *The Odyssey*?"

"No."

"Okay, let me get the blankets and we'll do math. But then we should read."

With the wool blankets wrapped tight around them, they paged through their math textbooks. "I won't be able to come on Monday. I have to go shopping–" Marty lifted his head and she stopped. She was about to say she was getting a new coat and boots. "My cousin's birthday is soon."

"Okay," he said and opened his textbook.

The Boy in the Woods

Jess turned the pages and tried not to think about how Marty's cloth coat wasn't warm enough.

On Monday, Jess found Annie standing next to the black car parked outside the high school. Dressed stylishly again, Annie had on a fitted dark blue suit with a matching hat. Waving goodbye to Louise, Jess headed to her with a grin and gave her a tight hug.

"Ready to go shopping?" Annie asked.

"Yes."

James drove them to the two-story department store on Main Street, and Jess chose a long brown wool coat and matching pair of fleece-lined winter boots. Then she tried to find a gift for Doug. Wandering among the display racks, nothing seemed right. He already had plenty of clothes, she'd never seen him read a book, and he didn't listen to music except on the radio in his car. What do you get the richest boy in town for his birthday? Trying to come up with something, she thought of the gifts she'd given her dad.

"I know what I want to get him," she said to Annie. "I want to get aftershave lotion." It was something Doug could use every day, and she could pick out one with a nice smell. Donna would like that.

"Are you sure?"

"Is there something wrong?" Jess said, noticing the troubled look in her eyes.

"They don't sell that here."

"I know. Can't we go to a drugstore?"

"Why don't you get him a tie?"

Jess made a face. "He already has a lot of ties."

The Boy in the Woods

Annie didn't reply but it was clear she still didn't like the idea.

"This is what I want to get him."

"Well, okay," Annie said with a resigned sigh.

When they stepped out of the store, James got out of the car to take their packages. "We're walking to Dwyer's," Annie said.

She led Jess down the sidewalk towards a large sign that said 'Dwyer's Drugs.' As they approached the store, Jess debated whether to get Doug the same aftershave lotion she'd given her dad, or a different one. If the scent reminded her too much of her father, it might make her sad.

Annie pulled the door open, and when Jess walked in, she was delighted to see a soda fountain along one wall. A short middle-aged woman wearing a white apron over her flowered dress was waiting on several teens sitting on stools at the bar. Jess recognized a few familiar faces and decided to ask Annie if she could have a chocolate malted.

"Miss Montgomery!" It was a man's deep voice, and even though it was a greeting, there was a harshness to the tone, and Jess spun around. A tall elderly man with thinning gray hair was looking at Annie, and the coldness in his piercing blue eyes made Jess take a small step back.

"Mr. Dwyer," Annie replied in a tight voice.

Neither of them said anything while he continued to glower at her, the tension between them unmistakable. Jess wondered why he seemed so angry at someone as kind as Annie. His eyes shifted to Jess and the intensity with which he stared at her while his brow furrowed made her uncomfortable.

"This is Jess." Annie placed an arm around Jess's shoulders. "She's – Doug's cousin."

The Boy in the Woods

Jess knew she'd avoided using her uncle's name. No doubt Mr. Dwyer was another citizen of the town who hated him.

"Jess is living with us now."

He seemed confused for a moment, and then his face fell. "Billy?" he gasped, and Annie nodded.

Jess had to look away, her grief rising up like a black wave. She moved closer to Annie, needing her comforting presence.

"His wife too," Annie said, rubbing her back.

"Why?" Mr. Dwyer cried. "Why is it always the young ones?" He turned his attention to the soda fountain, then bowed his head and walked away.

On the wall behind the soda fountain was a framed black-and-white portrait of a handsome young man in a military uniform. Jess recognized it as an army uniform because her dad wore the same one in a similar portrait that had hung in their Manhattan apartment. Unlike her dad, who'd been smiling and happy in his picture, this young man's expression was serious, as if he was already concerned about what was coming. Then she noticed the small red-and-white service flag with a single gold star hanging next to it. Mr. Dwyer had lost his son in the war.

"Come on, Jess," Annie said, sadness evident in her voice. "Let's find your gift."

Searching for the barber section while Annie followed, she wondered if Mr. Dwyer's son and her dad had known each other. Perhaps they'd signed up to join the military together. Her dad had never liked to talk about what happened in the army, but once he'd told her how he and his friends had enlisted the day they graduated high school. After Pearl Harbor, they'd felt it was their duty. Her dad had come home, but Mr. Dwyer's son hadn't.

The Boy in the Woods

She focused on the aftershave lotions to push the thoughts of the young man's death from her mind. After considering all of them, she chose one that was different from the ones her dad had used. When they went to the cash register, Mr. Dwyer was waiting for them. He and Annie didn't speak while he rang up their purchase. When Annie counted out change from her coin purse, he scrutinized Jess with his vivid blue eyes. She pretended not to notice, but it unnerved her and she was glad when they left the drugstore.

On the way to the black car, she was about to ask Annie if Mr. Dwyer's son was a friend of her dad's, but changed her mind. Annie's eyes were straight ahead, but seemed unfocused on their surroundings, pain evident in her expression. Jess guessed she must be remembering Mr. Dwyer's son.

Once they were settled in the back of the car, James pulled out of the parking spot and headed to the two-lane highway. Annie faced the window on her side of the car, and Jess looked out the opposite window. Then her heart skipped a beat.

It was Marty.

He was coming towards them with his eyes down. She kept watching him, praying he would lift his head and notice her. But as their car drew closer, a woman stepped out of a store, almost walking into him. His shoulders curled inward as he shied away from her and hurried his pace. The car passed him, and Jess had no choice but to face forward.

As Jess replayed the scene, his huddled walk and how he shrunk away from that woman when she got too close to him, she felt a profound sadness. Was that how bleak the world was for him?

The Boy in the Woods

While Marty walked down Main Street, he debated whether he should give up and head back to the cabin. After Jess had told him she wouldn't see him after school, he'd decided to stay in town and try to find odd jobs. He had to get his hands on some money, and soon. It wouldn't be long before Principal Petersen and his teachers were breathing down his neck about his hair. If he didn't have the money for a trip to the barber by then, he'd have to stay out of school until he could get it.

But the day had been a bust. He'd already knocked on the doors of almost half the town with no luck. Since it had been cold for so long, the grass was no longer growing and the flower and vegetable gardens were fallow. There weren't even any leaves to rake since they'd all fallen long ago. *Why had he waited so long?*

"Hey," a man shouted behind him, and he stiffened, sensing danger.

"I want to talk to you."

His heart began hammering in his chest. He knew the man was shouting at him.

"Stop!"

When adults were shouting 'Stop,' he had enough sense to know it was time to run. His body coiled with adrenaline as he leaned forward, but then he heard the last thing he ever expected to hear.

"Aren't you Stevie's little brother?"

Chapter Nineteen
It's Not for Me to Say

HEARING HIS BROTHER'S name for the first time in years caught Marty off guard, and he stumbled as he stopped. He turned around to find the elderly man who owned the drugstore approaching him. This wasn't good.

"You're Stevie Cappellini's little brother, aren't you?" the man repeated.

He was too close, close enough to grab Marty, and Marty leapt back. "If he stole something from you, I don't know where he is," he snarled, balling his hands into fists. "I ain't seen him in years."

Shock registered on the man's face before it smoothed out and his expression became neutral. "Stevie didn't steal anything from me."

Marty scoffed. It would be a miracle if his brother hadn't stolen something from him. "I don't know where he's at." He turned and walked away.

"Wait, son. That's not what I was going to ask you."

The Boy in the Woods

Marty quickened his pace.

"I wanted to ask you if you wanted a job."

A shock went through Marty at the word 'job,' and his feet stopped moving on their own. He should keep going, get away from this man as fast as he could, but his body wouldn't behave.

"You see, son."

Marty could tell he'd come too close again. Spinning around, he walked backwards to keep the man from getting any closer.

The man stopped and raised his hands. "You see, Stevie used to work for me and–"

Marty barked out a laugh. "No, he didn't." It was obvious the man was lying. Stevie never had a job. He didn't need one when he could steal anything that wasn't nailed down.

"Yes, he did, son. Stevie was my delivery boy for almost two years."

Marty opened his mouth to deny it but at the same moment, memories flooded his mind. Stevie was always taking off on his bike, only saying he was going into town. When he'd come back, he'd have the things he'd stolen, telling Marty not to tell their old man.

He hadn't always been a thief. But when their older brother, Ray enlisted and left home at eighteen, life got a lot harder for Stevie and Marty. Ray had worked alongside their old man at the filling station outside of town to bring in extra money. What little of their earnings that wasn't spent on drink, had put food on the table. With that money no longer coming in, Stevie began stealing to feed the two of them.

Or he had until the night he'd run off after a fistfight with their old man. He'd sworn he'd never return, and he'd been good on his word. Marty hadn't seen him since, but he didn't care. He didn't want to see either of his brothers again. Both of them knew what their old man was like once he started drinking, but they'd left anyway, abandoning him to deal with it alone.

While the man waited, Marty wondered if he might be telling the truth. Had Stevie been lying about the stealing to cover up the fact he had a job? The more Marty considered it, the more he realized that's exactly what Stevie had done. If their old man had gotten wind of it, he would've taken the money he was earning like he'd done with Ray. Even Marty kept any money he'd earned well hidden.

"What's your name, son?" the man said, breaking the silence.

Marty looked away. He should leave now before he got sucked into this any deeper, but *a job*. "Marty," he muttered.

"I'm Mr. Dwyer." He held his hand out.

Marty considered it, then shook hands while keeping his eyes on the ground.

"You see, Marty, I'm in a bind. My delivery boy quit on me and I need to find another one right away. That's why I wanted to talk to you, to see if you wanted it."

"Why me?" Marty said with a sneer. He was still suspicious.

There was a flicker in Dwyer's eyes, but his face remained impassive. "Your brother was a hard worker."

Marty snorted, unwilling to believe it. He'd never heard an adult say anything good about either one of his brothers. Both of them were worthless.

"I'm willing to give you a shot, if you're interested," Dwyer said, ignoring Marty's reaction.

The Boy in the Woods

Marty didn't trust him. There had to be another reason why he was offering him a job. But as he looked into the old man's blue eyes, there was something about them that reminded him of the way Jess looked at him. A genuineness. A few of his teachers had started to look at him that way too. But could he really take a chance when he didn't know him? And then he realized it didn't matter if he could trust him or not. "I ain't got no bike."

The disappointment on Dwyer's face confirmed that without a bike there was no job, and Marty turned away.

Going down the sidewalk, he shoved his hands in the pockets of his coat, feeling awful. If it wasn't a trick, that job would've solved a lot of problems. But why should he be surprised it didn't pan out? Things never worked out for him.

"Marty, wait."

He lowered his head and kept walking. Why wouldn't Dwyer leave him alone?

"I think I have a solution."

Marty walked a few more feet and then stopped. *Don't do it. Keep going*, a voice inside him said, but he turned and faced the man. *Darn it!* The uncertainty in Dwyer's eyes let him know he should have listened to his instincts.

"Maybe it'll work," Dwyer said, more to himself. He motioned for Marty. "Come with me, son."

He headed back to the drugstore, and Marty watched him, his anger rising. What was he doing standing there like an idiot? He needed to knock on more doors before any more of the day was wasted. But curiosity kept him rooted to the spot. What was Dwyer's supposed solution?

Dwyer walked past the store's entrance and disappeared down an alley. Marty took a few deep breaths as he looked around, fighting with himself. Then he ducked his head and headed for the alley. By the time he reached the rear of the building, Dwyer was in front of an old garage behind the drugstore, pushing open its large wooden door. It creaked as it rolled across its track, revealing cardboard boxes, old furniture, and Christmas displays, all stacked haphazardly. Then Dwyer walked in, poking around until he disappeared in the mess.

This is stupid, Marty thought.

"Here it is," Dwyer called out from the back of the garage, and then the top of his head became visible as he wove his way through the junk. When he came into view, he was pushing an ancient bike. "Well? What do you think?" He pressed on the kickstand with his foot. It was covered in so much dust, the black frame appeared gray. The tires were flat and the rubber, cracked in places.

Marty scowled. "I don't think so."

"It needs some work, but once it's been fixed up you could use it."

Marty shook his head. It was clear Dwyer didn't get it. "I ain't taking your bike." He'd never taken a hand out, and he wasn't about to start now.

Dwyer's eyes held his. "It's not my bike, it was my son's."

"Won't he get mad when he finds out you gave it to *me?*"

Dwyer's blue eyes became more intense. "No, he wouldn't."

It made Marty uncomfortable, and he looked at the bike to avoid Dwyer's gaze.

"He'd want it to be used by someone who could help me out of a bind."

The Boy in the Woods

Why wouldn't the man give up? Didn't he understand this wouldn't work? "I ain't got no money to buy new tires."

"I'll buy the tires and you can pay me back out of your wages." Marty began to object, but he continued. "The tool box is on the floor over there." He pointed with a nod of his head. "Other than that, it needs some oiling. Oil can's on that yonder shelf."

Marty kept his attention on the bike. "Ain't got no place to keep it." It was a lie. If he brought it home, the old man would sell it for booze. That's what had happened to Stevie's bike.

"You can leave it here."

Marty tried to think of another excuse.

"Are you taking the job, son?"

Staring at the bike, Marty felt Dwyer's eyes on him. He should go, walk away now before it was too late. Why would this man be so eager to help him? It didn't add up. Everyone knew his old man was a drunk. Since he'd been little he'd often been treated like an unwelcome stray dog by the people in town. *Don't trust him,* the voice inside him was screaming. But it was like he was frozen, unable to move or speak. Dwyer waited, and the silence became more uncomfortable by the second. Not knowing what else to do, Marty shrugged.

Dwyer sighed.

That's it. He's given up. When Marty lifted his head, Dwyer was smiling, but then it was gone, his expression impassive again.

"Come on," Dwyer said as he turned.

Marty watched him head to the rear door of the drugstore. *Now what?*

The Boy in the Woods

When Dwyer reached the door, he pulled it open and waited. Marty dropped his head before shuffling forward. He followed Dwyer through a back room filled with stacked boxes. Against one wall was a long table and above it, shelves of glass jars holding powders, liquids, and pills. When they entered the main part of the store, Marty saw a soda fountain crowded with teens from school. One of them noticed him and nudged the boy next to him. Within seconds, all of them were gawking at him. He glared at Mr. Dwyer's back. Why hadn't he taken off when he had the chance?

A slightly heavy woman in a flowered dress and a tight perm was standing behind the cash register. Her eyes widened when she spotted Marty behind Dwyer, and he grew even angrier. If she gave him a hard time, he was leaving.

"Mildred, this is Marty, our new delivery boy," Dwyer said.

She gazed at him with surprise. "Oh."

Marty kept his eyes on the front door, ready to bolt if she made a comment.

"It looks like someone needs you over at the counter," Dwyer suggested.

She hesitated, appearing reluctant to leave the cash register, but after Dwyer raised an eyebrow, she left. He stepped behind it and pushed a button. With the ring of a bell, the money drawer slid out. After taking out something, he pushed it closed and walked around the counter.

"Here." He held out a ten dollar bill.

Marty's mouth dropped open before he caught himself and closed it. It was more money than he'd seen at one time in his whole life.

"Go down to the hardware store. When you get the tires, be sure to buy inner tubes too. I know the old ones are shot. Bring back the change and a receipt so I know how much you owe me."

Was he serious? That was more money than his old man made in a day.

"Go on," Dwyer urged, thrusting the bill closer. "Daylight's wasting, son."

Marty reached out hesitantly, still unsure if this was a trick, but Dwyer's hand didn't move. After taking it, Marty went to the door, and walked out without looking back.

Heading down the sidewalk with the bill in his fist, he couldn't believe Dwyer was crazy enough to have done that.

While they waited for James to unlock the gate, Jess peeked up at Annie. She'd been quieter than usual during the car ride home from their shopping trip.

Noticing Jess examining her, Annie smiled and patted her hand. Jess debated whether to bring up Mr. Dwyer's son. She was dying to know if he'd been friends with her dad. Then another question came to her.

"Do you know why the gate is always locked?"

"It's to keep people from coming on the property."

"Like who?" Jess said, thinking of Marty.

Annie shifted on the bench seat. "Uh, kidnappers."

"Is that common around here?" Jess asked with alarm.

"I don't think so," Annie hedged. "But the fence was built a long time ago when your daddy was a little boy. There was a famous kidnapping of a baby back then, the Lindbergh kidnapping. Did you ever hear about it?"

"Charles Lindbergh, the pilot?"

"That's right. They kidnapped his infant son for ransom, but they killed him anyway, the poor thing." She shook her head. "Your grandma was afraid it would happen to her little boys, your daddy and your uncle, since they lived so far from town. They had the fence built right after that."

"Maybe it doesn't need to be kept locked now," Jess suggested, keeping her tone innocent so Annie wouldn't get suspicious. If her uncle allowed the gate to remain open, she could leave the property and go places with Marty.

Annie faced forward as James got back in the car. "Your uncle won't agree to that. It's important to him that the family is safe."

"I suppose," Jess muttered, facing the window so Annie wouldn't see her fuming. Uncle Jonathon was only worried about Doug. He wouldn't care if something happened to her.

"Since I'm running late with dinner, do you want to help me?"

"Sure." Even though she'd rather go to the cabin, there was no point since Marty was still in town.

Jess set the table while Annie mixed a meatloaf and put it in the oven, then the two of them peeled potatoes.

"Was my dad friends with Mr. Dwyer's son?" Jess asked.

Annie looked up. "Why do you ask that?"

Jess was surprised by the intensity of her question. "There was a photograph of him in the drugstore. He was wearing the same uniform my dad wore, and Mr. Dwyer seemed like he knew my dad."

Annie leaned back in her chair with a sad smile. "A lot

of people knew your daddy, Jess."

"Because he was a Blackwell," she said, unable to keep the bitterness out of her voice.

Annie put her hand on Jess's. "I meant a lot of people knew him because he was so kind. Everyone liked him. I'm sure many considered him a friend."

"Like Mr. Dwyer's son?"

Annie appeared troubled as she dropped her eyes to the potato in her hand. "He knew him, but I don't know if they were friends, exactly."

"Did they enlist together? Is that how they both went into the army?"

Annie lifted her head, her hazel eyes sad again. "No, pumpkin. Walt had already died in action when your daddy enlisted."

"Oh." Jess dropped her head. She concentrated on peeling her potato and tried not to think about her dad or the handsome, serious young man in the black-and-white photo.

Later that evening, Annie set the bowl of mashed potatoes on the dining room table between Doug and Jess. "We haven't had a chance to talk about your birthday party yet," she said to Doug. "Do you know how many people you're inviting?"

"It'll be thirty."

"I need to send the invitations out tomorrow, if they're going to make it on time," Annie said.

"I have the list here." He pulled a folded piece of paper out of his back pocket, but instead of giving it to Annie, he handed it to his father.

Uncle Jonathon unfolded it and scanned the list. "Charles Stewart is not on here."

"Uh," Doug said. His eyes flickered over to Jess and she straightened, realizing her uncle was referring to Chuck. "I, uh, don't see him anymore – socially."

"Why not?" Uncle Jonathon said.

Doug licked his lips while Jess's heart raced. What was he going to say? In the sudden silence, even Annie seemed to have noticed the charged atmosphere. She remained still, as if she was trying to be invisible.

"He did something, something I didn't like and I haven't talked to him since then." Uncle Jonathon opened his mouth, but Doug interrupted him. "He was rude to Jess."

Jess held her breath, terrified of what was coming next.

"And I don't want to be around someone like that anymore," Doug finished.

A muscle in Uncle Jonathon's cheek moved as he clenched his jaw. "Is this something I need to speak to his father about?"

No, Jess thought. Then it would all come out.

"No, sir. This is between the two of us and I've already taken care of it."

Uncle Jonathon continued to gaze at him, and Jess waited, afraid he would demand the details. "Very well." He handed the list to Annie. "I'll consider it dealt with."

Jess worked hard to hide her relief.

"I'm pleased to see the way you've handled this, Douglas."

"Thank you, sir."

While his father was busy filling his plate, Jess tried to let him know how grateful she was. He gave her a slight nod, his blue eyes letting her know he understood.

Chapter Twenty
What a Difference a Day Makes

"YOU DROPPED SOMETHING."

Jess glanced down as Louise bent to pick up a small folded piece of paper lying next to her locker. "I didn't drop that." She tried to shove her new coat out of the way so she could reach her books. Why hadn't she considered how small the lockers were before choosing such a long coat?

"It's got your name on it," Louise said as Jess grabbed her social studies textbook. "It says, 'Late today.' I wonder what that means?"

Jess straightened, her stomach lurching. Her name was written on the back of the paper in Marty's handwriting.

"Why is a boy giving you a note that says, 'Late today?'" Louise asked as Jess took it from her and scanned the other side. To her relief, it only held those two words.

"What makes you think it was a boy?" She folded the paper while avoiding her friend's eyes.

Louise took the paper out of her hands and reopened

it, holding Marty's note up so Jess could see it. "Look at that messy handwriting. Girls don't write like that." Then she leaned closer, her eyes widening. *"Jess,"* she said in a hushed voice. "Are you seeing a boy?"

"No." Jess snatched the note out of Louise's hand, feeling heat flush her face.

"You *are*."

"Do you really think my uncle would let me see boys?" Jess demanded, angry that Louise had figured out the truth.

"Oh, right," Louise said with disappointment.

Jess walked down the hallway to hide her telltale blush and Louise fell in step beside her. "What do you think the note means?" she asked.

"How should I know?"

"*Boys*," Louise said, disgusted. "They're so stupid sometimes. Can't they even figure out how to write a simple note that makes sense?" She put her hand on Jess's arm. "I know what we can do," she said with excitement. "We'll get handwriting samples from all the boys. We'll tell them we're doing an experiment or something, and then we can compare them to the note."

Jess shook her head, panic rising. "No."

"Come on, Jess."

"I don't care who sent it."

"But it's a mystery. We can solve it like Nancy Drew."

Jess couldn't help laughing. "I don't think so."

"You're no fun," Louise grumbled.

"I'm sorry." And she was. If the note had been anonymous, it would have been fun to investigate it with

Louise. But what if Louise asked Marty for a handwriting sample? Jess didn't want to take that chance, especially because Louise wouldn't hesitate to approach him.

As they got closer to their social studies class, Jess slowed her pace, letting Louise go in first. She walked in behind her, glancing towards the back of the classroom. Marty was already at his desk, watching for her. She gave him a slight nod, and he leaned over his open textbook.

While she waited for class to start, she wondered why Marty would be late coming to the cabin. She was glad he'd let her know so she wouldn't worry about him, but it was a close call with Louise finding the note. Louise was a smart girl, but it was still astonishing how fast she'd figured out the truth. Even though she didn't want to, Jess had to warn Marty never to do that again.

Life would be so much easier if she could confide in Louise, but when she considered telling her friend about Marty, her uncle loomed in her mind. Louise would never disclose her secret on purpose, but if there was a slip and he found out, Jess knew all of her secrets would be exposed. Then everyone she cared about would be hurt. Uncle Jonathon would make sure Marty could never see her again, and Annie would be banished from their home. She couldn't take the chance on any of that happening. She hated lying to her friend, but there was no other choice.

When she and Doug got home that afternoon, she went up to her room. Sitting on her bed, she opened her purse and took out Marty's note. She ran her finger over his handwriting and smiled. This was the first thing of Marty's she'd brought home. It was solid and real, like a piece of him was with her.

"Are you coming down?" Annie called up the backstairs.

Jess jumped off the bed.

"I packed your basket."

"I'm changing!" She folded the paper. "I'll be down in a minute." She looked around for a place to hide it. Annie would be sure to find it while cleaning if she didn't, and Jess didn't doubt she'd figure out what the note meant even quicker than Louise had.

A hand-carved wooden jewelry box on her dresser caught her eye. During a visit to China Town, she was fascinated when a street vendor showed her a secret compartment on the bottom and she'd begged her parents to buy it for her. Sliding different pieces of wood until she'd opened it, she pushed the note inside. Then she threw on a pair of jeans, a sweatshirt, and saddle shoes before running down the backstairs with her school books and coat.

"See you later, Annie." She took the basket.

"Be careful," Annie warned.

"I will," Jess replied with a sober nod.

The crisp fall breeze chilled her, and she clutched her books tight to her chest while picking up her pace on the path. As she expected, there was no smoke coming from the cabin's chimney. Inside, it was as cold as it was outside, and she decided to light the fires.

In the kitchen, she opened the firebox to the cast iron cookstove and put in pieces of wood until it was full. Marty always added newspaper, so she crumpled up a few sheets and shoved those in as well. She struck a match and lit the newspaper. Once small flames caught on the paper, she closed the door. After a minute, she opened it to check the progress of the fire. To her dismay, the paper had burned away, leaving the wood untouched. Crumpling up more newspaper, she put it in and struck another match. This time she watched the newspaper burn until it was a pile of black ash on top of smoking wood, and then the wood stopped smoking.

Why wouldn't it burn? Marty never had any trouble getting a fire going. Frustrated, she went to the fireplace in the living room. This time, she put the crumpled newspaper under the pieces of wood, hoping that might work better. To her delight, the smaller pieces of wood caught fire, and she watched the flames grow as the bigger pieces began to burn. With a blanket wrapped it around her, she sat on the floor to watch the flames.

She was still there when the door opened. "Hi, Marty."

"Hi." He started to take off his heavy cloth coat, but pulled it back on. "How long ago did you light the fires?"

"I couldn't get the one in the stove lit." She followed him as he headed to the kitchen. "No matter how hard I tried, it wouldn't catch fire."

When he opened the firebox, he laughed. "What did you do?" He pulled out the wood she'd packed in there.

She pouted. "I put in wood and paper and lit it."

"You're only supposed to put in a little until it gets going. The fire can't breathe otherwise."

"I didn't know. I'm not used to making fires."

He shook his head. "City kid." He reloaded the firebox with smaller pieces of wood.

Jess put her hands on her hips. "You know, Louise found your note. She guessed right away a boy wrote it. It's a good thing you didn't put your name on it or we'd be in big trouble."

He smirked while he crumpled newspaper. "Which is why I didn't put my name on it."

"She wanted to get all the boys to give us samples of

The Boy in the Woods

their handwriting so we could find out who did it. Believe me, I had a hard time convincing her not to."

"You should have. It would've been funny."

"What if she asked you?"

"I would have told her 'no.'"

"Oh." She dropped her arms. "I didn't think about that."

He shook his head again with a smirk, and struck a match.

"So why were you late today?"

"I got a job." He leaned forward to light the paper.

"You did? That's swell, Marty!"

He shrugged as he straightened, but Jess could tell he was trying not to smile. It was so typical of Marty, pretending it wasn't a big deal when it obviously was.

"Where are you working?"

He took the kettle to the pump to get water. "At the drugstore."

"Which one?" she said, wondering if it was Dwyer's Drugs.

He barked out a laugh. "There's only one drugstore in town, Jess."

Jess dropped her head. She turned to open the dishcloth lining her basket. "I knew that. I forgot for a minute, that's all."

When Marty returned the kettle to the cookstove, Jess looked up. He'd been laughing a moment before, but now his expression was more serious. From the look in his eyes, he'd seen right through her lie, and shame burned through her like the fire in the cookstove.

"I know you knew it." Marty's brown eyes were kind, and there was a hint of humor. "I was teasing you."

Her heart warmed, touched by his kind gesture.

He pulled out a stool to sit. "We better start with math since we don't have much time."

"Good idea."

Jess finished her assignment before Marty did, and she picked up a cookie, watching him work while she ate it. He took more time doing his math problems because he did the counting using his fingers. But he no longer had a hard time understanding the concepts once she'd explained them. She smiled, thinking how much better his life would be now that he had a job. He could buy all sorts of things, most importantly food. Far too often, she'd seen him walk through the small gym at lunch time without a paper sack.

"How did you get the job, Marty?"

Marty lifted his head. "Old man Dwyer asked me if I wanted to do deliveries for him."

"Right out of the blue?"

"Yeah."

It was hard to believe Mr. Dwyer was kind enough to offer Marty a job, considering how severe he'd been to Annie. "Is he nice?"

"He's okay."

She waited for him to say more, but he returned to his math problem. Watching him scratch an answer with his pencil, she knew he wasn't going to elaborate. It was times like these she wished he would talk more. She just hoped Mr. Dwyer wasn't mean to him.

By the time they'd checked over their answers, it was getting dark and Jess hurried to gather her things.

The Boy in the Woods

When she stepped out from behind the garage, the lights of the black car swept across the yard as it came out of the trees. Leaping back, she hid behind the garage, her heart banging against her ribs, terrified she'd already been spotted.

The car crunched to a stop, and the engine turned off. She pressed her back against the building and tried to quiet her rapid breathing. Car doors slammed and crunching footsteps followed as Uncle Jonathon and James walked across the gravel. She heard doors open and close, and then it became silent. She waited a few seconds more, then crept to the front of the garage. When she peeked around the corner, she saw her uncle through a window, fixing a drink in the grand parlor with his back to her. It was the best opportunity she would get. She ran around to the kitchen door and let herself in.

Annie glared at her from her spot in front of the stove, but said nothing. Jess mouthed '*Sorry,*' while putting the basket on the counter before racing up the backstairs.

She felt terrible as she yanked off her sweatshirt and kicked off her saddle shoes. Coming home so late she almost got caught wasn't good. There was too much at stake for her to be making stupid mistakes like that.

The next day, Jess was chatting with Louise in homeroom when Louise gasped. A hush fell over the classroom, and Jess turned to see what had everyone's attention.

Marty had entered the room and she covered her mouth with her hand when she saw him. His left eye was a dark purple and so puffy it was almost closed. He went to his desk with hunched shoulders and slid into his seat. Leaning forward, he kept his eyes on his desk, his mouth set in a grim line.

As Jess turned to face forward, Louise shook her head, her eyes full of pity. Jess kept her attention on the chalkboard and tried to keep her emotions under control.

What happened? When she'd left him the night before, he'd been in a good mood, eager to get back to his homework. He must have been hit after he went home. Sorrow and anger seared through her that anyone would hurt someone as sweet and gentle as Marty. She wished she could go talk to him, but she was stuck.

All through homeroom and the classes that came after, she couldn't shake the sick feeling in the pit of her stomach. At lunch, she pulled food out of her paper sack even though she wasn't hungry.

"Oh, my gosh. Do you see that?" Patty said, and Jess lifted her head. Marty was walking through the gym, his black eye visible across the large room.

Cheryl turned to Jess with a triumphant grin. "I told you he always gets in fights."

Jess's hand twitched to slap her, but she stuck her tongue out at her instead.

Janet was peeling limp lettuce off her open sandwich. "I'd hate to see the person he beat up this time."

"I hope he gets caught and suspended again," Patty said in her usual catty tone.

Jess fought the urge to lunge at her.

"He needs to be kicked out of school. He's just a troublemaker."

Jess stood. "I have to go to the bathroom." She had to get out of there or she would be the one suspended for getting into a fight.

"Do you feel okay?" Louise asked.

"I'm fine." Jess didn't want Louise to offer to come with her. "I just can't wait."

"Okay," Louise said, but her brow was furrowed.

Jess left the gym as fast as she could, but as soon as she was alone in the hallway, she slowed her steps. Near her was a door that led outside. After checking that she was alone, she ran to it and burst out into the chilly autumn air. In the distance, she saw Marty at the edge of the football field and then he disappeared behind a shed. She sprinted towards him, grateful the windows of the gym were too high for anyone to see her.

When she reached the shed, Marty was sitting on the ground, leaning against it. Hearing her heavy breathing, he looked up with surprise, his puffy eye squinting in the sunlight. "Don't look at me like that," he snapped, shifting his eyes to the trees in the distance.

She swallowed and tried to make her expression neutral. "What happened?" she said, hoping she sounded breathless instead of shaky.

"Nothing."

She knelt in front of him, the cold grass prickling her legs. "Marty, please tell me."

"You don't want to know."

"Was it your dad?" she whispered.

He began pulling up handfuls of grass. "I hate that old man."

She watched him tear out chunks of grass, his body rigid with rage, and it hurt too much. She wanted to comfort him, to take his pain away, but she didn't know how. Why did his dad continue to hurt him? How could any father be that cruel?

She reached out and took his fist. After gently prying open his fingers, she brushed away the grass and dirt, then held his hand in both of hers.

He frowned at her hands holding his, but his other hand stilled. His skin warmed inside her hands while she sensed his anger draining away. It was having an effect on her too, the pain in her heart easing. When both of them were at peace, she let go even though she hated to do it.

Disappointment crossed his face before he hid it.

She stood and brushed the grass off her knees. "I better get back before someone comes looking for me."

He stared at the trees in the distance. "Yeah."

She didn't want to leave while he still needed her, but with each passing second, the risk of getting caught was increasing. "I'll see you at the cabin, Marty."

"Sure."

She hesitated, but he kept his eyes on the trees. As soon as she stepped out of the shelter of the shed, a biting wind blew through her thin sweater, and she ran back to the school. When she took her spot at the table, Louise turned to her with concern. "What took you so long?"

"Uh, it was Miss Gillis," Jess said, thinking fast. "She saw me in the hallway and talked to me about doing sports again."

"Oh."

To her relief, Louise seemed to buy it.

"What's wrong with her?" Louise said, suddenly angry. "Why won't she leave you alone?"

"I don't know." Jess unwrapped her sandwich, the weight of yet another lie settling over her.

Once she'd changed out of her school clothes that afternoon, Jess debated whether she should wait before going to the cabin. Marty would be at work for an hour or more. But while she thought about staying at home when she was so desperate to talk to him, she didn't know if she could stand it. Deciding she'd rather be alone in the cold cabin with her troubled thoughts than home, she pulled on a pair of wool trousers and an extra thick sweater.

After promising Annie she wouldn't be late again, she stepped outside. She took her time walking the path, trying not to think about how bad his eye had looked, or imagine how horrible it must have been when his dad beat him. But when she stepped into the clearing, her heart leapt into her throat.

Smoke was rising from the chimney. *Oh, no.* Had he lost his job?

She ran to the cabin and threw open the door. Marty spun around, startled by her entrance. When she remained frozen in the doorway, his face screwed up and he turned away. She closed the door and crossed the room, using the time to compose her expression. "I thought you'd be at your job," she said, bracing herself for bad news.

"I don't work every day, Jess," he said as if it was obvious.

"You don't?"

"Old man Dwyer won't let me," he said with a scowl.

"Why not?" The image of Mr. Dwyer's intense blue eyes glaring at Annie came into her mind.

"He said he's got to check my grades before he gives me more hours. He says he won't give me more until he's sure I won't fall behind."

"But – that's good."

Marty's face darkened.

"I mean, I know he'll give you more hours as soon as you show him how good your grades are," she said, trying to boost his spirits. "You're real smart, Marty. He'll see that."

He studied her. "You really think so?"

"I know so."

His expression changed, a wily grin spreading across his face. "I guess I'm smarter than a city kid who can't build a fire."

She stamped her foot. "Stop calling me a kid," she said, but she was laughing.

Chapter Twenty-One

Silhouettes

THE SMELL OF roast chicken surrounded Jess when she left her bedroom, carrying Doug's birthday present. Annie had spent the whole day preparing Doug's favorite dinner which filled the house with the aroma.

Uncle Jonathon was looking through his mail when she entered the dining room. Wrapped presents were at the opposite end of the table arranged around a cake, devil's food with vanilla icing.

After setting her gift near the others, she went to her chair, studying the extra place setting next to it. "Is someone eating with us?"

"Annie always joins us on Douglas's birthday," Uncle Jonathon said, without lifting his eyes.

Jess tried to hide her excitement. For the first time, Annie would eat with them.

Doug appeared as Annie pushed through the swinging door with the last of their food. "This looks nice," he said.

The Boy in the Woods

Annie beamed. "Thank you, Doug." She sat next to Jess and the three of them smiled at each other. Uncle Jonathon held his hand out for Doug's plate, and even though he was his usual formal self, Jess sensed his mood was happier too.

During dinner, Annie told stories about Doug, recounting the funny things he used to say and do when he was little. Doug pretended to be embarrassed, but Jess could tell he was enjoying it. After the birthday cake was served, his father handed him two slim boxes, and he unwrapped them between bites. They both held cuff links.

"I don't want you wearing them to school," Uncle Jonathon said. "They're solid gold."

Doug's eyes widened. "Really? Gee, thanks, Dad."

Seeing Doug's excitement as he examined them, Jess fought back the familiar jealousy. She wasn't surprised her uncle would give him such an expensive gift, but it hurt that he still fought over every dollar he spent on her.

Uncle Jonathon straightened in his chair. "Now when you go to the office, you'll be able to dress the part."

"That reminds me," Doug said. "I wanted to talk to you about something."

Uncle Jonathon frowned.

"I've decided to quit the basketball team."

"Doug," Annie said in a hushed voice.

"If I stay on the team, I'll be too busy during the season to work."

"You love basketball," Annie insisted.

"I like it, but not as much as working at the mine. That's what I love."

"I wanted you to play sports because I never had the opportunity," Uncle Jonathon said. "My father didn't see the benefits, and I didn't want you to miss out."

"I know, but the longer I'm on the team, the more they're going to rely on me. I don't want to let the fellows down. Now is the best time to quit, before the season starts."

Uncle Jonathon didn't reply, seeming to struggle with himself.

"Please, Dad. I don't want to be playing for the next three years. I'd much rather work with you."

That clinched it. "Very well, son. If that's what you'd prefer, you have my permission."

Doug smiled. "Thanks, Dad."

Annie handed her present to him. When he opened it, Jess was almost as excited as he was. It was a large stack of 45s, all of them rock and roll. "I thought this year, you and your friends might like to have a dance for your birthday party. Now you have the music."

"That'll be fun. Thanks, Annie."

Then it was Jess's turn. Doug pulled the paper off the box of after shave lotion and looked at it with confusion. Jess waited for him to say something, but he remained silent, and her stomach sank. "I thought you might like it," she said, hoping it would prompt him.

Doug opened his mouth to reply but his father spoke.

"What is it?"

Doug held it up. "After shave lotion."

"That is a very nice gift." Uncle Jonathon's eyes traveled from the box to Jess. There was something odd about the way he scrutinized her, and she kept her focus on Doug to avoid his gaze.

"Yeah, Jess. Thanks." Doug was still looking at the box instead of her.

Jess felt worse by the second. It was clear he hated it.

"You should smell it," Annie suggested.

"Yes, Douglas. Why don't you open it?" Uncle Jonathon said.

Doug pulled up the top of the box and took out the clear glass bottle. After unscrewing the cap, he sniffed it.

"Can I?" Annie asked with her hand out, and he gave it to her. When she brought it close to her nose, Jess caught a spicy whiff. "It's nice. You picked a good one," she said to Jess.

Jess tried to smile. "Thanks."

"Yeah, it's good," Doug said.

He took the bottle back from Annie, still not looking at Jess, and she wished she'd thought of something else to give him, something more expensive.

"Do you know which dress you're wearing to Doug's birthday party?" Annie asked Jess.

"Uh, I didn't think I was attending." Jess glanced over at Doug. His head was still down while he closed the lid to his box. "I thought it was just going to be Doug's friends."

"Of course, you're attending!" Uncle Jonathon said.

"You have all day tomorrow to choose something," Annie said. Her hazel eyes were kind as she patted Jess's hand under the table.

"Yes, ma'am."

Doug hunched over his plate, jabbing his fork into the remainder of his cake. She knew how he felt. She didn't want to attend his birthday party. It was bound to be awkward since she didn't know any of the older teens who were his friends, and he probably didn't want her there either.

There was a flurry of activity as the house was prepared for the party. Workmen arrived early in the morning and directed by James, the furniture in the grand parlor was arranged around the edges of the room. The oriental carpets were rolled up and taken away and the dining room table was brought in.

Instead of spending the day with Marty, Jess was on kitchen duty with Annie. The two of them made finger sandwiches filled with egg and ham salad, canapes, dozens of deviled eggs, and a giant salmon mousse in a fish-shaped mold. By the time Annie sent her upstairs to get ready, Jess was tired and ready for a long soak in the bathtub.

After she'd brushed out her wet hair and put on her undershirt and petticoat, she stood in front of her open wardrobe. Knowing how much of a big deal was being made over the party, her school dresses wouldn't be fancy enough, so she pushed them aside. A dress she hadn't worn since the previous spring caught her eye, but off the hanger it seemed smaller. She tried to pull it over her head, but it was tight and she dropped it on the floor. She chose two more dresses, but they soon joined the first one. That left only two.

With a sigh, she pulled out the mint green dress she'd worn the day Uncle Jonathon took her from Manhattan. It went over her head more easily than the others, but her hopes sank when she buttoned up the back. There was no denying the dress was too tight. Filled with anger that she even had to go to Doug's stupid party she yanked it off and threw it on the others. Then she took the last dress off the hanger with dismay. It was the pale blue plaid one she'd worn the night she'd gone out with Doug. She'd never wanted to wear that dress again after what had happened with Chuck.

She hoped it would be too small so she would be forced to wear one of her school dresses. The buttons fastened, but then she noticed the skirt was short, reaching her knees. She debated removing her petticoat since it would make the skirt appear longer, but Annie would never approve. Her shoulders hunched in defeat, she went to her bathroom to deal with her hair.

Once she was ready, she walked down the stairs, her petticoat swishing against her legs. Near the entrance to the grand parlor an empty table was set up with a white tablecloth over it. At the far end, Annie was fussing over the dining room table that had been brought in, and Jess joined her. Platters of the food she and Annie had made were set out. A giant punch bowl was filled with red punch and cut up fruit, and for anyone who didn't want punch, bottles of Coca Cola were lined up.

"What's that table for?" Jess asked, pointing to the empty one at the other end of the room.

"It's for the presents," Annie said. She straightened and placed her hands on her hips, surveying the table. "Am I missing anything?" she said to herself, and then gasped. "Napkins."

She rushed out of the room and Jess wandered to the high-fidelity stereo. Sliding the lid open, she found Doug's new 45s. She sorted through them, putting the records she liked best on top so they would be played first.

"*What* are you wearing?" Uncle Jonathon shouted, making her jump.

Annie appeared from the doorway with a stack of napkins. "What's wrong?"

"Did you see this?" he said, pointing a finger in Jess's direction.

Annie looked at Jess, and the color drained from her

face.

"Why is she dressed like that?" he demanded.

"I'm sorry, with all the preparations, I–"

"What am I paying you for if you can't be responsible enough to attend to details like these?"

"Jess, go upstairs and change before the guests arrive," Annie urged.

"It's the only dress I have that fits."

Uncle Jonathon waved his arms. "This is just *perfect*."

"Annie didn't know my dresses were too small," Jess said, wanting to protect her from Uncle Jonathon's wrath. "When it was time for me to get ready, that's when I found out."

Uncle Jonathon's eyes flashed with red-hot anger.

"Next time I'll make sure to check ahead of time," Jess added.

"I certainly hope so." He stalked out of the room.

Jess could see Annie was fighting back tears. She cleared her throat. "Come on, let's put these on the table." While they arranged the napkins in a fan pattern, she said in a low voice, "I should have warned you. Some days bring up memories for your uncle, memories that are hard for him to deal with, and Doug's birthday is one of them."

Jess didn't want to make Annie more upset by arguing with her, but she didn't think it was an acceptable excuse. No matter how bad he was feeling, he shouldn't be shouting at Annie. It was a terrible way to treat the woman who was raising his son.

"Ah, Douglas," she heard Uncle Jonathon say in the hallway.

The Boy in the Woods

Doug walked in, followed by his father. He looked handsome in his dark blue suit and tie, the color making his blue eyes stand out. His hair was shiny with hair cream, the dark waves swept up and off his forehead. "This looks really nice, Annie."

"Are you excited, son?" Uncle Jonathon asked.

"Yes, sir."

Uncle Jonathon clasped Doug's hand and grasped his upper arm with his other hand, his brown eyes filled with love. "I only want the best for you."

Jess had to turn away. The way her uncle had looked at Doug reminded her of how her father used to look at her. She swallowed against the lump in her throat as the doorbell rang. Annie rushed to answer it, followed by Doug, and Jess returned to the stereo.

"What are you doing?" Uncle Jonathon demanded, and she halted.

Now what?

"Are you not a member of this family? Go greet the guests!"

"Yes, sir," she said through gritted teeth, and left the room. She *hated* him. And as soon as she graduated from high school, she was moving as far away from him as she could.

Feeling out of place, she stood next to Doug while he welcomed his friends. The boys eyed her, no doubt wondering why she was there, but the girls were worse. They were all in formal ball gowns, with their hair styled and lacquered in place with hair spray. The looks on their faces as they took in her too-short little girl's dress made her want to sink into the floor. To cover up her unease, she took jackets and directed people to the gift table.

Once the last boy had arrived and Annie had hung his

letterman jacket in the closet, she returned to the grand parlor. Jess looked at the stairs with longing as she followed. Doug was surrounded by his friends, laughing and chatting, while Annie walked around inviting them to eat or offering to get them drinks. Jess stayed at the fringes of the room, wishing she could sneak away to her bedroom.

Uncle Jonathon appeared in the entryway with a glass of brown liquor in his hand, and she headed for a group of teens surrounding Doug before he yelled at her again. The closer she got to Doug, the more uncomfortable she became, knowing he wouldn't want her hanging around. She glanced over her shoulder, but Uncle Jonathon had disappeared, so she changed course and went to the stereo.

Looking at the stack of Doug's 45s, Elvis Presley's song "Don't" was on top, and she got an idea. After placing it on the turntable, she turned it on and set the needle down. The volume was too low and she turned it up so the teens could hear. When it finished, she chose a faster song, and to her delight, a few of the couples began dancing. With record after record playing, she kept the party music going until Annie announced it was time for them to light the candles on Doug's cake.

After they sang "Happy Birthday" and he'd opened his presents, everyone wanted to dance. Jess kept busy mixing the records in different combinations and stacking them on the spindle so they were ready to go. She tapped her foot while she watched the couples, admiring how the girls' skirts sparkled and flared out as they twirled. Then she saw Doug standing by the food table, watching his friends. He hadn't danced once that evening. If he'd been allowed to invite Donna, he'd be dancing like everyone else. Not wanting him to be alone at his own party, she joined him.

"Hi Jess," he said when she reached him.

She stood beside him and watched the dancers. "I'm

sorry you couldn't have Donna here."

He dropped his arms. "What?"

"I said, I'm sorry you couldn't invite Donna."

He scanned the room, then leaned close to her. "Why would you say that?" he hissed.

"Because you like her."

"You don't know that," he whispered, his blue eyes hard.

"But I thought–"

"You don't know my feelings."

"I'm sorry, Doug. I assumed since–"

"Don't assume."

"Okay."

"Because you're wrong."

"Okay, okay, I get it," she said, trying to calm him down.

"Good." He turned his attention back to his friends, crossing his arms over his chest.

Did he really not care about Donna? All the times Jess had seen Donna walking with him in the hallways or sitting beside him at lunch, they seemed in love. Then it hit her. Uncle Jonathon had been popping in and out of the room all evening. If he'd overheard her talking about Doug's girlfriend, Doug would be in trouble. She felt terrible for bringing Donna up.

A short thin boy with a bad case of acne came up to them.

"Hello, Phil," Doug said.

"Hiya, Doug." Then he stepped in front of Jess with

his hand out. "Do you, uh, want to dance?" he mumbled to the floor.

She stared at him with astonishment, not knowing what to say.

Doug took her hand. "Sorry, Phil. Jess already promised me this dance."

Jess's mouth dropped open as he pulled her towards the dancing teens.

"Uh, yeah. Sure thing, Doug," Phil said to their backs.

When they were in the middle of the floor, Doug faced her. She gaped at him, and his shoulders drooped. "I thought I'd save you from having your feet stepped on." His eyes were darting around the room. "Phil's a terrible dancer."

"Thanks, but I might step on *your* feet. I've never danced before." She wanted to give him the opportunity to change his mind before it was too late.

His brow furrowed as he studied her, and then he grinned. "Don't worry about that. It's easy." He took her hand and held it up while he placed his other hand on her back. "Follow my lead."

He waited, and she realized what she was supposed to do. She put her free hand on his shoulder, feeling his warmth coming through the fine wool of his jacket.

"Now watch my feet," he said.

She tried to match his steps, and before long she'd caught on to the simple movements. It turned out Doug was not only a good teacher, he was a good dancer, and soon Jess was having a wonderful time gliding around the floor, swaying to the music as record after record played. Doug seemed to enjoy himself as well, smiling and laughing as he twirled her.

The Boy in the Woods

Then something changed. He was no longer smiling and his dancing was flat, like he was going through the motions. She wondered what was wrong, but he wouldn't meet her eyes. As soon as the song ended, he let go of her and looked in the direction of the food table. "I'm ready for a drink."

"Okay. I guess I am too."

He started for the table without a backward glance and she followed him. He poured a cup of punch and handed it to her. She turned to watch the dancers as she took a sip, and her heart leapt into her throat. Uncle Jonathon was at the far end of the room, leaning against the wall. With his glass in his hand, his bloodshot eyes blazed at her.

She pretended not to notice and sipped her punch, concentrating on the dancing teens, but she could feel his eyes boring into her. Doug walked away to talk to two unattached boys, leaving her alone. Uncle Jonathon vanished again and she let out a breath.

She set her glass down and returned to the stereo to resume playing records. An hour later, the party ended and Jess helped Annie hand out jackets while Doug said his farewells. After the last couple had left, Annie went back into the grand parlor and Jess joined her.

"Thanks for everything, Annie. It was a great party," Doug said, while Jess picked up discarded Coca Cola bottles.

"I'm glad you had a good time, Doug."

"I did. Good night."

"Good night." Annie turned to Jess. "You look tired, pumpkin." She took the bottles from her.

"I am tired," Jess admitted.

"You should go to bed. I'll get the the food put away and take care of the rest of this tomorrow."

Jess gave her a hug. "Good night, Annie."

"Good night."

Once Jess had her nightgown on and had brushed her teeth, she climbed into bed, exhausted. She was pulling up the blankets when she heard loud muffled voices through her door. Wondering what was happening, she got out of bed and slipped on her robe. She opened her door as Uncle Jonathon's voice boomed from the staircase. "Lea' me alone!"

It was clear he was angry, and she pushed the door closed – almost. She left it open a crack so he wouldn't hear the latch click.

"Please. Not so loud," Annie said, her voice lower. "You'll wake the children."

"So?"

"Let me help you upstairs," she pleaded.

"No, I don' need help."

"Please, Mr. Blackwell."

Jess heard stumbling, and then a thump. Her uncle swore.

"Johnny, please let me help you! You're going to break your neck."

"Alrigh', alrigh'. Why's it so hard to climb the stairs?" he slurred, his voice closer. "Why's everything gotta be so hard?"

Jess could see them now. Uncle Jonathon had his arm over Annie's slim shoulders and she was holding him around his waist while he lurched up the stairs.

"I don't know," she said.

"Why'd she haffta die? *Why?*" he said, his voice cracking with emotion.

The Boy in the Woods

"I don't know, Johnny." There was sadness in her voice too.

"Why'd *he* have to die?" he cried, and Annie shushed him. They were walking down the hallway now, their backs to Jess. "If he hadn't died, everything would be so much easier. *None* of this crap with her–"

"Johnny, don't talk like that!" Annie closed his bedroom door behind them.

Her uncle's reply was too quiet, and Jess opened her door wider, trying to catch what he was saying. Doug stepped out into the hallway in his pajamas, and she froze. He was looking at his father's bedroom door, not having seen her. She didn't want him to know she'd seen his father drunk, but if she moved, he'd notice for sure.

Doug turned to go back to his room, and their eyes locked. His face was grim, but he lifted his chin as if he was daring her to say something. She remained still, not knowing what to do. He went into his room and closed the door.

She closed her own door. The wood floor had chilled her bare feet, and she shivered while she slipped under her covers. Burrowed deep under her blankets, she tucked her knees up to her chest. Poor Doug. It had to be embarrassing to have his father get drunk at his birthday party, and to know she'd seen it too.

Something her uncle said didn't make sense. "Why did she have to die?" He must be referring to his dead wife. But then he'd said, "Why did *he* have to die?" Who was the "he," she wondered. It must be his baby son. Things would be easier if his son had lived, and it had to do with a "her." She was trying to figure out who he could be talking about, and then a searing pain tore through her as it all came together.

She was the "her" he was referring to, and the "he"

was her father. If her father hadn't died, Uncle Jonathon wouldn't have to take care of her.

Tears filled her eyes as she hugged herself under the blankets. She'd felt his anger from the moment he'd arrived in Manhattan to oversee her parents' funeral. And when he'd brought her back home with him, he'd barely tolerated her presence in his home. But until that moment, she'd never known the degree with which he hated her. For the first time since her parents' deaths, she realized she was truly alone and unwanted.

As she wept, the tears soaked into her sheet, leaving it cold and damp against her skin. It was as if she'd been dropped into a deep well of grief, one she'd never climb out of. She hugged herself tighter, trying to comfort herself, but it didn't work.

It was a long time before she fell asleep.

Chapter Twenty-Two
You Send Me

JESS WOKE TO a sunlit-filled bedroom. Squeezing her eyes shut, she rolled over and pulled the blankets over her head to escape the light. The man who was raising her didn't want her in his home, and had never wanted her.

A fresh tear rolled down her cheek, and she wiped it away. Her uncle may not want her, but she *was* loved. She found strength in that. Annie was every bit as much a mother to her, and even though it had been rocky with Doug at the beginning, he'd stepped into the big brother role. There was her best friend, Louise, and then there was Marty. If there was one person who made her happy she lived with her uncle, it was him. She pulled the covers off her head and flung her legs out of bed. She wouldn't allow her uncle to make her forget all the good she had in her life.

Annie was frying bacon and humming along with the country song playing on the radio. She looked up from the frying pan and smiled. "Good morning."

"Good morning, Annie," Jess replied, and went to get a hug. She was relieved Annie was in a happy mood. It must have been hard dealing with Uncle Jonathon when he was drunk and belligerent the night before.

"Did you get a good night's sleep?" Annie asked.

"Yes," she lied. "How was your night?"

"I slept very well."

Jess searched her eyes, but Annie seemed untroubled.

"Have a seat. Breakfast is almost ready."

Jess sat at her spot and listened to Annie's humming while she sipped her orange juice.

Annie set Jess's breakfast in front of her. "What do you have planned for this beautiful day?"

"I'm going to–"

"Stop that racket!" her uncle's voice thundered through the room. He leaned against the doorway to the butler's pantry with his hand over his eyes.

"I'm sorry, sir." Annie rushed to turn off the radio.

"I need Aspirin," he snapped, lowering his hand and glaring at her through squinted, bloodshot eyes.

"Yes, sir."

Annie hurried to her bedroom, and as his eyes followed her, they fell on Jess. She slumped in her chair, knowing what was coming.

"What are you doing in here?" he bellowed while she picked up her plate and cutlery. "How many times do I have to tell you? We eat in the dining room."

"Yes, sir." She walked towards him, but as she got closer, she noticed his hands balled into fists and she hesitated. Was he going to hit her? She didn't want to near him, but if she didn't go to the dining room, he'd hit her for sure. Her body tensed while she squeezed past him. He glared down at her, but he didn't move and once she was on the other side of the swinging door, she leaned against the wall, breathing deeply.

"Please don't be angry with Jess," she heard Annie say. "It's not her fault. I thought you'd be sleeping late this morning."

"You know I don't like it when you make assumptions."

"I know, but... it's hard not to... sometimes." The sadness in Annie's muffled voice came through the door with clarity.

"I need water to take these," he grumbled.

"Why don't you sit at the table and I'll–"

Jess raced to her seat, not waiting to hear the rest. The last thing she needed was to be caught eavesdropping again. She was shoveling food into her mouth when Uncle Jonathon pushed through the doorway. Annie followed him a minute later with a glass of water and a pot of coffee. Her eyes were red-rimmed, and Jess lowered her head, pretending she hadn't noticed.

"Your eggs should be ready soon," Annie said to Uncle Jonathon.

He grunted in response as he worked to unscrew the cap on the bottle of Aspirin.

Jess attempted to make as little noise as possible while she ate her breakfast, not wanting to give him another reason to get angry at her. For the hundredth time, she thought about how much she hated him for being so mean to her and Annie.

On the way to the cabin after breakfast, a frigid wind blew through the forest and Jess clutched her coat tighter. Dark gray clouds flew past the swaying tree tops, and it seemed like the temperature was dropping by the second. The cabin came into view, and when she saw smoke rising out of the chimney, she hurried to get inside. She flung the door closed behind her, not wanting to lose any of the precious heat. Marty was whittling in front of the fire, still in his heavy cloth coat.

Seeing him lifted her spirits. "Hi."

"Jess," he said with a nod, closing his pen knife.

She set her books and basket on the table in the kitchen, and he got up to join her. It wasn't long before they were wrapped in blankets and reading. But while Jess tried to make sense of the politics leading up to the Revolutionary War, her mind kept drifting to her uncle's behavior over the last twenty-four hours.

Giving up on reading, she lifted her head. Marty was bent over his textbook, already answering the questions at the end of the chapter. His golden brown hair was neatly trimmed, but he'd let his bangs grow out a bit. Free of the hair cream he only used when he was at school, they flopped over his forehead. It was a sign that the money from his new job was helping him.

Noticing her watching, he looked up from his paper. "What?"

"Nothing," she said automatically.

He went back to his work, and she looked down at her chapter, but there were too many thoughts swirling in her head for her to concentrate.

"Marty?"

He leaned back with a smirk, like he'd been expecting her to say something. "Yeah."

"Do you live with your mom and dad, or, just your

dad?"

His smile disappeared. "Why do you want to know?"

"I was just wondering. Never mind," she said, now sorry she'd brought it up. You don't have to talk about it." She leaned over her textbook, determined to force the historical facts into her memory.

"I live with my old man."

She looked up.

He was hunched forward, his expression bitter.

"What happened to your mom?"

"Died."

With that one word, her heart broke for him. She'd lost her parents only six months ago, and the grief could still swoop out of nowhere to savage her. "I'm sorry, Marty."

He shrugged and picked at the binding on his textbook.

"How did she die?"

He was concentrating on what his fingers were doing. "Got cancer."

"Do you miss her?"

He gave her a look that let her know it was a stupid question. "No."

She tried to hide her shock. How could anyone not miss their mom? "How old were you when she died?" she asked, wondering if he'd been too little to remember her.

He went back to picking at the binding. "Seven."

That was old enough to remember, Jess thought, and then another, more terrible explanation came to her. "Was she... a good mom?" she said, afraid of what he might say. She didn't want to know that his mother had been as cruel as his father.

"I don't know," he said, continuing to pull at the threads he'd worked loose from the binding. "She used to read to me," he said, quieter. "All the time." His brown eyes came up and met hers. "And then she got sick."

For a brief second, Jess saw a flicker of grief in his face. His mother *had* loved him. She fought hard to keep her tears back. "She sounds like she was real nice," she said when she thought she could keep the emotion out of her voice.

Marty shrugged in response.

"I miss my mom and dad. I miss them a lot... especially because–" She took a deep breath. "My uncle hates me."

Marty's brow furrowed.

"He doesn't want me. He's mad he has to take care of me." She squared her shoulders. It felt good to admit the truth to someone. "He's mad at me all the time, no matter what I do."

Marty leaned forward, his eyes full of intensity. "Does he hit you?"

"No!" she said, shocked he would think it. And then she remembered how scared she was that morning when she'd had to pass him on the way to the dining room. "But... sometimes I think he's going to." She dropped her head as shame descended on her, but she didn't know why. She hadn't done anything wrong.

"Is he like that with your cousin?"

"No. He loves Doug." The bitter truth of it crushed her, and the lump in her throat became much larger. The emotions she'd felt the night before came rushing back. She was unwanted, alone, hated by a man who could love his son but not her. Her vision blurred, and she blinked hard.

Marty reached across the table, picked up her hand, and held it in his. She wiped her eyes, and looked at him with wonder. He had the same intense expression he'd had a moment ago, but he was focused on his hand holding hers, as if it was too difficult to face her while doing something so intimate.

The warmth of his skin spread through her body, chasing her sadness away. She had Marty. He would always be there for her no matter what. She took in a deep breath, and when she let it out, the pain vanished.

Neither of them spoke, but it wasn't needed. Drinking in the solace of his friendship, she listened to the wood crackling in the fireplace. When he let go, he leaned over his book as if nothing had happened, and she returned to hers, now able to read.

Hours later, with their homework finished, they sat in front of the fire in the living room. Marty worked on his piece of wood, flicking the shavings into the fireplace where they made a pop when they hit the flames while Jess read. She noticed the room darken, and she lifted her head. Fluffy white flakes were flying outside.

She put down her book and went to the window. "It's snowing," she said, turning to Marty with a smile.

Marty closed his knife. "Didn't it snow where you came from?"

"Yes, it snowed a lot, but the first snow of the year is always special, don't you think?"

He scoffed. "No."

Jess was about to argue the point, then decided against it. A boy who struggled to keep himself clothed and fed wouldn't think snow was anything to celebrate. She looked back out the window at the flurries. Her mother had always celebrated the first snowfall of winter by making hot chocolate with whipped cream. With a sigh, she took off the blanket wrapped around her. "I should get going." With her uncle in such a bad mood lately, she had to make sure she got home well before him.

Once they were bundled up and ready to leave, they stepped outside. Jess was surprised there was already a thick white coating on the ground. They started across the clearing, but then she stopped, turning to Marty with fear. "Footprints!"

Marty looked behind them at their tracks.

"What if my uncle sees them? He'll find out I came from the cabin."

"Follow me." Marty set off in a different direction. Stopping at the edge of the clearing, he turned to her. "I reckon you better get something to write with." He paused and grinned. "Since you're a city kid, you're bound to get lost if you don't."

"Ha. Ha. Very funny." Then she looked in the direction they were supposed to walk. There was no path. He might be right.

She pulled a sheet of paper from her notebook, and followed him while he pointed out trees, rocks, and fallen logs, as if each one of them was unique. It was apparent he knew the route well, and she did her best to note the characteristics of all of them, trying to see them the way Marty did. When they stepped out of the trees, Jess was surprised to find herself on the winding drive that led to the house.

"You got it all?" Marty said, while she folded the paper and tucked it inside one of her textbooks.

"I think so."

He smirked. "I'll know what happened if I never see you again."

"Stop." She tried to push him, but he jumped back, laughing. "I won't have any trouble," she said, even though she wondered if that was right.

"I reckon we'll find out." His brown eyes were sparkling with amusement.

"I guess we will."

"You better get going," he said, his tone more serious.

She didn't want to say goodbye, but he was right. "Okay, I'll see you tomorrow." When a wily grin spread across his face, she added, "At *school*."

"Yeah, I'll see you, Jess," he said, his smile turning genuine.

He headed back into the woods and she watched him until she couldn't see him anymore. With snowflakes falling around her, she walked home, not feeling the cold at all.

Chapter Twenty-Three
The Secret of Christmas

December 1958

JESS CROSSED HER bathroom and opened the door to the back stairs. The smell of pancakes and bacon rose to greet her and she hopped down the steps.

"Good morning, pumpkin. Hungry?" Annie said.

"Yes, ma'am." Turning towards the table, Jess stopped mid-step, astonished by the view out the window. "What's that?" she said, although it was obvious. A large horse wearing a harness was standing outside the garage, clouds of steam coming from its nostrils.

"It's Mr. Lindstrom's horse from the farm up the road. Every year we hire him to bring his draft horse and help James get a Christmas tree from the woods."

Jess's heart skipped a beat. "The – woods? Oh, that's good." She took her seat at the table, feeling faint.

What if they stopped by the cabin and went inside? Marty was bound to be there since it was Sunday and the drugstore was closed. Even if he hid, there would be no way James wouldn't figure out someone was using it.

"While they're out getting the tree, I'll need you and Doug to help bring down the decorations from the attic." Annie set a plate of pancakes in front of her. "Once the tree is set up, we'll have a decorating party. Doesn't that sound like fun?"

Jess attempted to smile. "Yes, ma'am."

"What's wrong?"

Looking into her hazel eyes, Jess tried to figure out how best to approach it. "The blankets," she said in a whisper. "They're still at the... you know."

Annie's expression relaxed. "They're not going to go there. I told you, Jess. No one is allowed."

"Okay," Jess said, but she wasn't so sure Annie was right. If Annie was willing to let her go to the cabin as long as it was a secret, what was to stop James from doing the same thing?

"I need to wake up Doug. He looks forward to decorating the tree every year."

Jess forced down her pancakes while she watched the horse, her anxiety increasing. The image of James entering the cabin and then rushing out to alert her uncle about the intruder filled her mind. She might be able to convince Uncle Jonathon she'd been the only one using the cabin, except for Marty's carved animals. It would be impossible to explain where they came from.

Doug entered the kitchen with messy hair, looking like he'd just rolled out of bed.

"Morning, Doug," she said when he joined her at the table.

The Boy in the Woods

He grunted a response, refusing to meet her eyes, and she suppressed a sigh. He was still being distant.

Ever since the night of his birthday party, Doug had been different. He barely said more than a word or two when she tried to talk to him during their drives to and from school. And when he was home, he kept to his room, only coming out for meals. She was hurt by his sudden rejection of her, especially because she now knew how much her uncle hated having her there.

She'd tried to figure out why he'd changed, but the only answer that came to her was that he was ashamed. It had to have been embarrassing for him to know she'd witnessed his father being drunk and out of control. And he had to have heard his father had said about her. Eventually he'd get past it, Jess had decided. In the meantime, she was trying to be patient with him.

After breakfast, Annie ushered them through the butler's pantry. As Jess passed the diamond-paned window in the dining room, she saw James and an old man who had to be Mr. Lindstrom coming out of the garage. They were bundled up and James was carrying an enormous saw. Jess's heart began racing as she walked behind Annie and Doug, knowing the men could head in the direction of the path.

"I have to go to the bathroom," she blurted out when they reached the stairs to the attic. She knew she'd been too loud by the look of concern on Annie's face. "I won't be long," she said in what she hoped was a more normal tone.

"Okay," Annie said. "I'll be waiting for you up there since you won't know where to find anything."

"Yes, ma'am." Jess turned towards her bedroom door with her heart in her throat. She couldn't stop James from going to the cabin, but at least she could warn Annie they were about to be in big trouble.

The Boy in the Woods

As soon as she closed the door, she raced to her window, but the men were nowhere in sight. *Oh, no.* Had they already gone behind the garage? She ran to the window on the opposite side of her room and sagged with relief. James and Mr. Lindstrom were striding across the large yard with the horse trailing them. Satisfied, she went to find Annie.

The attic was enormous, filled with castoff furniture, steamer trunks, rolled carpets, and boxes.

"Over here, Jess," Annie said, and Jess spotted her in a far corner. "Be careful with these." Annie handed Jess a stack of boxed Christmas ornaments. "They're glass and they've been in your family for a long time."

She took the boxes with trepidation. Not wanting to take any chances, she navigated the stairs one step at a time. Uncle Jonathon would be sure to punish her if there was so much as a crack discovered in any of them. Once she'd delivered them safely to the grand parlor, she collapsed on a couch.

"What are you doing?" Annie said after setting her boxes next to Jess's. "There's a whole bunch more to bring down."

Considering the three large stacks they'd already carried, Jess wondered how they could need more. It took several trips before they had brought down everything, and surveying the multitude of lights and decorations, Jess thought there had to be enough for five trees.

Annie had Doug and Jess plug in the strings of Christmas lights and replace burned-out bulbs. While they worked, she turned on the record player and the sound of a harp plucking the first notes of "Ave Maria" filled the room. When Frank Sinatra's deep voice began singing, Jess dropped her head over the lights in her lap. She pictured her mother singing along with the record, her eyes closed as she lost herself in the music. The glowing lights blurred, the colors running together, and she blinked hard to clear away her tears.

Afraid she might break down if she continued to dwell in her memory, Jess turned her thoughts to a problem that had been plaguing her for the last week – what to get Marty for Christmas. Whatever it was, it had to be small so she could hide it until it was time to give it to him. And it shouldn't be expensive. Marty wouldn't want her to spend a lot of money on him. But she wanted his gift to be meaningful, something that would let him know how much his friendship meant to her. Thinking through all the possibilities, she'd rejected each one as not quite right.

"They're back," Annie said with excitement.

The three of them went to the front door where Annie handed them their coats. When they stepped outside, Jess couldn't get over the size of the tree James and Mr. Lindstrom had brought. It was far bigger than the tiny Christmas trees her dad would bring home from the corner grocery store.

"Do you always have a tree that big?" she asked Doug, who was standing beside her.

"Yeah," he said, watching the men unfasten the horse's harness from the massive pine tree.

Doug stepped forward to help them stand it upright and shake the snow off the branches. It was so large, Jess wasn't sure they could bring it inside, but Annie opened the second half of the double door, widening the front entrance. *No wonder we brought down so many decorations*, she thought, hurrying out of the way so Doug and the men could drag it in.

Once the men had it secured in an iron tree stand, Annie gave Mr. Lindstrom a plate of Christmas cookies to take home and they left. With Christmas records playing on the stereo, the three of them strung the lights, and then hung the ornaments. When the last of the tinsel was dripping from the branches, they stood back to admire it.

"It looks real pretty this year," Annie said in a wistful voice.

The ornaments and tinsel glittered in the afternoon sunlight, bringing memories to Jess of decorating Christmas trees with her mom and dad in their little Manhattan apartment. The trees may have been small, but they'd always seemed magical to Jess. Thinking about those happy times, grief engulfed her. She'd never get to share those moments with them again.

Annie put her arms around Jess and Doug. "It's all thanks to my helpers." When she looked at Jess, her smile disappeared. "Are you okay?"

"Yes, I'm fine," Jess said, smiling to reassure her. There was no way she could talk about what she was feeling without losing control, and it would be embarrassing to cry in front of Doug.

"I better get started on dinner. You guys are done here." Annie kept her tone cheerful, but her eyes let Jess know she understood.

Jess went up to her room, trying to keep her tears from coming until she was alone.

"I've had my girl put together the guest list for the office Christmas party," Uncle Jonathon said at dinner that night, holding out a folded piece of paper for Annie.

She set a pecan pie in front of him before taking the paper. "Alright." She opened it. "I'll send the invitations out tom–" She stopped mid-word.

"What is it?" Uncle Jonathon said.

"The date of the party. It's the twenty-second."

Jess looked up with surprise.

"What about it?" he said.

"That's Jess's fourteenth birthday."

Uncle Jonathon fixed his attention on Jess. "I suppose you're expecting a grand affair."

"No," Jess said, trying her best to keep the anger from her voice. He'd been more than happy to give Doug a big birthday party a few weeks earlier. "I wanted to have a family dinner."

"On the twenty-second?" Uncle Jonathon raised an eyebrow as if it was her fault her birthday was the same day as his office party.

"I don't mind if it's a different day, but I want Annie to eat with us."

Her uncle's eyes flashed at the demand, but this was one thing she wouldn't back down on. While the muscles in his cheek twitched, Jess waited, wondering how hard she'd have to fight for it. "Very well," he said.

Doug and Annie shifted as the pressure in the room broke.

"Make the arrangements with Annie later."

"Yes, sir."

"And Annie," he said in a louder voice, turning on her. "Make sure she has an appropriate dress for the Christmas party. I *don't* want a repeat of what happened last time."

"I'll make sure. We'll go dress shopping tomorrow, alright, Jess?" She sounded excited at the prospect.

Jess tried to smile. "That'll be nice." She wished

Annie would tell him it wasn't right for him to talk to her like that.

After school the next day, Annie was waiting by the black car when Jess came out, and she ran over to her. Annie looked beautiful as always, wearing a stylish wool coat with a soft fur collar that Jess rubbed her face on when she gave her a hug.

"Ready?" Annie said.

"Yes," she said with a grin. She'd asked Annie that morning if it was okay for her to shop for Christmas presents after they'd found a party dress. That way she'd get to shop for Marty's gift, now that she knew what she wanted to get him.

Their first stop was the department store. There, she and Annie discovered she'd grown tall enough to fit into the dresses in the Junior Miss department. They chose a velvet, forest green dress with long sleeves and a sweetheart neckline. It hugged her body, unlike her school clothes, enhancing her newly developing curves. Admiring herself in the mirror, Jess thought for the first time she looked like a real teenager.

In the men's department, Jess found a silk tie for her uncle, and then looked at the sweaters. Since Doug's birthday present was such a flop, she wanted to be sure to get him something nicer than aftershave lotion for Christmas. After examining all of them, she chose a soft one in a shade of blue that matched his eyes. She was sure Donna would approve.

While they waited in line to buy them, Jess said, "There's one more thing I need to shop for. I need to go to Dwyer's Drugs."

Annie's expression darkened.

"I mean I'm going *alone*," Jess said. "That's where I'm going to get your present."

"You don't need to get me anything," Annie said, but the deep concern in her hazel eyes was about more than a Christmas present.

"But I *want* to get you something."

Before Annie could reply, it was their turn at the cash register. While she paid for the clothes, she still looked troubled, and Jess worried she would refuse. The one chance she had to get both Annie and Marty a gift was slipping away. She had to do something. When Annie had taken their purchases from the saleswoman, Jess took Annie's free hand while they walked away. "Please let me. It won't be Christmas if I don't have a gift for you."

Annie let out a sigh. "Okay."

"Thanks, Annie."

Annie didn't answer, and Jess didn't press her luck by saying anything else. Once they'd stepped outside, James got out of the car to take their bags.

"I need you to drive us to Dwyer's," Annie said.

Jess was elated her plan had worked. She just hoped Marty wasn't in the store. It would be wonderful to see him, but it would also be more difficult to shop for his gift.

While James parked the car in front of the entrance, Annie looked in her purse. "I'm all out of small bills." She pulled out a five dollar bill. "I don't want you to spend all of this on me," she warned, handing it to Jess.

"I won't," Jess said, while James opened the door for her.

She walked into the drugstore, making the small bell on the door ring. Marty was nowhere in sight, but a few classmates were at the soda fountain, and she waved. Not wanting to waste any time, she headed for the perfume section and located a bottle of Shalimar. Annie would like the sweet vanilla scent. Then she searched for the gift for Marty. When she saw a red leather diary with a lock and key, she thought of Louise. It would be perfect for her. Happy she now had a gift for her friend, she continued looking up and down the aisles, but when she reached the last one, she became worried. What if she couldn't find it?

"Can I help you?"

It was a man's deep voice. She turned around, and then took a step back. Mr. Dwyer's eyes widened when he recognized her, then his expression became unreadable. "Were you looking for something?"

She swallowed, her heart racing. What if he was hostile to her like he'd been with Annie? She had the urge to flee, but she needed to get Marty's gift. She'd already taken too long trying to find it, and she couldn't have Annie come into the store looking for her.

"Y-yes, sir," she stammered as his eyes drifted past her. "I was looking for–"

"Marty," he called out, and Jess whipped her head around.

Marty stepped out of the back room wearing his cloth coat, his cheeks red from being out in the cold. He approached them, but when he noticed Jess, he looked alarmed, then dropped his eyes. Jess faced Mr. Dwyer, working hard to keep her composure.

"You know those screws I was using to shore up the shelves?" Mr. Dwyer said to Marty.

Jess was struck by the change in his tone. It was softer, but firm.

The Boy in the Woods

"Yeah," Marty said with his head still down.

She peeked up at him through her lashes. Under his red cheeks, his face was flushing.

"I need you to go down to the hardware store and get more of them." Mr. Dwyer peeled off a few bills from a roll. "Might as well get a whole box. When you get back, there'll be a couple packages ready for you to deliver."

"Okay." With the money in his hand, he walked to the front door without looking back, and Jess watched him leave with longing.

"Now what did you say you were looking for?"

Jess pulled her eyes away from the door. "I need fish hooks."

"I don't carry those. You'll need to go to the hardware store."

A wave of despair washed over her. She couldn't go there. Annie would see her and ask what she was doing.

"Is there a problem?"

"It's a gift," she said, looking at the spot where Marty had left. "It won't be a surprise if he sees–" She stopped, realizing she'd almost given herself away. "What I mean is, if they see me go to the hardware store, they'll guess what it is."

He studied her, then turned his head in the direction she'd been looking. She hoped it was the black car he was gazing at through the window, rather than guessing she'd been talking about Marty. He nodded as he faced her. "I understand now."

He knows.

"I think I might be able to help you."

"You – you can?" she said, startled by his offer.

267

The Boy in the Woods

"I'll be right back." He strode to the back room before she could ask him what he meant. After a minute, he came back with a small clear plastic box. There were four compartments, two held fish hooks in different sizes, one had plastic bobbers, and one held small lead weights. "I bought this last summer, but I never used it. I can sell it to you for what I paid for it. The price tag is on the bottom."

She beamed at him. "Thank you, Mr. Dwyer. This is perfect."

A look of pain crossed his face, and he turned towards the cash register. "Let's get you rung up," he said, his voice rougher.

He wrapped the gifts in plain white paper and tied them tight with string. Jess was grateful since there would be no way Annie could see what was inside them.

He handed her the change. "You know, you look a lot like your dad."

"Did you know my dad?" Maybe he'd be willing to share more information about her dad's friendship with his son than Annie had.

"Well..." His eyes drifted off, his expression somber. "He came to the soda fountain a lot."

"He did?" She waited, but he seemed to be somewhere else, staring in the direction of his son's photo.

His shoulder's shook as he turned his attention back to her. "I hope you have a Merry Christmas, Jess," he said with a sad smile. "You and your fisherman."

She opened her mouth to reply, but he turned and headed in the direction of the back room.

When Jess joined Annie in the car, her eyes widened, seeing the packages in Jess's hands. "I hope that's not all for me?"

"No. I, uh, got something for some girls at school," Jess said, thinking fast. "I hope that's okay."

"Of course it is, pumpkin."

As James put the car in reverse, Jess spotted Marty. He was approaching the entrance to the drugstore carrying a small paper bag. When their eyes met, she had an overwhelming urge to wave, but with Annie there, it was out of the question. Instead, she placed her hand on the glass and Marty gave her a small nod, the corners of his mouth twitching.

James drove down Main Street while Jess hugged her packages. She couldn't wait to give Marty his present.

Chapter Twenty-Four
Gonna Give Myself a Party

JESS WAS AWAKENED by someone rubbing her back.

"Happy birthday, Jess."

She rolled over to find Annie leaning over her, lit by her table lamp. "Good morning." Jess stretched her arms above her head.

"How does it feel to be fourteen?"

Jess sat up and hugged her knees. "It feels pretty good." And it did. Unlike previous years when she'd felt no different than the day before, now she felt like she wasn't a little kid any more.

"If you're ready to get up, I made a special breakfast for us."

"Us? You mean we're going to eat together?"

"Yes, but we have to eat now." Annie's smile faltered before it returned. "I have a lot to do today."

Jess understood. Annie wasn't just referring to the fact

that Uncle Jonathon's Christmas party was later that day. She wanted to make sure they finished with their breakfast before he woke.

"I'll get dressed."

"See you downstairs." Annie headed for the door.

Jess had kicked off her warm blankets and when her bare feet touched the cold wood floor, she shivered. With goose bumps covering her skin, Jess yanked on an angora sweater and jeans. Walking down the backstairs, she was enveloped by a sweet smell mixed with bacon. The table next to the window was set with a tablecloth and pretty china for two.

"Thank you for this." She gave Annie an extra tight hug at the stove.

"Have a seat. I've got everything warming in the oven."

Annie carried a plate mounded with waffles to the table. She'd made Jess's favorite recipe, the one that had to be started the night before. Jess smothered them with butter and maple syrup, and when she took a bite, she closed her eyes. They were crispy on the outside, yet melted in her mouth. "These are the best waffles ever," she said as soon as she'd swallowed.

Annie cut into her waffle. "So what are your plans for today?"

"Uh, I thought I would help you get ready for the party."

Annie laughed. "I wouldn't make you work in the kitchen all day on your birthday, Jess. And besides, we could never do it all by ourselves even if we wanted to. Your uncle's Christmas party is too big. I hire women to help prepare the food. Most of them are old friends and we have a lot of fun catching up on our gossip."

Jess realized she'd get to spend her birthday with Marty. "Then I'd like to go out today."

Annie picked up her coffee cup. "Why do you like going to the cabin so much? Don't you get bored spending all day there?"

While Annie sipped her coffee, Jess's heart beats came faster. She didn't want to lie to Annie again. Not after Annie had been so kind. "*Well*," she said, drawing it out while she tried to think. "When I'm there, I'm... happy. It's peaceful."

Annie smiled and Jess was pleased she'd found a way to tell the truth.

"It reminds me of my old home, the apartment where I used to live in New York, because it's so small."

Sadness crossed Annie's features. "I'll make you a nice birthday lunch. How does that sound?"

"Wonderful." Not only was she going to spend her birthday with Marty, they would have a special lunch to celebrate.

"You can't stay out too late. You have to get back in plenty of time to get ready for the party."

Jess understood the warning. "I will. I promise."

Even though it would be a while before Marty showed up since he worked Saturday mornings, Jess went to the cabin early. She wanted to get the fires lit so it would be warm when he arrived. While she waited, she set the food out on the table. He was always starving after riding his bike in the snow, making deliveries. She wrapped herself in a blanket and settled into a chair in front of the fireplace. The door opened some time later, and she set down the book she was reading.

Marty's face lit up when he saw her. "Hey, I thought you weren't coming today."

"It turns out Annie didn't need me after all."

"That's good."

She watched him take off his coat, hugging her sides while her heart sang. This was the first time he hadn't tried to hide his reaction to seeing her. *He really likes me*, she thought giddily.

Heading for the kitchen so she wouldn't embarrass herself by looking goofy in front of him, she said, "I got our lunch ready."

"Look at that spread," Marty said, taking in meat loaf sandwiches, baked beans, cabbage slaw, and cupcakes with pink icing.

Jess and Annie had made the cupcakes for her to share with the girls at school. She'd made more than she needed on purpose in the hopes she'd have extra ones for Marty. "It's my birthday today." Jess sat on her stool.

"Is it?" His mouth was already full of meatloaf sandwich.

"I'm fourteen."

"Happy birthday, kid."

"You can't call me a kid anymore. I'm the same age as you now."

Marty barked out a laugh. "Not hardly. I'm fifteen."

"What? When was your birthday?"

He shrugged. "A while ago."

"How long ago?"

"Months."

"Why didn't you tell me? I would've celebrated with you."

Marty considered his sandwich. "Not everyone makes a big deal out of it, you know. It's just a day."

She was about to disagree, but when he looked up at her, her heart clenched. Even though her uncle hated her, she would still have a special dinner and presents to celebrate. But at Marty's home, there was no celebration to mark his birthday. It was another reminder that Marty's life was much worse than hers.

"Next year, I'm going to celebrate it with you."

He studied her for a moment, and then a mischievous grin spread across his face. "Maybe I won't tell you when it is." The twinkle was back in his eyes.

"Don't you worry, I'll find out."

"How do you reckon you'll do that?"

She wagged her finger at him. "I have my ways."

He laughed before taking another bite of his sandwich.

While she helped herself to a sandwich, Jess wondered how she could find out the date. She knew Marty well enough to know he'd refuse to tell her, if only for the enjoyment of torturing her by keeping her guessing. She was determined to get it out of him though. Marty deserved a birthday party, and she would make sure he had one next year.

Marty picked up a cupcake. "Old man Dwyer said he'd give me more hours today."

Jess beamed at him with pride. "That's swell, Marty."

"When I showed him my report card, he said he was impressed. He reckoned I can handle deliveries after school every day now."

"I knew you'd be able to show him. I told you, you're real smart."

"I reckon." He concentrated on peeling the paper off his cupcake and tried to hold back a smile.

Jess watched him lick pink icing off his fingers, deciding this was better than any birthday party she could've had.

After they finished clearing the table, they opened their books to do homework. When Jess looked up from her chapter a while later, it was darker outside. She closed her textbook. "I better get going."

"Do you have to?"

"Yeah, my uncle's having a party tonight and I have to get ready."

"Okay." It was clear he was disappointed.

Once she'd gathered her things, they pulled on their coats and headed out. At the edge of the forest where she would step out onto the drive, Jess stopped. "I wish I didn't have to leave so early," she said.

He kicked at the snow. "Yeah."

"I'm glad I got to spend my birthday with you."

With his head down, he smiled. "Yeah, it was nice."

"Does that mean you're going to tell me when your birthday is so we can do it again?"

He looked up, his eyes full of mischief. "I ain't giving up that easy."

"You're such a tease, Marty." Still, she was smiling. "I better go. I'll see you tomorrow."

"See you."

After a quick bath, Jess put on her new green velvet dress, and examined herself in her mirror. Running her hands over the soft fabric, she admired how her skirt flared out from the tight bodice. It wasn't so bad wearing a petticoat after all.

She found her new black ballet flats, then went to the bathroom to deal with her hair. It was past her shoulders now, and while she brushed it, she couldn't decide if she should wear it up or down. She needed help from an expert. With brush in hand, she opened the door to the backstairs, and the sounds of unfamiliar women's voices rose, along with delicious smells.

In the kitchen, a group of middle-aged women in cotton dresses covered with aprons were busy preparing food. Their loud voices and laughter filled the warm room as they chatted with each other. Every surface not being used for cooking held silver serving platters with artfully arranged finger food.

"Don't you look pretty?"

Annie's voice ringing out got the attention of the women and there was a sudden silence as they all turned towards Jess. There were exclamations of admiration as she descended, heat flushing her cheeks.

Annie took in Jess's dress with glowing eyes. "I'd hug you, but I don't want to take a chance on getting anything on your dress."

"Can you help me with my hair?" Jess asked, desperate to escape the attention focused on her.

Annie took off her apron. "Sure I can, pumpkin. Let's go to my bathroom."

Annie brushed her hair into a high ponytail and formed it into a perfect curl. Then she finished it with a heavy layer of hair spray. When she was done, the two of them looked at her reflection in the mirror. With her hair pulled back, her face was thinner, and her brown eyes stood out below her short bangs.

"You look so grown up," Annie said, her eyes becoming shiny. She turned away from the mirror. "I need to hurry and get the food set out."

Jess walked through the kitchen as Annie directed the women on which platters to bring out first. On her way down the hall, Jess peeked in the rooms. Annie's decorating had transformed each of them for the holiday. Pine boughs tied with red bows hung over the doorways, windows, and along the staircase. The grand parlor was beautiful, with the colored lights on the tall Christmas tree reflecting off the tinsel and glass ornaments. The furniture was moved to the edges of the room and the dining room table brought in. Covered with a festive tablecloth, it was ready to hold food.

Jess spotted her uncle mixing a cocktail at his bar cabinet, and she paused. While she waited for him to notice she was there, her stomach twisted, wondering what his reaction would be.

"Hi, Dad," Doug said behind her. He was as handsome as ever, wearing the same blue suit he'd worn to his birthday party. "Oh," he said as his eyes swept over her.

"Douglas," Uncle Jonathon said as he walked towards them with his drink, but his attention was on Jess. She held her breath while he examined her. "I see you've dressed appropriately." The coldness of his words stung.

"I think you look real nice, Jess," Doug said.

His kindness was a refuge. "Thanks, Doug. You look nice too."

"Uh, thanks." A blush crept up his cheeks. "Music," he said, heading to the stereo.

The Boy in the Woods

Jess had to suppress the urge to laugh while she watched him escape. It was funny to see him get so embarrassed over a simple compliment. Then she noticed Uncle Jonathon studying her while he sipped his drink. It made her uncomfortable. She considered going to help Doug pick out music, but Annie came in, followed by the other women, carrying trays of food, and she followed them to the table.

Annie was pointing out where to put the different trays when the doorbell rang. "Oh, dear. They're here already," Annie said. The women hustled back to the kitchen and Annie headed to the front door. "Come along, Jess."

As a steady stream of men arrived, there was back slapping and hand shaking while Doug and Uncle Jonathon loudly greeted them.

When she introduced herself, she got the same reaction almost every time, "You're Billy's kid." making her grit her teeth with annoyance. Didn't they notice she wasn't a kid? Then it occurred to her that no wives had been invited to the Christmas party, and her heart sank. What was she going to do all evening with no other women to talk to? Deciding she'd been called 'kid' enough, she offered to take coats and fedoras so she'd be too busy for introductions.

Soon the grand parlor was filled with raucous laughter and a haze of cigar and cigarette smoke, Uncle Jonathon in the center of it all. The men surrounding him hung on his every word and laughed at his jokes. It reminded Jess of how Doug was always surrounded by his friends in the high school lunchroom.

This was their world, the world her father had left behind. She could understand why Doug liked it. He'd been raised in this life. He belonged here, but she felt out of place. Watching Doug listening to his father tell a story with rapt attention, she hoped he wouldn't turn out to be like him in every other way too. With nothing else to do, she shadowed Annie, helped her with drink orders, passed out food, and emptied ashtrays.

Later in the evening, she handed a large Tom Collins to a man with ruddy cheeks talking to her uncle.

"You're Billy's kid, aren't you?"

"Yes, sir," Jess said, forcing a polite smile.

He nudged Uncle Jonathon with his elbow. "Too bad she wasn't born a boy. She could've helped Doug run the mine."

"Douglas doesn't need help running the mine," Uncle Jonathon hissed through his teeth, and stalked away.

The man laughed, leaning towards Jess with a wink. "Uh, oh. I've angered the boss."

Even without smelling the alcohol on his breath, Jess knew he was drunk. There was no other explanation for him not being terrified he was about to lose his job.

"He's right about Doug though." He staggered and put his hand on Jess's shoulder to steady himself. "That boy's got iron ore running through his veins. If there was someone born to run a mine, it's Doug!"

She wanted to leave, but he kept his hand on her shoulder and wouldn't let go. "That's nice." She searched the crowded room, trying to find Annie.

"Why, speak of the devil!" the man said, pointing with his glass and spilling a little of his drink in the process.

To her relief, Doug appeared.

"How's it going, Mr. Ingalls?" Doug was smiling, but there was a tightness in his features as he took Ingalls' hand off her.

Mr. Ingalls threw his now free arm over Doug's shoulders. "I was just talking about you."

"Let's find you someplace to sit," Doug said.

"I was telling the little lady how you were born to run the mine."

"Annie's looking for you," Doug said to Jess. He seemed miserable, and Jess's heart went out to him.

"*Thank you*," she mouthed before leaving him to deal with the drunken Mr. Ingalls.

She found Annie at the bar cabinet.

As soon as Annie saw Jess, she put down the cocktail shaker she was holding. "You look tired."

"I am tired," Jess admitted.

"No wonder. It's way past your bedtime." She steered Jess out of the room. "The party won't be over for hours. There's no point in you staying up." When they reached the bottom of the stairs, she gave Jess a hug. "I hope you had a good birthday."

"I did, Annie. I had a really good birthday. Thank you."

"I'm glad. Good night, pumpkin."

With one last hug, Jess climbed the stairs, suffused with happiness. Christmas was a few short days away, and she couldn't wait to celebrate that with Marty too.

Chapter Twenty-Five
Let's Start the New Year Right

THE FOLLOWING NIGHT, the family celebrated Jess's birthday. The mood was more subdued than it had been for Doug's birthday since Uncle Jonathon remained silent. Jess pretended not to notice, unwilling to let him ruin her celebration.

"You know, Jess." Annie took Jess's hand under the table. "I remember how excited we all were when you were born."

"You were?"

Annie's smile turned sad. "With the war and everything that was happening, it was nice to be happy about something. I crocheted the cutest little jacket for you, and your Aunt Helen knit you a blanket."

"Aunt Helen?" Jess asked. The name sounded familiar, but she couldn't place it.

"Doug's mother."

Jess had never thought about Doug's mother being

excited about her birth, considering her uncle's attitude towards her. But maybe things were different back then.

A memory tugged at her. "Wait," she said to Annie. "Was it a white blanket with a yellow ribbon border?"

Annie's face lit up. "Yes, it was. Helen was a swell knitter, but I had to help her sew on the ribbon."

"That was my favorite blanket." Jess smiled at Doug. "I used to carry it everywhere. I called it my 'Baba.' It was so soft."

"She was–" Uncle Jonathon's choked voice got their attention. His face was a mixture of pain and sorrow as he struggled to speak. "A good woman," he finished.

"Yes, she was," Annie said, looking at him like she might cry.

"Is it time for cake yet?" Uncle Jonathon grunted.

"I think so," Annie said, turning to Jess.

"I'm ready," Jess said.

While they sang "Happy Birthday," Jess watched the fourteen glowing candles on her chocolate cake and thought about all the things she could wish for. But by the time they'd finished, she'd decided there was only one thing she wanted most: that Marty would always be in her life.

While they ate cake, Doug handed Jess his gift. Her suspicion of what it might be was confirmed when she opened it. They were books, the first three volumes of the *Penny Parrish* series. She tried not to laugh, imagining Doug picking out girl's books. "Thanks, Doug."

"Annie helped pick them out," he said, perhaps sensing her bewilderment. "Since you read all the time, I thought you'd like books."

"They look good."

Annie's box was much smaller. It contained a delicate silver watch. "It's so pretty!" Jess slipped it onto her wrist and held her arm out, admiring it.

"Now you'll never be late." Annie gave Jess a pointed look.

"It's perfect. Thank you, Annie."

"Jessica." Uncle Jonathon handed over a flat black velvet box.

When she lifted the lid, she didn't know what to say. Nestled on the white satin lining was a pearl necklace. "Thank you." She tried to sound as excited as she'd been for the other gifts.

"Those belonged to your grandmother."

"Oh." Jess thought of the painting of her that hung in the living room. A stylish, pretty young woman with bobbed brown hair. She'd studied it often, trying to see the family resemblance. Her grandmother was more beautiful than she was, but they had the same eyes, and definitely the chin. Her grandmother was wearing a pearl necklace in the portrait. This might be the same one.

She rubbed her finger over the lustrous spheres, feeling their cool smoothness. What was the woman who once owned this necklace like? Would her grandmother have loved her or would she have resented her presence like Uncle Jonathon? Holding something that belonged to her, Jess wished she'd had the chance to meet her.

"They're real, of course, and I expect you to take care of them," Uncle Jonathon said, his tone turning stern.

"I will, sir." It wouldn't be difficult. She didn't know when she'd ever wear a pearl necklace.

"I have homework." Doug shoveled the last of his cake into his mouth before jumping out of his chair.

"It was a great dinner, Annie," Jess said.

"I'm glad you liked it."

Jess stacked plates after she stood.

"I don't think so." Annie took the dishes from her. "Birthday girls shouldn't have to wash up."

Jess laughed. "Okay, good night." She wanted to hug Annie, but with her uncle there, she decided it would be best if she didn't. Instead, she gathered her presents.

Upstairs, she passed Doug's bedroom. He was reading at his desk. After setting her new books and watch on her bed, she took the box with the pearl necklace to her dresser. She placed it in an empty drawer and closed it. Then she got an idea and opened the bottom drawer where she kept the things from her previous life.

Among the old toys, porcelain figurines, and favorite picture books, she found what she was looking for. Even though it was more of a dingy gray than white after years of being carried around, it was still as soft as she remembered. She ran her fingers over the yellow satin border of the knitted blanket, noticing the fine hand stitching. Were those Annie's stitches, or her Aunt Helen's?

Closing the drawer, she refolded the blanket, then returned to the hallway. When she knocked on Doug's door frame, he looked up from his book. "Yeah?"

"I wanted to show you something." She crossed the room. "This was the blanket your mom made for me."

"Oh," he said, frowning.

She held it out to him. "I thought you might like to have it."

He didn't say anything, examining the blanket, his frown still in place, and she wondered if he didn't want it.

"Thanks." He took it from her and set it on the desk next to his open book.

He resumed reading, and she turned to leave, disappointed by his reaction. Having his mom's blanket didn't seem to mean as much to him as she thought it would.

When she reached the hallway, she glanced over her shoulder. Doug had stopped reading and was looking at the blanket. Then he reached out, rubbing it with his fingers to feel the softness. Jess continued to her room so he could be alone.

On the day before Christmas, Jess took wrapping paper and Scotch tape upstairs after breakfast to wrap presents. When she finished wrapping the gifts for Annie, Doug, and Uncle Jonathon, she went to the dresser holding her summer clothes. Sliding her hands under her dresses, she pulled out the small clear plastic box of fishing tackle for Marty. While she wrapped it, she couldn't stop smiling, imagining his delight when he opened it.

After putting on her winter coat in preparation to leave for the cabin, she tucked Marty's present under her arm, holding it tight against her body before fastening the buttons. She debated bringing her textbooks, then decided it was stupid to take them since she had no intention of doing homework on Christmas Eve.

She was surprised Annie wasn't in the kitchen working on their dinner, but she could smell turkey roasting in the oven. She took the basket from the counter and left.

Excited about celebrating Christmas with Marty, she hurried to the cabin.

Marty came from the kitchen when she opened the door. "Hey."

She set the basket on the table between the two chairs and unbuttoned her coat.

"Where's your books?" he said. "I thought we were going to get started on our history project."

Jess laughed, more from nerves than anything else. "It's Christmas Eve, Marty. I don't want to spend it doing homework." She was still holding his present under her arm and didn't know how she would get her coat off without him spotting it.

"Suit yourself. I reckon you'll be the one with a bad grade." He took the basket and returned to the kitchen.

Jess shrugged off her coat and put it on a chair, making sure the present was well hidden. "I thought we could sit in front of the fire while we eat." She joined him in the kitchen where he was setting out his books. "We can have a picnic."

"I don't know." He eyed his stack of books.

"Come on, Marty." She didn't want to give him his present over history homework. "Please?"

"If you insist," he said, giving in with exasperation.

She spread a blanket out in front of the fireplace for the two of them and they sat. When she laid out the food, Marty's eyes widened. There were miniature pigs in a blanket, cheese puffs, deviled eggs, and finger sandwiches as well as two bottles of Coca Cola.

"Is all of that for us?" he said with astonishment.

Jess smiled. "Doesn't it look good?"

"Didn't they get suspicious when you made all this?"

"It's the leftovers from my uncle's party. Annie wanted to make sure it all gets eaten."

"Oh." He picked up a deviled egg, looking at it like he wasn't sure it was edible, then sniffed it. With a shrug, he popped it in his mouth. While he chewed, his eyes lit up. Before he'd finished it, he took another one.

"It's good, isn't it?" Jess took out a bottle opener. She removed the top off a bottle of Coke and handed it to him.

Marty took a long drink and then burped. "This is swell." He chose a finger sandwich filled with cream cheese and chipped beef.

When they'd eaten their fill, Marty leaned against a chair, patting his stomach. "I reckon I'm going to need a nap before I start on the project." He closed his eyes.

It was the moment Jess was waiting for, and she reached into the folds of her coat to get his gift. "Marty?"

"Hmm?" His eyes were still closed.

"I have something for you."

"What is–" He stopped when he saw the wrapped present in her hand.

She held it out. "Merry Christmas."

He stared at it without moving.

"Go ahead," she urged.

He took it from her with both hands. Hunching forward, he examined it in his lap.

Jess waited with breathless excitement while logs crackling in the fireplace filled the silence. "Open it."

He hooked a finger in a fold of the paper and tore it off with one slow deliberate motion, unwrapping the tackle box. Jess smiled, expecting his reaction, but he thrust the box towards her.

"I can't take this."

"What?"

"I can't take it." He tried to hand it back to her.

"But it's your Christmas present."

"I ain't taking it!" He dropped the box on her lap before jumping up and stalking into the kitchen.

"Marty." She scrambled to get up and follow him.

He stood facing the back door.

"What's wrong?"

"I didn't get you anything," he said to the door.

"That doesn't matter to me."

"It matters to me." He spun around. "Don't you get it? I *can't* give you anything."

Behind his anger, she saw shame, and realized the mistake she'd made. Of course he'd be wounded by having it brought up he couldn't afford presents. But then she had an idea. "Marty, you do have something you can give me."

"What do you mean?"

"You can give me one of your carved animals."

"You'd want one of those?"

"Yeah. I told you I thought they were good."

He examined her as if he was trying to decide if she was lying, then walked past her to the fireplace. "Which one you want?" he said, looking at the animals on the mantel.

"You choose," she said, but her eyes found the beaver. It was the first one she'd watched him make.

"Here," he said. He was holding his fist out to her. Not knowing which one he'd chosen, she held her hand out, and he placed it on her palm. It was a sitting cat with its tail curled around its feet. Marty had cut slight notches into its body to mimic the stripes in its fur, marking it as a tabby. "You like cats, don't you?"

She beamed at him. "Yes."

He shrugged. "I reckoned, since you're a girl."

"It's beautiful, Marty. Thank you."

"We should start on that project." He pivoted towards the kitchen, but not before she saw him blushing.

She put away the remaining food and when she went to the kitchen, Marty walked past her, bringing wood to the fireplace. She sat at the table and placed the cat in front of her. Then she noticed Marty standing in front of the fireplace with the clear tackle box in his hands, looking at it. Moving the animals, he cleared a space in the center of the mantel and propped it up before stepping back. By the time he'd turned to come back to the kitchen, she was pulling his textbook towards her, pretending to look for their chapter.

"Merry Christmas, pumpkin."

Jess opened her eyes. Annie was leaning over her, and she panicked. She'd gone to sleep holding her little carved cat, but it was gone.

"Time to get up and dress."

Jess felt around under her blankets.

"We're going to have breakfast and then open presents."

"Okay," Jess said, relieved when she located the cat lying near her hip.

After Annie left, Jess lay in her bed with her eyes on the ceiling, then pulled off the covers with a sigh. Rubbing her fingers over her cat, she wondered why she wasn't excited that it was Christmas morning. Instead, a vague heaviness pressed on her. She wanted to lie back down and pull her covers over her head, but Uncle Jonathon would get mad at her for being late to breakfast.

The dining room table was covered with delicious food, and it was clear Annie had gone to the effort to make their favorite breakfast dishes. Jess remembered her mom used to do the same thing, and grief rose up, making her eyes sting.

"Jessica," Uncle Jonathon said with a curt nod, coming into the room.

She had to swallow before she could speak. "Merry Christmas, Uncle Jonathon." She tried to lift her spirits by concentrating on the extra place set next to her chair. Annie would be eating with them.

Doug came in looking tired but happy, and Annie appeared through the butler's pantry with a pot of coffee.

"This looks good, Annie," Doug said.

They began eating, and Annie and Doug took turns sharing memories of past holidays while Jess slowly chewed. Even though everything had looked delicious, she found she wasn't hungry.

After she helped Annie clear the table, they joined Doug and Uncle Jonathon in the grand parlor to open presents. The tie Jess bought for her uncle was met with a tepid response, but she didn't care. He'd hate whatever she gave him. She was more interested in what Doug thought of his sweater. While she watched him unwrap his box, she hoped it wouldn't be a repeat of his birthday.

"It's swell, Jess. Really," he said, holding it up, but Jess thought it seemed forced rather than genuine.

Before she could reply, Annie spoke. "That color blue

will look nice on you. It's the same shade as your eyes."

"Oh, yeah," he agreed, folding it and putting it back in its box without looking at either of them.

Jess wished just once she could choose something he'd like.

Annie loved her gift, a bottle of Shalimar perfume.

Then Jess opened her gifts from Uncle Jonathon and Doug. When the paper was off, she was astonished by what they'd given her. She had a new record player and a stack of rock and roll 45s. Jess suspected Annie had been the one to pick them out. More than anyone else in the family, Annie knew how much she loved music.

With the last present opened, Annie gathered the torn wrapping paper and Jess rose to help her. "I'll see all of you tomorrow," she announced, when they'd collected the last of it.

Jess's mouth dropped open. "You're leaving?"

"I must not have mentioned it. I usually spend the rest of Christmas with my mom and sister."

That's why they'd woken early, Jess realized with a sinking feeling. The family had needed to eat and open presents so she could leave.

"Let's take the paper to the kitchen." Annie turned to Doug and Uncle Jonathon. "Have a nice rest of your Christmas Day."

"Annie," Uncle Jonathon grunted without looking at her.

"Bye, Annie," Doug said. He alone seemed unfazed by the fact she was leaving.

Jess followed her to the kitchen with the heaviness from that morning pressing on her even more.

"Are you okay?" Annie said.

"Yes," Jess lied.

Annie went into her room and came out with an overnight bag and her coat already on. Doug must have called James, because Jess saw him pulling the black car out of the garage through the kitchen window.

"I'll be back tomorrow morning, pumpkin."

"I know." Jess had tried for cheerful, but Annie saw right through it.

She stepped forward to give Jess a hug.

"I hope you have a nice Christmas with your family." Jess rubbed her face on Annie's fur collar.

"I will." She let go. "There's no need for you to cook tonight. There are plenty of leftovers and Doug and your uncle are used to fending for themselves for Christmas dinner." She placed her hat on her head and secured it with a pin. "I'll see you at breakfast."

"Okay."

Annie left through the back door and Jess approached the kitchen window. Before she got in the car, Annie waved and Jess waved back. As James pulled away, Jess waved again, and watched until they were out of sight. Turning from the window, she looked around the empty kitchen. The only sound was the humming motor on top of the icebox.

Her footsteps echoed through the rooms as she headed down the hallway. When she entered the grand parlor, it was empty. Doug and Uncle Jonathon had already left, taking their presents with them. She gathered her gifts and went upstairs. Closed doors and silence greeted her when she reached the second floor and she continued to her room. She set her gifts on the bed, then found her carved cat.

The Boy in the Woods

While she rubbed her fingers over the cuts Marty had made, she thought about how different this Christmas was from years' past. Her parents had always invited friends who lived too far away from their own families to come celebrate at their apartment. Back in Manhattan, Christmas had always been filled with laughter, food, and friends to play with. Here she was entirely alone and it wasn't even lunchtime.

Outside her window, the garage doors were closed, and the woods behind the building beckoned her. She slipped the little cat under her pillow and retrieved her coat from the wardrobe. Within seconds, she was in the kitchen. There wasn't much time before James would return, and she rushed to fill her basket with whatever she could find; the last of the party food, a turkey leg, and dinner rolls. Then she sprinted out the back door and down the drive.

When she opened the front door of the cabin, Marty jumped out of his chair with alarm, his pen knife in one hand and a small piece of wood in the other.

"Sorry," she said.

He closed his pen knife. "What are you doing here?"

"Everybody just – kind of left." She took off her coat. The emotions she'd been struggling with rushed up, and she turned away to hide her face, laying her coat across a chair. The clear plastic tackle box was on the table next to it. He'd taken it off the mantel to look at it. That lifted her mood a little. "I don't know if you've eaten already, but I brought lunch."

Marty shrugged and looked away. "If you want, I reckon we can eat."

If he was going to that much trouble to make it seem like he didn't want to eat, he had to be hungry. "Let's sit in front of the fire again," she suggested. After laying out the blanket, she opened the dishcloth in the basket.

Marty's eyes widened when he saw the turkey leg.

"Do you want it?"

He nodded, and she handed it to him.

He tore a huge chunk off with his teeth. When he tore off another hunk before he'd finished the first mouthful, she tried to hide her sadness. With the drugstore closed for the past two days, he'd spent most of his time in the cabin. Had he not been able to bring anything to eat?

She leaned against a chair to watch the fire, taking a finger sandwich.

"Aren't you hungry?" Marty asked after a while.

Jess looked down at the uneaten sandwich in her hand. "I had…" She was about to say she'd had a big breakfast, but that wasn't true. She'd eaten little of it. When she tried to put her finger on why she wasn't hungry, the heavy sadness that had been weighing on her all day rushed back. "I really miss my parents." Tears stung her eyes, and she wiped them away while staring at her lap. She didn't want to break down in front of him.

After a moment, Marty put the remaining food back in the basket. After he'd finished, he surprised her by crawling over to sit beside her. Then, to her utter amazement, he reached out and took one of her hands to hold in his. His hand was warm as his fingers curled around hers. It was a sweet gesture, a soothing one, and the heaviness lifted somewhat. Instead of being alone, she was celebrating Christmas with her best friend. Jess closed her eyes and concentrated on the feel of his warm hand.

"Jess."

Jess blinked her eyes open to find her head resting on Marty's shoulder. "Sorry." She pulled away from him.

"Nah, it's okay, but it's getting late. You should go

home."

"Oh." She looked out the window. It was almost dark. How long had she been asleep?

He let his fingers slip from hers and stood, then held his hand out to her. She looked at it, realizing he was offering to help her up. He'd never done that before. She put her hand in his and he lifted her up, bringing her close to him. His brown eyes held hers for a long moment, then he dropped her hand and turned to collect his jacket. She took in a deep breath, realizing she'd been holding it, and reluctantly picked up her coat.

They walked through the darkening forest, their feet crunching in the snow. At the edge of the drive, they stopped and Jess turned to face him. "Thanks for spending Christmas with me. I feel a lot better now."

"Sure thing, kid," he said, with a mischievous grin, and then it fell away. "I liked it too."

"I'm glad."

"See you tomorrow, Jess."

"See you, Marty."

Chapter Twenty-Six
My Happiness

May 1959

"GET YOUR HEAD back in the car, Jess," Doug said with irritation. "It's dangerous to lean out like that."

They were on their way home from school, and Jess was trying to catch the wind. She lifted her bangs so the breeze could cool her forehead. "It's hot."

"I'll put the blower on for you." Doug fiddled with the controls and a blast of hot air hit her.

"That's even hotter, Doug!" She snapped the vents closed.

"I can't help it," he grumbled, turning off the air. "The car was sitting in the sun all day."

The weather was getting warmer as summer approached, but that late-May day had been the first hot one. Even with the windows open in every classroom, it had been sweltering, making the students and teachers miserable and putting everyone in a bad mood.

As soon as they got home, Jess ran upstairs, eager to peel off her wool jumper. As she surveyed the too-small cotton dresses she'd worn the previous summer, she realized she had nothing to wear. Choosing a pair of jeans, she cuffed them to shorten the legs. Since the button-down shirt she was already wearing was the lightest one she owned, she rolled up the sleeves and went to the kitchen.

"What's wrong?" Annie said as soon as she saw the pout on Jess's face.

"It's hot and I don't have anything to wear."

To Jess's surprise, Annie smiled. "I suspected as much. I already planned to talk to your uncle about it tonight."

"What if he says no?" Uncle Jonathon was always so disagreeable when asked to buy her clothes. She wasn't looking forward to the fight.

Annie put her hands on Jess's shoulders. "Don't worry. I'm going to take care of it. We'll be shopping tomorrow, I guarantee it. And we can get your uncle's birthday present at the same time."

"I don't know what I'd get him. He hated the tie I gave him for Christmas."

"I'll think about it, alright? I'm sure I can come up with something he'd like."

"Okay." Jess took the basket and headed out the back door, still in a sour mood.

Walking down the drive in the direction of the gate, she glanced towards the garage. Even though the snow had melted long ago, Jess had continued taking the route through the woods. She'd decided it was safer than taking the path. If anyone saw her, she was sure they wouldn't guess where she was going since she was heading in the opposite direction of the cabin.

The front door was closed as she expected when she entered the clearing, and inside the cabin, she was enveloped by hot, stuffy air. She opened windows as she made her way to the kitchen, where she propped open the back door. Fanning herself with a paperback, she leaned against the threshold. If Uncle Jonathon refused to buy her summer clothes, she was going to be miserable.

"Hi, Jess."

She turned around, her spirits lifting. "Hi, Marty."

His face was flushed and his T-shirt sweat-stained from making deliveries on his bike after school. "It's a hot one, ain't it?" He headed to the water pump.

"It sure is."

He took a long drink from the spigot.

"I might not be able to come here tomorrow. I might be shopping after school," Jess said.

"Will you be going to the drugstore?"

"I'm not sure. Annie and Mr. Dwyer don't get along."

"Huh."

"Are you asking because you hope I'll come?" she said with a coy smile.

"Nah, I just wondered." He took his place at the table.

She would love to see him at the store, but she knew Annie would be too uncomfortable. *Why did life have to be so complicated?* she wondered as she plopped on her stool.

That night at dinner, Uncle Jonathon was in a particularly good mood. Annie had outdone herself, cooking a standing rib roast. But he was also happy because the school year was drawing to a close. There was excitement in his voice while he talked with Doug about him working at the mine over the summer. Jess hoped he'd still be as cheerful when Annie brought up the clothes.

She entered the dining room carrying a lemon meringue pie, one of Uncle Jonathon's favorites, and gave Jess a covert wink.

Jess shifted in her chair, her stomach tightening.

Annie placed the pie in front of Uncle Jonathon. "I would like to take Jess shopping for summer clothes tomorrow." She handed him the pie server. "She's outgrown everything she wore last year."

He pursed his lips, observing the pie server.

Jess held her breath.

"I suppose," he said.

Jess leaned back in her chair, and Annie gave her another wink before leaving through the butler's pantry. Jess tried hard to keep her expression neutral, and then she noticed Doug smiling. He was happy for her too.

That Saturday, Jess put on her new swimsuit after breakfast. It was a navy blue one-piece with a short, swingy skirt. Posing in front of the mirror, she decided she finally looked her true age of fourteen instead of like a little kid. She slipped on a sundress and sandals before going to the bathroom to pull her hair into a ponytail.

After the hot weather of the previous week, she was looking forward to swimming. Even better, this was the first holiday weekend of the summer. She and Marty had an extra day together since the drugstore would be closed on Monday. She raced down the drive, not caring that sweat beaded on her forehead. The water was going to feel wonderful.

To her delight, the front door of the cabin was already open. Marty must have finished his deliveries early. "Ready to swim?" she said as she leapt inside.

"Hold your horses," Marty said, a smirk playing on his lips. "You just got here."

Jess bounced on her toes. "Come on, Marty. I've been waiting all week for this."

He held his hands up. "Okay."

When they reached the pond, the water glittered in the hot sun, and she couldn't wait to jump in. Marty turned his back to her as she kicked off her sandals. She was about to pull off her sundress when Marty took off his T-shirt, and she stared open mouthed.

The summer before, he'd been so thin his bones were visible under his skin, but having a steady income over the winter had made a difference. With a better diet, he'd filled out, and his shoulders were broad. When he turned around, unfastening his jeans, she saw hair on his chest.

She spun away, her face flaming, and went behind a large bush to hide. While her stomach fluttered, she took off her dress and tried to collect herself. This was Marty. There was no reason to be surprised he'd changed. She'd changed since last year too. It was natural since they were getting older.

Marty was already splashing into the pond in plaid swim trunks when she stepped out from behind the bush. He dove and swam underwater a few feet, then came up, tossing his head to get water out of his eyes.

Jess's feet touched the water, and goosebumps erupted all over her. "It's *freezing*," she said, laughing, but she kept going. The further she went in the icy water, the more she slowed, letting her body get used to the cold bit by bit. When it was up to her thighs, she stopped. "How can you stand it?" When Marty didn't answer, she looked up.

The Boy in the Woods

He was staring at her, water dripping off his bangs.

She waved her hand. "Hello."

He blinked as if he'd awakened.

"How can you stand the cold?"

"You've got to jump in. Get it over with all at once."

"No, thank you. I'll do it my own way."

He swam towards her with a mischievous grin. "Maybe I should help you."

"Don't you dare!" She tried to run back to shore, but the weight of the water dragged at her legs. A wave of frigid wetness hit her back, making her body seize up. She rounded on him. "Marty Cappellini! I'm going to kill you."

Laughing with delight, Marty reversed course, and she followed, diving into the water to increase her speed. When she got close enough to the opposite shore she could touch bottom, she leapt forward, landing on his back. He turned in an attempt to slip out of her grasp, but she held onto his shoulders. She shook him while he laughed. "I can't believe you did that."

"You're not cold anymore, are you?" he said when she let go.

"That's not the point."

"I was just trying to help you," he said, smiling sweetly.

There was feigned innocence in his brown eyes, and she struggled to keep from smiling. "I'm still mad at you," she said, but they both knew it was a lie.

"Hey, I'll race you to the other side. I bet I can beat you."

Before she could say anything, he lunged away, and

she swam after him, determined not to let him win.

When they'd exhausted themselves, they headed back to shore. Sitting still in the shallow water, the coldness seeped into Jess's body. "I'm getting out."

"Don't go." Marty tried to grab her hand as she stood. "Swim some more."

"It's too cold, and I'm tired."

She dried off under the willow tree, and Marty joined her. In the tree's shade, she shivered, still chilled from the water. She wrapped her wet towel around her, but it did little to warm her.

"Why don't you lay in the sun?" Marty said. He took the folded blanket and headed to an area where the grass had grown tall. After spreading it out, he motioned for her. "Go ahead."

It looked inviting, like a puffy pillow. She stretched out on it, and he joined her, close enough that his arm was touching hers. She was surprised his skin was already warm. She thought he might adjust to put space between them, but he didn't.

In the seconds that passed, all she could think about was how near he was to her. She tried to think of other things, but it was as if an electric current was passing from through their skin from him to her. It caused the strange fluttering in her stomach to return. Then the image of him taking his shirt off came into her mind, and her face burned. She turned her head away from him, trying to concentrate on the tall grass surrounding the blanket, but it didn't work. The heat coming from Marty was spreading through her body, making her heart skip beats.

What was *wrong* with her? She'd taken plenty of naps by the pond with Marty before. She'd even fallen asleep resting on his shoulder on Christmas Day. Remembering that night, she thought about how good it had felt when he'd held her hand. The fluttering intensified. She wanted him to hold her hand now. He hadn't tried since that day, but she hadn't tried to hold his either. Perhaps she should. All she'd have to do was move a little closer, and–

Marty sat up. "I'm going to fry. Let's go back in the water."

The sudden loss of his warm skin left her chilled. "I don't want to." She sat up and rubbed her arms. "I don't think the pond is warm enough for swimming yet."

"Yes, it is. You were just swimming in it."

"Let's eat instead. Aren't you hungry?"

He shrugged. "I reckon."

He stood, and she gathered the blanket and followed him to the willow tree.

"When school's done, old man Dwyer said I can work more hours." Marty opened his paper sack while she set out food from the basket. "He reckons I can work the cash register in the morning while he gets the orders ready."

"That's swell, Marty," she said, but then her smile fell. That meant he'd be spending less time with her. She would be lonely all those hours without him. "I wish I could get a job."

Marty laughed. "Jessica *Blackwell? Working?* I don't see that happening."

Jess put her hands on her hips. "It's 1959, Marty. Women can have careers if they want." She jutted out her chin. "I've decided I'm going to college and get a degree so I can have a career."

He looked at her with incredulity. "Doing *what?*"

"I haven't decided yet." Until that moment she hadn't considered what she wanted to do. She knew what careers were open to women – secretary, teacher, nurse – but none of those interested her. Were there other options?

Marty snorted.

"What's so funny?"

"If any *girl* was going to go out and get herself a career, I reckon it'd be you."

"Oh, thanks, Marty," she said, warmed by his compliment.

"I don't know anyone who's more stubborn than you are."

She put her hands back on her hips. "I'm not stubborn."

"If you say so," he said with a smirk.

A week later, Jess was awakened by Annie shaking her shoulder. When she opened her eyes, Annie had her hands clasped to her chest.

"What's going on?" Jess sat up.

"Your uncle's decided he's going away to celebrate his birthday. He'll be gone for the whole weekend so we can't have his birthday dinner tonight."

"Oh." She tried not to seem happy by the news.

"We have to do a birthday breakfast instead. He wants to eat now so he can leave early. Get dressed, and bring your present."

"But it's not wrapped."

Annie stopped on the way to the door. "What? Oh." She waved her hand. "That won't matter to him. Bring it anyway, the box is nice enough."

The Boy in the Woods

Jess kicked off her blankets. He wasn't going to like it anyway, but not having it wrapped was sure to make him hate it more. Why couldn't he have left on his stupid trip?

When she was ready to go downstairs, she pulled a small black box out of her desk drawer. Doug stepped out of his room at the same time she did, looking sleepy and carrying a large wrapped box. "Hey, Jess," he said, and then yawned.

Seeing his gift, Jess was even more dismayed about the small unwrapped one she was carrying.

In the dining room, Uncle Jonathon was seated and reading his newspaper. There was a mound of fresh baked biscuits on a plate and a bowl of fruit salad already on the table. Annie must have woken extra early to start breakfast.

"Happy birthday, Dad."

Uncle Jonathon lifted his head and beamed. "Douglas." He held his hand out, and Doug shook it before handing him his present.

"Happy Birthday, Uncle Jonathon." Jess stepped forward and held her gift out to him.

"Jessica." He took it and then turned his attention to the swinging door where Annie entered with a large tray filled with more platters of food.

She set scrambled eggs, ham slices, and a pitcher of gravy on the table between the three of them. Jess wasn't surprised when Annie disappeared back into the kitchen. Of course her uncle wouldn't include her in the celebration, but it wasn't right. She was as much a part of the family as any of them.

"Where are you going for your birthday?" Doug asked, handing his plate to his father.

"The boys are flying me to Chicago."

The Boy in the Woods

"That sounds like fun."

"I expect we'll be–" He stopped, glancing in Jess's direction. "Let's just say, we'll be having a good time." He gave Doug a knowing wink and Doug grinned.

Jess could only imagine what he meant by a 'good time,' remembering all the drinking that had gone on during the Christmas party.

After they ate, Uncle Jonathon opened Doug's gift, a marble fountain pen holder with a perpetual calendar for his desk. Of course, he loved it. Jess watched him lift the lid of her small black box with dread. He looked at the contents for a moment, then said, "It's very nice, Jessica," as if it was difficult for him to admit it.

"What is it?" Doug said.

"Cuff links." He held out the box to show Doug.

They weren't just any cuff links. They were made from real gold nuggets, the most expensive ones in the department store.

Doug's eyes widened when he saw them, and he let out a whistle. "Those sure look swell."

At that moment, Annie came in with the tray to clean up.

"I'll need my suitcase ready," Uncle Jonathon said to her.

"I'll have plenty of time to get it packed before you leave," Annie said.

Jess excused herself and returned to her room. She changed clothes, putting her swimsuit on under a dress, then went down the backstairs. Her basket wasn't ready and Annie wasn't in the kitchen. She must still be packing Uncle Jonathon's suitcase. Jess noticed the black car was out of the garage and James was leaning against it, smoking a cigarette. She returned to her room, deciding she should wait until her uncle left. After a while, she heard noises in the hallway and guessed it was time to say good bye to him. When she stepped out of her room, it was quiet. *They must be outside already*, she thought.

She was halfway down the stairs when the front door flew open and hit the wall with a resounding bang. She froze, watching her uncle stalk in, his face full of rage. Tendrils of panic seized her. Whatever was happening was bad.

Then Jess grabbed onto the banister to keep from falling, unable to breathe. James had staggered through the doorway, wrestling Marty in front of him.

Chapter Twenty-Seven
Am I Losing You

"OH, MY GOODNESS! What *happened*?"

Marty looked up a staircase while Blackwell's driver wrestled him to a stop inside the house. Jess's face was full of terror – and she was looking right at him. *No, Jess. Don't let them guess you know me.*

Realization came into her eyes as she understood the mistake she'd made. "Uncle Jonathon, what's going on?" she repeated in the same voice, now looking at Blackwell.

"Is this really necessary?" the maid, Annie, pleaded from the doorway.

Blackwell ignored both of them. "What are you doing on my property?" he roared, striding to Marty.

There was a sound like a crack of thunder followed by a terrible stinging pain as Blackwell slapped him hard across the face.

"Don't hit him!" Jess cried.

"*Johnny,* he's just a boy," Annie said at the same time.

The Boy in the Woods

Marty gritted his teeth to keep from making a sound. While his cheek throbbed, he glared up at Blackwell, and struggled against the tight grip of the driver. If only he could get his hands free, he'd give Blackwell a broken nose.

"What's your name?" Blackwell shouted.

Let the old man figure it out, Marty thought while he continued to glare at him.

Blackwell headed to a small table that held a telephone. "Alright. We'll see if the police can convince you to talk."

"You're calling the police?" Jess said, her voice shrill.

Marty's stomach knotted. *Don't do it, Jess. Don't give yourself away.*

"Am I supposed to allow him to trespass on my property?" Blackwell said. "Who knows what he was intending to do to us? I'm going to make sure he's locked up for a long time." He picked up the receiver and put it to his ear.

"What's that piece of trash doing in our house?"

Jess's smarmy cousin was walking down the stairs. Her expression was livid as she spun towards him. But Marty didn't hear what she said because old man Blackwell bellowed over her words. "Do you know this delinquent?"

Instead of answering his father, Doug gaped at Jess.

"Douglas!"

Doug tore his eyes away from Jess. "I, uh, I don't know him, but I've seen him at school. His dad's that drunk who works at the filling station on Mesabi Road."

Blackwell sneered at Marty. "He does, does he? That will make things much easier for the police."

"Wait, Uncle Jonathon!" Jess walked down a step, clutching the banister, her body trembling. "I – I know him."

No! Marty hadn't realized he'd been struggling until he was lifted off the ground. Searing pain flared across his shoulders, and he wondered if his bones might snap. He ground his teeth to keep quiet.

"He's – he's–" Jess stammered. "He's in some of my classes. He's not a bad boy."

Blackwell snorted.

"He made a mistake. I'm sure he won't do it again."

"I'm not going to argue with you about this, Jessica." Blackwell began to dial the phone.

She came down another step. "It just doesn't seem fair to ruin his life over one mistake."

"Johnny, he's so young," Annie said behind him, but Blackwell ignored her as well.

"Dad, wait. I think they're right."

Both Blackwell and Marty looked up at Doug with incredulity.

"He's just a stupid punk kid," Doug said. "He won't come back now that he knows what will happen if he does."

Blackwell stared at his son, and a second later, to Marty's amazement, he placed the receiver back on its cradle.

"Alright." Approaching Marty, he grabbed the neck of his T-shirt in his fist and leaned close enough that Marty could smell coffee on his breath. "If you ever come on my property again," he hissed. "It'll be years before you see the outside of a jail. Do you understand?"

Marty willed himself not to break away from Blackwell's steely gaze. "Yes, s-sir," he said, stumbling as he forced the word out.

"Escort him off the property."

Blackwell let him go, and while Marty was jerked towards the door, he glanced up at Jess before he was shoved outside. She looked like she was in agony.

He and the driver stumbled down the steps, and Marty worried he was going to fall face-first into the gravel. When they reached the bottom, the driver took hold of the back of his neck, his other hand gripping Marty's upper arm like a vice.

They continued down the drive, and Marty's instinct was to break loose and run, but he fought the urge. Even though the driver was gripping him tight enough to hurt, it was best to keep his cool. They were letting him go, and now wasn't the time to be making any more mistakes.

"Yer thinkin' ya got away with somethin', don't ya?" the driver said in a heavily accented voice once they were hidden from the house by the trees.

There was a coldness in his tone that put Marty on alert.

"Yer thinkin' maybe the family's a soft touch. But ya'd be makin' a mistake ta think that. I know what ya are," he hissed in Marty's ear, digging his fingers even deeper into Marty's arm. "Trash, like the young master said, and I know how ta deal with trash."

Marty's heart raced. The driver was baiting him like his old man liked to do before he hit him. The gate came into view and he kept his eyes on it. It wasn't that far. In a minute he'd be away from the driver.

"If ya come around here again," the driver said when they were almost at the gate. "Jail will be the least of yer worries, I'll tell ya that right now."

Before Marty could wonder what he meant, he was pushed hard from behind and landed against the iron bars, his forehead hitting the metal. Scrambling to keep from falling, he wheeled around, his hands balled into fists to defend himself.

The driver pulled one half of his suit jacket away from his body, revealing a holstered pistol under his left arm. "Now ya see, don't ya?" he said with a leer. He took a step towards Marty, and Marty stepped backwards, hitting the gate. "If I catch ya anywhere near Mr. Blackwell's property again, I'll be puttin' a bullet in yer head. Do ya hear me?"

Marty nodded once, his heart banging in his chest. From the iciness in the man's gaze, he had no doubt he meant it.

"Don't ya move, boy," he warned, pulling out a set of keys.

Marty's body shook with fear, but he remained where he was while the driver unlocked the gate.

Grabbing Marty's neck, he shoved him through the opening. "Now go on with ya."

Marty stumbled but quickly recovered, and tore off down the dirt road, fearing he was about to be shot. But instead of gunfire, there was only the sound of his own shoes hitting the packed dirt.

When he reached the highway, he was winded. Putting his hands on his knees, he sucked in air while his body trembled. Being out in the open, he felt unsafe, and he wedged himself behind a bush next to the iron fence. He sank to his knees, coughing and wheezing. His lungs burned while waves of humiliation and anger washed through him.

As the minutes passed, his heart rate slowed. Straightening, he pushed through the branches and stepped out into the open. He wandered alongside the fence, his ears open to the sounds of approaching cars. At the dirt road that led to his house, his eyes rose to the tree branch he used to get over the spikes at the top.

If went back to the cabin, he could get shot. But if he never went back... *Jess*. He saw her anguished face in his mind, but she wasn't on the stairs watching him being dragged out of her house, she was standing over his dead body.

He closed his eyes and shook the image out of his head. There were no more options, and it was time to accept it. His luck had run out. His time with her was over.

Curling his fingers, he dug his nails into his palms, and forced his feet to move down the dirt road that led to his house.

Chapter Twenty-Eight
It's Time to Cry

JESS STRUGGLED TO keep from crying as she watched James drag Marty out of the house. Uncle Jonathon slammed the door closed behind them and strode to the telephone, lifting the receiver. Was he going to call the police after all? she wondered, panic rising.

"What are you doing?" Annie said, and Jess wondered if she was worried about the same thing.

Uncle Jonathon's finger dialed the numbers with quick, harsh movements. "I have to tell *someone* I'm running late."

Annie put her hand on his arm, trying to soothe him. "You still have time to make your flight. James will be back soon."

He shot her a harsh look and held up his hand to signal her to be quiet. "Leonard," he barked, turning his back to her. "I've been delayed."

As he continued to speak, Jess ran up the stairs. Now that she knew Uncle Jonathon wasn't going back on his word, she needed to get to her room so she could see what was happening to Marty.

"Jess," Doug said as she passed him, but she didn't stop.

He followed behind her and she quickened her steps, not wanting to talk to him. When she reached her bedroom door, he was still behind her and she wheeled around. "What?"

"Do you really think that?" he asked, searching her eyes. "Do you really think I'm mean like my father?"

She felt guilty for her outburst. Doug wasn't a bad person. "No, I don't think you're mean, but calling someone you don't even know a piece of trash? That's a terrible thing to say, let alone think. That's how your father treats people."

He hung his head, not saying anything while precious seconds were slipping away.

"I don't want to talk about it now." She was inside her room with the door closed before he lifted his head. Rushing to the bay window, she saw James escorting Marty down the drive, but just as she feared, they disappeared behind the trees within seconds. No longer able to hold back her emotions, she collapsed on her bed, crying. What if Uncle Jonathon had convinced him to never come back on the property again?

Through her open window, she heard car doors slam shut, and sat up, wiping her face. The black car drove down the drive, and one thought filled her mind – she had to go to the cabin. Running through her bathroom, she eased the door open and listened. The icebox motor was the only sound she heard.

After slipping out through the back door, she ran down the drive so fast that by the time she'd entered the woods, she had to slow down and rub the stitch in her side. But she didn't care about the pain. She had to know if she'd lost Marty.

When she saw the cabin, a thrill of joy ran through her. The front door was wide open. *He came back.* She sprinted to the cabin, shouting, "Marty!" but the only sound that greeted her were the birds chirping outside. Looking at the empty rooms, she realized Marty must have left the door open before he'd been caught.

Surrounded by the quiet stillness, an icy dread spread through her body. Her legs turned to jelly beneath her, and she stumbled to a chair, gasping. Even though she'd lied to everyone she loved, even though she'd been so careful to keep their secret, he'd still been taken from her. She covered her face with her hands and sobbed.

"Jess."

She lifted her head, and like a miracle, Marty was in the doorway, his brown eyes full of worry.

"Marty!" Jumping out of the chair, she threw herself at him and he held her tight, burying his face in her shoulder. She shed fresh tears while her heart ached with relief. "You came back. You came back." She pulled away. "What happened? How did you get caught?"

His expression was grim. "I was stupid. I went to the house to see if you were coming and your uncle saw me." He hugged her again. "Did he hurt you?"

"He didn't hurt me, Marty. I'm okay."

"I was afraid, because you were crying," he murmured into her neck.

"I was crying because I thought you weren't coming back."

"I wasn't going to," he said. "I started walking to my house but…" He took in a deep breath and when he let it out, he leaned into her. "It hurt."

The Boy in the Woods

While he held her tight, the enormity of those two words settled over her. She'd always known he needed her, but to hear him admit it made it more powerful. She relaxed, breathing in his musky boy-smell of soap mixed with sweat. They'd had a close call, but they were okay now. Marty was still with her.

What if he gets caught again? a voice inside her head said.

Remembering her uncle slapping Marty, her fear returned. There would be no way to save him from her uncle's wrath a second time. He'd make sure Marty went to jail. If he was locked in a tiny dark cell for years, never able to see the sky, or feel the grass under his feet, it would destroy him.

There was only one option, and she was going to have to do it. She moved, and he let go of her. Looking into his brown eyes hurt too much, and she shifted her gaze away. "Marty, are you sure you made the right decision?"

He gaped at her. "I thought you were happy I came back!"

"I am happy. I felt like I was going to die when I thought I'd never see you again, but maybe you shouldn't come here anymore."

"You think I'm going to let them push me around?" he shouted. "They're no different from my old man. Just because they hit me and threaten me, doesn't mean–"

"I'm not saying that at all," Jess said, cutting him off. She needed to reason with him. If she couldn't, she could lose him forever.

"Why do you want me to stay away?"

He sounded frantic, and it broke her heart more. Tears threatened to return, and she struggled to remain in control. "I don't want you to get caught again. If you did, I – I…" She covered her face with her hands.

Marty put his arms around her. "Don't cry, Jess."

"I'm scared."

He sighed and laid his head against hers. "I know."

She wrapped her arms around him, her tears soaking his shirt. The pain was unbearable, but she struggled to pull it together. "You know my uncle will put you in jail if he catches you. If I'm going to lose you–" She paused to steel herself. She had to do this for him. "At least I'll feel better, knowing you're free."

He didn't say anything, and she buried her face in his T-shirt again. She focused on his firm chest, his steady heartbeats, and how tight he was holding her, wanting to memorize everything about him. It wouldn't be long before she'd have to say goodbye.

"I'd be lying if I said I'm not worried too," he said after a minute. "But I don't know if I can stay away."

"You have to, Marty."

"I don't want to lose you." His voice cracked, and she squeezed him tighter.

"I don't want to lose you either. But I don't want my family to hurt you, to take away your freedom and ruin your life."

He dropped his arms. "It only happened because I went where someone could see me. I was careless, but it won't happen again. Your uncle didn't figure out we've been seeing each other, did he?"

"No," she admitted. "He left on a trip."

"See? He thinks he's scared me off. As long as I stay away from the house, I'll be fine."

The Boy in the Woods

She was dismayed to see hope in his eyes. Trying to come up with a reply, she remembered the look of panic on Marty's face when he was dragged into the house, and the helplessness she felt when her uncle slapped him and threated to send him to jail. She had to think of something to convince him he was wrong.

Marty took her hand, his eyes were begging her. "I've been coming here for years and nobody ever had a clue. The cabin was abandoned long before I found it. If no one from the house comes here, how will they see me?"

She couldn't deny he made a certain amount of sense. She'd lived here a whole year, and in all that time she was the only one who'd ventured into the woods. Maybe her uncle's arrogance would work in their favor. He'd never consider the possibility Marty would defy him.

Then she thought about what Marty would go through if she convinced him to never come back. It was dangerous for him to be at home where his father beat him. He could spend his days at the drugstore, but would that anger Mr. Dwyer? How much patience would the man have for Marty hanging around his shop? And he'd be lonely, without a single friend. "You're right," she said. "I don't think he will figure it out."

Marty's expression lightened with relief. "We'll be more careful."

He felt better, but her heart was heavy. "We have to." There was no other option. "I better go."

"Do you have to?"

"I better. No one knows I left the house."

"I reckon you're right," he said, disappointed.

She continued to look up at him, unable to move. She needed to leave, but after almost losing him, it felt like torture to tear herself away.

"Come on, Jess." He took her hand and led her out of the cabin.

He kept holding her hand while they crossed the clearing, and when they reached the edge, he stopped. "I'll say goodbye here." He sounded firm, but she could tell he didn't like the decision. He pulled her, closing the distance between them, and wrapped his arms around her. "Don't worry, Jess," he said into her hair. "I'm not going to let them do anything to me. They're not going to take me away from you. Promise."

"Okay."

He chuckled. "You can look forward to me giving you a hard time for a lot of years to come."

She smiled into his shirt. "I don't mind."

He let go of her. "See you later, kid."

"Bye, Marty."

He gave her a mock salute, and headed back to the cabin.

She went into the woods, and slowly walked home, her mind too exhausted to think. The house came into view, and she was relieved the garage doors were closed. If she could slip inside without Annie noticing, she could pretend she'd been in her room the whole time.

Opening the kitchen door, she was surprised she didn't smell anything cooking. Usually Annie had begun working on dinner by lunch time. Then she spotted Annie sitting at the kitchen table with a cup of tea in front of her, a grim expression on her face. Jess's stomach dropped. Something was wrong.

"Hi, Annie." She closed the door behind her.

"Come here, Jess."

It wasn't her usual warm greeting, and Jess's heart rate increased. She crossed the room with quivering legs and sat across the table from Annie. She waited, but Annie continued looking at her. "Is something wrong?"

"I want you to tell me the truth, Jess. I want you to tell me the truth about that boy who came to see you."

Chapter Twenty-Nine
Heartaches by the Number

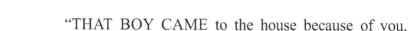

"THAT BOY CAME to the house because of you, didn't he?" Annie said.

While she waited for the answer, Jess considered denying it, but from the look in Annie's hazel eyes, it wouldn't work. Annie already knew it was true. She hung her head. "Yes, ma'am."

"Did you ask him to come here?"

"No! I would never do that."

Annie's face softened. "I didn't think you would." Her expression became serious again. "I'm assuming you met him at school. I can understand why you never brought him up, the way your uncle is."

Jess stared at Annie as her hopes rose. She hadn't guessed the whole truth.

"He would never approve of your friendship with that boy, and he'd be right."

Jess couldn't believe what she'd heard. Why would

Annie say that?

Annie reached both hands across the table. She wanted to hold hands, and Jess complied. "I know you're a good girl," she said solemnly. "But I want you to listen to me because this is very important."

Jess's stomach sank. Annie had never spoken to her in such a serious way.

"You must never spend time alone with that boy. It's too dangerous."

Jess pulled her hands out of Annie's. "Marty would never hurt me."

"He may not *intend* to hurt you, but if you're alone with him, especially now that you're getting older, something might happen."

"Marty would never hurt anyone. He's a good person."

Annie dropped her eyes and shifted in her seat. "Jess, when boys and girls are alone together," she said, her face flushing. "That's when girls can get – in the family way."

Jess found it difficult to breathe all of a sudden, understanding what Annie meant. "I thought only married ladies can have babies," Jess said faintly.

"Any girl who is old enough can have a baby, and *you're* old enough," she said, looking at Jess with meaning.

"How? How does it happen?" Jess tried to keep the panic out of her voice. Could she and Marty have already done whatever it was?

Annie leaned back in her chair. "I never thought we'd be having this conversation, at least not until you're ready to get married." She gazed at Jess while she chewed her lip. "You're too young to know the details, but... you have to be close to the other person with your clothes off."

Jess was horrified. "I would never do that!"

Annie slapped the table. "It *does* happen. I know girls it happened to, good girls like you. Girls you think would never do something like that."

Could that be true?

Annie leaned forward. "Jess, if it happened to you, your life would be ruined. Can you imagine the scandal it would cause? Everyone in town, maybe the whole state would be talking about you. The family name would be dragged through the mud, and the company could be affected too. What if other companies refused to do business with Blackwell Iron and Mining because they thought the family had loose morals?"

Jess wiped away the tears that had sprung to her eyes. "But Marty and I are just friends."

"I know you would never do it intentionally, pumpkin. It's never something someone plans, but I can tell you already care a lot about him. You're growing up and soon those feelings will get stronger, to the point where you forget about everything but being with him. All it takes is one momentary mistake for your life and this family's name to be destroyed. I'm sorry, Jess. You can't be alone with him ever again. We just can't take that chance."

Jess covered her face with her hands as her tears came in a flood. She couldn't bear the thought of never seeing him again.

Annie went to Jess and pulled her into a hug. "You understand why, don't you, Jess? I'm trying to protect you."

Jess nodded against her. As terrible as the pain was, Annie was right.

"When you see him at school, I want you to tell him

he's not to try to see you alone again."

"Yes, ma'am," she choked out as she pulled away. All she wanted now was to go to her room where she could be alone with her grief.

"Why don't you go wash your face and have a rest? If you're hungry later, let me know and I'll fix you a plate. Doug is with his friends tonight, so it's just us for dinner."

As soon as she was in her room, she sprawled across her bed and sobbed, not only for her loss, but for Marty's too.

When she woke, her eyes were sticky. Blinking at the sunshine pouring in through her bedroom window, she realized she'd slept through the night. Then she remembered her conversation with Annie, and burrowed into her blankets. She had to tell Marty she couldn't see him anymore, and the pain was unbearable. She didn't know how she could do it. The news would devastate him. What if he begged her to see him anyway. Would she be strong enough to resist? Maybe she should wait until Monday when they were at school. She could sneak away at lunch and tell him then. That way she'd have an excuse to leave before he could change her mind.

She heard a quiet knock on her door before it opened. "You're awake." Annie approached her bed.

"I just woke up."

"You missed dinner. I came to check on you but you'd fallen asleep."

"I was tired."

"I don't want you to miss breakfast. You need to eat."

"Yes, ma'am," Jess said, even though she wasn't hungry.

While she sat at the kitchen table waiting for Annie to

The Boy in the Woods

bring her plate, she looked at the woods beyond the garage. She imagined Marty sitting on the front stoop, waiting for her, and had to fight back tears.

Annie set her breakfast in front of her. "Are you going out today as usual?"

"No ma'am." She kept her head down so Annie couldn't see her face. "I thought I'd stay inside and read."

Annie returned to the stove. "I don't want you staying inside all day. You need fresh air. I know you're sad, but it'll do you good."

Jess hung her head, knowing there was no point in arguing. "Okay." Pushing her scrambled eggs around the plate, she contemplating her choices. She shouldn't see Marty, but where else would she go? She'd have to hide from him. Meanwhile, he'd be worried about her, at least until she could talk to him at school tomorrow. What if he got so upset he shouted at her when she told him? Someone could hear him and tell Doug, and if Doug told his dad, she'd be in worse trouble.

As hard as it would be to say goodbye at the cabin, maybe that would be best. Tears threatened to bubble up while she took her dishes to the sink. This would be the hardest thing she'd ever have to do.

Annie went in the direction of the butler's pantry. "Give me a minute to get your basket ready."

She didn't want Annie to pack any food since she wasn't going to stay long, but Annie would be suspicious if she asked her to stop.

When she entered the clearing a while later, the front door was wide open, and she felt worse. It would only be minutes now before she'd have to hurt Marty.

He was sitting in a chair, whittling on a piece of wood.

"Hey, Jess," he said, a smile lighting up his face.

Her heart ached. He was so happy to see her.

"Are we swimming?" He stood and closed his pen knife.

"No, I…"

He looked at her, waiting for her to finish the sentence.

"I left my suit at home."

He shrugged. "Okay. What do you want to do?"

She should say it now, but a lump had formed in her throat, making it too difficult to speak. She swallowed, but it didn't help. The seconds were ticking by and he frowned, studying her. She went to the kitchen sink. A drink of water might ease her throat.

"I know what we can do. We can fish. We haven't done that since last year. Want to?" he said, following her.

She pumped the handle and took a drink. When she straightened, she made a decision. She'd give him this one last day. They'd do something he loved and before she left, she'd tell him the news. "Okay."

"Give me the bucket and I'll get the worms."

While they walked on the path to the pond, she watched his back. Tall and straight, shoulders relaxed, he looked at ease. She would miss these quiet moments with him.

When they reached the field of tall grass, it was beautiful as always, sprinkled with wild flowers. She would miss this beautiful place too, and the pond. After he cast out the fishing line, he sat on the overturned tree and stretched his legs out. She joined him, keeping her eyes on the red bobber so she wouldn't look at him.

The Boy in the Woods

She tried to convince herself he would be all right without her. If he wasn't visiting her, he could work more hours. That extra money would be a big help. He was doing well enough at school that he'd be fine doing his homework without her. And Mr. Dwyer would make sure he kept up with his studies. When she'd first met him, he'd had so little good in his life. He'd miss her, but he wasn't all alone anymore.

Over the next hour, Marty caught two fish, both too small to eat, and he let them go. After he watched the second one swim away, he turned to her. "You hungry?"

"Sure," she said, even though she wasn't any hungrier now than she'd been at breakfast.

He spread a blanket out under the tree and they settled on it. She pulled a thick roast beef sandwich out of the basket and offered it to him. He gave her one of his peanut butter and jelly sandwiches. After unwrapping it, she looked at it. When would she get to have peanut butter and jelly again?

"Jess, is something wrong?"

He was studying her again, his expression worried. Now that he'd brought it up, she should get it over with. With the decision made, tears pricked her eyes. She struggled to keep them at bay.

"Did something happen?" he asked.

She couldn't look at him. "Annie figured out that you came to the house to see me."

"What?" he gasped.

"She didn't figure everything out. She thinks it was the first time you came here. She thinks we met at school."

"Is that why you're upset?"

"She said I can't see you anymore. I can't be alone

The Boy in the Woods

with you."

His eyes narrowed. "Let me guess," he said through his teeth. "It's because of who I am."

Jess wiped a tear that ran down her cheek. "Sort of."

"And you agreed with her?"

"Yes," she whispered.

He jumped up. "Why did you do that?" he shouted. "Is that what you think of me?"

"No!" she cried, standing to face him. "You know I don't care about things like that."

"Then why would you agree?"

She should tell him what Annie was really worried would happen, but she couldn't bring herself to say it. It was too personal, too embarrassing. "She had other reasons, and I think she's right."

He shook his head, looking at her like she'd betrayed him. She didn't blame him.

"I'm sorry, Marty."

He turned and stalked away, knocking the willow branches out of the way.

She took out the rest of the food and picked up her basket to leave. When she came out from under the willow tree, he was standing at the water's edge. She longed to go to him, but she couldn't. She should leave now while he wasn't watching. It would be better that way. The tears were coming so fast now, she was finding it difficult to see, but she kept putting one foot in front of the other. Then she heard a sound that made her stop.

Marty was still at the edge of the pond with his back to her, wrenching sobs shaking his body, and her resolve crumbled. She couldn't do this to him. Dropping the basket, she ran to him. She laid her hand on his back, and he turned to face her. In his tear-filled eyes, she saw the little boy who'd lost his mother, and she held him while he buried his face in her shoulder.

"Don't leave me, Jess. Don't leave me," he sobbed while he clung to her.

He'd already experienced so much pain in his life, she couldn't be responsible for hurting him more. "I won't, Marty. I promise I won't ever leave you." She rubbed his soft T-shirt, and the grief she'd been feeling since the previous evening eased. She was glad still had him. But as the pain left her heart, she realized what a terrible situation she was in.

She'd promised Annie to never see him alone, and now she'd gone back on her word. It wasn't fair. No matter what decision she made, she would hurt people she cared about.

Marty let go of her and wiped his face. "I can't almost lose you anymore. This is too hard."

He took her hand, and alarmed, she eased her hand out of his. She and Marty had become too comfortable holding hands, and hugging too. She couldn't allow either to happen anymore. It was the only way to make sure she protected both of them.

"Do you want to eat, or go back to the cabin?" he asked.

"We might as well eat. I dropped the basket on the path. I've got to go get it."

With the weight of her responsibility settling over her, she trudged to where the basket lay. After she returned to the tree, she sat on the blanket a little further from Marty than usual, but he didn't seem to notice.

Chapter Thirty

Don't You Know

WITH THE SUN lower in the sky, the afternoon was drawing to a close. Marty walked Jess to the edge of the clearing. When they stopped, Jess looked up into his brown eyes. They were filled with a sad resignation.

"Are you sorry you changed your mind?" he said. After swallowing, he looked away. "Because you can, you know, stay away. I can take it. I just lost it for a minute, that's all." He was trying not to cry, and her heart went out to him.

"I'm not sorry I changed my mind. I don't think I could have stayed away. It was hurting me as much as you."

"Then why are you still sad?"

"I made a promise to Annie, and I broke it. She's like my mom. I don't want to keep lying to her. I love her." She dropped her head. "I don't know what to do."

Marty raised his hand as if he was going to put it on her shoulder, but let it drop. "I don't know either."

"I have to go. I'll see you at school tomorrow."

The Boy in the Woods

On the way back home, Jess knew the moment she saw Annie she'd have to lie to her, and she was dreading it. She wracked her brain, trying to think of a reason that would convince Annie to change her mind about Marty, but it was useless. When she reviewed everything Annie had said, there wasn't anything she came up with that countered her arguments.

Annie was shelling peas at the table by the window when Jess let herself into the kitchen.

"Hello," Annie said. She tossed the peas she was holding into a bowl and stood, wiping her hands on her apron.

Jess set the basket on the counter and Annie joined her.

"Did you have fun outside?" Annie, said opening the dishcloth.

"Yes," Jess said. It was the first lie, but the worst ones were coming.

Annie stopped emptying the basket and examined Jess. "You're still upset about that boy, aren't you?"

"Yes." Jess was grateful she could at least be truthful about that.

Annie took her hand. "Come sit with me."

Jess slid into the seat opposite Annie and eyed the mound of pea pods on the sheet of newspaper between them. She plucked one from the pile and rubbed her fingers over it's smooth surface.

"You can still see him at school. You can still be friends," Annie said.

"That's not true. Uncle Jonathon won't let me be friends with a boy like him. If he finds out, he might make me leave school. And Marty's not the only friend that I have to keep secret." She couldn't hold back now that she'd started. "There's a girl named Louise. She's really nice, but Doug told me not to talk about her because she's not rich."

Annie winced. "You have to remember, your uncle grew up a long time ago. Things weren't the same back then as they are—"

"But my dad wasn't like that! He didn't care who my friends were, or if they were rich or not."

"Your dad was different. Billy was always more open and accepting, but he could afford to be."

Jess was taken aback. "What do you mean he could afford to be?"

"Your dad wasn't going to inherit the mine. He could *choose* a different life. Your uncle didn't have that choice."

"You mean Uncle Jonathon didn't want to run the mine?"

Annie looked at the mound of peas. "I wouldn't say he didn't want to, but it was expected from the moment he was born. That's what I meant when I said he didn't have a choice."

Jess tried to picture what it would be like to be born with her whole life already planned out for her. She couldn't imagine anything more horrible. She'd often been comforted by the knowledge that she could do whatever she wanted once she was old enough, including moving away and getting out from under her uncle's control.

"He's been expected to behave a certain way from the time he was little," Annie continued. "Everything he said or did was scrutinized because he was going to be the head of Blackwell Iron and Mining. It's a difficult way to grow up, and it's why it's hard for him to see things from a different perspective. This is the only life he's ever known."

The Boy in the Woods

"Like Doug," Jess said, as the realization came to her.

"Like Doug," Annie repeated. "He's raising Doug like he was raised, preparing him to take over the mine when he's old enough. When *you* grow up, you can make your own choices, live any kind of life you want."

"Like my dad."

Annie nodded. "You'll have choices that Doug will never have."

Jess was struck by the revelation. She'd felt trapped and stifled in her uncle's home, but now she realized how free she was compared to Doug and her uncle. Was that why her dad had been so happy while Uncle Jonathon was always so disagreeable and angry?

She remembered a conversation she'd had with Doug in the school parking lot the previous fall. He'd said it wasn't always fun to be a Blackwell, but he was grateful. She didn't know how he could be so positive about it. If she were the one destined to take over the mining business, she'd probably be as angry as Uncle Jonathon.

But none of this changed the fact that she still had to live by her uncle's rules. "I don't want to lie and keep my friends secret. I feel like I'm hurting the people I care about, like you, but if I'm honest and tell the truth, I'm going to lose them. What can I do when no matter what decision I make, I'm hurting someone I care about?"

The sadness in Annie's eyes told her she didn't know what the solution was either. Jess's fingers found each hard pea in the pod she was holding, imagining the next four years of lying and sneaking off to see Marty. It was a horrible way to live.

"You're right," Annie said.

Jess slouched in her seat with shame, and Annie

reached out to take her hand. Her expression had softened and her eyes were kinder. "Being a good friend, no matter the other person's background, is an admirable quality. Do you remember what we talked about yesterday, about how important it is to not do anything to bring shame on the family?"

"I would never do it, Annie. I could never hurt you or Doug. I know how much the mine means to him. I would never do anything to hurt the business."

"You're such a kind person, Jess. Your momma and daddy raised you well." Her expression became more serious. "As long as you stick to your principles and always do the right thing to protect yourself and the family, whatever you do away from the house should be your own personal business, and not something you should feel guilty about."

Jess blinked. "Really?" It sounded as though Annie had given her blessing for her to see Marty.

"Yes."

She jumped out her chair and gave Annie a tight hug, smelling the Shalimar perfume she'd given her for Christmas. "Thank you, Annie," she said. The weight of lies Jess had been carrying ever since she'd met Marty lifted.

"You're welcome." Annie patted her back. When Jess let go of her, she was smiling. "Are you going to stand here, or are you going to help me shell these peas so I can get dinner on the table on time?"

Jess sat back in her seat and began shelling peas, feeling lighter.

"Since your uncle's still away, we're going to have hamburgers for dinner. How does that sound?"

Jess grinned. "That sounds good."

"You know what I think?" she said when they'd

finished with the peas. "We should eat here in the kitchen. Won't that be fun?"

"Yeah."

Annie took the peas to the stove and dumped them in a pot of boiling water. "Maybe it will lift Doug's spirits. He's been out of sorts the last couple of days."

Jess remembered the last time she'd seen him. It was outside her bedroom right after Marty had been dragged out of the house.

"I expect he's missing his dad," Annie said. She set a bowl of potatoes on the table for them to peel. "Your uncle has always taken him when he's gone out of town, but then it's usually been for business."

Jess kept her head down as she worked on a potato, the guilt creeping back. It was her fault Doug was feeling so low. After he'd called Marty a piece of trash, she'd been so angry, she'd said the first thing that came into her head, *"You're as mean as your father."* She regretted it now. Doug shouldn't have said it, but he wasn't mean or cruel.

Once the potatoes were in boiling water, Jess threw away the peels while Annie prepared the hamburger meat. After Jess had set the table, Annie said, "Why don't you let Doug know it's almost time for dinner?"

Jess was grateful. It would give her a moment to talk to Doug alone.

Upstairs, Doug's bedroom door was open a few inches and she knocked on the frame.

"What is it?" Anger was evident in his voice.

"It's me. Can I come in?"

There was a moment of silence. "Sure."

She pushed the door open with trepidation.

The Boy in the Woods

He was lying on his bed, throwing a baseball towards the ceiling and catching it in a mitt. "What do you want?" he said, concentrating on throwing his ball.

"I wanted to talk to you."

"What about?" He threw the ball hard enough that it hit the ceiling with a thump.

"I'm sorry, Doug. I shouldn't have said you were mean."

He caught the ball and sat up to face her, his eyes hard. "I'm not blind, you know. I know you don't like my dad. A lot of people hate him. He's tough on people, but it's because he expects them to do better." He kept his eyes leveled on her, challenging her to disagree.

"It's okay to expect people to do better," she said, choosing her words with care. "But you don't have to make people hate you to get them to do what you want."

His expression changed as he took in what she said, and then his face fell. "Do people hate me?"

Jess went to him. "No."

"How do you know?"

"Because I know *you*, you're a good guy. A lot of people like you."

He searched her eyes. "You really think so?"

"Yes."

"Are you coming?" Annie called from downstairs.

"Just a minute," Jess yelled back. "I was supposed to come get you for dinner. It's ready."

He leaned forward and put his head in his hands. "Right. Tell her I'll be down soon."

"We're eating in the kitchen tonight."

"Okay." He didn't move.

Jess turned towards the door. She hated leaving him when it was obvious he still had so much doubt about himself. On the way down the stairs, she felt bad about the situation Doug was in. He loved his dad, but it had to hurt to know his dad was wrong to treat people the way he did. No wonder he was worried he'd turn out the same. But she couldn't imagine Doug ever being as cruel as his father. It wasn't in him.

In the kitchen, Annie was placing the last of the food on the table. "Where's Doug?"

"He said he'd be down soon."

"How did he seem?"

"Sad."

Annie sighed. "Poor fellow. He'll be better once his dad gets back. You know what? I have some biscuits left over from breakfast the other day. If you whip some cream after dinner, I can slice strawberries and we'll have strawberry shortcake for dessert. That ought to cheer him up."

"Yeah." Jess tried to sound optimistic, but she suspected Doug's problems were bigger than strawberry shortcake could solve.

On Monday morning, Jess found Louise in the crowd outside school and waved. Louise walked to Jess with a spring in her step, her bouncing red curls gleaming in the sun. "Only two weeks of school left," she said in a sing song voice. "And *boy*, am I ready for summer." She threaded her arm through Jess's and they headed to the entrance. "No more homework, no more boring classes, no more tests, sleeping in every day. Well, at least until Jack wakes me. He's still an early riser."

The Boy in the Woods

"The way you talk about him, he sounds like fun," Jess said, imagining what it would be like to have a little brother running around the big house.

Louise scoffed. "Fun, huh? You're lucky you're not woken up every day by a five year old jumping on your bed."

Jess laughed. Even though Louise complained about her siblings, it was clear she loved them. Their home sounded like a lively one, and Jess envied her for it. She was certain Louise was never lonely like she often was.

Once seated in homeroom, Jess kept her attention on the door. Marty would come in at any moment, and she hoped to catch his eye when he did. She wished she could tell him that Annie had approved of her seeing him, but that good news would have to wait.

He appeared in the doorway and she waited for him to look up at her, but he turned to the back of the room without lifting his head. His expression was sad, and she wondered if he was still worried about her lying to Annie.

In social studies class, she arrived early so she could be there before him. He went to Mr. Miller's desk to drop off his homework, and when he turned around, she kept her eyes glued on him, but again, he passed by her, his face still somber. With a sigh, she got out paper and a pencil.

The hours dragged, and when lunchtime finally arrived, Jess was glad half the day was over. She and Louise joined the other girls at their usual table. She'd just opened her lunch sack when Marty came into view, walking along the wall. He didn't have his paper bag. To keep her sadness for him from growing, she shifted her focus to the other problem that had been needling her. How was she going to tell Louise she couldn't see her over the summer?

She couldn't hurt her friend's feelings by telling her she wasn't rich enough for Uncle Jonathon to allow their friendship. Nor did she want to admit how terribly she was treated by him. It would be humiliating to admit she was kept locked up for the entire summer. Lying to cover the truth wasn't something she wanted to do either. But if she didn't address it soon, Louise would want to make plans to see her.

Pretending to be busy unwrapping her sandwich to hide her shame, she said, "Louise, about this summer–"

"I was going to talk to you about that," Louise said. "I won't be able to see you."

Jess's head snapped up. "You won't?"

"Summer is the busiest time for us since so many people come through town on their way up north. I have to watch my brothers and sister so my mom can work all day at the restaurant, and I'm not allowed to have friends over when I'm babysitting."

"I wasn't going to be able to see you either. I was worried you'd feel bad about it."

"I was worried about that too, but we'll see each other when school starts. I hope we'll be in lots of classes together again."

"I hope so too."

"I'm awful glad you moved here, Jess. It was a fun year because of you."

"Thanks, Louise," Jess said. "I'm glad I moved here too." And she was. After living here for a year, this now felt like home. She still missed her parents, but the pain of losing them had subsided to a dull ache. The memories of her old life would always be with her, but she was moving forward.

When Jess entered the clearing, the cabin door was closed. She walked inside, enjoying the aromatic pine smell of the floorboards. After opening the windows, she heard footsteps alerting her to Marty's arrival. He looked as grim as he had at school.

"Marty, you won't believe what I have to tell you."

He eyed her warily. "What?"

"I had a talk with Annie last night. I told her how I was feeling, how I didn't like having to lie about my friends, and she said if I wanted to see them, it wasn't anyone's business."

"What does that mean?"

"It means I can see you here, and I don't have to feel guilty about keeping it a secret."

He studied her, and then shook his head with a bitter smile.

"It's good news, Marty," Jess said, confused by his reaction.

"I know."

"I thought you'd be happy."

"I was going to tell you…" He sighed. "I was going to tell you I wasn't coming back here anymore."

"Why?"

"I can't stand to see you hurt because of me."

"Oh, Marty." She stepped closer and took his hand. "It wasn't because of you. It's because of my uncle."

His head was still hanging, but he leaned forward, closing the space between them. She knew what he wanted, but hesitated. She'd promised herself she wouldn't hug him anymore. Then she thought about what he'd been through all day. While she'd been waiting for school to be over so she could give him the good news, he'd been dreading it, knowing he would lose her.

She reached out to pull him close and he encircled his arms around her. With his breath warming her through her cotton blouse, the meaning of what he'd been planning to do sank in. He'd been willing to give up their friendship to protect her. It was so selfless.

"I told you being friends with me would cause problems," he said.

She tightened her hold on him. "Don't say that. There's nothing wrong with us being friends. If I'd met you when my parents were still alive, they would have liked you as much as I do."

He let go of her. "But your dad – he was a Blackwell."

"He wasn't like my uncle. He didn't judge people because of how much money they had."

Jess pictured bringing Marty home to her apartment in Manhattan. As soon as Cora saw how little he had, she'd make sure he was well fed. Her mom would have treated him the same as all her friends, accepting and kind. There would be no sneaking around, no lies, no secrets. The two of them would spend their free time playing in the nearby park, or having endless stickball games with the other kids on her street. And in the evenings, she'd tell her parents about their adventures. She had no doubt they would have cared about him like she did.

"I wish I could've met them," Marty said.

"Me too." Memories of her mom and dad flooded her mind, bringing a twinge of sadness, like an old wound.

"I reckon we ought to study for our final exams."

"Okay, but let's study at the pond."

"It'll be easier if we do it here, you know, at a *table?*"

The corners of his mouth tilted up. He was being difficult on purpose, but she laughed.

"Come on, Marty. It's hot. We can have a quick swim to cool off and study under the tree."

"It'll be harder to concentrate, and I don't know about you, but I'm planning on getting all A's."

"Then I'll have to work extra hard so I can beat you, but after we have a swim."

He raised his hands in surrender. "If you insist."

Chapter Thirty-One
Five Feet High and Rising

July 1959

JESS LIFTED HER head from her book and brushed aside the hair that had fallen over her face. Marty strode across the clearing with a paper sack in either hand. She jumped up from the front stoop of the cabin and approached him. "Hi, Marty. It's nice today. Not too hot."

"Yeah, it wasn't too bad making deliveries this morning with the breeze."

"What do you got in the other bag?" She was practically bouncing as she walked beside him.

He grinned. "You'll see."

"I want to see now."

"Hold your horses. I'll show you when we eat."

She crossed her arms over her chest and pouted. "You're torturing me on purpose. It's not nice, you know."

He shook his head and laughed. "You make it too easy."

She huffed and looked away.

"Come on. I reckon it won't kill you to wait until lunch."

She still refused to look at him. "I guess."

"I'm ready to swim. How about you?"

"Okay."

His eyes were twinkling with humor. "Besides, it'll kill time while you're waiting."

She lunged to grab him, but he was ready for her, dodging sideways.

Later, when they were sitting on the blanket under the willow tree, Marty opened the smaller of the two paper sacks and pulled out a peanut butter and jelly sandwich. He held it out to her with a knowing smile. She took the sandwich and handed him the sliced roast pork sandwich she'd made for him without a word. She was dying to know what was in the second sack, but she wasn't about to give him the satisfaction of asking.

He unwrapped the sandwich and took a big bite. Jess watched the water ripple through the swaying willow branches. Sometimes, when the branches moved just right, she caught a reflection in the water of the puffy white clouds crossing the blue sky overhead. Suppressing a sigh, she dropped her eyes to her sandwich and unwrapped it. Normally she loved afternoons like this, but today, she was restless. Paper rustled as Marty opened the second bag. She didn't look up.

"Want a Coke?"

He held a bottle of Coca Cola in his hand, but she was determined not to let her excitement show. "I suppose," she said with a shrug.

He took a bottle opener out of the bag and popped off the cap. When he handed it to her, the glass was still cold.

She took a long drink, the carbonation burning her throat. "It's good."

"I thought you'd like it."

After opening his own bottle, he pulled the wax paper holding Annie's bread and butter pickles towards him. Jess watched him take one, noticing how tanned his skin was from all the time he spent outdoors. It contrasted with his golden brown hair streaked with sun-bleached blond strands. He bit into a pickle, his eyes meeting hers. "What?"

"Nothing." Jess looked out at the water. When she glanced at him to see if he'd noticed, his focus was back on his food.

There was something about Marty lately, an appeal that Jess found difficult to ignore. She'd been studying him for a while, trying to figure out what it was. He wasn't handsome like Doug, with the kind of looks that made girls swoon when he walked by. His face was thinner, his chin more pointed, and his nose was a little big and turned up at the end, but she still thought he was every bit as good looking.

When he let his more serious side show, there was an unexpected sweetness in his personality, surprising for a boy. He had a gentle kindness in his quieter moments, often reflected in the warmth of his brown eyes. She'd decided his eyes were his best feature. They had long lashes that made them prettier than most girls', even though he'd hate it if she pointed it out. His eyes frequently drew her in, making her forget she was staring at him. She supposed her fascination was due to spending so much time with him, but it wasn't like she had anything else to do.

Marty sprawled out on his back, settling in for a nap,

The Boy in the Woods

and Jess wrapped her arms around her knees. Her restlessness had been with her for weeks, slowly building the longer she'd been out of school. In the month since classes had ended, she hadn't been off the property once and the monotony of the endless summer days was getting to her. She missed having schoolwork to do and being with all her friends.

Her time with Marty had become monotonous too, with them always doing the same things. A few times she'd asked him to take her exploring in the woods, but it was endless forest, all looking the same. He showed no signs of being bored with their activities, but he had a job. She wished she had one. Instead, the isolation was making her edgy.

"Marty?"

He stirred, but his eyes remained closed. "Hmm?"

"Can you show me where you climb the fence?"

He opened one eye and squinted at her with a frown. "Why do you want to see that?"

"I don't know. I just want to see it."

He sat up. "It's not a good idea."

"Why not?"

"We could be seen."

"We'll be careful," she said, but he still seemed troubled. "I don't want us to get caught either, but taking a look won't do any harm."

He shook his head.

"Please? I'm bored always doing the same things."

"Well, maybe we can, if we're careful."

She grinned. After he showed her where he climbed the fence, maybe she'd see it wasn't that difficult.

"But just a quick look," he added.

The Boy in the Woods

Instead of going to the path back to the cabin, Marty headed in a different direction through the tall grass. Jess walked beside him, running her hands across the green seed heads, excited about this new adventure. He pushed through the brush at the edge of the woods and held the branches aside for her.

The forest floor was littered with fallen logs and rocks, and he slowed his pace, stopping to hold her hand when she climbed over the debris. It had been a while since he'd held her hand, and his soft, gentle grip warmed her. They walked long enough that Jess was sweating in spite of the breeze. Then Marty stopped, and she almost walked into him.

"It's not far, just beyond those bushes," he said, but there was worry in his face.

"Okay."

"We could be seen as soon as we step through so you need to wait until I say it's okay." He went to the bushes and paused, appearing to listen.

She listened too, but all she heard was the rustling of the trees and birds singing. He stepped through and she waited for him to give her the signal. She began to wonder what was taking so long, but then he pushed aside a branch and waved her forward. Once she'd stepped out, she was in an open area. In front of her was the wrought iron fence, twice as high as she was. Through the bars, she saw the two-lane highway running alongside it and past that, a dirt road lined by large trees.

Marty had been right about having to be careful. If anyone drove past, they'd see them. Studying the spikes at the top of the fence, it looked impossibly high.

"This is where you climb?" she asked.

Marty was scanning the highway. "Yeah, over by that tree." He pointed, but his eyes stayed on the road. One large branch of the tree hung over the fence.

"Are the spikes sharp? Can they cut you?"

"Nah, they're rounded off, but I reckon it wouldn't feel good if you fell on them. I use the branch to help me get over them."

"Will you show me?"

He gaped at her. "Jess, this ain't a good idea."

"I want to see how you do it."

"We shouldn't even be standing here."

"You climbed the fence a few hours ago. You've done it lots of times, haven't you? You never got caught before."

He seemed to weigh the decision.

"You can do it right now while the road is empty."

"Okay," he said with exasperation. "But you stand in the bushes to watch. There's no point in both of us being out in the open."

She hurried to hide in the brush.

Marty pressed his face against the iron bars, looking in both directions, then he looked up at the tree branch, adjusting his position so he was beneath it. Grabbing onto the bars, he reached up with each hand, pulling himself higher while gripping the bars with the bottoms of his rubber soled shoes.

Jess gaped, watching him climb. The muscles in Marty's bare back, arms, and legs strained as he made his way to the top. He looked so strong, as if it was nothing. It was the most amazing thing she'd ever seen him do. When he reached the top, he grasped onto the branch with one arm. With his foot on the gap between two spikes, he lifted his body up and over. Once on the other side, he let go of the tree

The Boy in the Woods

and made his way to the ground.

"That's amazing, Marty," she said from behind the bush while he looked up and down the highway. Without responding, he grabbed onto the bars and hoisted himself up. This time, Jess studied how he was doing it.

As soon as he reached the ground, he headed into the brush to join her. "Satisfied?"

"I want to try."

His mouth dropped open. "What?"

"I want to see if I can climb it."

"No, Jess."

"Yes."

"This is a *really* bad idea."

"Marty, I need to try. If I can get over the fence, we can go places. Places where we won't be seen," she added when his expression turned to alarm.

"Someone could see you climbing it."

"I live here. The worst that would happen is my uncle would tell me not to climb the fence."

He considered her, then let out a sigh. "Okay, but be careful. I don't want you to fall and break your neck."

"I'll be careful."

He checked again that no one was coming and sent her out. Standing next to the fence, she looked up at the tree branch and positioned herself underneath it. It seemed even higher, and a nervous tremor traveled down her spine. She looked back at Marty who was watching from behind the leaves. He looked just as nervous. She faced the fence with newfound determination. If he could do this, she could too, and she wasn't about to let fear stop her.

"Take off your sandals. You can grip the bars better with your feet," Marty said.

She slipped them off and wiped the sweat from her hands onto her dress. Then she grasped onto the bars as high as she could reach and pulled. The metal was cool in spite of the heat of the day. She tried to use her hands and feet for leverage so she could climb, but they slid down the smooth metal. Struggling, she grabbed onto a bar a little higher, but her legs continued to slide. She wasn't making any progress.

Marty came out of the brush and grabbed onto her feet. With him lifting her, she moved her hands up the bars. He held her foot at waist height, but she still had a few feet to go before she could reach the tree branch. She pulled with all her strength. "Can you get me higher?"

With a grunt, he heaved her up, and she grasped onto the bar that ran across the top of the fence. "Now grab the tree branch," he said. "Use that to lift yourself over the spikes."

By now, her muscles shook from the effort, and she was drenched in sweat. With one final push, he raised her high enough and she got hold of the branch, grateful her sweaty palm could grip the rough bark without slipping. Getting her other hand on it, she yanked herself upwards, her arms burning from the effort. Marty let go of her feet.

"*Marty!*" she screamed, terrified she was going to fall, and he grabbed onto her feet again.

Panting, she looked at the ground on the other side of the fence. Even if she managed to get over, how on Earth was she going to get down without falling? And how would she get back? She had hardly any strength left.

"Pull, Jess," Marty said, encouraging her. "I can't lift you any higher."

"I'm coming down."

The Boy in the Woods

She let go of the branch and grabbed onto the fence. Her hands were slick with sweat, and Marty had to hold onto her to keep her from sliding straight to the ground. As soon as her feet touched the grass, he took her hand and dragged her into the brush so fast, the branches scratched her bare skin. Once in the shelter of the forest, he let go and a car whizzed past on the highway.

"I don't think they saw us," Marty said breathily. He turned to her, his face full of concern. "You don't want to try again, do you?"

She shook her head. Her body was still trembling from the scare she'd had when she thought she would fall.

His face relaxed. "Let's go back to the pond."

"My sandals," she mumbled.

He glanced at her feet. "I'll get them."

He hesitated at the brush, listening for cars and then disappeared from sight.

Jess let out a jagged breath and rubbed her aching arms. Tremors were still going through her. She wished they would stop.

Marty appeared with her sandals and waited while she put them on. Walking behind him in the forest, Jess's legs were like jelly, and she felt like she was suffocating.

Marty reached a fallen log, and turned, offering her his hand. "Hey, are you okay?"

"Yes." A tear betrayed her, and she wiped it away.

"Jess," he said in a quiet voice, taking her hand.

She turned her head away, angry and embarrassed she couldn't hold back her tears.

"He doesn't let you leave, does he?"

The Boy in the Woods

She kept her face averted. The tears were coming too fast now.

He pulled her closer, wrapping his arms around her. His chest was smooth against her cheek while she sobbed. "Don't cry, Jess." He rubbed her back. "I hate seeing you hurt."

After a minute, she gained control.

"Okay now?" Marty said, when she pulled away.

Jess wiped her face. "Yes."

He smiled, but his eyes were sad. "Let's go." He took her hand and helped her over the log, but when she was on the other side, he didn't let go.

Walking beside him, holding hands made her feel better, but she knew it wouldn't last. There was more than a month of summer vacation left. How was she going to keep her sanity?

That night at the dining room table, Doug asked, "How was your day, Jess?" He'd been attempting to include her in the conversation during meals more, and she was grateful. But today's question caused a lump to form in her throat.

"It was okay," she managed.

"That's good. It was busy at the office today."

"Jessica." Uncle Jonathon held his hand out for her bowl.

Giving it to him, she was compelled to say something. "Uncle Jonathon, I was thinking. I might go into town tomorrow, if that's okay." She'd tried to sound confident, but her voice faltered when he stilled at the word 'town.'

His eyes searched hers as if he was trying to guess her true intentions. "What were you planning on doing?"

"I was thinking I could walk around a little." Her heart sank when his expression hardened.

"I will not have you idling about town like a vagrant," he said. "You're a Blackwell. Think of the example you'd be setting for the young people of the town. And what, may I ask, is James supposed to do while you're *walking around?*" He waved the soup ladle he was holding in his hand. "He has better things to do than sit in a car, waiting for you. The answer is no. There's plenty of room to walk around here." With the matter finished, he gave her back her bowl and filled his own. "Doug, you go out most nights. Why don't you take Jessica along with you?"

The startled look in Doug's eyes let her know he didn't want her tagging along, but she didn't want to go with him either. The last thing she wanted was to spend the evening with his older teen friends, especially after that one disastrous night. Or worse, be the third wheel on a date with Donna.

"I wanted to see *my* friends," Jess said.

Uncle Jonathon set his bowl down. "Very well."

Jess stared at him with shock.

"If you wish to visit Mr. White's daughter or Mayor Melville's daughter, you have my permission. James will drive you to their homes and you will call him to pick you up when you're done."

Jess's heart sank. She wouldn't be able to fake a visit to Patty or Janet's homes. Not with James there, watching to make sure she went inside.

"But I do *not* want you wandering around town with them," Uncle Jonathon continued. "That is not how a Blackwell behaves. Do I make myself clear?"

"Yes, sir." She picked up her spoon, her hopes of

freedom dashed.

He started discussing the mine with Doug, and she took a mouthful of stew. While she chewed, she tried to convince herself that six weeks wasn't that long.

Chapter Thirty-Two

Tell Him No

THE NEXT DAY, JESS folded their towels before she and Marty went to the pond, Marty came out of the kitchen carrying the bucket. He took the towels out of her arms and held the bucket up to her with a grin.

"What's that for?"

"Take the bucket." He moved it closer to her.

"Are we going fishing?"

"No, *you're* going fishing. I'm going to teach you."

She looked at him like he was crazy, because it *was* crazy. She'd never had any desire to fish because so many aspects of it were disgusting. The thought of touching worms and skewering them on a fishing hook, made her shudder. And she'd have to touch a live fish. "That's okay. You can do all the fishing."

He thrust the bucket towards her. "Come on. Didn't you say you were bored always doing the same things?"

Her smile dropped. "Yes."

The Boy in the Woods

"I reckoned if I teach you how to fish, that would be something different."

Jess was about to explain why she'd hate it, but hesitated when she saw the excitement in his eyes. "Okay." She took the bucket.

He grinned and reached into his pocket. "You're going to need this to get the worms." He handed her the pen knife. It was warm from being in his pocket, the black plastic hilt, bumpy like tree bark. "Go on." He held his arm out, directing her to the back door. His eyes were full of humor, and she wondered if it was because he knew she was going to hate what she'd have to do.

She headed in the direction of the trees and once she'd pushed through, she examined the forest floor, looking for an undisturbed area. When she found a good spot, she sat on her heels, and opened the knife. Using the blade, she pushed away the layer of rotting leaves to expose the dark dirt underneath. She dug into it the way Marty did, and a fat worm rose to the surface, its body glistening as it wriggled, trying to rebury itself.

"Don't let it get away," Marty said, smirking.

She made a face at him and then picked it up with two fingers. It was as squishy and slimy as she'd imagined. "Ugh." She dropped it in the bucket, shuddering again.

Marty laughed. "Don't be such a baby, Jess. It's just a worm."

"It's disgusting."

"You need more than one, so you better get on it. At this rate we won't even make it to the pond before you've got to go home."

"Fine." She poked through the ground and found five more slimy worms before Marty said she had enough. He sprinkled a layer of loamy leaves over them to protect them from the sun and they returned to the cabin to gather their things.

This time when they walked to the pond, Marty carried the blanket, towels and food while she carried the fishing pole and bucket. It was a hot day and by the time they arrived, Jess was sweating through her swimsuit. With the sun beating down on her, she stood at the edge of the water. It looked cool and inviting.

"Let's swim first," she said when he joined her.

"Are you *trying* to scare the fish away?"

"I'm sweating, Marty."

He snorted.

"Let's swim for a while and then I'll fish. They'll come back if they see something to eat."

"Okay," he grumbled, letting her know he didn't think much of the idea.

She stowed the bucket of worms in the shade and pulled off her dress. Once they were in the water, Marty's mood recovered and he chased her, splashing her with waves of water. With all thoughts of fishing gone, Jess swam hard, chasing Marty and being chased until her arms and legs were too heavy to push her through the water.

"Let's eat," she said, when she got out of the water.

"I thought you were going to fish after we swam!"

"I will, but I'm too hungry now. And besides," she said with a triumphant smile. "This will give the fish a chance to come back."

He scowled, angry he couldn't argue with her logic, and she went to the willow tree, delighted she'd won. He groused behind her, but he wouldn't be grouchy once he started eating.

When she was unwrapping the banana bread for their dessert, Marty said, "You know what? I've changed my mind."

"Changed your mind about what?" she asked, laying the open waxed paper on the blanket between them.

"I'm not sure you *can* learn how to fish."

She looked up at him.

"After all, you're a girl."

"Just because I'm a girl doesn't mean I can't learn how to fish, Marty."

"You can barely hold a worm." He picked up a slice of banana bread. "If you can't hold a worm, you can't bait a hook, and if you can't bait a hook, you can't fish. I guess that's why girls don't fish." He took a bite of the bread and chewed, meeting her glare with a mild expression.

"If that's what you think, then you're wrong." She jumped off the blanket. "You'll see. I can put a worm on a hook as good as you."

Snatching the handle of the bucket, she stalked to the fishing pole lying against the log. She sifted through the loamy soil and uncovered a few worms. Choosing one, she gingerly picked it up. She wanted nothing more than to drop it back in the bucket, but she was determined to prove Marty wrong. He joined her, and she hid her revulsion as she prepared to pierce its body.

"Don't poke yourself." Instead of the smirk she'd expected, he was looking at her with concern.

"I'll be careful." She gritted her teeth and speared its body, once, and then twice. It might not be baited as well as Marty's worms, but it wasn't going to fall off.

"Now let's see you catch something," he said, his smirk back in place.

She walked to the edge of the water and Marty sat on the log to watch. Pulling her arm back like she'd seen Marty do dozens of times, she threw it forward in what she hoped was a fluid motion, but something went wrong. Instead of the bobber landing in the middle of the pond like it was supposed to, it landed with a plop six feet in front of her.

"Naw, Jess." Marty stood as she reeled in the line. "Don't release it when your arm is going down."

She huffed, angry she had failed.

"Your arm should go part way, then use your wrist to cast it out the rest of the way."

"O-kay?" she said, unsure what he meant. Had he used his wrist when he cast out the line? She drew her arm back to try again.

"You can do this."

She looked over her shoulder.

He was smiling, his brown eyes warm and encouraging.

She felt a familiar tug, the one that made her want to keep gazing at him, but forced herself to face forward. She moved her arm back and then cast the line out again. This time the bobber landed ten feet ahead of her and she turned to Marty with frustration.

"I'll show you what I mean." He came closer. "Reel in the line."

When she had it ready, she held the rod out to him, but he didn't take it.

"It'll be better if you hold it." He stepped behind her.

The Boy in the Woods

Taking her hand that held the rod in his, he moved closer, so close his chest was now pressed against her bare back where her swimsuit dropped down. Her heart skipped a beat at the contact of his skin.

"You don't want to bring it down all the way." He lifted her arm up and back. Then he moved it forward to demonstrate, but all she could think about was his body pressed against hers.

"When your arm is about halfway down, you use your wrist like this." At that point, he tilted her hand. "That's what makes it go far. See?"

She nodded because she didn't trust her voice enough to speak. Her breathing had become too erratic.

"I'll show you again," he said, and put his hand on her stomach.

He held her tight against him while he made her arm go through the motions, but she was no longer aware of what he was doing. The warmth of his hand was spreading through her body, creating a heat she'd never felt before. While her heart banged in her chest, he moved her arm through the motions one more time.

"See, Jess?" he said close to her ear, but his voice was lower, huskier. "It's easy."

His chest was moving, his own breath quickening, and she knew whatever she was feeling, he was feeling it too. He laid his head against hers, and then his fingers moved on her stomach, caressing her through the fabric of her swimsuit. She closed her eyes, his touch making her melt inside. His head dropped further, nuzzling into her neck and her knees almost gave out. With his hot breaths going through her hair, she was lost, falling through time and space. Every nerve in her body alive and on fire, and she never wanted it to stop.

Then a voice came into her head. *Soon those feelings*

will get stronger – to the point where you forget about everything but being with him.

Her eyes flew open, remembering Annie's warning.

All it takes is one momentary mistake for your life and this family's name to be destroyed.

She pushed Marty's hand off her stomach and wrestled her other hand out of his grip. "I think I know what to do," she said shakily, going to the water's edge to get away from him.

Still in shock and with her nerves jangling, she pulled her arm back to cast out the line, praying it would work this time. Somehow she got it to land some distance away, although nowhere near the middle of the pond. While she stared at the red bobber, she tried to understand what had happened.

She and Marty had hugged lots of times, and she'd never experienced anything like that. She was astonished at how fast things had escalated, and how strong the feelings were. Annie had said she'd known girls who'd given in to those feelings, and now Jess understood how dangerous it could be. What if Annie hadn't warned her ahead of time? What would she and Marty have done?

"I'm sorry, Jess," she heard behind her, and turned. Marty's head was hanging. "I shouldn't have done that."

"It's okay." She was just as guilty as he was for what happened.

He looked up at her, his eyes begging her not to hate him. "I won't do it again. I promise."

"Marty, it's really okay."

"I don't know why, why I…" He stopped, seeming to search for words.

"I'm not mad about it."

"You're not?"

She was dismayed when his expression lightened. This wasn't good. He had to understand how serious this was. "But it can never happen again," she said, resolved to make it clear what the stakes were. "Or I can't see you anymore." His face fell, and she cringed inside, knowing she'd hurt him.

He lowered his head again. "I know."

"Let's go sit," she suggested.

He followed her and took a seat on the log a few feet from her. While he stared at his clasped hands in his lap, she watched the bobber, feeling awful. She wanted to comfort him, but she couldn't take that chance now. She had to protect him for the sake of both their futures, even if it meant hurting him.

There was a yank on the line, and it startled her. She tightened her hold on the rod as there was another, longer pull. She was surprised by how strong it was and turned to Marty. "A fish," she gasped. "What do I do?"

His face lit up. "Reel it in!"

She stood as the fish pulled harder, cranking the reel while trying to keep the pole from being dragged out of her hand. "It's strong."

"It's a big fish, Jess. Don't let him get away."

Now that he was happy again, she was determined not to let him down. Using all her strength, she wound the line on the spool, inch by inch. When the bobber came close to shore, the fish appeared, splashing at the surface as it fought to break free. Jess pulled on the rod, the top of it bending from the weight of the fish. "Marty, grab it."

Marty splashed into the water and lifted the wriggling fish into the air. "Look at him, Jess. You did it."

She grinned. It was as big as any of the fish Marty had caught.

"Now you got to take the hook out."

Her smile fell. "I don't want to touch it."

"You got to. You can't leave the hook in his mouth. It's cruel."

She set the rod down and prepared herself. Grabbing onto its cold, wet body with both hands, she watched its mouth open and close, the barbed hook pierced through it. It wasn't as slimy as the worms, but its body was slippery, and it almost wriggled out of her grasp. She tightened her grip. "I don't think I can hold it and get the hook out."

Marty stepped forward. "Try to keep him still."

After he'd worked out the barb, there was a trickle of blood, and Jess fought the urge to look away. Marty dumped the worms out of the bucket and filled it with water. He set it on the ground and Jess came forward. She lowered the fish into it and as soon as its tail touched the water, it began splashing and she let go. It was terrible watching it flail and thump into the sides as it tried to escape the too-small bucket.

"I ought to take care of it," Marty said.

Jess straightened, understanding what he meant by 'take care of it.'

His eyes were serious when they met hers. "We shouldn't let it suffer."

"I want to let it go."

Marty's mouth dropped open. "After all that, you don't want to eat it?"

"No."

He shook his head. "It's your fish." He picked up the bucket, and set it in the water, tipping it until the fish leapt out. With one last flip of its tail, it disappeared in the water. "Caught the biggest fish ever your very first time, and you let it go."

"Yep," Jess said, beaming.

"City kids," he said under his breath.

"Don't call me a kid," Jess said, but she was laughing.

Chapter Thirty-Three
Arrivederci

September 1959

"GREAT DINNER, ANNIE," Doug said, when Annie brought out a blueberry cobbler and a dish of whipped cream for dessert.

Her face lit up at the compliment, and Jess added, "It was delicious."

Annie had made Doug's favorite roast chicken dinner and added Jess's favorite macaroni and cheese. "I wanted it to be special since you're starting school tomorrow," she said.

Excitement rippled through Jess. She couldn't wait for tomorrow morning to come.

"This is a big year for you, Doug. I can't believe you're a senior. Your last year of high school," Annie said wistfully. She turned to leave, but not before Jess saw her tear up.

"That's right," Uncle Jonathon said, holding his hand out for Doug's dessert plate. "Soon you'll be taking your place, working beside me at the mine."

By the sudden change in Doug's expression, Jess could tell the news was unexpected, but Uncle Jonathon didn't seem to notice as he spooned cobbler onto his plate.

"You've worked hard, Douglas. You've earned this. I'm proud of you, son." He handed the plate back to him, and cleared his throat. Uncle Jonathon dropped his eyes to the cobbler, and Jess wondered if he was ashamed that he'd allowed himself to become emotional.

"Thanks, Dad," Doug said, but he looked concerned.

"Jessica." Uncle Jonathon held his hand out without looking at her, and she gave him her plate. "I was planning to give you the corner office that Reynolds is using," he said while Doug frowned at his cobbler. "Unless there's another one you'd prefer. You can have any one you'd like, except mine, of course." He chuckled at his own joke and handed Jess her plate. "But someday that one *will* be yours."

"Uh, Dad," Doug said. "I wanted to talk to you about that."

Uncle Jonathon dug into his cobbler. "Yes?"

"As soon as I graduate, I want to start working right away and–"

Uncle Jonathon smiled. "That's fine, son. It's good to see you so eager to begin."

"The thing is, uh, I was thinking I would work through the summer and go to the state university in the fall."

Uncle Jonathon's smile vanished as he stared at Doug. "Why would you want to do that?"

"I thought it would be a good idea for me to learn more about the business," Doug said, voice wavering.

"I never had to go to college to know how to run the

mine."

"I know, but–"

"How long is this going to take?" Uncle Jonathon's face was turning red as his voice rose.

"It's a four year program."

"Four *years?*"

"I won't be gone the whole time."

Uncle Jonathon shook his head. "It's absolutely out of the question."

"I thought I could–"

Uncle Jonathon's fist banged on the table and he leaned towards Doug. By now his face was almost purple, and Jess didn't know how Doug wasn't cowering in fear. "My father dropped dead of a heart attack when I was nineteen years old. I wasn't off at some college when that happened, I was right there beside him. I took over the entire operation from that day on. If he hadn't prepared me for it from the time I was a boy, this family could have lost everything."

"I know that, Dad."

"I *thought* that's what I was doing with you."

"But there are new technologies, new processes–"

Uncle Jonathon waved his arm. "That's what we hire engineers and scientists for."

"I could take business classes too."

"What was the point of all these years of hard work if you were going to up and leave the minute you turned eighteen?"

Doug looked stricken. "That's not what I'm doing."

"And I thought you wanted this," Uncle Jonathon

said, shaking his head.

"I do!"

"I thought the mine and this family were important to you."

"They are," Doug said, his voice cracking, and tears appeared in his eyes.

"Then you listen to me, Your duty is here at home with me," he said, jabbing the table between them with his finger. "I have big plans for you, but they're not going to happen if you're wasting time at some school."

Doug hunched over his plate.

"So what's it going to be? Do you want to take your place at the mine? Or do you want to leave?"

"I want to work at the mine."

Uncle Jonathon straightened now that the matter was settled. "I'm glad you've come to your senses."

Jess picked up her spoon and took a mouthful of her dessert, but it tasted like cardboard. All three of them were silent, the argument poisoning the air around them. Even though he'd had his way, Uncle Jonathon's face was pale. He seemed shaken, and Doug wasn't much better. He was slumped over his plate, jabbing at his cobbler with a spoon, eyes red-rimmed. Jess's heart broke for him, knowing his dream of going to college had been shattered.

She remembered a discussion she'd had with Annie a few months ago. As bad as she felt being trapped on the property, at least she could escape in a few years. She could decide never to come back if she wanted, but it wouldn't be like that for Doug. As soon as he graduated, he'd be tied to the mine for the rest of his life. Even though it was what he wanted, the confinement had to weigh on him.

"May I please be excused? I'm finished," Doug mumbled.

Without looking up, Uncle Jonathon grunted in response, and Doug left.

Uncomfortable being alone with her uncle, Jess hurried to finish the last of her dessert. She didn't want to linger in case he turned his anger on her. Luckily, he seemed lost in thought, and only grunted again after she excused herself.

At the top of the stairs, she noticed Doug's bedroom door was open partway, and she peeked in. He was standing in front of his desk with his hands on the back of the chair. She knocked on his door frame. "Doug?"

He wiped his face. "What is it?" His voice was rough.

She pushed the door open and took a couple steps into the room. "Are you okay?"

"I'm fine."

She joined him by the desk. "Do you want to talk about it?"

"No." He sniffled.

She put her hand on his back while he continued to wipe his face. "I'm sorry your dad won't let you go to college."

He let out a sob. "He thinks I don't love him."

"That's not true, Doug." She moved in front of him. Seeing his tear-streaked cheeks, she didn't hesitate to hug him. "He knows you love him. It's just that it's been the two of you for so long. He doesn't want to lose you, like he lost your mom."

Doug was quiet for a moment. "Do you think so?" A note of hope had crept into his words.

"I know he loves you a lot. That's why he doesn't want to let you go."

Doug was quiet again, but he kept his arms around her. It was different from hugging Marty. Doug was taller and his chest was thicker. Unlike Marty, he smelled of aftershave.

He released her. "I never thought about it that way, but you're right."

There was a mix of gratitude and wonder in his face, and she smiled, happy she'd helped him.

"You know, Jess, I'm glad you came to live with us." He said it as if the thought had just occurred to him.

"Oh," Jess said, startled by his admission. "Thanks, Doug. I'm—"

His face fell. "I didn't mean – I wasn't trying to say – I'm not glad about your parents," he sputtered.

"I know."

"Because that's not what I meant at all."

"It's okay. I know you didn't mean it that way."

"It's better here than it was before with you living here. That's what I meant to say."

Jess was so used to feeling unwanted, to hear Doug say he appreciated her presence meant everything to her, and her emotions welled up. She headed for the door before he could tell she was about to cry. "I have to go wash my hair."

"Good night, Jess," he said, and she stopped.

He was looking at her with that sense of wonder again, and she smiled. "Good night, Doug."

The next morning, when Jess went down for breakfast, Uncle Jonathon was already seated and reading his newspaper.

The Boy in the Woods

"Good morning, Uncle Jonathon," she murmured, sliding into her seat.

He kept his attention on the news. "Morning."

She examined him out of the corner of her eye as she put her napkin in her lap. Had what he'd gone through when he was hardly older than Doug hardened him so much he didn't care he'd hurt his son? She imagined him as a young man, tied to the mine after he lost his father. Meanwhile, his younger brother was free to do whatever he wanted. How did he react when her dad moved across the country to start a new life? Was he glad he had the business, or did he feel trapped?

"Hi, Dad. Morning, Jess," Doug said behind her.

Uncle Jonathon's face lit up. "Have a good night's rest, son?"

"Yes, sir." Doug took his seat. He smiled, but it didn't reach his eyes.

"The first day of your last year of school," Uncle Jonathon observed. "I'm proud of you, son. I know you'll accomplish everything you set out to do this year."

"Thank you, sir." While Doug put his napkin in his lap, a look of sadness crossed his face, and then the mask was back. Even though he might understand why his father wouldn't let him go to college, it didn't change the fact he still wasn't going.

On the car ride to school, he was quiet and Jess left him alone with his thoughts. When she got out of the car, she heard Louise call her name. She turned to greet her, and then had to conceal her shock. Louise's red curls were straightened and shaped into the popular tight hairstyle that most of the girls had. It wasn't as flattering as her natural hair.

"How was your summer?" Louise asked, giving Jess a tight hug.

"It was good. Yours?"

"Busy, but fun," Louise said. She tilted her head and posed, patting her hair. "Well? What do you think?"

"It's pretty," Jess lied.

"I always wanted to do something with my hair and my mom finally let me get it styled. It was a lot of money, but she did it to pay me back for all the babysitting."

"That was real nice of her."

"Get your schedule out." Louise pulled an index card out of her purse. "Let's see how many classes we have together." Jess complied, and they held them up side by side. "Oh, no. We're not in the same homeroom."

"But look, we have English, gym, chemistry, and typing together. That's pretty good."

Louise pouted as the bell rang. "I wish it was more, but I'll take it."

"Come on." Jess took her arm and strode towards the building. "I'm happy we get to see each other every day again."

"Me too."

The moment Jess came through the doorway of her homeroom, her eyes went to the back of the class, but Marty wasn't there. Taking a seat near the door, she greeted the teens she knew as they came in, her excitement and nerves increasing with every passing second.

And then he walked in. His warm brown eyes held hers, reflecting the same happiness she was feeling before he turned towards the back of the room. She leaned forward, resting her elbows on her desk, and covered her cheeks with her hands to hide her blush. They had homeroom together. But her luck didn't hold. Jess was disappointed to discover

The Boy in the Woods

that Marty had only one of the next three classes with her. At least studying world history with him would make it less boring.

When she and Louise entered the small gym to eat lunch, Louise scanned the room, then headed for a table filled with the same girls they'd eaten with the year before. There were greetings all around as they took their seats. Jess opened her lunch sack and pulled out a sandwich, keeping an eye out for Marty. When he appeared, she was relieved to see him carrying a paper sack of his own.

"Jess, I, uh, need to check my hair in the bathroom," Louise said. "Will you come in case I need help?"

Jess was about to laugh. Surely Louise didn't need help with her hair, but from the look in her friend's eyes, something was up, and she set down her sandwich. "Sure thing."

When she and Louise stepped out into the empty hall, Louise glanced around and then leaned close. "My birthday is this Friday," she said in a low voice. "My mom said I can celebrate after school with a few friends. Do you want to go out for ice cream?"

"Yes!"

"I didn't want to ask at the table since I can't invite everyone. You're my best friend, and those other girls... Well, I'd rather just celebrate with you."

Jess understood what she meant. She'd chosen not to have a party for her birthday since she couldn't invite Louise. "Wait," she said, her excitement disappearing. "My cousin takes me home right after school. I don't have any other way to get home."

Louise's smile fell, but then it returned, her eyes much brighter. "Why don't you ask him to come with us? My mom said I could invite a few people, and then he can take you home after we're done."

Jess tried not to let her amusement show. Louise's excitement wasn't just because she'd figured out a solution to the problem. Almost every girl in school had a crush on Doug, and it was funny to see her friend was smitten too. "I'll ask him." Jess opened the door to the bathroom, and when she stepped inside, she was surprised to see a group of girls huddled together at the far end of the room.

They all turned, and from the looks on their faces, she knew she and Louise had interrupted something. Then she saw who was in the center of the group, and her heart sank. Donna's delicate features were swollen and tear stained, and it was clear the girls were trying to console her.

She lifted her head, her light blue eyes full of pain, but then she saw Jess and her expression changed. *"You!"* she said in a strangled cry. As she stepped out of the circle, her face contorted in fury. "Are you happy now?" she demanded, stalking towards Jess.

Jess shrank back. "What's the matter?"

"He broke up with me! He broke up with me because of *you*."

"You're crazy," Louise said, stepping in front of Jess to protect her. "He didn't break up with you because of Jess. She's his *cousin,* in case you hadn't noticed."

Jess came out from behind Louise. "It's because of his dad. He has these ideas about money, and status, and who Doug should have as friends."

Donna searched her eyes with confusion.

"He's the reason Doug broke up with you, not me. I'm sorry, Donna."

Donna's face crumpled and she began sobbing. The girls surrounded her, murmuring comforting words.

Jess felt helpless, watching them.

"Come on." Louise tugged on her arm. "We should go."

Jess hesitated, not wanting to leave when Donna was so distraught, but she followed Louise out. It couldn't be a coincidence that Doug had ended his relationship with Donna the day after the fight with his dad. Was he trying to be a better son by breaking up with a girl his dad didn't approve of? No wonder he'd been sad that morning.

"Is your uncle really like that?" Louise asked as they walked back to the lunch room. "He doesn't want Doug to date Donna because she isn't rich?"

"Yes," said Jess with a resigned sigh. The truth had to come out sometime and it might as well be now.

"Oh."

Jess was too ashamed to explain further. Louise must now realize her uncle didn't approve of her either. When they took their seats at the table, Louise was silent. Jess tried to swallow her shame along with bites of her sandwich, which she'd lost all appetite for.

Later that afternoon, as she exited through the school's double doors, she spotted Doug walking across the parking lot, and she ran to catch up with him. From the stony look on his face, she guessed he was just as upset as Donna.

"Are you okay?" she asked once they'd closed the car doors.

"I'm fine," he said through clenched teeth.

"I know what happened with–"

"Don't." He cut her off with a glare. "Just don't." He turned the key in the ignition, and the engine roared to life.

"Do you remember my friend, Louise?" Jess said,

deciding it would be better to change the subject. "Her birthday is on Friday and she wants to take me out after school to celebrate. You're invited too, and then we can go home after."

"Yeah, sure."

He didn't want to talk, so she faced the window, her heart breaking for him. If only her uncle wasn't so rigid. Doug would be free to date the girl he loved and pursue his dream of going to college. She could be open and honest about her friendships with Louise and Marty. Instead, he ruled over all of them with an iron fist, his skewed beliefs on status and power making them all miserable.

"Hi, Jess," Marty said, entering the cabin an hour later. He set his textbooks on the table and got himself a glass of water. "Looks like we got some good classes."

Jess sat on her stool. "Yeah, I think it'll be a fun year."

"I told Mr. Dwyer I got chemistry. He said he'd teach me some things." He puffed up with pride. "He reckoned I could make some of the simple compounds if I get good enough."

"That's swell, Marty."

They worked on their geometry assignment, and when Jess stopped to nibble on an oatmeal cookie, she thought about how much Marty had changed since she'd first met him. The lonely boy with the shaggy hair and grimy, tattered clothes was gone. Now he had a job that paid well enough that he could afford new clothes and haircuts. Perhaps with Mr. Dwyer's help, Marty could even become a pharmacist. Having a career like that would ensure he'd never have to worry about money again.

Marty lifted his head and smirked. "What?"

"Nothing." She leaned over her book, flustered that he'd caught her yet again.

Chapter Thirty-Four
He'll Have to Go

"YOU MADE PLANS with Doug so he can drive us for my birthday, right?" Louise asked. She was standing next to Jess's locker while Jess pulled out the books she'd need for the weekend.

"Yes, we'll meet him in the parking lot."

"Good. We're going to the soda fountain at Dwyer's."

Jess straightened. "You mean Dwyer's Drugs?"

"That's the one."

"Uh, okay." Jess turned back to her locker, her chest tightening. She knew Doug hadn't seen Marty at school since he'd been caught on their property. Marty had made a point of avoiding him.

What if Doug saw him at the drugstore and said something? It would be terrible if Louise's birthday was ruined because he caused a scene. But Marty made deliveries after school, she reasoned. Doug most likely wouldn't see him.

Pushing aside her fears, she found the paper sack holding her wrapped present for Louise and added it to her stack of school books. It wasn't possible for her to go shopping for Louise's birthday present without raising questions from her uncle, so she'd asked Annie to get the gift for her.

In the parking lot, Doug was leaning against his car. As they stepped off the sidewalk, Louise put her hand on Jess's arm.

"Oh, no. I forgot to bring *The Grapes of Wrath*. I'll get too far behind in my reading if I don't have it. I'll just be a minute." She rushed back to the building.

When Jess reached Doug, he stepped away from the car. "What happened to your friend?"

"She forgot a book. She'll be back soon."

"So are we going to her house, or to her family's restaurant?"

Jess leaned into the back seat to set down her books, keeping her face hidden from Doug. "No, uh, we're going to the soda fountain at Dwyer's Drugs."

"What?" Doug said loudly, and when she faced him, she was dismayed by the alarm in his eyes.

"We're going to Dwyer's D–"

"No," he said, his blue eyes turning to ice.

Jess gaped. "What?"

"We're not going there. Tell her to choose somewhere else."

"I can't make her choose somewhere else. It's her birth–"

"Forget it then. It's off. When she gets here, tell her

I'm taking you home."

Jess stared at Doug, speechless with shock. She couldn't believe he was going to make her cancel with Louise. Then a wave of emotions hit her, and she stepped closer to him. "This is the first time I've done *anything* with a friend the whole time I've lived with you," she said, tears stinging her eyes. "I was stuck at home all summer while you got to work and go out with your friends."

His eyes widened, but then became hard again and she knew he wasn't going to change his mind. She stepped even closer and glared up at him. "If you don't take us, I'll *never* forgive you, Doug. *Never.*"

"Sorry it took me so long," Louise said behind Jess.

Jess didn't move unwilling to back down from her threat.

"Uh, is something wrong?"

Doug broke eye contact, his shoulders hunching. "Let's go." He went to the driver's door.

Jess let out a breath, then plastered a smile on her face before she turned around.

"Is everything okay with you two?" Louise asked.

"Yes, it's fine." Jess opened the car door. "We just had a stupid argument, that's all." She scooted across the bench seat.

"Okay," Louise said, but she still appeared concerned as she sat next to Jess. She leaned forward to address Doug. "Thanks a lot for doing this, Doug. I really appreciate it."

He grunted and turned the key in the ignition.

"I'll spend most of the weekend studying for that chemistry quiz," Jess said, hoping Louise didn't notice the tension in the car.

"Me too. I know that class is going to be the hardest one this year."

Thankfully, Louise kept talking, comparing the classes she thought would be easy and difficult. When they parked in front of the drugstore, Jess reached into the back seat and retrieved the sack that held Louise's gift.

Doug held the store door open for the two of them and as Jess stepped inside the drugstore, she prayed Marty was nowhere in sight. She scanned the store but the only person she saw was Mr. Dwyer going into the back room. They each took a stool at the empty counter and Jess glanced around for Marty again.

"What's that?" Louise pointed to the paper sack on Jess's lap.

Jess handed it to her. "It's your birthday present."

"Wow. Thanks, Jess. You didn't have to give me a gift."

While she opened the sack and peered inside, Jess took another opportunity to check over her shoulder, but did a double take when she saw Doug. He was leaning forward, his face pale and grim as he stared at the counter. She heard paper tearing and turned back to Louise. Not wanting Doug's sour mood to ruin her friend's birthday, Jess leaned in to block Louise's view of him.

Louise looked at the books in her hands. "These are great. Thank you."

"I hope you like them. I've read those over and over," Jess said. Then she heard Doug snarl, "*You!*" and she turned around.

To her horror, Marty was behind the counter, lifting a white apron off a hook on the wall. While he put it on, he kept his eyes averted, avoiding looking at either of them. Seeing

Doug, Jess became alarmed. If he'd seemed upset before, now he was positively livid, his body coiled, like he was about to launch himself over the counter. Desperate to stop him, Jess put her hand on his leg and squeezed as hard as she could.

"Marty, I didn't know you worked here," Louise said.

Doug tore his gaze away from Marty, his blue eyes unfocused as he stared at Jess. "*Please* don't make a scene," she whispered. "*Please* don't ruin this for my friend."

"Yep, I work here," Marty said, struggling to tie the strings of the apron behind his back.

Recognition finally came into Doug's eyes and she mouthed, *'Please,'* one more time. He hunched forward, his eyes on the counter, and Jess was able to let out the breath she'd been holding.

"I've been working here about a year now." Marty stepped in front of Louise after having tied his apron strings. "What do you want?" he said, keeping his attention on her.

"Two scoops of chocolate ice cream with coconut," Louise said.

"Alrighty."

He stepped back and looked behind the counter. Spotting the ice cream dishes, he went to them and after deliberating, chose a large one. He set it on the counter, and opened the large metal freezer lids one after the other.

While Jess watched him, she noticed how quiet it was in the shop. She didn't know if Louise noticed it, but she kept herself positioned so Louise couldn't see Doug. Once Marty located the chocolate ice cream, he looked around for an ice cream scoop.

"How do you like your classes so far?" Louise asked

Marty as he dished up ice cream.

"They're okay," Marty said with a shrug. Jess recognized his familiar tactic of playing down his true feelings. He was as excited about the school year starting as she was.

"I haven't been here in a while. That's why I didn't know you worked here, but we're celebrating my birthday today," Louise said.

"That's swell, Louise. Happy birthday."

"Thanks."

"It's funny, though." He put a final mound of chocolate ice cream in the dish. "My birthday's coming up too."

Jess's head snapped up.

"It is?" Louise said.

Marty was looking at Jess, his brown eyes full of warmth. "Yep, it's in two days."

"I didn't realize our birthdays were so close. I hope you have a good one too."

"I think it'll be good," he said to Jess, and her heart melted. He turned his attention back to Louise. "You wanted coconut?"

"Yes, please."

Jess watched him lift the lids of different containers and examine the contents, giddy with excitement. She couldn't believe Marty had told her his birthday. Now she could give him the party he deserved.

Finished, Marty placed the dish in front of Louise. The ice cream was covered in so many coconut shavings it was hard to tell it was chocolate.

"What do you want?" he asked Jess, but his brown eyes flickered warily to Doug, and Jess peeked over at him.

Doug was still in the same position, but he had his arms wrapped around his stomach, and his face was shiny with sweat. What on Earth was wrong with him? When she turned back to Marty, her eyes landed on the wall behind him where the portrait of Mr. Dwyer's son hung.

"Did you, uh, want anything?" Marty prodded.

"Chocolate malted, please," Jess said, examining the portrait. Annie must have told Doug about her and Mr. Dwyer's son. That's why he hadn't wanted to come to the drugstore.

"Malted, malted, malted," Marty said under his breath while he looked around, and then went to a large red-and-white tin. While he read the instructions on the can, Jess noticed Louise looking at her dish of ice cream with her hands in her lap.

"Don't wait for me," Jess said.

"You sure?"

"I don't want your ice cream to melt."

By this time, Marty was at the milkshake machine, struggling to get the stainless steel cup to release. It occurred to her that he'd never used that machine before, or made a malted milkshake. How long was it going to take him to figure it out? Glancing at Doug, she made a decision. "That's okay, Marty."

He stopped struggling with the cup and looked at her.

"What she's having looks good. That's what I want."

He smirked, his eyes twinkling. "You sure?"

"I'm sure," she said trying not to smile and hoping neither Doug nor Louise were noticing their exchange.

The Boy in the Woods

"Suit yourself." He went to get an ice cream dish.

When he placed the ice cream in front of her, it was piled so high with coconut shavings that some of them spilled onto the counter. Then he looked at Doug, the humor in his eyes vanishing. "What do you want?" he said, his voice an octave lower.

"Nothing," Doug muttered.

Louise moved forward in an attempt to see around Jess, but Jess continued to block her view. "Order whatever you want, Doug. My dad worked out a deal with Mr. Dwyer. He's going to take it as credit at our restaurant."

"So, uh, you want something?" Marty said.

Doug's cheek twitched as he kept his eyes on the counter. "Cola."

Marty went to get a glass. After he set the drink in front of Doug, he went to wash the ice cream scoop at a small sink.

Louise talked about how her parents were taking a rare night off from the restaurant so they could all be together for a special family dinner. While Jess listened, she hurried to finish her ice cream. She would have loved to linger over it, spending as much time as possible with her friend. But with Doug acting so odd, it was best if they left soon.

"Marty." The short middle-aged woman Jess had seen working at the soda fountain had come into the drugstore and rushed to the counter. "Thank you for taking over. Did you find everything okay?"

"Yeah, I did." Marty tried to untie the knot on his apron strings, and she went to help him.

"Can we leave now?" Doug said under his breath.

Jess looked over at Louise, but she wasn't finished

with her ice cream. "A few more minutes, I promise," she whispered to him.

Once Marty had the apron off, he headed to the rear of the store. Jess watched him disappear into the back room with a mixture of relief and disappointment. By now, other students from the high school were coming into the drugstore and a group of freshman girls had gathered on the stools next to Doug. They peered over at him, whispering and giggling behind their hands.

"Jess," Doug hissed.

Her anger flared. Why couldn't he stop pushing her so hard to leave? She was about to tell him off, but stopped when she saw his eyes. They were pleading with her, tears appearing in them. If they didn't leave soon, she could tell he was going to fall apart. To her relief Louise's dish was now empty. "Are you done?" she asked.

"I think so."

Doug lurched off his stool and headed for the door.

"Can we give you a ride home?" Jess said, wanting to distract Louise so she wouldn't notice Doug stalking out.

"Thanks, but in a minute." She leaned forward to catch the eye of the woman who was serving the freshman girls.

While she waited, Jess sank in her stool. She'd kept anything terrible from happening between Marty and Doug, and Louise hadn't picked up on Doug's mood.

"Mrs. Schmidt," Louise said as the woman approached them. "My dad and Mr. Dwyer had a deal."

Mrs. Schmidt raised her hand. "I know all about it, honey. Mr. Dwyer told me yesterday. I hope you have a happy birthday."

"Thank you," Louise said, sliding off her stool.

"Tell your momma and daddy hello from me."

"I will."

Doug already had the motor running when they came outside, and while Jess walked to the passenger door, she examined him through the windshield. He still looked grim, his eyes on the steering wheel in front of him. "We're going to drop her off at home," she said with trepidation as she slid across the bench seat.

"Thanks, Doug," Louise said, sitting next to her and slamming the door closed. "It's not that far from here."

Doug put the car in gear. "Which way."

Jess went limp with relief.

Louise gave him directions and they soon pulled onto a street lined with one-story bungalows, several of which had small children playing in front. Louise pointed out her house and Doug pulled up to the curb.

As soon as Louise got out, Jess heard, "Weezie!" and a small boy with flaming red hair ran full speed at Louise. He jumped up to hug her, almost knocking her over.

"Jack! Be careful," she said, laughing while Jess got out of the car.

A miniature version of Louise, complete with bouncing red curls came out of the house next, followed by an older boy, also with red hair.

"Jess, this is Jack, the wild man." Louise ruffled the smaller boy's hair.

He swatted her hand away. "Stop," he whined, moving out of her reach.

"And this is Gary and Joyce. Say hello to Jess."

"Hi," Jess said with a small wave.

Jack ran off, already finished with the conversation, and the older ones were too shy to respond.

While Louise gathered her things from inside the car, a woman came out of the house, wiping her hands on an apron. Jess's heart clenched, watching her walk towards them. "You must be Jess," she said, holding her hand out.

"Yes, ma'am." Jess shook her hand, forcing a smile. Instead of red curls like her daughters, Louise's mom had thick dark hair and large brown eyes. She didn't look exactly like Jess's mom, but it was close enough that grief washed over her.

Mrs. Brooks put her arm around Louise's shoulder. "Did you two have fun?"

"We did," said Louise.

"That's good." She kissed the top of Louise's head.

Jess motioned to the car. "We have to go."

"Okay," Louise said, her disappointment evident. She gave Jess a hug. "Thanks for the books and for coming to have ice cream with me."

"Thanks for inviting me," Jess said.

"It was nice to meet you, Jess," Mrs. Brooks said when they let go.

"It was nice to meet you too, Mrs. Brooks." Jess kept her smile going as she got into the car. Doug put the car in gear as soon as she had the door closed and she waved while he drove off, calling out, "Bye."

Once out of Louise's sight, she laid her head against the back of the seat, blinking back tears, her heart engulfed with sorrow.

Free of the apron, Marty walked to the back of the drugstore, glad to get away from Jess's jerk of a cousin. Seeing how sore Doug still seemed about him trespassing on their property, it had been a good idea to stay away from him at school. If Jess hadn't kept him under control, Marty wondered if Doug would have tried to take a swing at him.

In the back room, Marty stopped short. Mr. Dwyer was in a chair with his back to Marty, leaning forward with his head in his hands. Marty had never seen Mr. Dwyer sit before. He'd even eat lunch while walking around the store taking care of things.

Marty moved closer to him. "Are you okay, Mr. Dwyer?" Maybe he was sick and that's why he'd sent Marty to work the soda fountain.

"I'm fine," he said, but his voice was rough. Then he straightened and faced the stack of packages on the table. "Did they leave?" he asked with his back still to Marty.

"No, Mrs. Schmidt took over. Do you want me to get started on the deliveries?"

Mr. Dwyer rubbed his temple. "Will you check and see if they're still here?"

"Uh, sure." Marty headed to the doorway. He peeked around the door frame, not wanting Doug to see him, but Jess and Louise were alone at the counter. "Not all of them," he said over his shoulder to Mr. Dwyer.

"Is it that boy?" Mr. Dwyer asked, his voice rising. "Is he alone?"

The Boy in the Woods

"No, Mr. Dwyer. It's just the girls."

Mr. Dwyer leaned forward, putting his head in his hands again. "Good."

Hearing the bitterness in the word, it dawned on Marty that it wasn't that Mr. Dwyer was sick. It was that he hated Doug Blackwell. Marty didn't blame him.

He peeked at the soda fountain again. Jess and Louise were climbing off their stools. *Turn around, Jess. Turn around*, he thought, but she didn't look back. Marty waited until she and Louise stepped outside, and then he faced Mr. Dwyer. "They're gone," he said with disappointment.

Mr. Dwyer rubbed his hands over his face and stood.

"Should I do the deliveries now?"

"No, Marty." Mr. Dwyer sounded tired. He picked up the packages. "I'll run these in the car. Will you take over the cash register?"

"You sure, Mr. Dwyer? I don't mind." He'd never seen Mr. Dwyer act like this before. Maybe he wasn't feeling well after all.

"It's getting late, son. It'll be quicker if I do it. I don't want to take any more time away from your studies."

"Okay."

Mr. Dwyer opened the back door, and Marty headed for the entrance to the store.

"Marty," Mr. Dwyer said, and he stopped. His boss was standing in the open door frame, the light from outside casting him in shadow. "You're a real good boy," he said slowly, emphasizing each word. "Don't ever let anyone tell you different, son."

The words hit him hard, and Marty swallowed a few times before he choked out, "Yes, sir."

Mr. Dwyer left, closing the door behind him. Marty took a few moments to compose himself before going to the cash register.

Jess got out of the car as soon as Doug stopped in front of the garage, and slammed the door shut before he'd turned off the engine. Doug's shoes ground in the gravel driveway as she headed to the kitchen. He went in the house through the front door, slamming it closed too, but she didn't care. He may not have ruined Louise's birthday, thanks to Jess's constant work to keep her friend from noticing, but he'd ruined it for her. It would take a long time for her to forgive him.

Entering the kitchen, she smelled ham baking in the oven. Annie was at the table cutting up peeled potatoes. "Did you have fun with Louise?"

"We had a nice time," Jess said, trying to sound convincing. She didn't want to make Annie feel bad by bringing up how Doug had reacted, knowing it was on account of Annie and Mr. Dwyer's son.

"Did she like the books?" Annie said, setting down her knife and wiping her hands on her apron.

"She loved them. Thanks for getting them for me."

"Where's Doug? I thought he'd want a snack."

"Uh, I guess he's too full."

"Are you full too? I was going to fix your basket but if you're not hungry–"

"No. I mean, I will be before dinner. I just had a little ice cream." She cringed, realizing she'd almost given away

The Boy in the Woods

where they'd gone. She prayed Annie didn't put ice cream and the soda fountain at Dwyer's together.

Annie returned to cutting the potatoes. "Go get changed and I'll pack the basket as soon as I get these in water."

When Jess got to the cabin, she wasn't surprised that Marty wasn't there yet since he'd been delayed making deliveries. After she was done setting out their food, he walked through the door, looking as relieved to see her as she was to see him. They grinned at each other for a minute, and then he shook his head. "What happened today?"

Jess laughed, the stress from that afternoon lessoning. "I don't know."

"Why didn't you tell me you were coming to the drugstore?"

"I didn't know. Louise sprang it on me at the last minute."

His smile dropped. "Your cousin's a real piece of work." He walked past her to the kitchen, and she followed him.

"I can't believe he acted that way. I'm sorry, Marty."

"Why are you apologizing for him?" Marty pumped the handle at the sink harder than normal. "He's the one who was being a jerk."

"He shouldn't have behaved like that, but I think I know why he did," she said, feeling the need to give Marty an explanation. "I don't know what happened between Annie and Mr. Dwyer's son, but it must have been bad. Doug was upset before he saw you. He didn't want to go to the drugstore at all."

Marty wiped his mouth, studying her with a frown, and then shrugged. "I reckon." He went to his stool at the table.

Marty unwrapped a sandwich, and Jess joined him. "I guess we're celebrating a birthday on Sunday."

A smirk spread across his face. "Will we?"

"Of course we will. You said that was your birthday."

"Maybe I lied."

"Marty, you did not lie. Don't try to get out of it."

He laughed. "I was joking. You're so easy."

"Nice try, but I didn't buy it for a second. And we *are* having a birthday party on Sunday."

"If you say so." He took an enormous bite from his sandwich. His eyes were sparkling while he chewed.

She opened her textbook, but now that she was thinking of Marty's birthday, she wondered what she should do to help him celebrate. She guessed he hadn't had a real birthday party since his mom had died, and this one had to make up for all the ones he'd missed. Pretending to read while Marty ate, she made plans.

Later that afternoon, when she let herself into the kitchen, she was pleased to see Annie at the stove. After setting the basket on the counter, she approached her.

"What's that?" She peered into a pan where Annie was stirring a brownish liquid with a whisk.

"It's gravy. You should wash up. I expect your uncle will be home soon."

"Yes, ma'am." Jess kept her eyes on the whisk. "I had a question though. I was thinking I'd like to bake something tomorrow."

"Oh?" Annie turned to deposit the whisk in the sink.

"Yeah, I was thinking about cupcakes."

Annie took a gravy boat from a cabinet. "What flavor?"

"Chocolate with vanilla icing?"

"That should be fine. You can be in charge of dessert tomorrow. Oh. There's your uncle."

Jess turned in time to see James driving the black car past the window.

"You better hurry and change."

"Thanks, Annie." Jess ran up the stairs while Annie poured the gravy into the gravy boat.

That was one part of Marty's birthday taken care of, but she still had another part to figure out. While she kicked off her shoes and pulled off her shirt, she wondered whether she should give him a gift. After his reaction to his Christmas present, maybe she should skip it. The last thing she wanted to do was ruin his day. But she couldn't drop the idea that it wouldn't be a real birthday party without a present.

If she *was* going to give him a gift, it should be something she made. It would be more meaningful too, like the wooden cat Marty had given her. She treasured that little carved cat even though she had to keep it stashed in the drawer with her old toys. Whatever she decided on, she'd have to have it finished before Sunday.

As she started down the stairs, Doug's bedroom door opened, and she heard his footsteps behind her. She wondered if he might try to explain himself, but he remained quiet. One thing was certain, she thought, bitterness surging through her. Until he apologized to her, she wasn't going to speak to him either.

Chapter Thirty-Five

16 Candles

———◆———

"JESS MADE DESSERT tonight," Annie said the following night at dinner, as she placed a plate of cupcakes on the table. "Don't they look good?"

Uncle Jonathon made a noncommittal noise in his throat and Doug was silent, but it didn't bother her. Examining the chocolate cupcakes with fluffy white icing, she smiled, imagining Marty's expression when he saw them. She noticed Annie was leaving. "Annie," she said to stop her. "I wondered if I could get a needle and thread from you. I need to repair a seam in one of my school dresses."

Uncle Jonathon's head rose and Jess felt his harsh glare on her, but she kept her eyes on Annie.

"Of course you can," Annie said. "I'll get it for you after dinner."

"Thank you."

It had been a gamble to bring it up at the dinner table, but it was the only way to keep Annie from asking too many questions. She needed the needle and thread to make Marty's

The Boy in the Woods

gift, and knew her uncle wouldn't approve of Annie lingering in the dining room.

When they were finished eating, Jess gathered dirty dishes without waiting for Annie. The sewing would take a while, and she was eager to get the dishes done so she could start right away.

"Jess," Doug said after his father had left the room. He was still in his seat, his expression sad. "I wanted to talk to you about the other day."

Was he really going to bring this up now? "It'll have to wait, Doug. I'm busy." She pushed through the swinging door with a stack of dishes. As she passed through the butler's pantry, her eyes fell on a drawer and she stopped. That's where Annie kept the box of birthday candles. Did she dare take one? Surely Annie wouldn't notice if only one was missing.

"All done?" Annie asked, and Jess almost dropped the dishes. She tightened her grip on them and stepped into the kitchen before Annie wondered what she was doing. "You can put those in the sink. I'll get my sewing basket."

Annie disappeared into her bedroom as Jess deposited the dishes in the soapy water. While she waited for her to return, she looked back at the butler's pantry. Should she take a candle now?

"What color do you need?" Annie said, reappearing from her room.

Jess went to her. "Uh, I'm not sure."

Annie set the basket on the table and opened it.

Jess looked at the different colored spools, trying to decide which one she should choose.

Annie closed the lid. "You know what? Why don't you take the basket so you can match the thread to your dress? The needles and scissors are inside. Do you need any help?"

"No, thank you. I know how to sew. Cora taught me."

"I can take care of the dishes tonight. You go up and get started on your sewing. If you need any help, let me know."

"Thanks, Annie," Jess said, already heading up the backstairs.

Once she was alone with her doors closed, she sat on the bed with the basket. A deep green thread caught her eye, and she took the spool out. It reminded her of the color of the fir trees in the woods. Then she spied a beautiful blue the exact shade of the water in the pond. Holding them in each hand, she tried to decide which one to use, and then smiled. Why not use both? Taking a needle from a paper packet, she threaded it with the blue thread and began to work.

Four hours later, she yawned and stretched the kinks out of her back, relieved she had finished. She changed into pajamas and climbed into bed, examining Marty's gift one last time. It hadn't turned out how she'd imagined it, but she'd done her best and all in all, it didn't look too bad. She just hoped Marty liked it. She put it under her pillow before turning off the light.

Sunshine woke her, and she stretched, happy but nervous at the same time. She wanted Marty's day to be special, but there was so much that had to go right.

Heading down the backstairs with Annie's sewing basket in hand, she heard sausages sizzling and country music playing. "Good morning," Annie said from the stove. "Did you get your dress fixed?"

"Yes, ma'am."

The Boy in the Woods

"Have a seat and I'll get your eggs ready."

Jess sipped her orange juice and looked at the woods beyond the garage.

"Going out as usual?" Annie asked, placing a plate in front of Jess.

"Yes."

"I'll pack you a lunch then."

Annie returned the stove, humming along to the song on the radio, and Jess picked up her fork, debating whether to bring up the cupcakes. If Annie didn't pack them, it would ruin one of the biggest parts of Marty's celebration. But she didn't want to make Annie suspicious by insisting. After considering it further, she decided Annie would most likely pack them.

Once she'd finished eating, she returned to her room to gather her school books. When she had everything ready, she pulled Marty's gift out from under her pillow and tucked it into the back pocket of her shorts. Walking down the stairs into the silent kitchen, she saw the basket on the counter. She peeked inside and was relieved to see the cupcakes. Did she dare take a birthday candle? Annie could walk in at any moment. Then Jess thought of Marty's expression when she put a cupcake in front of him with a lit candle.

She went to the butler's pantry, keeping her ears open to any sounds, but all she heard was her own heart pounding. She opened the drawer and rifled through it until she located the box of candles. More than half of them were gone already. That was good. Annie wouldn't remember the exact number. After pulling one out, she put the box back and eased the drawer closed. With the candle in her fist, she returned to the basket and tucked it inside. Heading down the drive, she grinned. Her plans had worked out so far.

The front door of the cabin was open, and she ran the

rest of the way. "Happy birthday, Marty," she said when she crossed the threshold.

Marty was in his chair in front of the stone fireplace. "Hey, Jess." He stood, closing his pen knife.

"You're sixteen today. Do you feel any older?"

He barked out a laugh. "No."

"I hope you're ready for a party," she said with a grin.

"After homework."

"We can do some, but then I'm giving you a party."

"If you say so," he said, but she could tell he was happy about it.

A few hours later, she took out their food, careful to keep the dish towel over the cupcakes so he wouldn't see them. What she'd put on the table included many of Marty's favorites, and he looked excited, picking up a thick ham sandwich.

After the last pickle was eaten, Jess decided it was time. She stood and retrieved the box of matches Marty used to light the cookstove then opened the dish towel. She blocked Marty's view of what she was doing, and set the candle in the center of one. After striking a match, she turned. singing *Happy Birthday*.

At first, Marty was startled, but then he laughed.

When she reached the end of the song, she set the cupcake in front of him. "Make a wish."

He looked up at her with amusement. "You really expect me to do that?"

"Come on, Marty. Don't be difficult."

"Okay." He closed his eyes, and after a moment, he opened them and blew out the candle. "You can sit now." He

The Boy in the Woods

gave her a gentle push, his face flushing.

Reaching into the back pocket of her shorts, her heart rate increased. She hoped the next few minutes went well. "I don't want you to get mad at me," she said, taking a seat while keeping his gift hidden. "But I have something for you. It's a birthday present."

Marty's smile disappeared. "I told you, I don't want you buying me things."

"I didn't buy it. I made it."

She kept her hand closed while she brought it out from under the table and held it out to him. He studied her, debating with himself, then he held his palm out. When she placed it on his hand, it partially unfolded, and with a quizzical expression, he opened it all the way. He examined it with his head down while she waited, holding her breath.

His eyes were full of humor as they met hers. "You made a handkerchief?"

"No, silly, it's one of mine. I embroidered it."

He tried to hide his smile. "I know." He ran his finger over the stitching. She'd embroidered his initials, M. C., with dark green thread and outlined them with blue. "I like it. I like it a lot."

He gazed up at her through his long lashes, his brown eyes saying so much more than his simple words. They drew her in, and then she realized she was staring at him again. She tore her eyes away. "I'm glad, Marty."

When they were done eating the cupcakes, she gathered their trash and he brought their school books to the table. "We should start with chemistry."

"Good idea."

She pulled her textbook towards her and flipped to the

beginning of the chapter. Then she noticed Marty folding his handkerchief so that his initials were on top. He put it next to his open textbook, and she ducked her head to hide her smile.

When it was time to go, she gathered her books and basket, and Marty joined her. While they crossed the clearing, she slowed her steps, wanting to draw out the last minutes of her time with him. At the edge of the trees, she stopped.

"See you, kid," he said with a grin.

"See you," she said, deciding to ignore his teasing.

His expression became more serious. "The birthday – I didn't expect you to do all that."

"I wanted it to be special for you."

"Why?" He was searching her eyes, and she could tell he didn't know.

"Because you deserve it, Marty, that's why."

He continued to frown at her, and then his eyes changed. There was a depth of emotion in them, wonder, gratitude, and something else. He leaned closer, closing the space between them as if he was about to hug her, and she suddenly felt it too, that pull to put her arms around him. *Don't do it*, a voice inside her warned. But the longing was stronger and she couldn't fight it another second.

She moved towards him, and he didn't hesitate to put his arms around her. He was holding her tight, and she closed her eyes. His soft T-shirt was against her cheek, and she breathed deeply, taking in his musky boy-smell. With the birds singing and the creaking of trees as they swayed in the breeze, she soaked in the comfort of being in his arms.

He let go, and she took a step back. She felt the loss, but he was glowing. "Goodbye, Jess."

"Bye, Marty. I'll see you at school tomorrow."

"Yep."

She pushed past the brush and headed for home, the whole way reliving their hug.

Chapter Thirty-Six
Come Go With Me

———————

"I'M SORRY ABOUT what happened on Friday." Doug steered his car out of the driveway and turned in the direction of the highway.

"You should be," Jess said through clenched teeth.

"I know your friend's birthday was important to you. I'm sorry you didn't have a good time because of me."

He sounded sincere, and her anger lessened. "Thanks, Doug. I know you wouldn't ruin it on purpose." He loved Annie as much as she did and because of that, Doug would feel protective over her. If Jess had been in his position, she might not have wanted to go anywhere near Dwyer's Drugs either.

When they got to the school, Jess went to open the car door but Doug put his hand on her arm. "Please don't go." For the first time, she noticed the dark circles under his blue eyes. "I want to make it up to you. How about I take you into town on Friday night?"

"No, thank you."

"Why not?"

"Because I'm not interested in going out with your friends, that's why," she said, irritated he didn't understand what should be obvious.

"No, that's not what I meant. It'll be the two of us." There was something in his eyes that made her hesitate. They seemed troubled.

"It's okay, Doug. You don't have to." She put her hand on the door handle.

"Wait, Jess."

She looked at him, and he bowed his head.

"Until you said it, I never thought about how you're cooped up all the time. I don't want you to be stuck at home just because you don't have a car. I thought maybe I could..." He sighed and lifted his head. "I'm trying to help you."

While Jess studied him, she realized that he was ashamed of the way his dad was treating her, and her heart melted. He was taking another step into the big brother role.

"Sure, Doug."

He relaxed. "Good."

Outside the car, she spotted Louise on the sidewalk and hurried to catch up with her. "Have a good birthday with your family?" Jess asked when she reached her.

"I did. I got some clothes and a bottle of perfume."

"That's nice." She saw Marty leaning against the trunk of a tree. He was watching her, trying not to smile.

"How about your weekend?" Louise said, as he gave Jess a slight nod.

"I had a good weekend too."

"What did you do?"

"I made cupcakes with Annie." Jess smiled as she thought of Marty's birthday.

"That sounds like fun." The bell rang, and they filed inside with the other students.

Later in chemistry class, Jess was doodling on a corner of her paper when Mr. Shaffer barked, "We'll be doing our first lab today. Choose a partner and choose wisely. This will be your lab partner for the rest of the year."

Jess smiled at Louise, knowing the two of them would be partners

Louise leaned close, a determined expression on her face. "There aren't an even number of students in this class."

"So?"

"Think about it. That means one group will have three people, and we need to be that group."

"Why?"

"Okay, maybe *we* don't, but *I* do. I almost failed that last quiz, but I know someone who got an A, someone no one else is going to pick for a partner. We need to get him before anyone else does."

Jess's stomach sank, but she hoped her guess was wrong. "Who?" she asked faintly.

"Marty Cappellini."

"No."

Louise straightened with surprise.

"We can do fine without him. I know we can," Jess said, trying to sound convincing. She'd done all right on that quiz, but only because Marty had explained some of the harder concepts to her.

"Let's not take all day," Mr. Shaffer said.

"Jess, *please*. I don't want to fail this class."

Jess glanced to the back of the room. Marty hadn't moved from his desk. Worse, he was scowling at the other students. It was futile to argue he'd get another partner. "Okay."

When Marty saw Louise approaching, he leaned back in his chair, eyes widening with alarm. She talked to him, and he hunched over his desk. Jess couldn't hear what Louise was saying over the loud chatter in the room, but when his eyes met hers, the grim expression on his face conveyed every bit of the trepidation she was feeling. She shrugged, trying to let him know it wasn't her idea.

"Miss Blackwell!"

Mr. Shaffer had come up behind her and she turned in her seat to see him glaring down at her. He'd never warmed up to her last year, even though she'd done her best to show him she was a good student, and he'd been just as unhappy to have her again this year.

"Is finding a lab partner too difficult for you, or do you feel none of the other students are good enough?"

"She has a partner, Mr. Shaffer," Louise said, before Jess could reply. She was walking back to Jess with Marty following, his eyes flashing daggers at Mr. Shaffer.

Disgruntled he couldn't give her more grief about not having a partner, Mr. Shaffer walked back to the front of the room, shouting at the class, "Go to the lab tables and put on an apron."

Heart pounding, Jess went to the nearest table while Marty followed behind her. How on Earth were they going to keep Louise from guessing they were friends? Louise took a vinyl apron, and to Jess's dismay, stood at the end of the table. Jess took her time slipping on her own apron, letting Marty take the spot next to Louise. If Louise wasn't standing right next to her, it would be harder for her to pick up on any clues Jess might give off.

"Today, you will be making acetylsalicylic acid," Mr. Shaffer said.

He turned to the chalkboard to write the name, and Marty said under his breath, "Aspirin."

"More commonly known as aspirin," Mr. Shaffer continued.

Louise leaned forward to catch Jess's eye, grinning triumphantly. Jess forced a smile in return. Marty didn't notice, absorbed in what Mr. Shaffer was saying. When he nodded with agreement at the instructions, she was relieved. If Marty could forget they were working together because he was focused on the lab work, maybe this wouldn't be as bad as she feared.

Mr. Shaffer finished his lecture, and sent the students to the storage shelves to get the ingredients and equipment they'd need. Jess tried to read the labels on the bottles, but they were all Latin names she couldn't begin to pronounce.

Louise leaned close to Marty. "I couldn't make heads or tails out of what Mr. Shaffer was talking about," she whispered. "What do we need?"

Without a word, Marty took glass measuring cups, beakers, bottles of liquids, and a small jar of white powder, handing them to Louise and Jess.

"Let's go," he said, after choosing a flask.

At the table, the girls set everything down and Marty measured out the white powder. While Jess and Louise watched, he poured it into the flask. As he measured a clear liquid into another glass, Jess asked him, "What's that called?"

"Acetic anhydride," Marty said.

A tremendous pride for him swelled inside Jess. It was clear Marty had made aspirin before, no doubt taught by Mr. Dwyer. There was nothing stopping Marty from having a career as a pharmacist now. With Mr. Dwyer's help, his future was set.

But while she watched him handling the equipment as easily as he carved lifelike animals, it occurred to her there might be even more possibilities open to him. He was smart enough to become a scientist, and if he was careful and saved the money he made working for Mr. Dwyer, he could go to college.

Goosebumps rose on her arms as another, more radical idea came to her. What if Marty went to the same college she did? She imagined them living somewhere far from her uncle's influence, a place where their friendship could be out in the open, and her excitement grew.

"Earth to Jess!"

Jess blinked while Louise snapped her fingers in front of Jess's face. Marty was behind her, the corners of his mouth twitching.

"What?" said Jess.

"We're going to the ice bath now."

"The what?"

"Never mind," Louise said with exasperation, taking her arm and leading her across the room. "Didn't you get enough sleep last night? You were spacing out."

"I guess not." Jess was trying to hold back her smile, thinking of a new future with Marty.

A small tub of ice water was set up in front of Mr.

The Boy in the Woods

Shaffer's desk and Marty set the flask containing a clear liquid in it. A quick look around the room confirmed to Jess that they were the first group to have reached this step. Marty stirred the liquid with a glass rod and it turned milky almost right away. As he continued to stir, it became more solid and then formed into a powdery substance.

"Oh my goodness, Marty. That's amazing."

He grinned at her.

"Is that aspirin?" Louise asked.

"Yep." He took it out of the ice water and headed back to their table.

"I *told* you," Louise whispered, as they fell into step behind him.

By the time class ended, Marty had the aspirin crystals drying and the three of them had washed and put away their equipment. They left the room while a flurry of other students rushed to finish their experiments. As soon as they were out the door, Marty headed down the hall without a backward glance at either of them. Jess watched him disappear in the crowd of teens.

"Aren't you glad we partnered with Marty now?" Louise said.

"I suppose so," Jess said, thinking about how hard it would be to keep Louise in the dark for the rest of the school year. "I still think we could have managed without him."

"Are you *kidding?* We'd still be in there now, trying to make aspirin if we didn't have him as a partner. You know Mr. Schaffer would be mean enough to make us stay until we finished."

"I guess."

"I don't know why you're so dead set against having

him for a partner," Louise grumbled.

Jess didn't say anything as they entered the lunchroom, deciding to let the topic die, but she looked across the room at Doug. He was surrounded by his crowd of adoring friends.

What would happen if he found out Marty was her lab partner? Would he tell his dad? If he did, her uncle could cause a scene at the school over it. Then Mr. Schaffer would hate her more than he did now. Uncle Jonathon might even decide to take her out of school.

Doug couldn't find out, and Jess wondered if she should ask Louise to keep quiet about it. But then she realized it was useless. In such a small school, Doug could hear it from any number of people. With the weight of yet another secret settling over her, she opened her sack and took out a sandwich, hoping it would all work out.

That afternoon, Jess set out food, listening for Marty while she worried what he would say.

His expression when he stepped through the door was as grim as she'd expected. "Why didn't you stop her?" he asked, not bothering with a greeting.

"I tried to talk her out of it, but she wouldn't listen to me."

"This is bad. *Real* bad. She could figure everything out."

"I know, but there's nothing we can do now."

"What if she tells your cousin."

"She wouldn't do that. Louise knows what my uncle is like. She won't want to get me in trouble."

"What's with her anyway? Why did she want to pick me?"

"Because she knows you're good at chemistry. Didn't you notice we finished before anyone else?"

"That don't mean nothing. It's because Mr. Dwyer already showed me how to make aspirin."

"That's not true. You're probably the top student in that class."

He considered what she said, his face brightening, but then his frown returned. "That don't change the fact she could figure out we know each other, and once she does, she'll start wondering—"

"Listen to me." Jess took his hand. "If she does, I'll talk to her. She won't tell anyone if I ask her not to."

While he searched her eyes, she hoped he didn't see her worry reflected in them. He'd been so focused on Louise, he hadn't thought about the fact that Doug might find out from someone else. Marty already lived with enough worry. She didn't want to add to his burdens.

"It'll be okay. You'll see," she added.

"I reckon." His shoulders dropped and he let out a breath, but then his brown eyes locked on hers. They were filled with trepidation, but also longing.

With his warm hand still in hers, she felt the same longing surge through her. Stepping back before they lost themselves in the moment, she pulled him with her. "Are you hungry? Annie packed the last cupcakes."

"Yeah," he said, a smile spreading across his face.

She pulled him into the kitchen, allowing herself to get lost in his eyes a little longer.

Chapter Thirty-Seven
Somebody's Back in Town

ON FRIDAY EVENING, Jess was in her bathroom getting ready to go to town with Doug. She began to put her hair up in a ponytail when she heard a knock on her bedroom door.

It was Doug, already wearing a jacket. "You ready to go?"

"Almost. I need to fix my hair."

"Oh, you–" he started as she turned away.

"What?"

He shook his head. "Nothing. Never mind."

"You don't have to wait in the hall." She opened the door wider.

"Okay."

She headed to the bathroom while he walked in. With her hair up and secured with an elastic band, she came out.

Doug was standing between her two beds, looking at

the framed wedding picture of her parents. "Sorry," he said when he saw her, setting it back on the nightstand.

"It's okay. I don't mind." She went to the wardrobe to collect her loafers. "Have you decided where we're going?" She sat on her bed and pulled on her ankle socks.

"I've got a couple ideas, but we'll see what looks good when we get to town."

She slipped on her last loafer and stood. "I'm ready."

"Alright." He held his arm out, directing her to walk ahead of him.

Jess thought Annie and Uncle Jonathon would be waiting at the bottom of the stairs, but neither of them were in sight and the house was quiet. Doug headed straight to the front door and opened it for her. When she stepped out, James was standing in front of the open garage smoking. He flicked the cigarette away and headed for the black car when he saw them.

While he unlocked the padlock, Jess noticed how quiet it was in the car. Doug must have noticed too because he turned on the radio and the song "All I Have to Do Is Dream" filled the silence. With the gate opened, Doug pulled out onto the dirt road. Jess looked at the iron fence and the forest behind it. Listening to the Everly Brothers' melancholy harmonies, her thoughts turned to Marty, alone at the cabin.

Did it bother him to say goodbye to her and then spend all those hours by himself before it was safe to go home? In a perfect world, *he'd* be the one taking her out instead of Doug. The next song came on, and Doug turned onto the two-lane highway.

He only broke the silence when they reached the edge of town. "Are you hungry?"

"Yeah."

The Boy in the Woods

She thought he'd talk about the places where they could eat, but he kept quiet. While he wove through the streets, Jess faced the window, her disappointed expression reflecting back at her in the glass. If he kept up like this, it would be a dull night.

Doug parked the car, and Jess leaned forward to read the name on the restaurant. She turned to him with a grin. "The Golden Skillet?"

"Since this is your friend's family's restaurant, I thought you might want to see what it's like."

"Thanks, Doug!"

They walked inside, and Jess looked around for Louise, but she was nowhere in sight. A row of red vinyl booths ran along the windows and cream Formica tables with chairs covered in matching red vinyl were lined up against the opposite wall. Doug chose a booth along the plate glass windows and Jess slid across the vinyl seat opposite him.

Doug leaned forward. "Don't tell Annie," he said with a conspiratorial smile as he handed her a menu. "But their pie is very good."

Jess beamed. "Okay, I won't."

"What can I get for you two?" a woman said. It was Louise's mom in a beige uniform. Her eyes widened when she recognized Jess. "Hello, Jess. What a lovely surprise."

"Hello, Mrs. Brooks. Is Louise here?"

"No, honey. She's at home. I expect she's putting Jack to bed about now."

"Oh, right," Jess said, remembering Louise watched her siblings so her mom could work.

Mrs. Brooks glanced at Doug.

"This is my cousin," Jess said, to introduce him.

The Boy in the Woods

"I've been here before, but we haven't been formally introduced." Doug held his hand out. "I'm Doug Blackwell. It's nice to meet you, Mrs. Brooks."

"It's nice to meet you too, D–, uh, Mr. Blackwell," she stammered, her face turning red.

He gave her a brilliant smile. "Please, call me Doug."

"Oh, uh, alright." She appeared more flustered.

Jess ducked behind her menu to hide her smile. It seemed even adult women weren't immune to Doug's charms.

"Do you know what you want?" Mrs. Brooks kept her eyes on her pad of paper, her pencil poised.

"I'm going to have a Coke, a hamburger, and fries," Doug said.

"And you, Jess?"

"That sounds good. I'll have the same."

When she left, Jess looked around the restaurant. There were a few families with small children, but most of the diners were couples, some elderly or teens like Jess and Doug.

"What did you do over the summer?" Doug asked, getting Jess's attention. "I mean, what did you do all day?"

Looking in Doug's curious eyes, she was wary. "Uh, I read a lot, and I walked, in the woods."

Much to her relief, Mrs. Brooks showed up with their sodas and they thanked her. Doug didn't say anything else, and she hoped he was satisfied with her answer. But while she chose a straw from the dispenser, she remembered what her summer had actually been like: long hours spent either alone or with Marty, always feeling restless and trapped like a caged animal, and her anger boiled over. "I tried to climb the fence."

The Boy in the Woods

"You did *what?*" Doug's voice was so loud that the other customers looked over at them. He leaned forward, his eyes filled with concern. "You could have killed yourself."

"Obviously that didn't happen," Jess said, unable to keep the sarcasm out of her voice. She realized it was mean to bring it up, knowing the shame he felt for the way his father treated her, but she couldn't hold it back.

"Did you manage to do it? Did you make it over?"

"No," she said, more bitterness creeping in. She leaned over to take a sip from her straw, keeping her eyes on the cars parked outside. Her mind went back to that day, reliving the crushing disappointment she'd felt when she'd realized her one chance of escape was impossible.

"I'm sorry, Jess." Doug was tearing his paper straw into small pieces. When his eyes met hers, she could see his shame, and she felt a pang of guilt. "I won't let it happen again next summer. While I'm still at home, I'm going to make sure to take you out. I promise."

Before she could respond, Mrs. Brooks appeared, placing plates with hamburgers and French fries in front of them. After she left, Doug reached for a bottle of ketchup.

"While you're still at home?" Jess said. "Are you going somewhere?"

He concentrated on unscrewing the cap. "I guess I forgot to tell you. Dad said I could go to college."

"What? That's wonderful, Doug."

"Yeah, it is."

He wouldn't meet her eyes, and there was something off in his tone. While he tried to shake the ketchup loose, Jess wondered what was going on. This was what he'd wanted, and yet he didn't seem happy about it. She was about to ask him what was wrong, and then she remembered stumbling

The Boy in the Woods

upon a distraught Donna in the girls bathroom. Was *this* the reason he'd broken things off with her?

She frowned at her plate of fries. After Uncle Jonathon had given in, Doug must have broken up with Donna so his dad didn't have a reason to change his mind. She opened her mouth to ask him, but then closed it, remembering how upset he'd been that day. "I'm glad you get to go," she said, trying for a cheery tone. "I'm sure you'll have a good time in college."

"Thanks, Jess." He gave her a half-hearted smile before taking a bite from his hamburger.

There was another long awkward silence between them while they ate.

Doug put the last of his fries in his mouth. "Do you like the woods?"

Jess shrugged, disappointed he'd brought up the subject again. "It's okay."

"My mom used to take me for walks in the woods."

Jess was surprised. This was the first time he'd ever talked about his mom.

"What kinds of things did you do there?" She wondered if he'd gone to the cabin.

"Not much," he said, avoiding her eyes.

She suspected he was evasive on purpose. She was dying to ask him what he knew about the cabin, but she didn't dare since it would give away the fact she knew about it too.

"I remember a big field, and water, like a lake," he said with a far-off look, and then he looked at Jess, his eyes intense. "Did you ever find a lake?"

"Uh, there's a small pond," Jess said, her wariness rising. "It's nothing like a lake." She didn't want Doug to decide he wanted to go swimming.

"I guess everything looks bigger when you're little."

"Do you remember much about your mom?"

"Not a lot." He leaned back in his seat and looked out the window. "I was so young when she died. Sometimes, I don't know if I really remember her, or if I only remember what Annie told me about her."

He continued to look out the window, and Jess thought of Marty. The two most important boys in her life had both lost their mothers at a young age.

"We had picnics by that pond. I do remember that. She had blonde hair and blue eyes, like mine. I always thought she was beautiful."

Jess pictured Donna and wondered if that's what had attracted him to her. Then she realized she'd never seen a photo of Doug's mom, not even in his room. It was probably at Uncle Jonathon's insistence, but it wasn't fair to Doug. He should have pictures of his mother. "Do you miss her?"

"It's been a long time. It doesn't hurt, but I wish I'd gotten to grow up with her. Do you miss your parents?"

"Yes. It's easier now, but when I first came here…"

Shame returned to Doug's eyes. "I'm sorry."

Jess knew what he was referring to. "It's okay."

"I know I wasn't very nice to you when you came to live with us."

"Doug, it's really okay. I know it had to be hard to get used to having another kid in the house, but it's different now, and that's what matters."

Mrs. Brooks appeared. "Do you want dessert?"

Jess looked at Doug. "What should I get?"

The Boy in the Woods

Doug studied her, and then he smiled. "We'll have two apple pies à la mode."

"You've made a good choice. That's Mr. Brooks' family recipe." She collected their empty dishes. "I'll be right back."

"What other kinds do they have besides apple?" Jess asked, not wanting to return to the subject of how he'd treated her.

"Blueberry, cherry, peach. They make a mean chocolate cream pie. We can have that next time."

"I'd love that."

After Mrs. Brooks brought their pie, Jess took her first bite and closed her eyes. It was the best apple pie she'd ever had, and that was saying something considering what good cooks Annie and Cora were.

"I was right, wasn't I?"

She opened her eyes, nodding while she chewed.

With her plate scraped clean, she set her fork down and patted her full stomach.

Doug picked up the bill and looked at his watch. "I guess it's time to go."

Jess slouched in her seat. "Are we going home now?"

"No, it's almost time for the late show. Unless, you'd rather–"

Jess straightened. "We're going to the movies?"

"Sure, why not." He put coins on the table for a tip.

Jess jumped out of her seat with excitement. She hadn't been to a movie since she'd left New York.

When Doug paid their bill, Mrs. Brooks called Mr. Brooks out from the kitchen. A short, stocky man dressed all

The Boy in the Woods

in white with a stained apron came out to greet them. "Good to meet you," he said in a gravelly voice, pumping both their hands in his strong grip.

Jess noted his kind face and hair that was every bit as red and curly as Louise's.

Once they'd said their goodbyes, Jess exited the restaurant and headed to the car, but Doug said, "It's a short walk from here."

By now the sky was dark and street lamps lit the sidewalk. The displays in the closed shop windows weren't as elaborate as Jess was used to seeing in Manhattan, but it was still fun to look at them as they passed.

They rounded a corner and she saw the movie theater marquee with a crowd of people milling under it. There were several teens she recognized from school, and her excitement grew. When they joined the line to buy tickets, Jess scanned the movie posters then turned to Doug with concern. "Are we going to see that?"

"Why, what's wrong?"

"I don't watch horror movies."

He laughed. "It's not scary, it's the *Return of the Fly*."

Jess looked at the poster, too embarrassed to say anything. She remembered the nightmares she'd had after her dad had taken her to see *War of the Worlds*.

"Look, it won't be that bad," Doug said, his face more serious. "I saw *The Fly* last year. It wasn't scary at all. It was funny."

Jess gave him a skeptical look.

"Come on. It'll be fun."

"Okay," she said, relenting.

As soon as she stepped inside, she smelled popcorn and it made her feel better. Maybe this would be fun after all. They sat in the middle of the theater which was already crowded with teens, and she took the time to examine the ornate interior. The chandelier overhead hung from a ceiling decorated with a plaster work and embellished with gold leaf. Red velvet curtains hung in front of the screen and underneath it was a pipe organ. For a small town, she was impressed they had such a beautiful theater.

The lights dimmed and there were whistles and loud laughter while the trailers ran for the coming attractions. Some people shouted jokes, but once the movie started, the audience settled down. Jess's nervousness about being frightened was forgotten as she lost herself in the story.

The action picked up when a corporate spy killed a policeman. He shoved his body in a machine that would dematerialize him, trying to get rid of the evidence. But when the policeman was rematerialized, it had gone horribly wrong. A guinea pig had been dematerialized earlier and now the two had swapped body parts.

The hokey, fake guinea pig arms on the policeman didn't bother Jess, nor did the rematerialized guinea pig with human arms. But before she could prepare herself, the killer stomped on the guinea pig. High-pitched squealing filled the theater as the guinea pig was crushed. Horrified, Jess grabbed onto Doug's arm and buried her face in his sleeve not wanting to watch.

"Hey," Doug whispered, but Jess clung to him harder, putting her hand over her ear to keep from hearing the guinea pig being murdered. Doug chuckled. "Are you scared?"

She nodded.

Doug shifted in his seat. "Come here." He pulled his arm out of her grasp and put it around her. "I'll protect you."

The Boy in the Woods

Jess could hear the amusement in his voice as she buried her face in his shirt, but she didn't care.

The guinea pig stopped screaming, much to her relief, and she straightened so she could resume watching. But when a scientist with a giant fly head stalked people, she hid her face in Doug's chest again. She didn't want to take the chance of seeing anything else that might cause her to have nightmares.

The music swelled and the lights came up, signaling the end of the movie. Doug let go of her, smiling at her in a bemused way. "Were you really that scared?"

"I told you, I don't watch horror movies," Jess grumbled, standing.

"Aw, it's okay." Doug stretched. "Movies like that used to scare me too."

"They did?"

"Yeah, when I was five years old." He laughed, and she stalked past him. He put his hand on her arm to stop her. "Wait, Jess. Don't be mad. I think it's kind of cute."

"It's not cute!"

He raised his hands in surrender. "Okay, I take it back. It's not cute." He was still smiling at her in that mischievous way. "Come on. Let's go."

Walking back to the car, Doug asked, "Did you have fun? I mean, except for the being scared part."

"Yeah, I did."

"I had fun too. Want to do something next Friday? We can go to the early show instead. It's usually a ladies' movie. Or we can do something else."

Jess studied him, unsure if he meant it, but he seemed sincere. "That would be real nice, Doug."

"Great."

Chapter Thirty-Eight
Put Your Head on My Shoulder

December 1959

"I SWEAR," LOUISE gasped, casting dark looks at Miss Gillis. "She always has us do laps when she's too lazy to teach."

Jess and Louise were jogging side by side while the gym teacher was sitting on the bleachers, watching girls run around the perimeter of the gym.

"I have a stitch," Louise cried, clutching her side. Jess grabbed her own side so she could walk without Miss Gillis blowing her whistle at her.

"How do you think you did on the chemistry test today?" Louise said when she'd caught her breath.

"Okay, I guess." Jess hadn't found it too difficult because Marty had helped her prepare for it, but she knew why Louise was worried. Louise had been struggling in chemistry class since the beginning of the year. Jess wished she could study with her so she could pass on the help Marty was giving her, but it wasn't possible. It was one more example of how her uncle's unreasonable rules affected the people Jess cared about.

A group of girls passed them, shooting angry looks that they weren't running. Louise ignored them. "I hope I did okay," she said.

"I'm sure you did," Jess said, wanting to encourage her.

"Thank goodness we have Marty to do the lab work."

"I guess." Jess looked away.

"If it wasn't for him, I'd fail for sure."

Jess remained silent, hoping Louise would drop the subject.

"You know, when we work with him, you're quiet. More quiet than usual."

"I hadn't noticed." Jess's stomach twisted. It was true she seldom spoke to Marty in science class. She'd been trying to keep Louise from guessing how close they were, but maybe she'd taken it too far.

"Sometimes he'll say something to you and, I don't know how to explain it. You smile at him like you're happy."

"I'm not allowed to be happy?" Jess said, angry that Louise was so perceptive.

"You are." Louise turned to her. "I have to ask you. Do you like Marty?"

"No!" Jess glanced over at Miss Gillis. Luckily they were on the opposite side of the gym and she hadn't heard. "I *don't* like him," she said more quietly.

"Are you *sure?*"

The skeptical look on Louise's face made Jess more nervous. She hated lying to Louise, but she had to do

The Boy in the Woods

something. Perhaps she should admit she liked Marty and hope Louise wouldn't dig any further. Still, if her uncle heard about it, even that bit of information would cause trouble.

"I know one thing for sure," Louise said. "Marty likes you."

Jess's heart sank. Louise had guessed more than she thought. "Why do you think that?"

"He watches you when he doesn't think anyone's looking. He's been doing it for a while."

"That doesn't mean anything."

"What's the big deal, Jess? I don't know why you're going to so much trouble to deny it. You're allowed to like boys."

"Look, Louise," Jess said as she made a decision. "The fact is Doug hates Marty."

Louise's mouth dropped open. "Why?"

"It's a long story, but if he knew Marty was my lab partner, he wouldn't like it. And if he told my uncle, it would be bad. He might even take me out of school."

Louise's eyes widened. "Your uncle would take you out of school for being lab partners with Marty?" Then her expression changed. "It's because he's poor, isn't it?"

"Yes."

"Gosh, I didn't realize. No wonder you've been so quiet around him. I'm sorry, Jess."

Jess gave her a sad smile and shrugged. "It's the way things have to be."

"I–" Louise was cut off by the shriek of a whistle.

"Ladies! Let's get *moving*," Miss Gillis shouted, and there were groans across the gym as girls began a tired jog.

"I *really* hate her," Louise hissed through her teeth while the two of them picked up their pace.

But Jess was grateful to Miss Gillis. She'd seen the pity in her friend's eyes, and shame seared through her. She hated that Louise knew how badly she was treated by her uncle.

Stomping snow off her boots, Jess entered the frigid cabin. With her coat still on, she lit the fires. The front door opened as she'd finished with the cookstove.

Marty shook snow out of his golden brown hair and grinned at her. "Happy birthday, kid," he said, his eyes twinkling mischievously.

"Thanks. Should we eat lunch in front of the fire?"

"Sure."

When Marty joined her on the blanket, his eyes became large, seeing the food she was setting out.

"My uncle's Christmas party was last night," she said. Annie had packed all her favorites from the leftovers, making her birthday lunch with Marty more special. When they'd finished eating, Marty reached over and slipped his hand into the pocket of his coat.

"I almost forgot. I got you something," he said, pulling out a flat parcel. It was the size of a book and wrapped in the same white paper she'd seen Mr. Dwyer use to wrap purchases at the drugstore.

"You bought me a birthday present?"

"Maybe," he said with a shrug, trying to hold back his smile.

When she took it from him, she noted it was too light to be a book. She took her time unwrapping it, wanting to prolong the moment. After she removed the paper, she smiled up at him. "Chocolates."

"I reckoned you'd like them."

"I love them. Thank you, Marty." She opened the box and held it out to him. "Do you want one?"

"You choose first."

She picked a round one and then offered the box to him. While he was deciding, she bit into hers. "Caramel. My favorite."

"Enjoy it because I'm not buying them again."

Jess laughed. "Why not?"

"They caused me too much grief, that's why."

"Why on Earth would a box of chocolates cause you grief?"

He scowled. "When I bought them, Mrs. Schmidt asked me if they were for a girl."

"What did you tell her?"

"I told her no, of course. Then she asked me who I was buying them for and I was so stupid, I said the first thing I thought of."

Jess was having a difficult time trying not to laugh. "What did you say?"

"I said it was for a teacher," he said, slouching.

Jess covered her mouth, unable to contain her laughter any longer.

"Then she asked me if it was for a *girl* teacher. It wasn't like I had a choice. I had to say yes."

By now, Jess was holding her stomach because it hurt from laughing so hard.

"Now she thinks I got a crush on one of my teachers," he muttered.

Imagining him dying from embarrassment while Mrs. Schmidt interrogated him, Jess fell over on the floor, howling, tears streaming from her eyes. "Stop it, no more, it hurts."

"It's *not* funny," Marty insisted.

"Yes, it is," she gasped. When she'd recovered, she sat up, wiping tears from her eyes. "I'm sorry about all the trouble, but I love my present."

"I reckon we're even. You bought me a gift and now I bought you one."

Jess put the lid on the box of chocolates, the humor of the previous moment vanishing. Now she understood what had motivated him to buy her a present. His pride was still wounded over the fish hooks she'd bought him for Christmas the year before.

"From now on, let's not buy each other presents," Marty said.

Disappointment pierced Jess. She'd already begun knitting a wool cap for him and was looking forward to giving it to him.

"We'll make them, okay?" he said. "I reckon that's better, don't you?" He seemed worried about her reaction, but when her expression changed, his face lightened.

"I agree. We'll make gifts from now on."

Jess cleaned up the mess from their meal while Marty pulled a small piece of wood and his pen knife out of the pocket of his jeans. He whittled, and Jess leaned back against a chair to watch the fire. In the silence, her thoughts turned to a topic she'd been mulling over for the last several weeks.

At first, she'd been reluctant to bring up the

possibility that she and Marty could attend college together, fearing his immediate reaction would be to reject the idea. He'd said he hadn't intended to go when the subject came up at the lake their first summer. Now that he was sixteen, he'd said nothing that indicated he'd changed his mind. But since school had begun, he'd excelled in all his classes, getting better grades than the year before. If he decided to go, she knew he'd have no problem keeping up with the workload.

As she considered her own future, she was in a terrible bind. She didn't want to leave Marty, but continuing to live with her uncle was out of the question.

"Have you ever thought about what you're going to do when you graduate from high school?" she asked, after spending several minutes working up the nerve.

"I reckon I'll work for Mr. Dwyer," he said, bent over his piece of wood.

"What about continuing with your schooling?"

His hands stilled and he lifted his head. "What do you mean?"

"I'm talking about college."

He scoffed. "No." He went back to his work.

It was the reaction she'd been expecting. "I've already decided I'm going to college."

Marty didn't stop working his knife, but his hands slowed as he frowned.

"If I'm at college, my uncle can't tell me what to do. He won't be able to control me anymore. I can go anywhere I want. I can be friends with anyone I want. *Anyone*, Marty."

He studied her, and then he shook his head as he realized what she meant. "I ain't got money for college."

The Boy in the Woods

"But you can save up for it if you start now. I knew people back in New York who didn't have a lot of money, but they worked over the summer and school breaks to pay for college."

"No one in my family ever graduated from high school."

"But that doesn't mean *you* can't. You're smart enough. You're the top student in our chemistry class. If you went to college, you could own your own drugstore instead of working at one, or even become a scientist."

"But I like working for Mr. Dwyer."

Jess let out a breath. Why hadn't she thought of Mr. Dwyer? From the way Marty talked about him, he viewed Mr. Dwyer as a father figure. She should have known he'd be reluctant to leave the man who'd shown him so much kindness.

Marty set aside his piece of wood and knife and moved so that he was sitting beside her. Reaching out to take her hand, he laced his fingers through hers. She laid her head on his shoulder and he rested his cheek on the top of her head. "Do you have to go?" he said, making her heart ache more.

"I don't want to leave you, but if I stay, even if I lived in town, he'd try to control me. He'd never leave me alone if he knew we were friends. I don't want to spend the rest of my life sneaking around."

His shoulders rose and fell as he sighed, and she closed her eyes. In a few years she'd have to leave without him. While she listened to the logs crackling in the fire, she tried to hold back her tears.

"Do you really think I could do it?" Marty said.

She lifted her head.

"You really think I could go to college?"

The Boy in the Woods

Hope rose inside her. "Yes. If you start saving now, you'd have a head start on the money you'd need, and I know you'd have no trouble with the classes."

A look of determination crossed his face. "Then I'll do it. I'll save my money so I can go with you."

"You will?"

He nodded.

With a squeal of joy, she threw her arms around him and squeezed with all her strength.

He chuckled and hugged her back, the sound tickling her ear through his shirt.

"I can't wait," she said.

"I reckon I can't either."

She smiled so hard her cheeks hurt. *This is going to happen.* In a few years, she and Marty would be free.

Chapter Thirty-Nine
Wishful Thinking

June 1960

"WHILE YOU'RE LIFTING your left foot, ease your right one down," Doug said.

Jess blew out a huff of air, but it did nothing to cool her face. Cicadas buzzed in the trees alongside the barren road where she and Doug were parked. They seemed as irritated by the heat of the late afternoon as she was.

After wiping sweat off her forehead, she gripped the steering wheel of Doug's car, feeling the vibration as the motor idled. Lifting her left foot to release the clutch, she pressed the accelerator with her right. The engine seemed to pick up, but then the car rocked forward and stalled. "Doug!"

"I told you already, you're still letting go of the clutch too fast. Come on, Jess. Try it again, but more slowly."

"Okay." She pushed the clutch to the floor and turned the ignition for the tenth time. *At least that part always works.* This time, she released the clutch slower and when she pressed on the gas, the car leapt forward into the middle of

The Boy in the Woods

the intersection. She took both feet off the pedals with surprise, causing the car to stall yet again. "This is hopeless."

"No, it's not," Doug said. "If I can learn how to drive, you can."

"It's too hot to do this now. I'd rather go home." It was true that the heat was ruining her concentration. But mostly it was that Doug had sprung a driving lesson on her while they were on their way home from school. Marty could already be at the cabin and the longer they took getting home, the less time she would get to spend with him.

"We'll go home in a little while. Look, Jess," Doug said, his expression serious. "I want you to learn how to drive because, well, I've been thinking about it. When I go to college next fall, I'm not going to need my car. And if I leave it here–"

"You're letting me use your car?" she said, eyes widening.

"Why not? This way, you won't be cooped up at home when I'm gone. You can go see your friends whenever you want."

"Doug! Thank you." She pulled him into a tight hug, and he laughed.

"It just seemed to make sense."

Now she'd have the freedom to go anywhere she wanted whenever she wanted. She imagined picking up Marty and taking him… she didn't know where, but any place off the property would be wonderful. She could visit Louise too.

"Ready to try again?" Doug said.

She grinned. "Yep."

After stalling the car two more times, she was finally

able to get it working. Driving down the deserted road, she concentrated on keeping the car straight. Then Doug talked her into trying to shift into second gear. Once the car was moving, it was much easier to deal with the clutch, and her change in gears was effortless. After another half hour of driving, she had no problem starting from a stop, and changing gears as easily as Doug.

"I guess we can go home now," he said with a proud smile. "But I'll drive if you don't mind. The quickest way back is on the highway and I don't think you're ready for that yet."

Jess laughed, giddy with excitement. "I agree." She opened the door so they could switch sides. The look on Marty's face when she told him about the car would be a sight. He'd be as excited as she was.

When Doug drove through the open gate, James glared at them, angry he'd been kept waiting, but Doug didn't seem to care and neither did Jess. She was too busy fantasizing about all the places she'd go once she had Doug's car.

Annie was stirring a pot at the stove when they walked in. "Oh, my goodness, you're late."

"Yeah, we took the long way home," Doug said. He winked at Jess on his way to the butler's pantry.

"It's too late for you to go out, Jess," Annie said after Doug had left. "Your uncle will be home soon."

"I guess so." Jess looked at the trees behind the garage. She was disappointed, but she felt worse for Marty. He'd been left waiting and soon it would be clear she wasn't coming at all. She consoled herself by thinking about tomorrow. When she told him about the car, it would more than make up for today.

"Since you're free, how'd you like to set the table for

The Boy in the Woods

me?" Annie asked.

"Okay," Jess said, still imagining Marty's joyous expression.

During dinner that night, Uncle Jonathon was in an unusually upbeat mood. "I'm proud of you, son," he said, slicing a peach pie into wedges for their dessert. "Graduating high school next week." He shook his head. "It seems only yesterday you were still in diapers, playing with your toy soldiers under my desk."

"Dad!" Doug glanced over at Jess, his face flushing.

She covered her mouth to hold back a giggle.

"And now, look at the man you've become." Uncle Jonathon cleared his throat and handed Doug his plate.

"Thanks, Dad."

Doug was as happy as she'd seen him. He seemed over his break up with Donna and college was right around the corner. She was excited for him.

When she took her plate from Uncle Jonathon, she reflected on how after two years, this felt like her family now. Even though she and her uncle still didn't get along, she'd formed a strong bond with Doug and Annie. They'd stepped into the roles she'd needed most, an older brother and mother.

"The Monday after graduation, you'll be taking your place by my side at the office," Uncle Jonathon sat back in his chair. "It's the moment we've been preparing for all these years. I wish it wasn't only for the summer." He frowned. "Are you certain about this college thing? You can still change your mind."

"It won't be forever," Doug said. "And I'll be working with you during school breaks and through the summers. You'll see. When I come back permanently, I'll help you more than I do now. It'll be good for the business."

"I certainly hope so." Uncle Jonathon took a bite of pie.

"Jess and I had fun today," Doug said, perhaps wanting to steer his father back to a happier topic.

"Oh?"

"Yeah, I took her way out on Franklin Road so I could teach her how to drive, like you did with me. She did pretty good for a first time." He looked at Jess with pride, and she beamed.

"Why would you bother doing that?"

Hearing the casualness in Uncle Jonathon's tone, Jess dropped her head. She should be used to remarks like this from him by now, but they still stung.

"She'll be almost sixteen in the fall," Doug said. "And I'll be–"

"The Blackwell women don't drive," Uncle Jonathon said, as if that fact ended the discussion.

Doug's face fell, and there was a sudden tightening in Jess's chest. "Uncle Jonathon," she said, hating how shaky and small her voice sounded.

He glared at her, but she dared to press on.

"I think in these times, it's important for women to learn how to drive so they–"

"The Blackwell women don't drive." Uncle Jonathon's voice was rising. "They've never driven. They don't have to."

"But Dad, I–"

Uncle Jonathon waved his hand towards the kitchen. "Annie doesn't even drive."

"I know but–"

Uncle Jonathon turned to Jess. "Did your mother drive?"

"We didn't use the car in the city," Jess said.

His brown eyes bored into her. "Did she know how to drive?"

Jess swallowed. "No, sir."

"There you go," Uncle Jonathon said to Doug. "It's best to give up this notion of teaching Jessica to drive. She'll always have someone to drive her like every Blackwell woman."

"But I already made plans with her," Doug said. "I'm leaving my car with her when I go to college."

Uncle Jonathon stared at him with disbelief, and then he fixed his glare on Jess. "Did you ask him to do this?"

"No!" Jess and Doug said at the same time.

"It was my idea," Doug said. "I thought if I left it for her, James wouldn't have to drive her back and forth to school. I don't need a car and it'll be easier for everyone if she can use it."

"How were you planning to get home from college?"

Doug opened and then closed his mouth.

"You said you were going to work with me during school breaks. Or did you just mean Christmas? Was that your plan?" Uncle Jonathon's voice was growing louder again. "I'm only going to see you at Christmas and then next summer?"

"No, I meant a lot more than that. I thought James would–"

"That's almost a four hour drive. Every holiday, your

birthday, he'll be driving for eight hours to get you and then turn around and do it again a day later. How is that easier for anyone?"

Doug wilted in his chair, and then looked at Jess. She didn't need to see the apology in his blue eyes to know it was over. Her freedom had been snatched from her before she'd even had a chance to experience it. The room suddenly seemed too small, and there wasn't enough air. She struggled to breathe while she fought back tears. She wanted to excuse herself, but she was afraid if she opened her mouth she'd lose control, and she would *not* cry in front of Uncle Jonathon.

"It makes more sense this way, Douglas." Uncle Jonathon picked up his fork. "You can come and go as you please without having to work around everyone else's schedule."

Doug hunched over his unfinished pie. "Yes, sir."

"And besides, even if you did leave the car, I wouldn't allow Jessica to drive it. We all know women can't drive."

Jess didn't know why he continued to belittle her. Wasn't it enough he'd won the argument?

"I bought you a beautiful car, and I don't want it to get dented every time she parks it, or sideswipes another car on the road."

Choking back a sob, Jess jumped out of her chair and ran out of the dining room.

"*Jessica*," her uncle bellowed, but she didn't stop. Halfway down the hall, tears filled her eyes. She took the stairs two at a time, even though she could barely see. When she reached her bedroom, she slammed the door behind her, and ran to her bed. Sobbing, she flung herself on it.

Why had she been so stupid? When Doug offered her

the car, she should have told him she didn't want it. Instead she'd been dumb enough to believe she'd be allowed to have some freedom. Uncle Jonathon had shown over and over he would never let her out of his control while she lived in his house.

The tears ran out, but she remained in bed, her soul aching. A knock interrupted the silence, but she didn't move.

"Jess."

It was Doug. She said nothing, hoping he would leave.

"Can I talk to you?"

"Go away, Doug."

"Please let me come in."

"Not now. I'm tired." When there was no reply, she was sure he'd left, then she heard the door open.

"I know you're not tired, Jess."

She rolled over. The door was open, but he remained on the other side of the threshold.

"Can I please come in?"

She turned away from him. What was the point of refusing when he ignored her? She heard the door close and his footsteps crossed the floor.

"I'm really sorry." She could tell by a squeak of springs, he'd sat on the other bed.

"You didn't do anything," she said.

"I should have talked to him before saying you could use it."

She rolled over to face him. "You know it wouldn't have made any difference, he still would have said no. He never lets me do anything."

The Boy in the Woods

Doug's shoulders drooped and he looked at his clasped hands in his lap. "He has old fashioned ideas about women. It's…" He sighed.

She turned away from him. "Save it, Doug. I don't care anymore." She wished it were true, but it wasn't. She felt more tears sting her eyes.

The bed creaked. "I promise I'll come home at least once a month," he said, his voice much closer.

She rolled over to find him kneeling next to her bed.

"I'm not going to abandon you, Jess. I won't leave you stuck at home. I'll take you out."

"Sure, Doug." She rolled away from him, her chest aching more. She should be grateful. He was doing his best to make it up to her. But once a month trips to see a movie with him were no substitute for being free to go out whenever she wanted.

"Good night, Jess," he said as he stood, but she didn't answer, not wanting him to hear the fresh tears in her voice.

A hand shook Jess's shoulder, and she blinked her eyes open. Annie was standing over her lit by the morning sun, concern in her hazel eyes. "You slept in your clothes last night."

"Oh." She rubbed her eyes and looked down at her school dress.

Annie put her hand on Jess's forehead. "Do you feel okay, pumpkin? Maybe you should stay home today."

"No, I feel fine." Jess sat up. "I was extra tired and fell asleep before I changed clothes."

"If you say so, but if you decide you don't feel well when you're dressed, let me know."

"Yes, ma'am. I will."

Looking in the bathroom mirror, her face was pale and her brown hair was a mess, sticking in every direction. Even worse, dark circles ringed her bloodshot eyes. No wonder Annie was worried. In truth, she'd gladly spend the day in bed so she could nurse her wounds, but if she stayed home from school, Annie wouldn't let her go to the cabin that afternoon and she needed to see Marty.

Once dressed, she walked down the stairs, her stomach in knots. She didn't want to face Uncle Jonathon after the things he'd said to her. With a deep breath, she entered the dining room. Doug and her uncle were already seated.

"Good morning, Jess," Doug said.

He studied her with as much concern as Annie had, but she dropped her eyes and took her place at the table. "Morning," she murmured, placing her napkin in her lap.

Annie brought out their plates, and she ate in silence while Uncle Jonathon talked to Doug as if nothing had happened.

When she and Doug arrived at school, Louise waved to her from the sidewalk and then skipped over to her. "Only one more week until schools out," she said.

"Yeah." Her friend's joy was contagious, and Jess was able to manage a small smile. She may not have a car, but she still had Marty, the cabin, and the pond. She took Louise's arm in hers and heading for the building. "Think you're ready for exams?"

Louise laughed. "No. I don't think I'm getting any sleep this weekend."

Jess scanned the yard while Louise chatted about their upcoming tests. She spotted Marty near the corner of the building. Anyone else might have thought he seemed relaxed as he leaned against the brick wall, but Jess saw the intensity in his eyes. She gave him an encouraging nod before turning her attention back to Louise. Louise was too preoccupied with detailing her study plans to notice their exchange.

As the day wore on, Jess focused on the last lessons of the year. The pain from the loss of Doug's car continued to ease, and by lunch time, she was in a much better mood. She'd never expected she'd have that much freedom, so the fact it was a possibility for a few hours shouldn't matter. Nothing had changed except that Doug would visit more often, and that wasn't a bad thing.

After the last bell rang, she and Louise said their goodbyes. While Jess walked back to Doug's car, she noticed a cool breeze had broken the heat of the previous day. It was perfect weather to hang out at the pond. Maybe she and Marty could even study for their exams under the willow tree.

"Do you want to try some more driving today?" Doug asked when he turned on the car.

"No, thank you. I would prefer to go home."

"I want you to know I don't agree with my dad, Jess. It's 1960. These are modern times, and I think women *should* know how to drive."

"Thanks, Doug." She put her hand on his arm in gratitude. Even if he couldn't overrule his dad, at least he was still on her side.

"Are you okay?" Those were the first words Marty spoke when he appeared in the cabin's living room.

Jess went to him. "I'm fine."

His eyes searched hers. "You didn't come yesterday."

"No, I–"

"Did he hit you?"

"No, Marty, he didn't hit me."

He pulled her into a tight hug. "Thank goodness. I was so worried."

Her heart went out to him, realizing what he'd been thinking all day. She rubbed his back. "I'm okay."

"This morning you looked... I know something happened."

"Doug was going to loan me his car when he went to college. I thought I'd get to go places with you, but then my uncle said I wasn't allowed to use it. I should have known he'd refuse, but I'm okay now."

He let go so he could examine her.

"It was a big disappointment, but we'll get to do whatever we want in a couple of years."

Marty's eyes softened. "When we're in college."

"That's right," Jess said, thinking about how that day couldn't come soon enough.

In the silence that followed, Marty's brown eyes held hers, and she was getting lost in them again. The familiar pull returned, drawing her to him, but this time she didn't want to resist. She wrapped her arms around him and he didn't hesitate to hold her close. With her cheek resting on his soft T-shirt, she closed her eyes and listened to his steady heart beats over the sounds of the woods outside.

Chapter Forty
The One You Slip Around With

JESS'S BED SHEET was damp from sweat, and she kicked it off. Even though it was early morning, the air was already thick with humidity. Doug's graduation ceremony was later that day and would be held outdoors in the high school's football field. Instead of enjoying it, she was going to be miserable in the heat.

After a cool bath, she covered her body with talcum powder, hoping it would keep her from soaking through her clothes. After putting on her stockings and petticoat, she slipped on a sleeveless dress covered in peach-colored roses and zipped up the side of the bodice. Stopping for a moment, she admired how the skirt flared outwards from the wide silk ribbon that nipped in her waist. It was the most grown-up dress she'd ever owned.

She brushed out her hair and put in the matching peach headband Annie had picked to go with it. Already feeling the effects of the heat, she took a new pair of white gloves out and slid into her heels. When she opened her door, Doug was exiting his bedroom. He was handsome in a gray

The Boy in the Woods

linen suit.

His eyes lit up when he saw her. "Hey, you look nice."

"Thanks. You look nice too. I wish it wasn't so hot though," she said as they went down the stairs.

"Yeah, I know what you mean."

Uncle Jonathon was in the dining room, reading his morning paper when they walked in.

"Hi, Dad," Doug said.

"Good morning, son." He beamed and stood, holding out his hand. "This is a big day. A *very* big day." He shook Doug's hand.

"Yes, sir."

"Your mother would–" He stopped, emotion filling his eyes.

Doug put his other hand over his dad's. "I know."

At that moment, Annie came through the swinging door, carrying a tray. Instead of wearing her usual black maid's uniform, she was dressed in a short-sleeved seersucker suit with an apron over it. "My goodness." Her eyes traveled back and forth between Doug and Jess. "Look at you both."

"Have a seat, son," Uncle Jonathon said, and they took their places while Annie set down their breakfast plates.

"Aren't you eating with us, Annie?" Doug said when she picked up the tray to leave.

"No, I've already eaten, and besides, I have a bunch of things to attend to before we leave if our luncheon is going to be ready when we get back."

"Annie will be joining us for lunch," Uncle Jonathon said.

"Good. It wouldn't be the same without you," Doug

said to Annie.

Annie returned his smile, but her eyes were misty. She ducked out of the room before her emotions got the best of her.

When he'd finished eating, Uncle Jonathon looked at his watch and stood. "It's time to go." Walking to the swinging door, he pushed it open. "Annie!"

Annie hustled into the dining room. Her apron was off and she was carrying her purse. At the front door, she pulled a hanger with Doug's black graduation gown out of the closet. "I'll carry this until we get there. I don't want it to get wrinkled." She reached to get his cap from the shelf.

James was waiting at the car with the engine running. He opened the rear door and Jess climbed in. When Doug joined her on the bench seat, she was surprised he hadn't waited for Annie. Uncle Jonathon climbed in and the door was closed. James opened the front passenger door, and watching Annie get in, Jess felt bad for her. Even though it would have been a tight fit with all four of them in the back, she didn't like how Annie was relegated to the servant's position in the car. It didn't seem right when she was as much a member of the family as the rest of them.

The high school parking lot was almost full when they arrived, and more families were walking from their homes. Senior boys and girls in long black gowns and caps were everywhere. Uncle Jonathon climbed out of the car and Jess heard people call greetings to him. Annie was out and helping Doug into his gown by the time Jess got out. Once his cap was on his head, Annie stepped back, pulling a handkerchief out of her purse. "You look so handsome and grown up." She dabbed her eyes. "I can't believe it's your graduation day already."

"Come on, Annie," Doug said, appearing embarrassed

and amused at the same time. "Don't start crying now. What's going to happen when the ceremony starts?"

Uncle Jonathon cleared his throat. "Let's go," he said, but his voice was rough.

Doug looked at Jess, shaking his head, and she gave him an encouraging smile before following Uncle Jonathon and Annie. She knew it made him uncomfortable that everyone was so emotional, but it was to be expected, considering what an important day it was.

While they walked among the other families, she thought of her own parents. They would have been as excited and proud to see her graduate as Annie and Uncle Jonathon were today. In two years time, would Uncle Jonathon even bother taking time off work to see her get her diploma? At least Annie and Doug would be happy for her.

Doug joined the other seniors going to the front steps of the school while the family continued down the sidewalk. On the football field, rows of seats were set up in front of a small stage. Annie, Jess, and Uncle Jonathon took seats in the bleachers overlooking it all.

While they waited for the ceremony to start, they sweltered in the sun. A trickle of sweat ran down Jess's forehead. Noticing it, Annie took another folded handkerchief from her purse and handed it to Jess. She wished she could take off her cotton gloves, but since Annie was still wearing hers, she knew better. Uncle Jonathon would be sure to say something if she removed them.

The band started playing the first notes of "Pomp and Circumstance" and everyone craned their necks. The seniors filed out of the building in pairs and made their way to their seats. Jess beamed when she saw Doug, feeling an intense pride for him. Annie looked like she might cry again, and Jess took her hand.

She wiped her eyes. "I'm okay, pumpkin."

Once the graduates were seated, the band finished, and Principal Petersen approached the lectern. After adjusting his Coke-bottle glasses, he welcomed the families and graduates. As his speech wore on, Jess looked down at the seniors, imagining her and Marty's turn. Her heart swelled, thinking of how anxious they'd be, waiting to be handed their diplomas to freedom.

The valedictorian, the football coach, and Mayor Melville also gave speeches, and as time wore on, people shifted in their seats and fanned themselves in an attempt to stay cool. But then came the moment everyone was waiting for, and the crowd stilled in anticipation. As the names of the graduates were called one at a time, each student walked across the stage to receive their diploma and a handshake from the principal.

They announced, "Douglas Blackwell," and Annie sucked in her breath. Doug looked confident and handsome striding towards Principal Petersen, and when he shook his hand, there was applause. Before he left the stage, he searched the bleachers and when he saw the family, he flashed a smile.

After the last name was called and the final student exited the stage, Principal Petersen instructed them to stand. They moved their tassels to the other side of their mortar boards, and then a cheer went up and caps were tossed in the air. The band began playing, and the families stood and slowly filed out of the bleachers.

When they reached the field, it was impossible to find Doug in the crowd, but suddenly he appeared with a big grin.

"Well done, son. Congratulations." Uncle Jonathon took his hand while gripping his upper arm with his other hand.

The Boy in the Woods

Annie was dabbing her eyes, unable to speak and Doug gave her a hug, making her more flustered.

"Congratulations, Doug." Jess held her hand out, but he surprised her by pulling her into a hug.

"Thanks, Jess."

A group of people surrounded them, wanting to shake Doug and Uncle Jonathon's hands, and Annie and Jess had to step out of the way to keep from being crushed. After a few minutes, Doug extricated himself from the group and approached Annie. "I need to get a drink of water. I'm parched."

"I suppose it'll be okay." Annie eyed Uncle Jonathon who was still surrounded by a crowd of well-wishers. "But don't take too long."

"I won't."

Sweat trickled down Jess's back while she watched her uncle being congratulated over and over. It made her uneasy to see how people fawned over him, but he seemed comfortable with all the attention. It reminded her yet again that staying in town meant she would always be a Blackwell instead of just Jess. Wherever she and Marty went to school, she'd make sure it was far enough away that no one would know or care about the Blackwell family name.

"We need to get going," Annie said under her breath while looking at her watch. "The roast is going to get overdone." Asking Uncle Jonathon to cut his conversations short was out of the question, and Annie looked more worried as the seconds passed.

"Do you want me to go get Doug?" Jess asked.

"Yes, you do that," Annie said.

Inside the building, cool air enveloped Jess. It was wonderful to be out of the heat. She walked down the empty hallways, looking for Doug in the open rooms, but he was nowhere in sight. Perhaps he'd gone up to the second floor.

When she entered the stairwell, she stopped, realizing she wasn't alone. Under the stairs, a couple still wearing their graduation gowns were kissing passionately. Jess was about to walk past them when the girl's face came into view. It was Donna – and a shock went through her as she recognized the dark wavy hair of the tall boy kissing her. Stepping backwards, she got out of sight before they noticed her, and tiptoed down the hall, her heart skipping beats.

Outside the building, the crowds had diminished and Annie and Uncle Jonathon were alone.

"Where's Doug?" Annie said, her face tight.

"I couldn't find him," Jess lied.

"This is ridiculous," Uncle Jonathon said. "People are leaving."

Annie put her hand on his arm to calm him. "I'll go inside and look for him."

Panic rose in Jess. If Annie found Doug with Donna, she might mention it to Uncle Jonathon, and then Doug would lose his chance to attend college.

"No, I'll do it," Uncle Jonathon said, and he stalked towards the door.

Jess felt frantic.

"Maybe he came out another door," Annie called out. "Jess and I can walk around the building and see if he's outside."

"You stay there," he said, his hand on the door handle. "I don't want to have to find you once I've located him." He wrenched the door open, jerking Doug forward as he was coming out of the building.

"Dad!" Doug said.

Jess could see fear in his eyes.

"Where have you been?" Uncle Jonathon demanded.

"I – I was saying goodbye to some of my teachers," he stammered.

"Everyone else has left already."

"I'm sorry. I didn't realize I was taking so long."

"Let's go." Uncle Jonathon turned to leave without looking at any of them.

Doug fell in step behind him, misery evident in his face. As they walked back to the car, Jess looked up at his slumped shoulders, wondering what was going on between him and Donna. Could they have been seeing each other all this time? That didn't make sense, though. She hadn't seen them together at school once since the break up, and both had been sad for weeks. Perhaps they'd run into each other inside the school after the ceremony and their feelings overtook them. In any case, she was grateful neither Uncle Jonathon nor Annie had found them together.

Back at home, Jess helped Annie clear the breakfast dishes and put out a celebratory luncheon of roast pork, cold salads, and buttered rolls. When they'd taken their seats, Doug seemed to have recovered from almost being caught and Uncle Jonathon was in much better spirits, serving everyone, even Jess, with a smile.

For dessert, Annie brought out a chocolate cake with *Congratulations Doug* piped in white icing and placed it in front of him. "Here you go." She handed him the cake server.

"Wait, son. I have something for you," Uncle Jonathon said. He nodded to Annie, and she went through the swinging door, reappearing with a large wrapped gift.

The Boy in the Woods

Doug took it from her. "Gee, Dad. You didn't have to get me something." He tore the paper off and held up a leather briefcase. "Wow, thanks."

"Now that you've graduated, I want you to take on a bigger role at the mine."

Doug snapped open the latches and lifted the lid.

"You'll need a way to carry your papers back and forth. And I suppose it will be helpful at school too." The last part was said in a more disgruntled tone, making it clear he was still unhappy that Doug was choosing college first.

"It will." Doug closed the briefcase.

"I have something else waiting for you at the office. We'll go after we're finished here."

"I can't wait to see it."

"I think you'll be pleased."

After the cake was eaten and the two of them had left, Annie surveyed the mound of dirty dishes in the kitchen sink. "I know I should tackle these, but I'm so tired."

"Maybe you should rest," Jess said.

Annie gave her a gentle smile. "Maybe I will after a quick bath. You look like you could use one too, pumpkin. It was hot out there."

"Or maybe I'll go for a swim." She studied Annie's reaction.

"I suppose that would be alright, just be careful about going in too deep. You've had a big lunch."

"I will."

"Your uncle had Doug's office made up, that's what he took him to see. I expect they'll be there a while, but you should be back by dinner time."

The Boy in the Woods

"Don't worry, I will," Jess said, already climbing the back stairs to her bathroom.

The front door of the cabin was open, but Marty wasn't there. Surveying the space, Jess noticed the fishing pole was missing. Certain Marty would want to swim, she went to the drawer in the bedroom where he kept his swim trunks. She gathered up their towels and headed for the pond with a smile. Marty would be surprised. He wasn't expecting her today.

She spotted him long before he noticed her. He was sitting on the log, fishing, his attention on the water. When she was almost upon him, he turned his head.

"Hey," he said, his face lighting up. "I didn't think you were coming."

"We're all done with the graduation. How's the fishing?"

He shrugged, still grinning. "Not that great."

"Want to swim?" She held his suit out to him, and he laughed.

"Am I supposed to change out here in the open?"

"I won't look, I promise."

"Okay, but only because you promised," he said, his eyes twinkling.

Jess kicked off her sandals and took off her dress while he disappeared behind a bush. She splashed into the deliciously cool water. As soon as she was deep enough, she dove in and swam underwater, letting the day's sticky sweat wash away. When she came up, she heard Marty splashing behind her and turned. The wily grin on his face let her know what he was up to, and she shrieked with laughter as she leapt in the opposite direction.

Later, they rested under the willow tree, side by side, propped up on their elbows.

"How was the graduation?" Marty said.

"It was kind of boring, but it won't be boring when it's our turn."

"I reckon not. So, what do they make you do?"

His voice was more serious, and she realized he might not have any idea what was involved with a graduation ceremony. "They have you wear a gown and a–"

"You mean I got to wear a dress?"

She laughed. "No, it's more like a long black overcoat, but lighter, and you wear a cap with a square thing on top. I don't know how to describe it but they call it a mortar board."

"It sounds stupid," he said with a grimace. "Do you *have* to wear that stuff?"

"Yes, you have to. It's tradition."

He scowled.

"Everyone else will be wearing it too, so you won't feel strange. The band plays "Pomp and Circumstance" while the seniors take their seats. People give speeches, and then they call everyone's name. When your name is called, you walk onto the stage and Principal Petersen gives you your diploma. That's it."

Marty looked out at the water. "That doesn't sound too hard."

"Just think, Marty. In two years, we'll be walking across the stage."

He smiled. "Yeah."

"And then, we can do whatever we want, go wherever

we want. It'll be grand."

"I reckon it will be," he said, his eyes filled with happiness.

Chapter Forty-One

The Twist

August 1960

"JESS. JESS, WHERE are you?"

Jess was surprised to hear Doug yelling for her. A moment ago, she'd seen the black car drive past the window bringing Doug and Uncle Jonathon home from work.

"I'm in the dining room." She placed the last of the silverware at her uncle's spot.

Doug appeared in the doorway with a flat paper bag. "There you are. Come with me."

"It's almost time for dinner. I'm helping Annie."

"She can spare you for a few minutes." He approached her. "You have to come. I want to show you something."

She thought he would open the bag, but instead he took her hand and pulled her out of the room. "What's going on?" she said, laughing. "Why can't you show me in the dining room?"

The Boy in the Woods

"Because I can't. It's a new dance." He smiled as he led her through the hallway. "Everyone's doing it."

They entered the grand parlor, and if Doug hadn't been holding her hand, she might have hesitated to continue. Uncle Jonathon was mixing a drink at the bar cabinet with his back to them. She hoped with Doug there he wouldn't chastise her for some reason.

"I went out on my lunch break to buy the record." Doug let go of her hand and took a 45 out of the bag. He placed it on the turntable of the high-fidelity stereo. The opening notes of a saxophone filled the room, and Jess recognized the song.

"I heard this on the radio. It's called "The Twist," she said.

"Yeah, they've been playing it non-stop." Jess stepped forward to dance with him, but Doug put his hands on her shoulders and moved her back a few steps. "Watch me."

He swiveled his hips while moving his arms in the opposite direction in time to the music, and Jess's eyes widened. She'd never seen anything like it, but it was especially surprising to see Doug dancing like that in his dark blue suit, his shiny shoes sliding on the rug as he twisted his body.

"Try it, Jess," he said with a grin.

She mimicked his movements, speeding up as she became used to the motions. Lost in the music, she felt free, keeping in time with the beats.

"It's fun, isn't it?" he said.

"Yeah."

"What on Earth are you two doing?" Annie was standing beside Uncle Jonathon, who was watching them while he sipped his drink.

"We're dancing," Doug said, not stopping.

"But you're not holding Jess." She seemed scandalized.

"You don't hold your partner with this dance. It's new." The song ended, and he put the needle back at the beginning.

"Can you believe how children are dancing now?" Annie asked Uncle Jonathon while the music started again.

"That's not dancing. And it's not music." With that, he turned and left the room.

"You two should come eat," Annie said. "Your dad won't want dinner to get cold."

"We'll come as soon as it's done," Doug said, and she left.

When the song ended, Jess was breathless and giddy. "I loved that," she said as they walked to the hallway.

"I know. As soon as I saw my friends doing it, I had to learn. I bet everyone at State will be doing it."

"You're probably right."

Doug was leaving for college in a week, and Jess could tell his excitement was growing by how much he brought it up. She was happy for him, but at the same time she was sad he was leaving. She would miss him.

"Do you want to dance some more after dinner?" Doug asked.

"Sure!"

The next day, Jess and Marty were under the willow tree in their swimsuits. They'd finished eating lunch, and Marty was lying on his side, taking a nap, but Jess wasn't tired. As the summer had worn on, she'd combated the monotony and boredom by swimming until she was exhausted and then reading late into the night. But today her restlessness was worse than normal.

"Hey." She put her hand on Marty's shoulder and jiggled him.

He lifted his arm and squinted at her with one eye.

"Get up. I want to show you a new dance."

He put his arm back over his eyes. "I don't dance."

"Come on, Marty." She jumped up. "It's real fun. Everyone's doing it."

He was trying not to smile. "Not everyone." He'd turned his refusal into a game.

She decided on a different tactic. Singing the opening line of "The Twist," she reached down to take his hand. Marty opened his eyes with surprise. While she sang the lyrics, she pulled and to her delight, he stood. From the way his brown eyes were glowing, she knew she had him. She continued singing and began swiveling her hips, her bare feet pivoting on the grass. Marty gaped as he watched her, but after a few minutes he still hadn't joined her.

"Try it. Move your hips," she said, continuing to dance.

He shook his head while he watched her. "They don't move like that."

"Try, Marty." Exasperated, she put her hands on his hips and tried to move them.

He barked out a laugh and jumped backwards. "You're tickling me!"

"If you don't do it, I'm going to tickle you for real."

"Okay," he said, laughing. "But I need music." From

The Boy in the Woods

the smirk on his face, she knew he was being difficult on purpose, but she was determined to get him to dance with her.

Starting at the beginning of the song, she sang while she danced the Twist. Marty made jerky motions with his body as if he was having a difficult time figuring out how to move. She had to work not to laugh, not wanting to discourage him. The longer they danced, he became better, although his movements were still awkward. Instead of enjoying it, he looked serious, as if he had to put all his concentration into moving his body.

As soon as she reached the end of the song, he stopped. "Can we quit? I'm tired."

"How can you be tired? I could do this all day, but, okay," she said, realizing it was a losing battle.

He dropped dramatically to the ground. "I'm going to need *two* naps now." He threw his arm over his eyes.

"Stop being such a baby." She sat beside him, and while she looked out at the water, her thoughts drifted. "I bet they have dances at college." She peered at him out of the corner of her eye, but he didn't move. "I bet they have them every weekend."

"I reckon."

"Will you ask me to go to them? And dance with me?"

"Maybe," he said with a shrug, but he was trying to hold back his smile.

She hugged her knees, imagining walking into college dances on Marty's arm. It was going to be the best.

Chapter Forty-Two
Let's Twist Again

JESS ENTERED THE cabin, and propped the door open. It was already getting hot, and she took a moment to wipe the sweat off her brow. Turning towards the kitchen, she saw a figure sitting in one of the chairs in front of the empty fireplace and stopped. "Marty?"

He was leaning forward with his head in his hands.

"I thought you were still at work."

"I didn't go to work," he muttered.

Knowing something was wrong, she knelt in front of him and he lifted his head. "Oh, Marty," she whispered, tears filling her eyes. His lower lip was split open and swollen, and his left eye had a deep purple bruise under it. But it was the anguish in his eyes that made her heart break. "What happened?"

"I thought he was asleep, but he was waiting for me."

"I'm so sorry." She caressed his cheek, wishing she could take away his pain. What kind of man would hurt his son like this? She started to stand. "I'll get a cold cloth for your swelling."

"Jess." He grasped her hand. "Don't go." He was struggling not to cry, and she hugged him. "He found it," he said, his voice cracking. "He found all of it."

"He found what?"

"The money, almost a hundred dollars. He took it all."

"Oh, no." She hugged him tighter.

"It was my college money."

"You can save more," she said, trying to give him hope. "You have enough time."

He shook his head against her shoulder. "No, Jess. I can't. He was mad I'd been holding out on him. He says I got to pay my own way now."

"What does that mean?"

"He says I got to pay him rent and help pay the bills. If I don't, he's going to throw me out. I ain't got nowhere else to go!"

"Marty, no." She couldn't believe this was happening, that his father had snatched away their plans. "Maybe I can find a cheap college. Then you wouldn't need to save as much, and in two years, you'd–"

He let go of her. "You don't get it. I can't make enough money to pay my old man making deliveries a few hours after school. I have to work full time."

"But you have to go back to school. You have to finish and graduate with me."

"I don't have a choice."

"What if you told your dad–"

"Do you think he cares about that?" he shouted. "I'll

The Boy in the Woods

be seventeen in two weeks. I told you no one in my family ever finished high school."

"But, Marty, what about your future? What about *our* future?"

"There is no future," he said in a flat voice.

"No!" She covered her face with her hands, sobbing.

"Please don't cry." He pulled her up and she climbed on his lap. "I'm sorry I said it like that."

"I don't want to leave without you."

"I know."

Jess continued to cry while Marty held her. After a while, her tears ran out.

"There has to be something we can do," she said, breaking the silence.

"I've tried to think of a way, but there isn't one. It was stupid for me to think I could go to college." Bitterness had crept into his words. "I'm going to be exactly like my old man, a worthless bum."

"Don't say that."

"I really liked school," he said, his voice lower.

She buried herself deeper in his arms. "I know you did."

"I should have never gotten my hopes up. I should have known it would never happen." He let go of her. "I have to leave."

"Where are you going?"

He tried to get up, but she stayed on his lap. "I have to tell Mr. Dwyer I'm quitting. My old man wants me to work for him at the filling station."

"You can't work with him! He hits you."

He looked at her, the pain back in his eyes. "Mr. Dwyer only needs me for deliveries. It's not enough to pay my old man."

She clung to him. This was too horrible. "Marty, please don't quit."

"I don't have any choice. Come on, Jess." He took hold of her arms and lifted her up.

When he stood, she took his hand. "I want to walk with you." To her relief, he didn't object.

On the way to the fence, she tried to think of someway to save him. He couldn't work with a man who beat him and stole his money. It would break his spirit.

"I'll see you, Jess," he said, when they'd reached the trees at the edge of the fence. His head hung low. He already seemed broken.

She hugged him, trying to comfort him back to being whole. "Don't give up hope yet. We'll figure something out."

He pulled her arms off him and turned to leave, disappearing through the brush without a backward glance. She moved a branch aside and watched him climb the fence. Once he dropped to the ground on the other side, he headed down the two-lane highway, shoulders hunched. She stepped out of the bushes and went to the fence, pressing her face against the iron bars. She didn't turn away until she could no longer see him.

As Marty trudged towards town, he tried not to think, but the sick feeling in his stomach wouldn't go away. His old man had ruined everything, but he was angry at himself too. He should never have brought his money home. It was as dumb as him thinking he could go to college. His dad had told him he was worthless his whole life and he was right. Wealthy people like Jess could do whatever they wanted, but his course was set the moment he was born. There was no use trying to fight it.

When he reached town, he kept his head down and didn't make eye contact with anyone he passed. A woman pushing a stroller gasped when she saw him, and he ducked into an alley. The day was already bad enough, he didn't want to be the town freak on top of it. When he reached the back door of the drugstore, he paused before entering. He wasn't looking forward to his talk with Mr. Dwyer.

The backroom was empty, and he waited. Mr. Dwyer wouldn't want people in the store to see him. While he waited, he looked around, but when his eyes passed over the wall of chemicals and medicines, it was too painful and he turned away.

"Marty! Where have you been?"

Mr. Dwyer sounded angry and Marty was glad. It would make what he had to do easier. He turned and Mr. Dwyer stopped short, his eyes registering shock.

"Who did that to you?"

"My old man."

Mr. Dwyer's face darkened. Marty looked at the floor. There wasn't anything Mr. Dwyer or anyone else could do about it. It was just the way things were.

"Let me get something for that cut," Mr. Dwyer said after a minute.

"I don't need anything, I came to tell you – I came to tell you I'm not coming back. I'm working somewhere else now."

Mr. Dwyer's eyes widened, but then his face became impassive. "I see." He leaned against the table where he filled the orders. "Where are you going to work?"

Marty didn't know why he was having such a hard time meeting Mr. Dwyer's gaze. "With my old man at the filling station."

"Is that what you want?"

"I ain't got no choice. I got to pay my old man rent."

"So you need to work more hours." Mr. Dwyer said it like a statement instead of a question.

Marty shrugged. "Yeah."

"What about school?"

"I'm quitting. I have to support myself." Marty hated how weak it made him look, his old man forcing him to quit the two things he loved most: his job and school. But if his old man threw him out, there was no place for him to go. The laws against vagrants in town were strictly enforced. He'd have to hit the road like his brother Stevie. He could imagine how bad it would be; sleeping under bridges, finding work when he could, starving when he couldn't. Even if working with his old man would be hard, at least he'd have a roof over his head, and he wouldn't lose Jess. She was the only good thing he had left in his life.

He heard Mr. Dwyer let out a breath, but he didn't look up. He didn't need to see the pity in his boss's eyes.

"You don't have to work for *that man*," Mr. Dwyer said, spitting out the last two words. "I'll give you more hours."

"No, sir. You already have Mrs. Schmidt. I know you can't pay both of us."

The Boy in the Woods

"Don't tell me what I can and can't do! You don't know that."

Marty met his anger with a glare. "I ain't taking a handout because you feel sorry for me."

Mr. Dwyer came away from the table. "Look, son. Mrs. Schmidt told me she wanted to work less a while ago. I asked her to wait until you graduated and could take on more duties. You're a hard worker, the best I've had in long while. There's a job here if you want it, son. This isn't a handout. It's *been* yours."

Marty opened his mouth and then closed it, stunned into silence.

"I can't keep this place running forever. I'll have to pass it on to someone, and with my boy gone–" He stopped and cleared his throat as he looked away. When he faced Marty, his eyes were red. "I've been thinking on it for a while now. I want you to take over this place for me someday. Will you stay, son?"

Marty swallowed. He'd had no idea Mr. Dwyer was considering giving him the drugstore. The night before, his world had come crashing down when he stepped into his house and his old man sucker punched him. For the first time since that moment, there was a tiny spark of hope inside him. What Mr. Dwyer was offering would solve everything. Then the spark vanished. "It won't work. I have to quit school, and without the learning I'll never be able to–"

"Let's not worry about that now," Mr. Dwyer said. "Maybe it'll take you longer to get your schooling done, but we've got years before you take over the store." He approached Marty, his hand held out. "Is it a deal, son?"

Marty stared at Mr. Dwyer's hand. The offer reminded him of the moment Jess had asked him about going to college. A world of possibilities had opened up for him that day, a future he'd never considered before, and it had changed him. He felt like he could accomplish anything. When it was ripped away, it gutted him. What if that happened again? His old man was expecting him to work at the filling station. If he didn't, his life at home could be made a whole lot worse. He didn't want to have his dream stolen from him all over again.

But when he lifted his head to tell Mr. Dwyer no, he saw something in the man's eyes he'd never seen in his own father's. Mr. Dwyer was fighting for him. *He cared.* There'd been so few people in his life who cared about him. "I don't know if I can, Mr. Dwyer. My old man might throw me out if I don't work at the filling station with him."

Mr. Dwyer frowned. "If he does, you'd still have a job here. I reckon you'd make enough you could rent a room in town."

The sick feeling in Marty's stomach eased as he realized it was true. He grasped Mr. Dwyer's hand. "Alright. It's a deal."

Mr. Dwyer smiled. "That's good, son. That's real good."

Chapter Forty-Three
Only the Lonely (Know How I Feel)

"JESS, WE'RE HERE," Annie said.

Jess closed her book and lifted her head. Doug was moving into his college dorm today, and she and Annie were in the black car, following Doug's car as he drove with Uncle Jonathon.

Annie strained to take in the large buildings of the university campus from the car window. "It looks so big."

Young men and women walked in groups or lounged together on the grass, enjoying the late summer weather. All of them looked happy and excited, and it made Jess's heart ache. She imagined her and Marty among them, walking out in the open together for the first time. Except now it would never happen since he couldn't graduate high school with her.

"What if Doug gets lost?" Annie said, her eyes filled with worry.

"He won't get lost. Doug will learn his way around like the other students."

Annie had been excited to help Doug get ready to move to college. But as the day of his departure grew closer, she'd become more emotional. Jess knew how she felt. She was sad he was moving away too.

"This must be his dormitory," Annie said when James pulled into a parking lot.

In front of them was a four-story brick building covered with ivy. The lot was filled with cars and more were parked on the grass. Everywhere, parents and students were pulling suitcases and trunks out of them.

"It's so big," Annie repeated as all of them got out of the cars. "What if you get lost?"

"Annie, I told you I'm going to be fine," Doug said. "I don't want you to worry about me."

"But it's your first time–"

"I'll be okay."

"I want to see what the dorm room looks like," Uncle Jonathon said through his teeth. "It better not be a dump."

"Dad," Doug said, exasperated. "It's not going to be a dump."

"You don't know that. They assign you a room, sight unseen. And who knows what kind of a person they've stuck you with for a roommate?"

"Dad, please."

"You should have had a choice, Douglas."

"That's how they do it for everyone."

Uncle Jonathon opened his mouth and Jess knew he was about to insist they weren't like everyone but Doug spoke again.

"I'm sure it'll be alright. Please don't make a scene,

okay?"

"If you insist, but if it's not up to par, the president and the board of regents will be receiving a very strongly worded letter."

Doug sighed and picked up his trunk. "Let's go."

With Doug leading the way, they carried his luggage into the dorm and climbed a crowded stairwell to the second floor. Walking down the hall, Jess heard male voices and music playing. She couldn't see her uncle's face as he walked ahead of her, but she hoped listening to rock and roll records wasn't something that warranted a strongly worded letter.

Doug went through a doorway, and when Jess walked in, she was relieved. The room was spare with two twin beds, two desks, and two dressers, but it looked clean and well kept. The walls were freshly painted and cheerful red and blue plaid curtains matched the plaid bedspreads on the beds.

"Hello," Doug said.

A young man in horn-rimmed glasses stood from the bed closest to the window. He was dressed in khaki trousers and a white button-down shirt with a tie. Surely Uncle Jonathon would approve of him.

"You must be my roommate." He approached while Doug set down his trunk. "Cornelius Steiner the third, but everyone calls me Con."

"Doug Blackwell," Doug said with a smile, shaking his hand.

There was a flicker of recognition in the boy's eyes when he heard Doug's name.

"This is my dad," Doug stepped out of the way so Con could shake hands with his father.

"Is your family associated with Steiner's department

stores?" Uncle Jonathon asked.

"Uh, yes, sir. They are." Con pushed up his glasses while his smile drooped. He didn't like being recognized for what his family did either.

"This is Jess," Doug said, breaking the silence.

Con came forward to shake her hand. "Sister? Or..." He raised an eyebrow, and Jess realized he was asking if she was Doug's girlfriend.

"I'm Doug's cousin."

His eyes lit up. "You're a *cousin*." He was shaking her hand longer than was necessary, all the while giving her a toothy smile. It made her uncomfortable.

"This is Ann – I mean, Miss Montgomery," Doug said.

Con let go of Jess and she moved out of reach, grateful Doug had come to her rescue again.

With the introductions over, Annie unpacked Doug's things and Jess helped her, hoping she'd appear too busy to carry on a conversation with Con. While they worked, Uncle Jonathon left to inspect the communal bathroom and the boys talked about classes and fraternities.

When the last suitcase was emptied and Doug's bed made, the family stood by, waiting. Noticing them, Doug broke off his discussion. "I guess it's time for you to leave."

It was quiet. No one wanted to be the first to say goodbye.

"I'll go see what they're serving for dinner," Con said, perhaps sensing an emotional family scene was about to occur.

"You won't forget to wear a hat when the weather gets cool," Annie said after Con left. "Winter will be here before you know it and you'll catch a cold."

Doug gave her a bemused smile. "I'll remember."

"Be sure to get enough sleep, and don't forget to eat. You need to keep your strength up."

"Stop smothering the boy," Uncle Jonathon said, but for once his tone was soft.

"Don't worry," Doug said. "I'll be fine."

He hugged Annie, and when he let go, she pulled a handkerchief from her purse and dabbed at her eyes, but she was beaming.

"Dad." Doug extended his hand.

Uncle Jonathon was silent while he shook it. He looked like he was working hard to control his emotions.

Then Doug turned to Jess. Looking up into his eyes, Jess's throat hurt. "Bye, Doug," she whispered.

"Hey." He put his arms around her, and she squeezed her eyes shut while she hugged him. "You know I'll be seeing you soon, and I'll call you in a couple days. Check to see how you're holding up."

She nodded into his chest, breathing in his aftershave.

"I'll see all of you soon." He let go of her.

"Let's go," Uncle Jonathon said, his voice gruff, and left the room.

Annie put her hand on Doug's arm, then followed him. Doug looked at Jess, his face full of emotion. She gave him an encouraging smile before she left.

Back at the black car, James opened the door for them and Jess climbed in first. After Annie had slid across the seat to join her, Uncle Jonathon got in and the door was slammed shut. That's when Annie broke down. She sobbed into her

The Boy in the Woods

handkerchief while Jess rubbed her arm, trying to comfort her. She wondered if Uncle Jonathon would say something to Annie, but he looked out the side window, keeping his face hidden.

"Thanks, pumpkin," Annie said after she'd recovered, but as they drove, she continued to wipe her eyes. Jess leaned against her window, her heart hurting for her whole family.

When a bump in the road jostled her, she blinked her eyes open. She must have fallen asleep. As she straightened, she saw Annie yank her hand out of Uncle Jonathon's and a jolt went through her. She turned to gaze out the window, pretending she hadn't noticed while her mind reeled.

They were driving down the two-lane highway through their town. She must have been asleep for hours, and even though it seemed impossible, Annie and Uncle Jonathon were holding hands. How did that happen? Annie would never dare to take his hand on her own. Had he decided to comfort her after all? Or was it because he needed *her* to comfort *him*? Jess wondered, anger bubbling up. It was just like him to be that selfish. Annie wouldn't hesitate to hold his hand if he let her know he wanted it, but when she'd been crying earlier, he hadn't given her one kind word.

James pulled up in front of the gate and stopped the car.

"I'm hungry enough to eat a horse," Annie said, while he unlocked the gate. She was smiling at Jess, and although her face was lined with exhaustion, the sadness in her eyes had lessened. "How about you?"

"I'm hungry too."

James climbed back in the car.

"Don't bother locking the gate," Uncle Jonathon said.

"Yes, sir," James said.

The Boy in the Woods

"When you get to the house, leave the engine running. It won't take me long to be ready to go."

"You're going somewhere?" Annie said.

"I'm going to the office," Uncle Jonathon said, his eyes on the drive ahead.

"What about dinner?"

"Don't wait for me. I'll send my girl out for something."

Annie dropped her head. "Oh."

Hearing the disappointment in her voice, an awful realization hit Jess like a fist to her chest. Annie was in love with her uncle. A flood of memories came to Jess. Conversations between Annie and Uncle Jonathon, only now they were shown in a different light. Annie had been in love with him for a long time, long before Jess had come to live with them.

Turning to face her window, Jess felt sick. She didn't *want* Annie to be in love with Uncle Jonathon. It was wrong. Not because Annie was a servant or poor, but because he treated her so terribly. How many times had Jess witnessed him bullying her, shouting orders at her, humiliating her? And she'd excused his behavior over and over. He didn't deserve her love, nor would he ever love her back. For him, Annie would never be worthy enough.

Once out of the car, Uncle Jonathon headed to the front door, and Annie turned to Jess. "I'll heat up the leftovers from Doug's dinner."

Her sadness had returned, and Jess cringed. "I'll just have a sandwich, if that's okay?" It would take the least amount of time to prepare.

"Sure, pumpkin."

They ate roast chicken sandwiches and cold gelatin salad at the kitchen table in silence. When the dishes were washed and put away, Jess gave Annie a good night hug, and then went up the backstairs.

The low sun cast long shadows on the walls of her bedroom. Knowing Doug was now living hours away from home, the house felt empty. Standing behind her desk, she looked out the bay window at the woods beyond the garage. Marty would be there now. She wished she could see him. It had been a trying day, and she didn't get to spend as much time with him now that he worked until late afternoon most days.

Then she noticed the garage doors were closed. James hadn't returned after taking her uncle to the office. That meant she and Annie were the only ones home. It was a risk to sneak out at this hour, but what harm could come from it? Annie already knew she visited the cabin. If she was gone for no more than an hour, she'd be back long before her uncle returned home.

Heart racing, she eased her bedroom door open and crept down the stairs. Once outside, she darted across the yard and headed down the path. The cabin door was open, but Marty wasn't there, so she hurried to the pond.

Marty was under the willow tree, leaning against its trunk and eating his peanut butter and jelly sandwich when he noticed her.

He jumped up. "What are you doing here?"

"Everything's fine. Annie's the only one home tonight and I really wanted to see you."

"Oh." He frowned at the sandwich in his hand.

"Go ahead and finish. I ate already," she said, not wanting him to think he had to share. She hadn't asked about his money situation, not wanting to pry, but she worried he

The Boy in the Woods

didn't have enough money for food now that he had to give part of his wages to his dad.

Marty sat back at the base of the tree, and she joined him. It was the latest she'd ever been out with him and in the still air the water was like glass, except for the ripples caused by fish breaking the surface to catch low-flying bugs. She tried to take comfort in being there on such a beautiful evening, but her thoughts were overwhelmed by the events of that day.

She was dying to talk to Marty about it all, but she didn't know if it was a good idea. He most likely wouldn't understand how she could be sad that Doug was gone since he didn't like him. And bringing up the fact that her cousin was at college would only remind Marty that his dad had crushed his dream to go. She didn't know if he could empathize with how awful it was to learn of Annie's feelings for her uncle, but she didn't want to betray Annie by disclosing her secret.

"How was your day?" she said when he'd finished his second sandwich.

He shrugged. "It was okay." He folded his sack and smoothed it flat on his leg. As sad as she was, she felt worse for Marty. He'd been ecstatic when he'd shared the news about Mr. Dwyer offering the drugstore to him. But in the days that followed, he wasn't interested in doing any of their usual activities.

At first she'd thought he was tired from working longer hours, but it soon became clear it was more serious. His dad had taken more than his money, he'd stolen Marty's plans to graduate with Jess. It was certain now, she'd be leaving him in two short years.

She laced her fingers through Marty's, but he pulled his hand away so he could put his arm around her. She leaned against him, and while they held each other, Jess's heart ached for both of them.

Chapter Forty-Four
It's Now or Never

September 1960

SOMEONE WAS SHAKING Jess's shoulder, and she moved away, wanting to sleep more.

"Come on, Jess. You have to wake up," Annie said. "You slept through your alarm."

Jess blinked her eyes open. "I did?"

Annie straightened and crossed her arms. "You've been sleeping in so late these last few days, I was afraid this might happen. I suppose you were reading when you should have been sleeping last night."

"Yes, ma'am," Jess lied. The truth was she'd been tossing and turning for the last several nights.

"You know it's not a good idea to stay up late when today's the first day of school." Annie dropped her arms with a sigh. "You'd better hurry. You don't want to keep your uncle waiting."

"Yes, ma'am," she grumbled. She wasn't looking

forward to eating breakfast alone with him.

She'd expected her uncle would miss Doug, but he seemed to be having a much harder time coping than her and Annie. He left for work early in the morning, before she got up, and returned home late in the evening, long after she and Annie had eaten dinner.

After dressing, she went to the bathroom to brush her hair. Looking at her reflection in the mirror, she was dismayed by the dark circles under her eyes, the evidence of her sleepless nights. She set her brush down, hoping the solution she'd come up with would work.

"Good morning, Uncle Jonathon," she said with trepidation when she entered the dining room.

He didn't look up from his newspaper. "Jessica."

Once seated, she glanced up at her uncle. He had dark circles under his eyes too. Annie entered with a tray holding their breakfasts.

"Do you need more coffee?" she asked Uncle Jonathon when she set down his plate.

He lifted his head with annoyance. "What?"

"More coffee?"

"No."

"Alright, but if you do, I have more in the pot."

He grunted, already back to his reading.

Jess dropped her head and cut into her eggs so she wouldn't see the disappointment in Annie's face. As she ate her breakfast, she looked at Doug's chair, feeling his loss. Was this what it would be like for the next two years? Silent meals while her uncle ignored her?

Uncle Jonathon refolded his newspaper and checked

his watch. "Hurry *up*, Jessica. We're leaving in five minutes."

"Yes, sir." She leaned over her plate while her stomach twisted. She'd known she would be driven to school by James. But until that moment, she hadn't realized she'd be riding with Uncle Jonathon.

When they were ready to leave, she followed him outside, carrying her sack lunch and purse. James was waiting in the driveway, standing beside the open car door. It was ridiculous that he was required to open the car door for them. It wasn't like they couldn't open it themselves, but she kept her thoughts to herself.

Uncle Jonathon climbed in after her and snapped open his paper. Jess looked out her window, the silence pressing on her. For the first time in her life, she wasn't excited about the first day of school.

Even though it had been hard to attend school with Marty while pretending she didn't know him, it would be a hundred times worse not seeing him at all. But as bad as she felt, she couldn't imagine what he must be going through. Instead of getting dressed and starting his second to last year of high school, he was going to work.

James drove the car up to the front entrance of the school and parked at the curb. The teens standing outside all turned to gape. Embarrassed by the attention the black car was drawing, Jess reached for the door handle, wanting to get out so James could drive away.

"Jessica," Uncle Jonathon hissed. "What are you doing? You will *wait* for James."

She dropped her hand. "Yes, sir."

By the time James reached the door, everyone outside was watching. With her face flaming, Jess clutched her notebook to her chest and climbed out, feeling every pair of eyes on her. Walking to the front steps of the school, she kept her attention on the sidewalk to avoid the stares.

"Jess, wait."

She lifted her head to find her friend. Louise ran to Jess and gave her a hug.

When she let go, Jess beamed at her. "Look at your hair."

Louise patted it with her hand. "Do you like it?"

"I love it!"

Her red curls were cut shorter and shaped into the latest poufy hairstyle.

"Who knew having curly hair would end up being a good thing?" Louise said with a laugh.

Jess opened her purse. "Let's see what classes we have together."

"Oh, no," Louise said when they compared their cards. "We only have one class together, English composition."

"Why are you taking bookkeeping and typing?" Jess asked, surveying Louise's list of classes. Most of them were business classes.

"So I can help my parents at the restaurant. I'm going to learn how to do their bookkeeping so they don't have to pay someone."

"That's a good idea."

"Why are you taking all those hard classes? Advanced algebra? And physics? You're crazy."

"I need to take those if I'm going to college."

Louise's smile fell. "Oh, yeah. I forgot."

The bell rang, and the two of them moved forward

The Boy in the Woods

with the crowd of students. Jess thought about how different Louise's plans were from hers. Louise had no intention of going any further than high school. She'd stay in the same town she'd grown up in, working at her parent's restaurant, living at home until she married, and then raising a family of her own. Jess couldn't imagine doing that.

Her morning with Uncle Jonathon had confirmed her intention to leave town as soon as she was able. But if her parents were still alive, would she and Louise be that different? Seeing the working women of Manhattan in their smart business outfits had inspired her own dreams of having a career, but with all the universities to choose from in the city, she probably would have lived at home while taking classes.

After saying goodbye to Louise in the hallway, Jess went to her homeroom. She waved to a few friends, but while she waited for the morning announcements, she couldn't help thinking of Marty. The two previous years she'd watched the door with excitement to see if he would be the next person walking in. That would never happen again.

As the day wore on, she went to classes, received textbooks, and wrote down assignments. Through it all, Marty's absence was foremost in her mind. He didn't pass her in the hallways, he wasn't seated in the back of her classes, and he didn't walk through the lunch room while she ate with the usual gang of girls. Wherever she was, no matter what she was doing, she was reminded of him.

When the last bell rang, she found Louise at their lockers.

"You know what?" Louise said. "I haven't seen Marty Cappellini all day. Is he in any of your classes?"

"No." Jess avoided looking at her by taking her textbooks from her locker and stacking them on her arm.

"That's weird. I wonder what happened to him?"

"Yeah, me too." Jess slammed her locker shut and headed for the exit.

Louise rushed to catch up to her. "I hope that doesn't mean he's not coming back. Now that Doug isn't here anymore, the two of you could have talked and gotten to know each other."

Jess halted and stared at Louise. Could that be true? She'd never considered the possibility she and Marty could have been open about their friendship with Doug no longer attending high school. "I don't think so," she said, shaking her head as another thought came to her. "Janet White's dad works for my uncle. I'm sure she'd mention it if she saw me talking to Marty, and then my uncle would hear about it."

"You're probably right. I wouldn't put it past her." Louise held the door open for her. "I guess I'll see you…" She stopped walking and her mouth dropped open.

Jess faced the direction Louise was looking, and groaned. James was standing at attention outside the black car, the back door held open. He stuck out like a sore thumb among the teens, who all stared as they passed him.

"See you tomorrow, Louise," Jess said, heat rising to her cheeks.

"Yeah. Tomorrow," Louise said, still focused on James.

Jess hurried to the car with her head down. Once she'd climbed in, James closed the door. Louise was still in the same spot, staring at her, and Jess forced a smile and waved while James started the engine. As soon as Louise was out of sight, Jess collapsed against the seat. *Could this day get any worse?*

The Boy in the Woods

"Uh, James." She forced a smile while he glared at her in the rear view mirror. "You don't need to bother opening the door for me when you pick me up. I don't mind opening it myself."

"And have yer uncle sack me for not doin' a proper job? I think not!"

Gritting her teeth, she thought again about how much she hated the man. When Doug was home next summer, she'd have him give her more driving lessons. And as soon as she was on her own, she was buying a car. James would never drive her again.

In her bedroom, Jess took her time changing into a pair of jeans and a flannel shirt. As much as she wanted to see Marty, she was dreading it at the same time. He'd been down for days, but today was bound to be worse. For someone who loved school as much as he did, being forced to stop going was cruel.

But there was something else she'd been agonizing over. She had homework assignments that needed to be completed, and Marty didn't. If she brought her school books to the cabin, it would be like twisting a knife into him. Even if she didn't bring them, he'd be sure to notice. Homework had been such a big part of their time together during the school year, and the absence of it was going to hurt him.

The worst part about it was that from now on she'd be moving forward in her life while Marty would be stuck where he was. It was that thought that had tortured her for the last several nights while she'd lain in bed, unable to sleep.

When she walked down the backstairs, the basket was on the counter and Annie was at the table shelling peas. "You should be back in time for dinner."

"I will."

"Even though your uncle hasn't called yet, he still

might come home."

"I know," Jess said, her back to Annie.

She took the basket and went out the door, not wanting to continue the conversation, or see Annie's sad eyes. It was clear Annie was hurt by Uncle Jonathon staying at the office for such long hours. She kept saying how worried she was about him, making Jess feel awful. How could she have never noticed Annie's feelings for him before? They were obvious now.

A cool wind picked up and dark clouds raced across the sky. Jess hurried her pace, hoping it wouldn't rain. She entered the empty cabin, closed the door, and set her textbooks on the kitchen counter, wondering how bad Marty's reaction might be when he saw them. She was setting the last of the food out on the table when she heard the front door open, but she didn't turn around. Instead, she folded the dishcloth that lined the basket while Marty crossed the living room.

"Jess."

She faced him. "Hi, Marty."

He was standing in the entryway, his face grim as he eyed her stack of textbooks.

Her heart ached for him. "Are you hungry?"

He shrugged, tearing his eyes away from the books.

"It's meatloaf sandwiches today." She sat on her stool.

He joined her at the table. "How was school?" he asked, not making a move to take any of the food.

"Terrible."

He lifted his head, his eyes stormy.

"I really missed you." Her voice wavered and she

swallowed. Now was not the time to break down. "I made a decision last night."

He glared at the food. "Yeah? What was that?"

"You're going to do homework with me."

He looked up at her with incredulity. "What's the point of that?"

"The point is, I don't want to continue on with my schooling without you. We're going to learn together like we always have."

She held her breath while his brown eyes searched hers. How much of a fight was he going to put up?

Then his expression changed. "I ain't got no say in this, do I?" He tried to keep from smiling, but the corners of his mouth twitched.

"Nope, so there's no use arguing," Jess said, keeping her tone serious, but inside she was rejoicing.

"What were you going to do if I said no?"

"Refuse to do my homework."

He shook his head. "Wow. You sure don't fool around." It was the most animated she'd seen him in days.

"We started high school together, and we're going to finish it together."

He picked up a sandwich, still shaking his head. "You and Mr. Dwyer."

"What about Mr. Dwyer?"

"He gave me some old chemistry books," said Marty, unwrapping his sandwich. "He says I got to start studying. He's even going to give me tests."

Jess grinned. "What a good idea. I'm going to give you tests too."

"Aw, gee, I shouldn't have said that."

Jess laughed. "Too late!"

Chapter Forty-Five
Swingin' School

October 1960

"HE'S HERE!"

Jess looked up from the bowl of boiled potatoes she was mashing and saw Doug's car drive past the kitchen window.

"Just in time," Annie said, beaming.

Jess and Annie took off their aprons and hurried down the hallway. They reached the front door as Doug walked in.

"Doug." Jess lunged at him. His chuckle rumbled in his chest, tickling her ear while she hugged him.

"Miss me?" he asked, once she'd let go.

"Yes." Even though he'd called her often, it was still hard not having him home.

"We've all missed you." Annie was gazing at him as if she hadn't seen him in years.

"Hi Annie," he said. His face lit up when Uncle

Jonathon appeared in the doorway of the grand parlor. "Dad."

"Douglas," Uncle Jonathon said, looking just as happy. He reached out to grasp his son's hand. "How are they treating you at that school?"

"They're treating me fine."

"You look thinner," Annie said. "I don't think they're feeding you enough."

"He isn't thinner," Uncle Jonathon said. "You're looking well, son. Very well, indeed."

For once, Jess agreed with her uncle. Even though he'd only been home for a few minutes, Jess noticed a change in Doug. The way he carried himself was different. He seemed more self-assured, more mature.

"We're going to have a good dinner tonight," Annie said. "Jess and I made all your favorites."

"They feed us well, but they can't compete with your home cooking, Annie. I've missed it."

Annie practically melted in front of them. "It's almost ready. Come on, Jess. Let's get back to work."

In the kitchen, Jess returned to the bowl of potatoes, but Annie brought her a stack of plates. "You set the table. I'll finish this and get the food in the serving dishes."

Jess noticed the number of plates in her hand. "You're eating with us?"

Annie's face was alight. "I asked your uncle, and he said it was okay."

"Doug will like that," Jess said, returning her smile, but it dropped when she went into the dining room.

She was glad Annie was taking her rightful place at the table as a part of the family, but she shouldn't have to beg for it. She wondered once again why Annie would love someone when he considered her beneath him.

With everyone seated at the table, Doug said, "This looks great. Better than anything they've been giving me at school." Jess had to work hard to suppress a smile. He'd said it for Annie's benefit, knowing how much it would mean to her.

It was one of those rare nights when Uncle Jonathon was in as good a mood as the rest of them. Between bites, Doug talked about his classes, his professors, rushing fraternities, and the new friends he'd made. It was obvious that college life agreed with him. Jess was happy he was having such a good time, but it was bittersweet. Marty would have thrived at college too.

"Your roommate seemed nice. Are you getting along with him?" Annie asked when they were finishing their apple pie.

"Con? Yeah, he's a fun fellow. We've rushed all the same fraternities, and we let them know they'd better bid for both of us because we'll only join together."

"You should invite him to come here for your birthday."

Doug appeared as startled by the suggestion as Jess was. "Uh, I'm not sure," he said. "He's from the city. He'd be bored by our little town." When his eyes shifted to Jess, she knew he'd said it for her sake. He hadn't missed Con's interest in her when they'd met in his dorm room. By keeping him away, he was saving her from a weekend of rebuffing Con's unwanted advances.

"Are you sure?" Annie said. "I can fix up the spare bedroom for him."

"I need Douglas at the office when he's here," Uncle Jonathon said. "He won't have time to entertain the boy."

Annie lowered her head. "I hadn't thought of that."

"It was a good idea, though," Doug said. "Dinner was the best, Annie."

Annie smiled. "I'm glad you liked it."

Doug stood. "I'm going to head into town for a while."

Jess looked up at him with hope, but he was gazing at his father.

"I want to say hi to a few friends and catch up."

"Don't be out too late," Uncle Jonathon said. "We'll be heading to the office first thing in the morning."

"I won't."

Jess gathered the dishes from the table, disheartened. Since Doug had been gone, she'd missed their trips into town. Maybe he'd forgotten he promised to take her out when he came home. Or maybe he'd decided he didn't want to when seeing his friends was more fun.

"Jess," Doug said. He was at the doorway leading to the hallway. "Want to catch a show after dinner tomorrow?"

"Sure," Jess said.

He grinned. "Cool."

The next day, while she waited for Marty to arrive at the cabin, Jess copied her notes so she'd be ready for him. Now that he was working longer shifts, she could only see him for a few hours and she hated it. With both boys away more than she was used to, the restlessness she usually felt during the summer had persisted into the school year. At least that weekend wouldn't be as bad as most. She was looking forward to going out with Doug later that night, and then she'd be with Marty all day tomorrow since the drugstore was closed on Sundays.

The Boy in the Woods

"It's getting chilly out there," Marty said when he walked into the cabin.

"I know. I started the cookstove a while ago."

"Good." He took off his jacket and laid it on a chair.

"I have to get back early today since Doug is home," Jess said. "But I have everything ready."

"Okay."

He took his place at the table and reached for a sandwich. She pulled her stool close to him while he ate and went over her notes, not wanting to waste any of the little time they had together. They'd worked out a system where she gave him an overview of her lessons while she was with him and then she'd leave the books she didn't need at the cabin so he could do the assignments in the evening after she left.

Marty threw himself into his schoolwork like never before. It was as if the chance to study after his dad had forced him to quit had lit a fire in him. Instead of his dad defeating him, he was determined to get his education as a way to defeat his dad. More importantly to Jess, focusing on the lessons made Marty's sadness disappear.

Marty got up for a mug of water. "Mr. Dwyer's having me make some of his compounds now."

Jess stretched the kinks out of her back. "That's real good, Marty."

"He reckons I could make all of them eventually."

"I'm sure he's glad to have that extra help." Jess looked at her watch. "I better leave."

"So soon?"

She could hear the longing in his voice. "I'll be here early tomorrow, and since Doug will be leaving, I can stay a little longer."

"Okay," Marty said, but his expression let her know he was disappointed.

When Jess and Doug walked out of the house for their trip into town, Jess noticed James wasn't waiting for them. Doug started the car and headed down the drive. When they reached the towering gate, Doug put the car in park and got out. Jess watched him go to the gate, pulling a set of keys out of his pocket to unlock the padlock.

"You have a key to the gate?" she said after he'd climbed back in the car.

"Yeah, Dad gave it to me when I went to college, that way I don't have to stop somewhere on the way home to call James." Past the gate, he stopped and got out to lock it behind them.

When he got in and pulled out onto the dirt road, Jess faced him. "Do you think I could have one too?"

He cast a sideways glance at her. "Uh, I don't know."

"Please, Doug. I promise I'd be careful with it. I wouldn't lose it or anything."

"I don't think Dad will allow it."

Jess crossed her arms over her chest with a huff. "Of course he won't."

"I'm sorry, Jess. He doesn't want to take a chance on anything happening to you."

"He doesn't care about me, he just doesn't want me to have any fun."

"That's not true. It's not safe for you to be out walking the roads by yourself. You'd be a target. Someone could kidnap you."

She scoffed. "That would never happen."

"You don't know that."

"What about you? Someone could kidnap *you*, Doug."

"I'm a grown man. I can take care of myself."

Jess let out an exasperated sigh.

"I don't want anything to happen to you either."

"I know," she said to the window.

"How are things going? With Dad, I mean?"

"Okay, I guess," she said with a shrug. "I don't see him except in the morning when I go to school."

"Why's that?" Doug asked, frowning.

"He's at work most of the time. Usually it's just me and Annie at dinner time."

"Oh." It was clear this was unexpected news.

"He misses you a lot. They both do." She studied him, wondering if he knew about Annie and his dad. She was dying to discuss it with him, but if he didn't already know, she didn't want to be the one to tell him. The news had been a shock to her, and she didn't want to do that to him.

"I knew it would be hard on him," Doug said. "But I didn't think it would be that bad."

Jess regretted not softening the information. She didn't want to make him feel guilty about being away at college. He should enjoy it and not worry about his dad.

"How has it been between the two of you, though?" Doug said. "That's what I meant."

"He's been okay," Jess said, surprised Doug had brought it up. "Like I said, I hardly see him."

"I talked to him about you. I said he shouldn't be so hard on you."

"Thanks, but you know he'll never accept me." She didn't need to see the confirmation in his eyes to know he believed it too, but at least he had the decency to look ashamed. "It's okay. I'm used to it by now."

"I don't think it's right that he treats you that way."

"I know you don't. You and Annie do a lot to make up for it. You make me feel like I'm a part of the family."

Doug gave her a grateful smile, but his eyes were still filled with shame.

On Monday, Jess took her time putting her papers in her notebook at the end of Mr. Taylor's advanced algebra class. When the last students filed out, she approached his desk. "Mr. Taylor?"

"Yes," he said.

"I wanted to ask you a question. What if someone couldn't continue with school because of family problems, but they kept up with their studies. Could they take the final exams?"

He stood and went to his filing cabinet. "That would be highly unlikely. I can't imagine anyone could keep up without attending school."

"But what if they *did?* If they could pass their final exams, couldn't they move up to the next grade?"

Mr. Taylor opened the top drawer of the cabinet and took out a paper sack. "I've never heard of anyone doing it that way."

"But if it's the only way they could graduate, they should be able to, right?"

The Boy in the Woods

He examined her. "Are you helping this person?"

Jess hesitated. She didn't want to say anything that might lead to someone finding out about Marty. But she needed the answer. "Yes, sir," she said, and held her breath.

"Now it makes sense." He sat back behind his desk.

"What do you mean?"

"Most girls can't do higher math, but since you've been teaching it to someone else, it's helping you learn it too."

While he opened his lunch sack, she was awash in relief. He wasn't going to demand a name. "So someone could take their final exams if they've been keeping up?"

"It is theoretically possible for someone to take their exams and move on to the next grade, but Principal Petersen would have to approve the plan. You'll have to ask him."

"Here you are, Jess," Louise said, appearing in the doorway, and then stopped short. "I'm sorry. I didn't realize you were getting help."

"We're all done," Jess said. "Thank you, Mr. Taylor, I'll do that."

He waved her out, biting into his apple.

"What was that about?" Louise said on the way to their lockers.

Jess didn't want to lie to her friend again. "I was asking about final exams."

"They're coming up fast."

"Yes, they are," Jess said, thinking about how little time Marty had.

While the girls chatted around her at their lunch table, Jess thought about how difficult the next step would be. There was no way she could approach Principal Petersen about the exams. That would lead to him finding out about her friendship with Marty. The only one who could ask for permission was Marty, which meant she had to figure out a way to convince him. Then he'd have to be persuasive enough for Principal Petersen to give him a chance. She sighed as the elation she'd felt a moment ago ebbed away. There were so many ways it could fail.

That afternoon, Jess and Marty were wrapped in wool blankets, sitting side by side at the kitchen table so they could read her world history book.

"Ready for the next page?" Marty asked.

"Not yet."

Marty helped himself to one of Annie's oatmeal cookies. Using the opportunity, Jess reached for one as well. He turned the page to continue reading.

"What if there was a way for you to pass the eleventh grade?"

His brow furrowed. "How would that happen?"

"You take the final exams."

He shook his head. "I don't think so." He returned to reading his book.

"Why not? I know you'd pass."

"You think the teachers will let me just waltz in and take them?"

"They will if it's arranged ahead of time. If you convince Principal Petersen you've been keeping up with your lessons, he could allow you to take them."

Marty frowned. "He'd never agree to that."

"How do you know if you don't ask? You've worked

so hard, you're doing better than me in some of our classes. Don't you deserve to graduate after all that work?"

He slouched forward. "I don't want to get my hopes up again," he said, his voice low.

She knew what he meant, and her heart went out to him. "It doesn't hurt to ask, does it?"

He shrugged.

"If he says no, then at least you know you did everything you could. And if he says yes, you can graduate with me."

"Maybe." There was a small bit of hope in his voice.

She could tell he was considering it. "You'll do it soon? There isn't much time before finals."

"I guess I could ask Mr. Dwyer for some time off work."

It wasn't a definitive yes, but she resisted the urge to push him. He had to do this on his own.

The next day, Jess couldn't help spending every moment between classes looking for Marty even though she knew it was stupid. Marty wouldn't be ready to talk to Principal Peterson so soon. After lunch, she had to force herself not to search for him. Why was she doing this to herself? she wondered, taking her afternoon textbooks out of her locker. *Get a grip*, she thought, slamming the door shut harder than she needed to. *You're going to drive yourself nuts.*

"You're so jumpy today," Louise said. "Are you okay?"

Her anger rose, knowing Louise had noticed her behavior. "I'm fine."

"Oh, my *word?*" Louise said, looking past Jess, and Jess spun around.

Mr. Dwyer was striding towards them with Marty a half step behind. Marty was wearing dark blue trousers she'd never seen before. His hair was combed back with cream and his face flushed bright red above a white button-down shirt – and he had on a tie. Students parted to get out of their way, and stared as they passed.

When they disappeared from view, Louise turned to Jess with wide eyes. "Marty looked so... so..."

"Handsome," Jess said, then ducked her head, realizing she'd given too much away. She headed down the hallway to hide her flaming face.

Louise caught up to her. "Why do you think he's here?"

"Who knows?"

"I wonder if he's coming back to school."

"Maybe."

"I bet *you'd* like him to come back," Louise said with a sly smile, nudging Jess with her elbow.

Jess laughed. "I'll admit it. It would be nice."

"Just nice? Oh, that stupid bell," she said, while it rang through the crowded hallway. "See you later." Louise rushed to the stairs.

Jess went to her class and took a seat, still picturing Marty walking down the hall. Mr. Dwyer must have given him those clothes, and he'd probably come with him to help convince Principal Peterson. She was filled with gratitude for the drugstore owner. With Mr. Dwyer's help, Marty's chances were much better.

Back home, she rushed to change so she could get to the cabin. After starting both fires, she paced the small rooms, too nervous to think about studying. She kept checking her watch until the door finally opened.

She bounded up to Marty. "Well?"

"Well, what?" His were eyes sparkling with humor.

"Tell me." She grabbed his arm and shook him.

He laughed. "Stop, you're going to rattle my brain loose, and that would be a shame, since I'll need it to take my tests."

He smirked while she screamed and threw her arms around him. "He *had* to say yes when you looked so nice," she said after she let go.

"I looked like a stiff, but I don't care. It worked."

"Why did Mr. Dwyer come with you?"

"Turns out he went to school with Principal Petersen." Marty shook his head. "He did most of the talking, and before I even got a chance to say a word, Petersen said yes."

"You're taking your final exams!" Jess said, jumping.

"Yep, I just have to show up." He beamed with pride. "And they're going to send the results to the drugstore so my old man won't find out."

"Marty, it's so…*wonderful*."

"Yes, it is."

Jess grinned so hard her cheeks hurt. Their dream of going to college was back on track.

Chapter Forty-Six
Where the Boys Are

May 1961

"WHO CAN'T WAIT for the spring prom?" Janet White asked the group of girls at the lunch table.

"Me," rose a chorus of voices.

"Next question." She raised her index finger. "Who do you want to ask you?"

"I've already been asked," Patty Melville said with a smug smile.

There were excited squeals. "You did? By whom?"

"How did it happen so fast?" Janet said. "They only put up the posters this morning."

"It was Bobby Baker. I guess he wanted to make sure he asked me before anyone else."

"You're so lucky," said Cheryl, and the other girls nodded.

Patty flipped her hair back. "He *is* the most handsome

boy in our class," she said.

Jess and Louise exchanged glances. It was so typical of Patty. She'd always been full of herself because her father was the mayor. But she was wrong about Bobby, Jess thought. Marty was the most handsome boy in their school even if he wasn't attending classes.

"I'm hoping Arthur Mullen will ask me," Janet said. "Or Vic Cromer. I can't decide."

While the girls debated the merits of each other's choices, Jess and Louise remained silent. Jess didn't know if Louise was hoping to be asked to the spring prom, but she wasn't, not that she wouldn't love to go. It was a relief when the bell rang and she could get away from all the talk about boys and shopping for ball gowns.

Back at their lockers, Jess heard someone clearing his throat behind her. "Uh, Louise?" She and Louise both turned around.

Harold Krueger, a tall, gangly boy who was so shy that Jess wasn't certain if she'd ever heard him speak, was standing in front of Louise. Four boys were behind him, trying to hide their grins. Jess had the impression they were there to back him up.

"Hello, Harold," Louise said with a warm smile.

He bowed his head. "Do you, uh, want to go to the prom?" he asked his shoes, his voice cracking on the last word.

Louise's smile brightened. "I'd love to."

He lifted his head with a stunned expression. "You would? Oh. I, oh," he stammered. He appeared unable to say anything else, and a boy behind him stepped forward.

"Okay, champ." He slapped his hands on Harold's shoulders. "Time to go. He'll talk to you later," he said to

Louise, pulling Harold backwards. "When he's recovered!" There were roars of laughter while he steered a dazed Harold away.

One boy remained, and as David Williams stepped towards Jess, her stomach sank. "How about you, Jess? Would like to go with me? We can double date."

Louise looked at Jess with a grin.

"I'm sorry, David. No, thank you."

David reacted as if air was let out of him. "I didn't realize you were already going with someone."

Jess felt for him. "I'm not going to the prom this year."

"You aren't?" His voice became hopeful. "Maybe next time we can go."

"Maybe," Jess said, not wanting to shoot him down twice in the same day.

"See you around, Jess." He walked away with a spring in his step.

"You're not going to the prom?" Disappointment was evident in Louise's tone, but then her eyes widened. "Don't tell me your uncle won't let you?" she said in a hushed voice.

"I'm sure he would, as long as the right kind of boy was taking me."

"And the boy you want to go with isn't the right kind of boy."

"Marty doesn't even go to school," Jess muttered, slamming her locker shut. "So it doesn't matter."

Louise put her hand on Jess's arm. "You should forget about Marty. There's plenty of other boys at school, boys your uncle would approve of. Isn't there at least one you like?"

"I'm not interested in any of them. They're all dumb."

Louise shook her head. "It's all that studying. You're getting too smart."

"You forget, I'm studying for a reason. Once I go to college, I'll be away from my uncle and I can see any boy I want."

"You don't want to wind up an old maid, Jess."

Jess laughed. "That's the last thing I'm worried about. And besides, maybe I'll meet that special boy in college."

Louise shifted her eyes away. "I suppose you're right."

"What's wrong?"

"I knew you were going to college, but I didn't realize you might not come back. I mean, if you find a boy your uncle doesn't approve of, you won't be able to bring him home."

Jess's smile evaporated. Louise was right, and it was something she'd been agonizing about over the last few months. Even if Marty went to college with her, when it was over, he'd come back to the same town where her uncle lived. She'd tried to think of a way she could come back with him, but there was no solution. Eventually she would lose Marty.

That afternoon, Jess sat beside Marty at the table in the cabin, listening to the scratching of Marty's pencil on paper. Their end-of-year exams were coming up soon, and thinking of the long summer ahead of her, Jess was already dreading spending so much time alone.

Marty set down his pencil and rubbed the back of his neck. He was tanned from his time spent making deliveries, and the blond streaks from the sun had returned to his hair. His eyes met hers. "What?" he said, a knowing smile spreading across his face.

"I wish school lasted all year."

"Yeah, I know." His expression was more sober.

"I decided I'm going to ask Annie to teach me how to sew," she said. "That'll kill a lot of time." She didn't want Marty to worry about her.

"Jess, I've got to tell you something."

She sat straighter, hearing the seriousness in his tone. "What?"

He smiled. "Don't worry. It ain't – I mean, it isn't anything bad," he said, correcting himself. "Now that I know I'm going to graduate from high school, I've been thinking about what comes next. I talked to Mr. Dwyer about it, and he thinks I should go to college right after I graduate and get a pharmacology degree. That way I can take over the drugstore when he's ready to retire."

"What are you saying?" Jess said, her breathing shallower.

"He reckons he can figure out a way to help me go, maybe a loan or something."

"Really?"

"It looks like we're going to college," he said with a grin.

"Marty, that's the best thing ever." She got up to go hug him. "We're going to have so much fun."

He chuckled. "I reckoned you'd be happy to hear it."

"We have to study extra hard." She returned to her stool. "We're not going to take any chances on you not passing."

"Yes, ma'am." He gave her a mock salute, his brown eyes twinkling. He leaned over the book to resume reading and Jess did too, but she couldn't focus on the words.

She would get to be with Marty for four more years, four glorious years where they would be free. With all that extra time, perhaps she could think of a way to stay with him forever.

Jess was still thinking about it that evening while she dried dishes next to Annie at the sink. Memories of the day the family had taken Doug to college ran through her mind, except now she imagined she and Marty were the ones moving into their dorm rooms.

"I can't wait for Doug to move back home next week," Annie said. "Things haven't been the same since he left."

"Yeah," Jess said, letting go of the image of her and Marty exploring the campus hand in hand.

"I thought your uncle would get used to Doug being gone, but he's so attached to him."

Uncle Jonathon was still taking his son's absence hard. Doug called his dad after his twice weekly conversations with Jess, but it hadn't made it easier for him. It was as if after his son had left he couldn't stand to be in the house anymore.

"At least this summer, everything will be back to the way it used to be," Annie said, smiling with happiness.

As Jess considered what that meant for Annie, Uncle Jonathon ruling over her, ordering her around, shouting at her, anger boiled up. "I can't understand–" She stopped before she finished the sentence.

Annie's hands stilled in the soapy water. "You can't

understand what?"

Jess searched Annie's hazel eyes, wondering if she should say it. If Annie understood the way Uncle Jonathon treated her was wrong, maybe she wouldn't love him anymore, and then he wouldn't have the power to hurt her. "I can't understand why you excuse his behavior."

Annie returned to washing dishes. "I know he's not easy to live with, but he wasn't always like that."

It was the same excuse she'd given when Jess arrived over two years ago.

"When your Aunt Helen died, he–"

"*My* parents died, but it didn't turn me into a terrible person."

Annie's mouth dropped open. "*Jess.* He's *not* a terrible person."

"How can you say that when he treats you the way he does?"

"Because of everything he's done for Doug." Tears sprang to her eyes. "I don't know of any man who would love that boy like he does."

"Of course he loves Doug! He's his son."

The color drained from Annie's face.

Jess took a step towards her. "What's wrong?"

"Your parents never told you," she said, her voice hushed.

"Never told me what?"

"I shouldn't have said it," Annie said shakily. She turned to the sink. "Forget I said anything."

"Annie, what's going on?"

The Boy in the Woods

She scrubbed a pot so hard it was in danger of losing its enamel.

"I don't understand what you mean. What didn't my parents tell me?"

A sob escaped Annie. "He'll be so *angry* when he finds out I'm the one who told you." She brought her apron up to wipe her eyes. "No one is supposed to talk about it."

"You know I would never tell him you told me."

"I suppose you have the right to know. Maybe your parents were waiting until you were older and could understand. Doug..." She took a shuddering breath. "Doug is adopted."

Jess gasped as a jolt went through her. "That's not possible."

"It's true."

Jess couldn't comprehend it. The boy Uncle Jonathon had devoted his entire life to wasn't his real son?

"Helen was in the family way when your uncle married her," Annie said, shame in her face.

That information was even more shocking. Her aunt had done *that* with another man when she wasn't married. "Did Uncle Jonathon know it when he married her?"

"Yes, he knew." Annie had tears in her eyes. "He did it to protect her from the scandal. And after Doug was born, he adopted him and the records were sealed so he would be protected too. No one outside the family can know." She grabbed Jess's hand. "It would bring terrible shame on Doug if anyone found out he was a bastard child."

Jess's mind reeled, struggling to make sense of it all. "Does Doug know he's adopted?"

"Yes, pumpkin. He knows."

"It's – it's–" Jess stuttered, searching for words, but she was speechless.

"I know it's hard to believe. But your uncle loved Helen deeply, even after she..." Annie's face flushed, and she looked away. "From the moment Doug was born, he loved him like he was his own. He gave him a name, a family, a future, everything he's had to give. Your uncle has his faults, but I don't know of any man who would be so selfless with a child that wasn't his. *That's* why I know he's a good man."

Annie resumed washing the pot while Jess stared at her. Her entire world had shifted. "What about Doug's real father? Who–"

"I won't discuss that!" Annie said, her attention on the pot. "I won't bring shame on another family by dragging them through the mud. What happened is in the past. Doug is your uncle's son now, and that's all that matters."

"Yes, ma'am," Jess said, her own shame making her cheeks flame. Annie was right. Doug didn't deserve to have her prying into his personal affairs.

"I'll finish the rest of these," Annie said, her voice kinder. "You should go up to bed, pumpkin."

"Okay." Jess was grateful for the excuse to be alone.

Upstairs in her room, she undressed in slow motion, memories of Doug and Uncle Jonathon flooding her mind. But this time, they were filtered through the knowledge that Doug was adopted.

Their love for each other had always been apparent, but there were moments when things didn't add up. Like when Uncle Jonathon had questioned Doug's loyalty to the family when he'd said he wanted to attend college. Doug had been so desperate to prove he was a good son, he'd broken up with the girl he loved the next day. And there was the time he'd told Jess he felt lucky to be a member of the Blackwell family. Now his words had a different meaning.

In some ways, Jess understood Annie's feelings for Uncle Jonathon. Annie had seen him at his best, and at his most vulnerable. When he'd been grieving the loss of his beloved wife and baby, Annie had been the only one to take care of him, and Doug. Going through that, the three of them had formed a strong bond.

Jess was climbing into bed when she heard the black car coming down the drive, bringing Uncle Jonathon home. She went to her window and peeked around the curtain, studying him as he walked to the house carrying his briefcase. She tried to see the man whose heart was so large, he'd loved another man's child, but she only saw the same Uncle Jonathon she'd always known. A man whose losses had made him bitter and cold.

In bed, she pulled the covers up, that old familiar ache returning to her chest. If her uncle hadn't closed off his heart to anyone except Doug, her life would have been different, and so would Annie's. Instead, all of them were caught up in his grief for his dead wife.

Chapter Forty-Seven
Run To Him

July 1961

JESS WAS EATING cereal in the kitchen when Doug walked in, and she straightened with surprise. She thought she was the only one in the house since it was summer and Annie was back to her usual schedule.

"Morning," he said. It was clear he'd just woken. He was barefoot, wearing a white T-shirt and shorts, and his hair was messy, dark curls falling over his forehead.

"What are you doing here?"

"I asked Dad if I could stay home today."

"Oh." She was astonished Uncle Jonathon agreed to let him have time away from the office. Since he'd come home for the summer, the two of them were never apart during the day.

Now that she knew Doug was adopted, she'd paid closer attention to their interactions, trying to see if she'd missed the clues. But her uncle was as devoted to Doug as he'd ever been, lavishing praise and attention on him, and Doug seemed equally devoted to his father.

But Jess wondered if he'd be happy to spend as much time at the mine if he didn't feel an obligation. It was clear he loved the business, but did he have to work *so* hard? Didn't most nineteen-year-old fellows want to be with friends once in a while, or have time off to relax? Then maybe that was the reason he'd asked for the day off.

"Do you know where Annie keeps the coffee?" He opened the cupboard where the plates were.

"Yeah, I do." Jess went to the butler's pantry and came back with the can of coffee grounds.

He took it from her and then looked around before giving her a sheepish grin. "I'm not sure how to make it."

"I can. I've seen her do it lots of times."

"Thanks, Jess."

She took the can from him and headed for the electric percolator.

Once he was seated at the table with his cup of coffee and a bowl of cereal, he took a sip. "It's good."

"Thanks."

"I asked for the day off because I wanted to spend it with you." He dug his spoon into his cereal.

"Are we doing more driving?" They'd resumed lessons in the evenings after dinner and she was now good enough to drive Doug's car on the highway.

"Uh, no. I was hoping you could take me to the pond."

Her heart began hammering in her chest while she watched him chew a mouthful of cereal.

His brow furrowed. "Is it alright? I mean, is there a

problem?"

"No, it's fine," she said, trying to think. How could she take him to the pond without him learning all her secrets? The only way she'd ever gone was using the path from the cabin. It would not only reveal that she knew about the cabin, he might want to look inside, and that would give away Marty.

"Annie said you swim there almost every day, and I thought—"

"She did?" Jess said, her breaths quickening. What else had Annie told him?

"Yeah, and I thought we could go swimming. Besides, I'm interested to see what it's like. If it's the same as I remember."

"Uh, yeah. We can do that." She'd go to the pond by a different route, they'd have a quick swim, and then she'd bring him home long before Marty was off work.

"Great. I thought we could pack a lunch so we could have a picnic, like I used to do with my mom. We'll make a day of it."

"That sounds fun." Jess struggled to keep her smile going. She stood to wash her breakfast dishes, her stomach doing flips.

This was a catastrophe. If the two of them were at the pond in the afternoon, Marty was going to show up, and there was no way to stop it. When Marty found the cabin empty, the pond would be the first place he'd go to find her.

Doug appeared at her side with his bowl and spoon and she took it from him to wash. "I'll go get ready," he said.

Jess looked at the wall clock. It was still early in the morning. Maybe after they'd been there a few hours, he'd be ready to leave. That way they'd be gone before Marty was on the property. After all, they could only swim for so long.

After cleaning up, Jess rushed to put together a picnic lunch for them, and then ran up the backstairs where she changed into her swimsuit. Once she'd pulled on a pair of shorts and a cotton shirt, she found her watch. She would need to keep a close eye on the time. When she returned to the kitchen, Doug was waiting for her with a towel, wearing swim trunks and a T-shirt.

"We need a blanket to sit on while we eat, but I don't know where Annie keeps the old ones," he said.

"I don't know either," Jess said, picturing the blankets at the cabin. "I sit on my towel."

"I guess that'll work."

"Let's go," she said. She needed to get them started.

They headed through the back door and Jess strode across the large yard. She tried to appear like she'd taken the same route lots of times. In her head she pictured a layout of the property, figuring out the best way to get to the pond.

She entered the woods and he followed. While they moved through the trees, she tried to gauge the direction they were traveling. When she saw the treetops thinning out, she moved faster, hoping she'd been accurate. Pushing through the dense brush, they emerged in the grass field.

She turned to Doug with a triumphant smile. "Almost there."

With the stand of willow trees to guide her, they were soon at the pond. She put her basket and towel under the willow tree. When she came out, Doug was at the edge of the pond. He didn't say anything as he looked at the water. She'd told him the pond was small. Was he thinking that she'd lied to him?

"Is it like you remember?" She watched his face.

"It's definitely smaller," he said. "But I can see why you like it here. It's pretty."

Jess suppressed a sigh of relief.

He turned and walked in the direction of the path, and Jess's smile fell. When he reached it, he stopped, and she held her breath. "The path is still here." He faced her with a grim expression. "Where does that path lead?" he asked, but she could tell he already knew the answer.

"The woods."

"This is the way I used to come with my mom. You know there's a cabin at the end of this path, don't you?"

She had no choice but to admit the truth. "Yes."

He approached her, his blue eyes intense. "Don't tell Dad you've been near it. He'll flip. No one is allowed to go there."

"I know. I won't tell him."

He didn't move, his eyes still intense, and she had the impression he was trying to decide something. Would he want to see it? If he did, she didn't know how she would stop him.

He broke eye contact and kicked off his loafers. "Let's swim."

She turned her back to him, taking several deep breaths, and then pulled off her shirt. That was a close call.

With her sandals off, she waded into the water, then dove and swam to the center of the pond. When she surfaced, Doug was standing at the edge, frowning at the water. It was the first time she'd seen him without a shirt on, and she was surprised that his skin was so white. But then he never spent any time outside like Marty. She was also surprised by his thin arms, and lack of visible muscles. It wasn't like Marty had huge biceps, but he had them. Doug's arms looked

The Boy in the Woods

scrawny in comparison. After spending so much time with Marty, she thought all boys looked like him with their shirts off, but it appeared she was wrong.

He hesitantly stepped forward and then looked across the water at her. "There aren't any leeches in here or anything, are there?"

She laughed. "No, there aren't any leeches. Do you think I'd swim here if there were?"

He took a few more steps while he grimaced and she wondered if it was because of the mud. She used to hate how it would squish through her toes when she first swam in the pond. "There are fish though."

Doug halted. "Fish?" he said, his voice rising. "How big?"

"Not big at all," she said with a grin. "Only like that." She held her hands wide apart while she treaded water.

"That's big!" He peered into the water. "Do they bite?"

She laughed again. "I'm only teasing, Doug. They're not that big, and believe me, they're more scared of you than you are of them."

"Right." He moved forward, but he still examined the water around him.

She remembered how Marty had given her such a hard time about being a 'city kid' who didn't know anything. Now she was the experienced one and Doug seemed like the city kid. It was ironic considering the property would belong to him some day.

She swam closer, intending to splash him, then decided against it. If he was having fun, he might want to stay longer, or even come back another day. She swam away from him, hearing splashing as Doug swam behind her. She ignored him, and swam laps back and forth like she did when she wanted to tire herself out. When she finished, instead of resting in the shallows, she left the water. While she was drying off, Doug joined her under the willow tree. She laid out her towel and sat with her back against the trunk.

"Don't you want to lie out in the sun?" Doug said.

"I don't need to. I'm warm enough."

"I meant to get a tan."

"I get enough sun. And besides, it makes my freckles stand out more."

"Oh." His shoulders dropped. He didn't seem to know what to do.

"You can lie in the sun if you want to." She considered saying he looked like he needed it, but decided not to. She didn't want to make him feel bad about being so pale.

"No, this is fine." He spread his towel out on the ground.

Jess looked at her watch. It was at least an hour before she could suggest lunch. What was she going to do? Wrapping her arms around her legs, she gazed at the water. Normally she found the pond peaceful, but she was a bundle of nerves. How long was Doug going to want to hang around after eating? Would he want to swim again? If he did, it would be at least another hour or longer before they left for home. That would be dangerously close to the time Marty would arrive.

"Is this what you always do?" Doug asked. "Swim and then sit here?"

Jess realized he was bored, and her spirits lifted. This might not be such a disaster after all. "I eat lunch too."

"Do you want to eat now?"

"Okay."

She laid out the food between them, and while they ate, she considered how different Doug and Marty were. Marty didn't mind hanging out at the pond all day, and the long silences between them were comfortable. When she was with Doug, she always had fun, but they were always doing something. When they ran out of things to talk about, the silence became awkward, and they'd fill it by turning on the radio, or one of them would start a different discussion.

After lunch, Jess leaned against the tree trunk. Out of the corner of her eye, she watched Doug fidget. He was getting antsy.

"What do you do after you eat?" he said.

"Sometimes I take a nap, or I read."

"Do you want to swim again?" From his expression, she knew the answer he was hoping for.

"No, thanks. I'm tired."

"Do you want to head back?"

"Sure."

He stood, appearing relieved.

The two of them gathered their things and set off across the field, going back the same way they'd come. She wondered if Doug thought it was odd they weren't taking the path since it would be quicker. But maybe he wanted to abide by his father's wishes and not go near the cabin. In any case, she was grateful.

"When I was little, I guess it was more exciting to visit the pond," Doug said when they reached the woods. "Don't get me wrong. I had a good time," he said when she looked up at him. "It's just too quiet for me."

"I can understand that," Jess said, filled with relief. It

sounded like he wouldn't want to swim again.

"I'm glad *you* enjoy going, Jess. It's great the property is so big you can find lots of ways to pass the time."

She opened her mouth to tell him he was wrong, that it wasn't enough to keep her from feeling trapped, but she clamped it shut. It might make him feel guilty enough to offer to swim with her again. During the rest of the walk, Jess was miserable. She wished she could tell him how much she suffered through the summers, but what could he do about it anyway? It was his father who insisted on it.

In the kitchen, Jess busied herself by emptying the trash from the basket.

"It's earlier than I thought," Doug said.

"Maybe you should go to the office," Jess said, hoping he'd take the suggestion.

"No. I was going to spend the day with you. I mean, we still have half the day. That's plenty of time–"

"Doug, I'm fine. I think you should go to work while it's still early."

"Are you sure?"

"I was going to read upstairs. I'm always tired after I swim."

"Okay." He smiled. "Dad will be happy to have me for a few hours."

"Sure, Doug. I'll see you tonight." Jess tried not to seem glad he was leaving.

As soon as he disappeared through the butler's pantry, Jess climbed the backstairs. She paced in her bedroom, chewing her fingernails. Finally, she heard Doug's car start. She moved to the window and watched until it disappeared behind the trees lining the drive, then she ran down the backstairs. Taking the basket from where she'd put it away, she packed a meal for Marty, and headed out.

She was sitting on the front stoop of the cabin when he stepped into the clearing.

"Hey, Jess. How's it going?"

"Not so great."

His smile vanished. "What happened?"

"Doug wanted me to take him swimming at the pond."

"Why did he want to do that?" Marty said, alarm in his eyes.

"He used to go there with his mom. I *had* to take him. Otherwise he'd be suspicious."

"Did he go in the cabin?"

"No, I took him a different way, but he knows about it. He didn't seem interested in seeing it, thank goodness."

Marty let out a breath.

"We were there for a while, but he got bored and decided he wanted to go home."

"We got lucky," Marty said, but he was grim.

Jess felt her emotions from that morning rising up. "I was so scared I wouldn't be able to get him to leave before you showed up."

"Come here."

He pulled her close, and she leaned against him, comforted by his strong arms. His T-shirt was soft against her cheek, and his firm chest warmed her skin while he rubbed her back. "If I hadn't been able to get him to leave before you…"

"It's okay. It didn't happen," he said into her hair.

She lifted her head. "What if he wants to go again? I don't know how I'll stop him."

"I'll tell you what. From now on, when I come here or go to the pond, I'll check to make sure no one else is around before I show myself. That way you won't have to worry."

She sighed, leaning against him. "That's a good idea."

He kept rubbing her back and she closed her eyes, concentrating on his steady breathing. For the first time since that morning she felt safe.

Chapter Forty-Eight
Tower of Strength

December 1961

JESS HAD HER notebook open as she sat in the back of the black car on her way home from school. Now that it was mid-December, first semester final exams were coming up, and she was making a list of which books she needed to bring home for her and Marty. He had two rounds of final exams to pass if he was going to graduate and she wasn't taking any chances.

When James reached the gate, he drove straight through and she lifted her head in surprise. The gate was unlocked and wide open. "Is something going on?" she asked.

"You'll be findin' that out when ya get in the house, won't ya?" James said, not even bothering to look at her in the rear view mirror.

Slapping her notebook closed, she ground her teeth. He pulled to a stop close to the house, and she got out of the car before he'd cut the engine, slamming the door closed as hard as she could. On the way to the back door, she felt a deep satisfaction, but when she walked into the kitchen it vanished. The room was empty and silent, absent of the usual smell of dinner cooking. And there were suitcases lined up near the door.

Annie emerged from her bedroom dressed in a matching wool skirt and jacket and carrying her winter coat. She was going out, but her hair was still in a bun instead of the chignon she always wore. Her eyes were red-rimmed from crying and Jess's heart leapt into her throat. *Uncle Jonathon had fired her.*

"Annie, what's going on?"

"Oh, Jess." She burst into tears, and Jess went to hug her. "I've had terrible news."

Jess pulled away so she could look at her. "What is it?"

"It's my sister." Annie wiped her eyes with a handkerchief. "She's had a stroke."

"Oh, no." Jess hugged her again.

"They don't know if she's going to make it. I don't know what I'll do if I lose her. After losing my brother, she's all I have left."

"I'm so sorry."

After a minute, Annie pulled away. "The three of us were close. When we lost my brother on D-Day, it was horrible. If I lose my sister, I'll be the only one left, and my mother–" She shook her head as more tears came.

"The doctors will do everything they can. They'll help her."

Annie put her hand on Jess's cheek and managed a watery smile. "Thank you. James is taking me to the train station. I called Mrs. Lindstrom up the road. Her daughter will come three days a week to clean and do laundry. Mrs. Lindstrom will be sending meals with her. I don't know if I'll be back in time for your birthday, or Christmas."

"Don't worry about that. That's not as important as your sister."

"Annie!"

Uncle Jonathon's sudden appearance startled Jess.

"I've made all the arrangements. There's a ticket waiting for you at the train station. When you get to Chicago, take a cab to the Carlisle Hotel. It's across the street from the hospital."

Jess stared at him with shock.

"I've told them you'll be keeping your room indefinitely. Dr. Baker will be in consultation with the doctors caring for Margie. He'll keep me informed of her progress."

"Thank you," Annie said, her voice trembling.

"When you get to the hotel, have them cash this for you, and have most of it deposited in the hotel safe." He handed her a check.

She gasped when she read the amount. "It's too much, Johnny."

"It's not too much. That's to cover your expenses, and anything Margie needs that the hospital won't provide. I want you to spend it. And when you run out, let me know, and I'll wire you more."

Tears welled in her eyes again. "You're too generous."

He turned away, looking uncomfortable. "It's time to leave," he said as he went to the window and waved at James. "I'll get my coat." He left the kitchen without a glance at either of them.

"Goodbye, pumpkin," Annie said, while James came into the kitchen to collect her luggage. "I wish I didn't have to leave you alone, but Doug will be home for Christmas break soon."

"Don't worry about me, I can manage. I hope you have a safe trip and that your sister will be okay."

Uncle Jonathon reappeared in the kitchen with his coat and fedora. "I'll be late tonight, Jessica. I'm heading back to the office after dropping Annie off."

"Yes, sir."

Annie slipped on her coat. "There's some pea soup in the icebox you can heat up for dinner." She looked at Jess with worried eyes and gave her another hug.

"We're going to be late," Uncle Jonathon snapped, looking at his watch.

Annie released her. "Goodbye, Jess," she said as Uncle Jonathon hustled her to the door.

"Bye," Jess said before it closed.

She stood at the window, watching Annie climb into the back of the car, heart aching for her. She couldn't believe the change in her uncle, that he'd done so much to help Annie. Maybe deep down he had feelings for her after all. Jess hoped that while they were in the car, he would comfort her. Annie needed it right now.

James drove off and Jess waved until the car disappeared from view, then she stepped away from the window. Facing the empty kitchen, the silence surrounded her.

"I have something special for you," Jess said to Marty later that afternoon at the cabin. He'd just arrived and was still knocking the snow from his pants and boots.

"Yeah?"

She motioned for him. "Come here."

He followed her to the kitchen, throwing his coat over a chair. "Are you cooking?" he said, when he saw a pot on the cookstove.

"No, I'm reheating soup."

"It's green," he observed with a frown.

"It's split pea. Haven't you ever had it?"

"No."

"It's delicious."

"If you say so," he said, sounding unconvinced. He leaned against the counter. "Annie packed soup for you? That's a first."

"No, I packed it." She pointed to the empty Mason jar in the sink, proud that she'd been so clever. "We're having dinner tonight." She took two coffee mugs from the cupboard. "Annie had to go to Chicago because her sister got sick and Uncle Jonathon is staying late at the office."

Marty dropped his arms. "Wait. Annie's gone?"

"Yeah, she had to go take care of her–"

"That means you'll be alone with him."

"I'll only see him in the mornings, and Doug is coming home soon."

"I don't like it. I don't like how he is with you."

"I'll be okay, Marty. He mostly ignores me."

"If it's only for a little while, I guess you'll be okay," he said, but the troubled look didn't leave his face.

While she filled the mugs with soup, her heart soared. Marty was so protective and caring. Despite his rough childhood with an abusive father, he had the biggest heart of anyone she knew. "You're going to like this." She put a spoon in a steaming mug and handed it to him.

He sniffed the soup and then blew on a spoonful before he tasted it.

"Well? How is it?" she asked.

"It's bad. Really bad," he said, his eyes twinkling.

She laughed while he licked the spoon clean. "Go take your seat. We have a lot of work to do."

Chapter Forty-Nine

Surrender

"DOUG!"

As soon as Jess had seen him park his car in front of the garage, she'd flown down the stairs and threw herself at her cousin as soon as he'd walked in the front door. She hugged him, feeling the cold air that clung to his coat against her cheek.

"How's it going?" he said after she let go.

"It's okay. It's been quiet without Annie."

His brow furrowed. "Oh? Well, I'm here now. Hopefully she'll be back before my Christmas break ends. She wrote to tell me her sister is recovering, but it's going to take a while."

"Yeah, she wrote me the same thing."

Jess was glad Annie's sister was doing better with Annie there to care for her, but the last week had been hard. Marty's worries about her being alone with her uncle had been unwarranted. As little as he'd been around before, she saw him even less now. He was no longer eating breakfast at home since Annie wasn't there to cook for him. The only contact Jess had with him was the ride to school, during which he read his newspaper.

In the house all by herself, she'd been lonely. She'd whiled away the hours alone by knitting a pair of mittens for Marty, but it didn't make the house seem less empty. If Doug hadn't come home, she didn't know how she would have managed now that school was out for the holidays.

"I guess Dad is tied up with a road commission meeting tonight," Doug said. "Is there anything for dinner?"

"Sort of," Jess grumbled.

He laughed. "What does that mean?"

"I'll show you."

She pulled the meal Mrs. Lindstrom's daughter had brought out of the icebox, and showed it to Doug.

He took a step back, grimacing. "What is that?"

"I think it's pickled fish in some kind of cream sauce."

"Is it any good?"

"I didn't try it. I'm not sure if it's cooked, or if I'm supposed to cook it, and it smells weird. I ate the last thing she sent, but only because I was starving. It didn't taste very good."

Doug contemplated the bowl of pale fish and then smiled. "How about we go grab some burgers?"

Jess grinned. "That sounds good."

After a meal of burgers, fries, and apple pie at the Golden Skillet, Doug suggested they go to a movie. Jess was thrilled when she found out it was *West Side Story*, knowing part of it was filmed in Manhattan. She wondered how many locations she'd recognize.

Later, when they left the theater, Jess barely noticed

The Boy in the Woods

the chill in the air. She hummed her new favorite song, "I Feel Pretty," all the way back to the car.

Doug opened the door for her. "That was fun. Let's go out again tomorrow night. I think you deserve it after being left alone for so long."

"Okay."

Doug turned the ignition, and the car radio came on. Jess reached for the dial to change the station, and then a shock went through her. Marty was on the sidewalk walking towards them – and he was with a girl.

While Doug backed the car out of the parking space, Jess stared open-mouthed as Sharon Allen, a girl from their grade, talked to Marty with a huge smile on her face. Then she moved closer, looping her arm around his so they could walk together, and Jess felt a searing pain in her chest. As Doug drove away, she dared to take one last look, and wished she hadn't. Marty was saying something to Sharon while she looked up at him adoringly.

What was going on? Why would Marty be with Sharon? And then a terrible realization hit her. *They were on a date.* What other explanation could there be for the two of them to be out together on a Friday night. And from the way Sharon was looking at him while she was holding onto him, it seemed like she was in love.

Jess kept her face turned to the window and blinked back tears. Had they been dating for a long time? Maybe Marty was going on dates with lots of girls. He was eighteen after all, already a man. Of course, girls would want to go out with him. He was a catch; funny, kind-hearted, smart, and with a great future ahead of him. By the time Doug had pulled his car into the garage, Jess was barely holding herself together.

How could she have been so stupid not to see this

would happen? While she was kept behind locked gates, Marty was free to move forward with his life. Sharon's family didn't have a lot of money, just like Marty's. She was much better suited for him, someone he could marry and raise a family with while he worked at the drugstore. Jess could never be that girl.

"Night," she said as soon as they were inside, and rushed up the stairs.

"Good night," Doug called out after her, but she didn't respond, afraid he'd hear the tears in her voice.

While she lay in bed, she wiped her eyes and tried to convince herself she'd been mistaken, that nothing was going on between them. But then she'd see Marty letting Sharon loop her arm around his and her adoring expression when she gazed at him.

Jess tossed and turned through most of the night, and when her room lightened from the rising sun, she decided she couldn't lie in bed any longer. After pulling on a sweater and a pair of wool trousers, she went downstairs, noticing a light snow falling outside the window.

She hesitated at the entrance to the dining room. Uncle Jonathon was seated at the table with his paper and a bowl of cereal in front of him.

"Good morning." She went to her seat.

He grunted in response.

Doug came from the butler's pantry carrying another bowl of cereal and the coffee percolator. "Good morning."

"Morning," she said.

Doug studied her. "You look tired. Bad sleep?"

Uncle Jonathon peered up at her.

"Uh, I read too late."

Uncle Jonathon shook his head and returned to his paper.

"Have a seat." Doug poured coffee for his dad. "You can have my cereal. I'll make another bowl."

He'd put sliced banana on top of the cornflakes.

"It looks good." She managed a smile.

When Doug returned with his bowl, Uncle Jonathon folded his newspaper and picked up his coffee cup. "That meeting last night was a waste of time. They're insisting on continuing Fairfield Lane north."

Doug scooped up a spoonful of cereal. "That's not going to work."

"Exactly. I demanded another meeting, but that means we'll be going over the maps with the geologist today. Don't expect us home for dinner, Jessica."

Doug stopped chewing, and his eyes met Jess's.

At that moment, she remembered he'd offered to take her out again that evening.

"Uh, Dad. I already planned to–"

"It's okay, Doug," she said, interrupting him. "We'll do it another night." She wasn't up for an outing with Doug anyway, and who knew how much worse she would feel after she'd talked to Marty.

"If you're sure."

"I am."

After they left for work, Jess paced through the house, agonizing over what she'd say to Marty, and what he might tell her. After a while, she decided she couldn't wait any longer. She'd go to the cabin even though Marty wouldn't be there for hours.

The Boy in the Woods

Snow was still falling, and the amount that had accumulated added to the foot already on the ground. It made walking through the woods difficult, but trying to avoid tripping over buried rocks and fallen branches gave her something to concentrate on while she made her way forward.

Once she had both fires lit, she paced in the small space until she heard the door open and Marty appeared. A thick layer of snow covered his shoulders and wool cap. Emotions flooded through her at seeing him: happiness, fear, heartsickness.

"Man, it's really coming down out there." He took his cap off and slapped it against his leg to knock off the snow. "They said we might get another foot, but it looks like it's going to be more." He draped his coat over a chair and went to the fireplace.

"I saw you in town last night," Jess said while he rubbed his hands near the fire to warm them.

"Yeah? I didn't see you."

"You were on Main Street and I was in the car with Doug."

"That's probably why I didn't see you."

"You were with Sharon Allen."

"Yeah, we went to the late show."

"Are you dating her now?"

Marty turned to her, his expressing darkening. She didn't mean for it to sound like an accusation but it had come out that way. "No, I'm not dating her," he said, his voice tight.

"Then why did you go to the movies with her?"

"I don't know," he said, his voice rising to match hers, "because she wanted to."

"Why didn't you turn her down? It's not that hard." She hadn't had any trouble saying no to David's prom invitation.

"I did turn her down. Lots of times."

Jess put her hands on her hips. "She must have been pretty persuasive then."

"She kept asking me to go out, and when I wouldn't say yes, she said she didn't think I liked girls. That's why I went out with her."

"That's a stupid reason to go out with her! Of course you like girls. You're a boy, aren't you?"

Marty studied her for a moment, and then his expression changed. "Are you *mad* about this?"

"Yes, I'm mad," she said, but until that moment she hadn't realized that's what she was feeling.

"Why?"

While he searched her eyes, she struggled to come up with an answer, but she realized there wasn't a valid one. What right did she have to be angry if he wanted to go out with other girls? It wasn't like she had any claim on him. "Just tell me the truth, Marty," she said, her voice breaking. "Are you dating girls now?"

"It *wasn't* a date. I don't even like her."

"You don't like her but you'll go out with her because she asked?"

Marty opened his mouth to argue and then closed it as he turned away. After taking in a deep breath, he faced her. "Look." He spread his hands out. "I had a pretty lousy time with her. She never stopped talking, even when we were watching the show, and then she practically attacked me when I took her home."

"What does that mean?"

"Let's just say that girls shouldn't try to kiss a fellow they don't even–"

"You kissed her?" Jess shrieked.

"I did *not* kiss her. *She* tried to kiss *me.*"

Jess turned her back to him, no longer able to hold in her tears. This was a disaster. With Marty going out with girls, it was just a matter of time before he found one he liked. Even if his date with Sharon hadn't ended well, there were other girls in town, lots of them. If he fell in love with one of them, she would lose him.

"Are you crying?" He put his hand on her shoulder, but she shrugged it off. He moved in front of her. "Why are you crying?"

She lifted her eyes to meet his. *Because I don't want to lose you,* she thought, but she couldn't say it.

He stepped closer and brushed away her tears with his thumb, his brown eyes full of concern as they searched hers. "What's wrong?"

She knew she might lose him when they graduated from college, but now it could happen before the end of high school. Did she only have a few precious months left with him?

"Jess." He continued stroking her cheek. "Please tell me what's wrong."

Placing her hand on the back of his neck, she stood on her toes and brushed her lips against his. They were soft, much softer than she'd ever imagined, and she rose up on her toes so she could feel them again. Gently caressing his lips, they tasted sweet mixed with her salty tears. Then his breathing changed and his arms wrapped around her.

The Boy in the Woods

A shudder went through her as his lips moved on hers. Clutching him tighter, she kissed him hard, her body charged with electricity. With his hot mouth on hers, a fire rose in her, consuming her from the inside out. Her breathing became shallow, leaving her gasping, but she didn't care. Marty's firm body was pressed against hers, his mouth hungrily kissing her, and she needed it more than she needed air.

When he pulled away, she opened her eyes. Both of them were breathing heavily.

"What are we doing?" he said, his eyes troubled.

"Kissing." She leaned in, eager for his lips again.

He pulled back. "Jess, I don't–"

She placed her hand on his mouth. He was going to question what they were doing. He was going to say it was a bad idea, that they should stop, and then that would be the end. "Please, Marty." She leaned closer while her tears welled up again. "Please."

He lowered his head with a sigh, his eyes showing his concern but full of longing as they searched hers, and then his mouth was on hers again. She closed her eyes and moaned, her fingers tangling in his hair as the heat from his touch burned inside her once again. She let the fire consume her, all thoughts leaving except the need for his kisses.

Jess didn't know how long they kissed. Time seemed to stand still, but when they stopped, they sat in front of the fire, holding each other.

Jess never wanted the moment to end, but after a while, Marty stirred. "It's getting late, Jess."

Jess sighed and squeezed him tighter. "I don't want to go home."

"I know, but I don't want you to take any chances with your uncle."

"Okay." She let go.

They put on their boots and coats, and Marty damped down the fires.

"You're going home?" Jess said.

"I think it's late enough, and I need to be at work early tomorrow. The old people can't get out when it snows and I'll be busy with deliveries for most of the day."

When they stepped outside, the snow was coming down so thick Jess couldn't see across the clearing. What had fallen was almost at her knees. Marty struggled alongside her as they tried to walk to the edge of the woods.

Jess stopped halfway across the clearing. "I don't think I can get home this way." Fat snowflakes swirled around her, stinging her skin before melting. "What am I going to do?"

"We'll take the path." He grasped her hand. "Your tracks should be covered by morning."

It was a much shorter distance, but it still took forever and when they reached the end of the path, they were panting. "Are you sure you should go home?" Jess said. "It's going to take you forever. Maybe you should stay at the cabin."

"I'm going back to town."

"No, Marty. It's too far! You'll never make it."

Marty shook his head. "The roads won't be too bad since they've been plowing. There shouldn't be any traffic. And I can stay at the store once I get there. If I don't go tonight, by tomorrow the snow will be too deep and I'll be stuck at home."

Jess nodded. She didn't want him to be trapped with his father.

"Don't worry. I'll be alright. Promise."

"Okay."

While he looked down at her in the dark, she knew what she wanted him to do, but she couldn't see his eyes to know if he wanted the same. Then he leaned closer, capturing her lips, and she deepened the kiss. He released her and their panting breaths created a cloud of mist around them.

"I'll see you, Jess."

"Goodbye, Marty."

She pushed through the snow-covered brush, and the powder rained down on her, coating her in white. She looked back, but she couldn't see Marty. Moving forward, she kept her hand on the side of the garage for support until she reached the front. She peeked around the corner. All the lights in the house were off except for the one in the downstairs hallway. Either no one was home, or everyone was already in bed. She went towards the house, but with nothing to use for support, it was a struggle not to fall.

If she went in through the front door, she could be quiet enough that no one would hear her. That would be far easier than fighting her way around to the back of the house. Holding onto the pillar of the front porch, she climbed the buried stairs and then brushed off as much snow as possible. After easing the door open, she stepped inside, and turned to close it, hearing the latch click into place.

"Well, well, well," Uncle Jonathon drawled behind her, and she froze. "Look what the cat dragged in."

Chapter Fifty

Take Good Care of My Baby

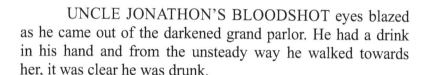

UNCLE JONATHON'S BLOODSHOT eyes blazed as he came out of the darkened grand parlor. He had a drink in his hand and from the unsteady way he walked towards her, it was clear he was drunk.

"Hello, Uncle J-J-Jonathon." She hadn't been cold when she was outside with Marty, but now her entire body was trembling.

He set his glass on the table where the telephone sat. "Where've you been?" he slurred.

To keep up the pretense that nothing was wrong, she removed her boots and unbuttoned her coat, but her shaking fingers fumbled with the buttons. "It looked so pretty outside, I decided to go for a walk."

She turned away from him to hang her coat in the closet, hoping he didn't see the tremor in her hand when she reached for a hanger. She tried to keep her panic down. She couldn't let him guess she wasn't telling the truth.

With the closet door closed, she turned. Uncle

Jonathon had moved between her and the stairs. "Good night." She stepped around him, but he grabbed her arm and yanked her back.

"Not so fast, missy." He held her upper arms in a tight grip, the smell of alcohol washing over her. "You must think I'm stupid."

"N-no, sir." She tried to pull her arms free. "I – I was – walking. I was–"

"Don't lie to me!" he said, shaking her.

Tears came to her eyes as she struggled. "Please, Uncle Jonathon. You're hurting me."

"I *saw* you," he shouted, giving her another shake. "How long have you been seeing him? *How long?*"

She'd never seen him like this. His rage was at a frenzied pitch, and an uncontrollable terror came over her. *"Let me go,"* she screamed, trying to get loose.

"What have you been doing with him? Tell me!"

"Dad, what are you doing?"

"Doug!" she sobbed, still struggling.

Doug appeared at his father's side in his robe and pajamas, pulling on Uncle Jonathon's arm. "Dad, stop. Let her go." As soon as he'd wrenched Jess away, she clung to him, sobbing into his chest. "What are you doing? Have you lost your mind?" he shouted.

"She's having an affair with James!"

"That's crazy."

"It's not crazy. I just caught her."

"No," Jess cried out. "It's not true."

"I don't believe it," Doug said. "Jess wouldn't do that."

"She was coming from the *garage*, Douglas. I *saw* her."

Doug didn't respond, and Jess lifted her head. He was looking down at her as if he didn't know her.

"It's not true," she said. "I *swear* it's not true. I was coming back from a walk."

"She's a lying tramp!"

"Don't talk about her like that," Doug roared, trying to take a step towards his father, but Jess's tight hold kept him back.

"You're going to take her word over *mine?*" Uncle Jonathon shouted, his hands balling into fists.

"No! Stop," Jess pleaded. With Uncle Jonathon drunk and Doug determined to protect her, she was terrified they might get into a physical fight. "Please, Doug, take me upstairs."

He looked between her and his father, seeming uncertain about what to do.

"Please," she begged.

"Alright," he said through his teeth.

"Douglas!" Uncle Jonathon shouted, while Doug led her up the stairs.

Jess wanted to run, terrified her uncle was going to come after them, but Doug kept walking, his arm around her waist.

"Douglas," he repeated, but Doug continued to her bedroom.

Once the door was closed, Jess leaned against him for support, her body shaking so much she feared her legs were going to give out.

The Boy in the Woods

"Are you okay?" Doug said. "Did he hurt you?"

"Yes," she said, the tears returning. She wiped them away with a trembling hand. "I thought he was going to kill me."

"Oh, Jess." He rubbed her back. "He wouldn't do that."

"I was so scared."

"You're safe now. What happened?"

What *had* happened? Uncle Jonathon must have been drinking in the grand parlor with the lights out. When he saw her walking from the garage, he'd assumed she'd been visiting James. She couldn't tell Doug the truth. Now that she'd seen what her uncle was capable of, it made her doubly terrified of what he would do if he found out about Marty.

"The snow looked so pretty, I decided to go for a walk. I went out the kitchen and walked to the woods behind the garage. I was going to walk around the edge of the yard, but the snow was too deep, and I came back. That's when Uncle Jonathon must have seen me."

Doug let go of her. "Jess," he said, searching her eyes. "Please be honest with me. You didn't go out there so you could see James, did you?"

"*No.* I hate him. Ever since I've lived here he's always been rude to me. I would *never* have anything to do with him."

He pulled her close. "I'm sorry. I didn't think you would do something like that."

"What am I going to do? Your dad doesn't believe me."

"I'll talk to him tomorrow. I'll make him see the truth."

"I want to leave. I don't want to stay here tonight."

"You can't leave."

"What if he comes in my room when I'm sleeping?"

"Jess, be reasonable. We couldn't leave now even if we wanted to. The snow is too deep to drive."

Fear constricted Jess's chest. He was right. She was trapped, and she started sobbing again.

"Don't cry." He tightened his hold on her. "I'll stay here with you. I'll sleep in the other bed, and that way you won't have to be scared."

"Okay." She gulped in some air, trying to gain control. "But I want to go tomorrow. I don't want to live here anymore."

"Jess, don't talk like that."

She was ready to argue, but he spoke again.

"Let's talk about it tomorrow, okay? It's late and we're too exhausted to think clearly."

She had the impression that what he really meant was *she* was too exhausted to think clearly, but that wasn't the case. She would never live with her uncle again after what he'd done.

"Why don't you change in the bathroom and we'll go to sleep."

"Okay," she said, deciding there was no use arguing with him any further. As soon as morning came, she'd make him take her away.

Once they were in their beds and the light turned off, fresh tears sprung to Jess's eyes. How could her life have gone so wrong? *Oh, Marty. I need you*, she thought. If he was there, he'd make her feel safe. Then she pictured Marty

The Boy in the Woods

walking to town in the dark through the deep snow. He was in danger too. A car could hit him, or he might slip and be too injured to walk. What would happen if he couldn't get out of the cold? She pushed the blankets over her mouth to muffle her crying so Doug wouldn't hear.

When she woke, sunlight was streaming through her windows. Rolling over, she was surprised to find Doug sitting on the other bed. He'd already dressed, and the bed was made.

"What time is it?" she asked.

He checked his watch. "After eleven. I talked to Dad."

She sat up with her stomach clenching.

"He doesn't remember last night."

Her mouth dropped open. "I don't believe it!"

"It can happen sometimes when you drink too much. It's called a blackout."

"How can he not remember what he did to me?"

"He feels terrible about it, Jess. He wants to apologize."

"No. After what he did, I don't trust him."

"Listen to me," Doug said, his voice pleading. "I know what he did scared you, but he won't do it again. He knows he made a mistake, a real bad mistake, and he wants to make it better. Please let him apologize."

She was about to argue with him, but Doug ground the heel of his hands into his eyes. This was the only family he had and it was being torn apart. She didn't want to hurt him, but when she considered forgiving her uncle, her mind balked. "I can't forget what he did to me, Doug."

"Will you at least listen to him? Let him explain? Maybe then you'll believe he's sorry."

She sighed. "Okay." Doug deserved at least that. "But I want you to go with me. I don't want to see him alone."

Doug's body relaxed. "Of course, I'll be there. You get dressed and I'll wait in the hall."

After he was gone, she looked out her window and her heart sank. There were drifts several feet high in front of the garage doors. Doug wouldn't be able to get his car out. And what about Marty? She had no idea if he'd made it to the drugstore. But if he had, he couldn't come back with the snow so deep. She was on her own with only Doug to protect her.

Doug walked with her to the library where they found Uncle Jonathon sitting in front of a fire, reading from a stack of papers. "Dad, Jess is here."

"Jessica," he said standing.

Jess moved closer to Doug.

"Douglas told me what happened last night. Apparently I'd had too much to drink and jumped to the wrong conclusion. It was wrong, and I hope you'll forgive my actions."

He waited, and Jess realized that was all he was going to say. It wasn't enough, she thought, anger rising inside her. Not after what he'd done.

"Jess?" Doug said. His eyes were begging her to accept.

"But – it might happen again," she said to Doug.

"It won't," Uncle Jonathon said. "I've promised Douglas, and I'll make the same promise to you. I won't drink at home while you're living here. He assured me that

The Boy in the Woods

you would never have anything to do with James, and I believe him. You don't need to worry about being accused again."

"See? It'll be okay," Doug said, his expression urging her.

In the silence, Jess felt the pressure increasing. She didn't want to say she forgave him because she didn't. But what other choice did she have? She didn't know when she could leave. If she refused to give him the answer he wanted, he could blow up at her again.

Jess dropped her head. "I… forgive you."

"Thank you, Jessica." There was relief in his voice.

She lifted her eyes, but he'd turned towards the fire to put in another log. Could he have been sincere?

"The snowplow from the mine is on its way," Doug said. "But it's going to take a while since they have to plow the roads to get here. We won't be able to leave until this afternoon."

Jess looked at him with relief.

"Uh, I meant Dad and I," he said with an apologetic expression. "We're going to work."

He wasn't taking her away?

"Are you hungry? You haven't had anything to eat yet," he said.

She felt a pain in her stomach when he said it. The last time she'd eaten was breakfast the previous day. "I guess."

Doug found eggs in the icebox and scrambled them while Jess made toast. At the table, she contemplated her food, blinking back fresh tears. She didn't know if Marty was okay or not, and she was trapped with no way to escape.

"Please don't be sad." He leaned forward to take her hand. "I know you still want to leave, but if you give it some time, you'll realize you have nothing to be afraid of."

He seemed convinced it was true and she wanted to believe him. She'd give anything to rewind the clocks back and have last night never happen. Maybe her uncle felt the same way. If he went back to ignoring her like he had in the past, she could hold out until she was able to leave for college.

After they ate, she excused herself, saying she would read in her room, but in reality she wanted to be alone. Now that her fears about her uncle had lessened a little, she was sick with worry about Marty. The only way she could make sure he was okay was to call the drugstore, but with Doug and Uncle Jonathon in the house, she didn't dare risk it.

In her bedroom, she picked up the mitten she was knitting for Marty's Christmas present, trying to keep her worries for him at bay. When she heard a truck engine, she put down her work and went to the window. An enormous snow plow was making its way down the drive. She watched as it pushed snow into huge piles on either side of the road, willing it to move faster. Upon reaching the house, the driver hopped out to help James shovel out the garage doors.

There was a knock on her bedroom door. "Who is it?" she asked, her heart beginning to race.

"It's me, Doug. Can I come in?"

She pushed the mitten and ball of wool under her pillow. "Yes."

He'd changed into a suit and tie. "We're going to work soon but I wanted to be sure you're alright. I can stay home if you need me to."

"No, I'm okay."

"Are you sure?"

"Yes."

He looked out her window at the garage. "They're going to plow the road to the Lindstrom's next so James can pick up something for dinner. I called over there this morning and gave Mrs. Lindstrom some suggestions for the kind of food we like. I figured I'd better before Dad realizes what she's been sending over. Dad will work late, but I'm coming home for dinner. I don't want you to be alone any longer than you have to be."

She hugged him. "Thanks, Doug."

He gave her an extra tight squeeze. "If you need anything, call me."

"I will."

She watched from her window until the black car disappeared from view and then ran down the stairs. Once she'd found the phone book she flipped through the yellow pages and dialed the number for the drugstore. Listening to it ring, she squeezed her eyes shut. *Please be safe, Marty.*

"Hello," a deep male voice answered. It was Mr. Dwyer.

"Is Marty Cappellini there?"

"No, he's not. He's out making deliveries."

She sagged against the wall.

"Did you need something?"

"Uh, no, I don't need anything. I just wanted to check, I mean, no, I'm fine."

"Who is this?"

"I'm a friend. Thank you. Goodbye."

She hung up the phone before Mr. Dwyer could ask

her more questions and collapsed on the stairs. Marty was safe, she thought, her heart swelling. Mr. Dwyer would probably mention a girl had called about him. As she stood to go back to her room, she imagined the smile on his face when he realized it was her.

That evening, she and Doug ate a delicious stew and a strange brown bread made by Mrs. Lindstrom that Jess thought was quite tasty. With her uncle out of the house and the knowledge that Marty was all right, she was much more relaxed. Doug had been quieter than normal throughout the meal, but she assumed he was worried about work. He'd mentioned how hard it had been for the employees to get to the mine, which had put them behind schedule.

When they finished, Jess stood and took their bowls, but Doug put his hand on hers and guided them back to the table. "Will you sit for a minute, Jess? I want to talk to you."

"Okay." She took her seat. From the serious look in his eyes, it had to be important.

He put his hands in his lap and slouched forward, frowning at the empty bowl in front of him. "I've been thinking an awful lot ever since last night. Seeing my Dad do that to you, it hurt me, and I think I finally know why." He took a deep breath and let it out. "You mean a lot to me, Jess."

Jess was overwhelmed with emotion. Almost the whole time she'd lived with Doug, he'd taken care of her and tried to protect her from his father. "You mean a lot to me too."

He looked up with surprise. "I do?"

"You've always been there for me when I needed you. You're like the brother I always wished I had."

He winced. "No, Jess. I mean I love you."

The Boy in the Woods

Jess's dinner became a rock in her stomach while she stared at him.

"I've been in love with you for a long time. For years, and I–"

"What about Donna?" she said, interrupting him.

Shock registered in his face. "Donna? I broke up with her a long time ago."

"I saw you kissing her on graduation day!"

His eyes shifted away and he hunched over, shaking his head. "That was nothing. It was a mistake."

"I don't care about what you did with Donna. I'm sorry, Doug, but I don't feel that way about you. I love you, but like a brother."

Doug hunched further, head hanging. "If it's because I'm your cousin," he said quietly. "You don't have worry about that. I'm not related to you by blood. I'm... adopted."

He looked so ashamed, that despite what was happening, Jess's heart went out to him. "I already know. It's not the reason."

"Please, Jess," he pleaded, his eyes full of desperation, but then his face became hopeful. "You said you didn't want to live here anymore. We can live in town! I'll buy you a house, and you can see your friends whenever you want. I'll give you anything you need. And we'll take our time. I won't expect you to love me right away."

"Doug, please. I can't–"

"Give me a chance, Jess. I love you and I want to spend the rest of my life with you. I know you can fall in love with me if you give it some time."

"I'm in love with someone else!"

There was a ringing silence as Doug gaped. "How? You're not dating anyone."

"I met him at school." She kept her eyes on his. "He's a nice boy, but he's not the kind Uncle Jonathon would approve of. That's why I haven't mentioned him."

"Is he in love with you?"

"Yes, he is. We've been in love for a long time."

Doug's face fell. Taking deep breaths, he stared at the table, fighting back tears.

Jess felt awful. She didn't want to hurt him. "I'm really sorry, Doug. I'm sure you'll find–"

Without a word, he stood and walked out.

Chapter Fifty-One
I'm Sorry

JESS'S BOOTS CRUNCHED in the packed snow while she walked down the winding drive. A blast of wind hit the trees and the powder that had fallen during the storm blew off the branches. Ice flakes surrounded her and dove down the back of her neck. She clutched her scarf tighter and hurried her steps.

She'd woken to an empty house, much to her relief. After Doug's bombshell admission the previous night, the last thing she wanted was to see him. Not only would it be awkward to be in the same room with him, knowing he was nursing a broken heart, she was sure he would be bitter and angry that she'd rejected him.

No matter how much she'd tried, she couldn't make sense of how he could have fallen in love with her. Had she done something that caused it? Maybe she shouldn't have been so affectionate with him, hugging him every time he came home. She'd never hidden how much she cared about him, and perhaps that had been a mistake. But in all the time they'd spent together, she'd never once suspected his feelings for her were any deeper than her feelings for him.

When she reached the spot where she had to enter the woods, she surveyed the snow bank on the side of the road that was taller than she was. With a sigh of resignation, she scrambled up the steep incline. The basket swayed precariously on her arm, threatening to spill its contents. After reaching the top, she half climbed, half slid down the other side, sinking knee deep in snow at the bottom. She took a step, but didn't raise her foot high enough and fell face-first into the powder. Struggling to stand, tears of frustration filled her eyes.

This was going to be more difficult than she'd expected, but she had to get to the cabin. She needed to see Marty. She wiped away the tears, then looked at her watch, noting the time so she'd know how long it took to get to the cabin. She couldn't risk being caught coming home by Doug and Uncle Jonathon. With a renewed determination, she forced her way through the snow.

She reached the cabin almost an hour later, out of breath and sweating. After kicking away the snow by the door, she let herself in. She gazed at the dark fireplace, reliving the moment she'd kissed Marty. It was magical, the most wonderful thing she'd ever experienced. Would he want to kiss her again? She hoped so, and a thrill of excitement went through her at the thought.

After building both fires, she wrapped herself in a blanket and sat on a chair to wait, her mind turning to what she would tell Marty. He was going to be angry when she shared the details of what Uncle Jonathon had done. But when she told him about Doug being in love with her, it could be far worse. She remembered how jealous she'd felt when she thought Marty was dating Sharon. What if he was angry enough to want to confront Doug? She'd have to make sure he understood how dangerous that would be, for both of them.

The Boy in the Woods

It wouldn't be pleasant for him to hear the details about everything, but she couldn't keep it from him. Her home life had turned into a disaster, and she needed help to figure out what she should do.

As the time Marty would arrive came closer, she set out their food in the kitchen and then went to the window that overlooked the clearing. She watched for him, more anxious with each passing minute. What was taking him so long? And then a terrible thought occurred to her. Maybe he wasn't coming at all. No, that couldn't be true, she decided. He'd do anything to see her, especially after they'd kissed. He must be running late because of the snow. But as more minutes crept by, her fears mounted. If he didn't hurry, she wouldn't have enough time to talk to him.

When she could no longer postpone leaving, she went to the kitchen with a heavy heart. Surveying the food on the table, she decided to leave it for him. He was bound to be hungry when he got to the cabin. She went to find a pencil and a piece of paper and wrote a quick note.

Dear Marty,

I'm sorry I had to leave before you got here, but I'll see you tomorrow.

She hesitated as she considered how she should end it. Should she write "Love, Jess" like she usually did when she ended letters? Perhaps it was too much. They should at least talk about their feelings before she wrote "love" in a message to him.

Enjoy the food and take care of yourself,

Jess

She left it on the table and then damped down the fires. After bundling up, she went outside, casting a longing glance at the spot where Marty would enter the clearing, but it was empty. With her scarf tight around her neck, she set off

557

The Boy in the Woods

towards the woods, grateful the path she'd created made walking easier.

By the time the black car had pulled into the garage, she had the table set. The meatloaf and mashed potatoes were heated and ready to be served. She watched Uncle Jonathon and Doug climb out of the car, her stomach twisting. Uncle Jonathon strode to the house while Doug trudged after him, his shoulders stooped.

Turning away, her jitters increased. She hadn't seen Uncle Jonathon since the morning she'd been forced to say she'd forgiven him and she had no idea how he was going to treat her. Nor did she know what to expect from Doug. What if Uncle Jonathon figured out why he was blue? She'd seen how out of control and angry he'd been when he thought she was having a relationship with James. How bad would it be if he knew his own son was in love with her?

She set the bowl of mashed potatoes on the table, hearing footsteps behind her as Uncle Jonathon and Doug entered the dining room.

"Hello, Jessica," Uncle Jonathon said.

"Hello." She avoided looking at him while she sat.

Doug was silent as he went to his chair.

"This looks very nice. Thank you," Uncle Jonathon said, surveying the table.

She looked at him with surprise. "Uh, you're welcome." That may have been the first compliment he'd ever paid her. Was this his way of trying to make things up to her?

Once Uncle Jonathon had served the food, he talked to Doug about the business like he always did. Doug hunched over his plate, murmuring one word answers, while Jess kept her attention on her food.

The Boy in the Woods

The pressure between them was palpable, and she couldn't understand how her uncle didn't seem to notice. But as usual, his focus was on himself rather than those around him, and for once, Jess was glad his selfishness was working in her favor. She just hoped Doug would get over his broken heart before his father figured out what was going on.

After they'd eaten, she escaped to the kitchen to do the dishes. While she washed them, she looked out the window at the dark forest beyond the garage. Marty had to be at the cabin. She wanted so much to see him, but she didn't dare leave the house.

The next morning, Jess looked up from her bowl of cereal to see Dorothy Lindstrom walk in from the butler's pantry carrying a bucket and a mop. "Good morning," she said.

"Morning," Dorothy said as she poured the contents of the bucket into the sink. "It's a fine day. Even when it's below freezing outside, all that sunshine makes a body happy."

"Yes, it does," Jess said, even though the sunshine was doing nothing to improve her spirits. She slowed her eating, watching Dorothy put away the bucket and mop.

Dorothy was a round-faced farm girl in her early twenties with a cheerful disposition. Jess appreciated that she did the cleaning quickly so she could get back to her farm chores. It meant she was too busy to hang around Jess, asking a lot of questions about what she was doing when she left the house. Seeing Dorothy locate an aerosol can of furniture polish and a handful of rags from the butler's pantry, Jess was glad. That would keep her busy for a long time, long enough for Jess to make meatloaf sandwiches for her and Marty and duck out the back door.

This time when she went to the cabin, it didn't take as

long. Not only had she cleared a passable path, the snow was hardening, making it easier to walk on. While she trudged through the woods, she wondered if Marty had written a message back to her last night. Maybe he'd say something personal, like how he felt about her.

Inside the cabin, she went straight to the kitchen with excitement, but as soon as she saw the table, a wave of despair hit her. The food and note were where she'd left them. Marty had never come.

Tears stung her eyes. There had to be an explanation. The roads must be worse than she thought. Or perhaps they were all right for everyone except the elderly people, and Marty was still busy with deliveries. In any case, he would be there today. It had been three days since the storm, plenty of time for the snow in town to have been cleared away.

She read while she waited for him, not wanting to brood over what she'd have to tell him. But when the time for him to be there passed, a terrible fear took hold. Something must have happened to him.

She lingered as long as she dared, watching through the window, but there was still no sign of him. By the time she'd pulled her coat on, she was sick with worry. On the way home, she tried to come up with another reason for his absence other than him being hurt, but nothing came to her. She had to call the drugstore and find out what was going on.

Back in the house, she looked at her watch. It was already late, and she had to get dinner ready before Uncle Jonathon and Doug came home. She rushed to heat up Mrs. Lindstrom's ham casserole and set the table, but she wasn't quick enough. Doug and Uncle Jonathon were waiting at the table when she brought out the last of the food.

Throughout dinner, Uncle Jonathon droned on about the mine while Jess's thoughts were on Marty. Images of what could have happened to him filled her mind even though she tried not to think about them: Marty riding his bike in the deep snow and falling, breaking a bone, or being struck by a vehicle.

Later, as she scraped her unfinished dinner into the garbage, she tried to console herself. She'd call the drugstore in the morning.

That night she dreamed she was fighting her way through the snowstorm, desperate to find Marty, but deep drifts dragged at her legs, keeping her from moving forward. Blinded by the swirling white powder, she screamed his name, but the howling winds blew her words away. She awoke the next morning, exhausted and unsettled.

After throwing on a robe, she ran downstairs to the phone. While she listened to it ring, she silently prayed.

"Hello?" Instead of Mr. Dwyer's deep voice, it was a woman. Jess guessed it was Mrs. Schmidt who worked at the soda fountain.

"Is Marty Cappellini there? I need to speak to him."

"He's in the back."

Relief washed through her. *He's not hurt.*

"Hold on while I get him."

She heard the receiver being set down and smiled. He'd explain what had kept him away so long, and she'd feel stupid for not having figured it out. He'd have a good laugh and tease her about it. Why had she let herself get so worked up? All that fear and worry, and it was for nothing.

"I'm sorry, dear," Mrs. Schmidt said, returning to the line. "I thought he was back there, but he's out making deliveries."

"Oh," Jess said, her chest tightening.

"Would you like me to give him a message?"

"Um, yes," Jess said, fighting back tears. He was safe, that was the important thing. "Can you tell him–" She paused as she tried to think how she could leave him a message that wouldn't give away too much information.

"Yes?" Mrs. Schmidt prompted.

"Can you tell him the friend who was waiting to see him yesterday will be at the same place today?"

"Uh, do you want to give me a name?"

"He'll know who it is."

"Well, alright. I'll tell him."

Jess hung up the phone and walked to the kitchen, the emptiness of the house pressing on her. The unsettled feeling from her dream came back as questions filled her mind.

That afternoon, she paced the cabin, checking her watch every few minutes. It was past the time Marty should arrive, and she was trying to keep her anxiety from rising. Then the door opened and he came in, stomping his boots.

"*Marty!*" She rushed to him and hugged him tight. Breathing deeply, she took in the smell of the cold winter air as it mixed with the familiar scent of his wool coat. "Thank goodness you're here. I've been so worried about you."

He moved and she let go. He unbuttoned his coat while he walked to the fireplace. "It's been busy because of the snow."

"I missed you." She drank him in while he held his hands close to the flames. "A lot has happened. I have so much to tell you."

"I have to tell you something too." He straightened and turned towards her.

The Boy in the Woods

Now that she had a good look at him, he didn't seem well. His face was more pale than usual and there were dark smudges under his eyes, like he hadn't been sleeping. "What is it?" she said, going to him. He wouldn't meet her eyes, and it made her more concerned.

"I'm not coming back here anymore."

It suddenly seemed as if all the oxygen had been sucked out of the room. "What?" she gasped.

"I'm not coming here anymore," he said louder, finally meeting her eyes.

Instead of the warmth she'd always seen, they were hard. She fought to breathe, her fear turning into panic. "I – I can't believe it. Why aren't you coming back?"

"There's no point to it."

"What do you mean there's no point?" she said, her voice rising. His eyes became colder, and she swallowed, forcing herself to be calm. "What about your schoolwork? How will you pass–"

"Do you think I can't figure it out on my own? Is that what you're saying? That I'm dumb?"

"No, Marty. That's not what I'm saying." She brushed away a tear that had escaped. "You know I think you're smart." She placed her hand on his arm, but he went to the fireplace to get away from her. "Did something happen? Is that why you're–"

"No, nothing happened," he said, rounding on her. "I already told you why."

"Marty, please, I really need you right now. I love you, Marty. I've loved you for a long time, and I know you love me. Whatever happened–"

"You're wrong about that," he said, his face like stone.

A cold dread gripped her heart. "Wrong about what?" she whispered.

"I don't love you."

She stared at him open-mouthed while a rushing sound filled her ears. *He's lying*. There was no other explanation. Memories came to her of moments they'd shared – the two of them splashing each other in the water, working on homework together, him holding her, comforting her, kissing her in front of the fireplace as if he couldn't get enough of her. How could the boy who'd done all that now claim he didn't love her?

Then another memory came to her. The troubled look in his eyes when he'd asked her what they were doing when she'd kissed him. He'd been the one to suggest they stop, making a stupid joke about their lips getting tired. She'd been too happy at the time to notice, but now she understood. That's when everything had changed. He didn't think they should be a couple. He didn't think he was good enough for her, and even though they were months away from escaping to college, he was giving up. She couldn't believe he would throw everything they had away, but from the steeliness in his eyes, that's exactly what he was going to do. After everything they'd been through, after all the plans they'd made, he was going to walk away and break her heart forever.

"You *coward*," she screamed, slapping his face as the enormity of his betrayal crashed down on her.

He covered his cheek with his hand, staring at her with shock and disbelief, but she didn't care. While her palm stung and her body vibrated, she glared at him, waiting for him to explain himself.

He dropped his hand, his eyes turning hard again, and went to the door. When he slammed it shut behind him, Jess fell to the floor, sobbing as her entire world shattered.

Chapter Fifty-Two
I Fall To Pieces

"JESS, ARE YOU in here?"

Jess had ignored Doug's knocking on her bedroom door, but he'd opened it anyway.

"What's going on?" he asked.

She heard his footsteps crossing the room.

"Why are you in bed?"

"I don't feel good," she said from underneath her blankets.

After Marty had walked out of the cabin, she'd lain on the floor and cried so long, both fires had gone out. When she could stand, she pulled on her coat, and staggered home, hardly aware of anything except an all-consuming agony.

"Aren't you coming down for dinner?"

"No."

"But it's your birthday. We bought you a cake."

It was her birthday? Marty had left her on her

seventeenth birthday, she realized, and a fresh wave of grief came over her. Had he remembered it was her birthday when he came to the cabin to destroy her, or had he lost track of the days like she had?

"Aren't you going to get up?"

She swallowed, trying to stop crying. "I'm sick," she choked out. "I'm not coming." There was silence, then she heard Doug let out a sigh.

"If you can't come down, I'll be back to check on you later. I'll bring you something to eat, alright?"

She didn't respond, and after another hesitation, she heard him walk away and close the door. Using her pillow to stifle the sound, she sobbed uncontrollably. It was like a part of her had been cut out, and everything left behind was bleeding from the loss.

"Are you awake?"

The words slid in through a haze, and her mind came into focus. Doug must have come back.

"I brought you some stew."

Now that she was conscious, the wrenching grief clawed at her again. Why wouldn't he leave her alone?

"Jess?"

"I don't want it."

"You have to eat. You need to take care of yourself."

"I'm not hungry."

He hesitated. "I'll leave it on your table in case you get hungry later. Okay?"

She didn't answer.

"Good night, Jess."

The Boy in the Woods

She waited until she heard the door close before she rolled over. Her hand went under the pillow, and she felt the half-finished mitten she'd been knitting for Marty. She sat up as she pulled it out. Turning it over in her hand, tears streamed down her cheeks. Didn't he care how badly he would hurt her?

She pulled the needles out and yanked on the yarn to unravel the knitting. When all that was left was a gray kinked pile of yarn, she shoved it to the floor. Collapsing on her bed, she writhed, wrenching sobs tearing through her. Marty had unraveled their relationship and tossed it aside as if it meant nothing more than that unfinished mitten.

"You didn't eat your stew!"

Jess stirred under her covers.

"Why didn't you eat it?"

"I told you I wasn't hungry."

"Pull your blankets down. I want to see you."

When she didn't move, she heard him step closer.

"If you don't, I'm going to pull them off myself."

She uncovered her head, but kept her eyes closed so he wouldn't see how much she'd been crying.

"Jeez, Jess. You don't look so good."

"I told you I was sick." She began to pull the covers back over her head, but his hand stopped her. She blinked her eyes open. The early morning light was too bright, and she had to look at him through slitted eyes.

"You didn't even put on your pajamas."

"I was cold," she lied.

"Are you going to get up and eat something?"

"I'm not hungry."

"That's it. I'm staying home and taking care of you today."

"No." She didn't want Doug hovering over her all day while she was grieving. Especially now that she knew he was in love with her. "I'll eat," she said, sitting up.

"Well, okay," he said, still frowning. "But if you need anything, call me at the office."

She turned her head away from him.

"I mean it, Jess."

"I will," she said, but she had no intention of asking him for anything.

After Doug left with his father, Jess wandered down to the cold, empty kitchen. She stood in front of the open icebox for a long time, unable to decide what to eat. After choosing a bottle of milk, she made a bowl of cereal, but when she sat at the table, all she could do was stare at it.

He's gone, she thought, wiping new tears as they leaked from her eyes. What was she going to do now? For over three years, she'd been with Marty almost every day. In many ways, her life had revolved around him. He'd been a constant presence, keeping her company over the summer, and doing homework with her every day during the school year. How could she go on without him? She took the bowl to the sink and poured the milk down the drain, then dumped the soggy cereal in the trash before heading back to bed.

An hour before Uncle Jonathon and Doug were due home, she took a bath, then warmed up leftovers for dinner.

"I'm sorry you were too ill to celebrate your birthday yesterday," Uncle Jonathon said when he entered the dining room. "But as they say: better late than never. This is for you." He was smiling, holding out a wrapped present. Doug studied her with concern behind him.

"Thank you," she mumbled, taking it and placing it on the table next to her plate.

While they ate, Uncle Jonathon talked to Doug about business as usual. She pushed her food around, wishing they would finish so she could go back to her room. But at the end of the meal, Doug brought out a chocolate cake with lit candles on it. She forced herself to go through the motions of blowing them out even though she had nothing to wish for. By the time she was unwrapping her present, she was barely hanging on.

"A record player with batteries," she said, attempting to sound excited. "Thank you, Uncle Jonathon."

While he cut the cake, she swallowed hard, trying to keep her tears back. She could have taken it to the cabin to play music for her and Marty.

"Jess, you don't look well," Doug said. "Maybe you should go to bed."

"Okay." She stood. By the time she'd reached the hallway, the tears had returned.

Chapter Fifty-Three
Blue Christmas

"I WISH ANNIE was here," Doug said, a few days later while they were eating cereal and toast for Christmas breakfast.

"Me too," Jess said. She'd been desperately missing Annie now that she spent her days alone in the big house.

Uncle Jonathon grunted in assent, while frowning at his coffee cup. "It's been too long."

"I loved the big breakfast she'd always make on Christmas morning," Doug said, a wistful expression on his face. "And the turkey dinner we'd have the night before."

Mrs. Lindstrom had sent over a ham and enough cooked vegetables to last them a few days, but it wasn't the same. Annie was the heart of their home, mothering all three of them. And if there was one thing Jess needed right now, it was a mother.

Doug stood. "I guess we should open presents."

Surrounded by books, records, clothes, and a bottle of

The Boy in the Woods

White Shoulders perfume, Jess realized that Annie had bought all her presents before her sister became sick. The only presents she was sure Uncle Jonathon had bought were the eight millimeter movie camera, film projector, and movie screen he'd given Doug. It was an over-the-top gift, exactly what he'd choose for his son.

Jess was anxious when Doug opened the presents she'd bought for him. Over the years, she'd chosen things she thought Donna would like, and this year was no different, a soft argyle sweater and a bottle of cologne. Now she wished she'd given him the same fancy fountain pen she'd bought for Uncle Jonathon. Knowing how he felt about her, her gifts seemed too personal. Was this one of the reasons why he'd fallen in love with her? By misinterpreting her gifts?

Doug held out a small box. "You didn't open my present to you, Jess."

She'd been avoiding it ever since she'd seen it under the tree. After taking it from him, she took her time tearing the paper off. Her stomach clenched when it fell away to reveal a small velvet box. She lifted the lid with dread. Inside was a silver filigree heart-shaped locket.

"Go on, open it," he said.

Oh, no. Did he put his picture in it? She pried it open, and when she saw the two small images, she couldn't hold back her tears. On either side were photos of her parents looking very young, younger than she was.

"That's your mom at thirteen and your dad at fourteen, the year they met," Doug said.

It was the same age she and Marty were when they'd met. She wiped her tears and fought hard to hold back her grief.

"Your mother moved into town that year," Uncle Jonathon said. "We hired her father to work as an engineer at the mine. Billy was quite taken with her."

"This is the second part of your present." Doug handed her a larger flat gift. "Maybe I shouldn't call it a present since it belongs to you anyway."

She took a steadying breath before she opened it. "A yearbook?"

"It's your dad's high school yearbook from that year. I found it in the attic and had someone in the office make copies of the pictures. I didn't want to ruin it by cutting them out."

She turned the pages until she'd found the sophomore class pictures. While she looked at her dad's boyish face, she considered how much effort Doug had put into his present. It was an unbelievably thoughtful gift, the kind of thing someone would do for the person they loved. He must have had it done before she'd rejected him, but he'd still given it to her. Was he hoping this would convince her to give him a chance?

"I'll help you clean up," he said, gathering torn paper as he stood, and she joined him, avoiding his eyes.

The rest of the day, she stayed in her room playing records until the shadows grew long, and she dragged herself out of bed to reheat their Christmas dinner. Doug's somber mood had returned, and she feared it was triggered by her less than enthusiastic response to his gift. She avoided looking at him while they ate, not wanting to see his sadness.

When they were having leftover birthday cake for dessert, Doug laid down his fork and cleared his throat. "I, uh, I've got something to say."

Jess's heart began to race as she stared at him. Was he about to confess his feelings for her?

"What is it, son?" Uncle Jonathon said.

"I'm not going to college."

Jess's mouth dropped open.

"Why, that's wonderful news!" Uncle Jonathon said. "This is the best Christmas present you could have given me, Douglas. Why did you wait until now to tell me?"

"I've been thinking about it for a while," he said, frowning at his plate. "I just made the decision."

"I've been waiting for you to come to your senses," Uncle Jonathon said, not seeming to notice Doug's sudden grimace. "Now you can take your rightful place at the mine."

"Thanks, Dad," he said with a pained smile, and then turned his attention to Jess. "Are you done? I'll help you clear the dishes."

"Okay," she said, taken aback by his offer.

Once the dishes were in the sink, she ran the hot water, aware that Doug was lingering behind her.

"Will you let me dry?" he asked.

"If you want," she said with a shrug, wishing she could tell him to leave. She suspected the reason he'd given up college was because of her. If he was home, that would give him the opportunity to try to make her fall in love with him.

"I hate that things are different between us," he said, after several minutes of silence.

"Why did you give up college, Doug?" she demanded, anger that he wasn't respecting her wishes coming to the surface.

"I didn't feel like I had a choice."

"If you did it because of me, then you made the wrong choice."

He appeared shocked, and then his expression changed. "Yes, I did it because of you, but it's not what you think. I made a promise that I wouldn't abandon you, and I'm not. We don't know when Annie is coming back and I'm not leaving you alone with Dad."

She stepped back from the sink, her wet hands dripping on the floor. "You think he's going to attack me again?" she said loudly.

"No, I don't think that," he hissed. "And keep your voice down." He glanced at the doorway to the butler's pantry. "I know the two of you don't get along, and I think it's best for me to stay here, in case there's a – a disagreement."

That sounded to Jess like he *did* think his father might try to hurt her.

"I've seen how hard it's been for you without Annie, and I don't want you to be alone. I'm not giving up college entirely. I can go back next fall, Annie is bound to be back by then."

If Uncle Jonathon will allow it, Jess thought.

"Look, Jess. You don't have to worry about me. I don't have any ulterior motives, I promise."

His blue eyes were sincere, and her anger dissipated. She'd lived with Doug long enough to know that deep down he was a good person. He'd always done what he could to protect her. "Okay."

"I wish things could have been different."

The sadness was back in his eyes, and Jess returned to the dishes to avoid looking in them. She hadn't wanted to hurt him.

"But..." He shrugged. "We just have to manage the best we can."

The Boy in the Woods

Jess kept her attention on the soapy water. There was no mistaking what he was saying. He was still in love with her even though he was trying to get over it. She hoped with all her heart he wasn't feeling the same pain she was over Marty.

A week later, Jess got out of the black car to see Louise bounding in her direction, her breath trailing behind her in the frigid January morning.

"How's it going?" she said. "Did you have a good Christmas?" Louise's smile fell as she examined Jess.

Jess hugged her to hide her face. She knew she looked pale and tired. "It was okay. I got sick over Christmas. How about you?"

"That's too bad. I had a good Christmas, and you'll never guess what," she said, her eyes lighting up. "Harold asked me to go steady."

"That's – wonderful." Jess forced her smile to stay, but inside, grief seared through her. "You're so lucky," she said, barely able to hide her bitterness. Louise's parents didn't care about Harold's social status or how much money his parents made. What mattered to them was that he was a kind fellow who treated Louise well. If Jess's family had treated Marty the same way, he'd still be in her life.

"Don't worry, Jess. You'll find that special someone too. He's out there somewhere."

Thank goodness, the bell rang at that moment. She didn't know how much longer she could keep her despair hidden. Jess looped her arm through Louise's and they walked to the building side by side. She was grateful they had almost no classes together. That meant she could go through her day without having to pretend everything was all right, because it wasn't.

The Boy in the Woods

Painful memories of Marty were everywhere. Not only was she constantly remembering him in the halls or in her classes, but when she opened her notebook to take notes in her first class, it hit her that she was no longer taking notes for both of them. Instead of helping her forget him, being back at school was full of grim reminders of everything she'd lost. By the time the last bell rang, she was desperate to go home so she could climb into bed and hide from all of it.

With a wave to Louise, she hurried to James who was waiting by the open rear door. As soon as he'd closed it, she leaned against the bench seat. When she went to college, she would choose somewhere as far from this town as possible. Maybe she'd go back to her hometown of Manhattan. Even though she'd have to deal with memories of her parents, it wouldn't hurt as much as being here. Then she could forget all about Marty Cappellini.

Jess gasped. Marty had appeared as if summoned by her thoughts. Riding his bike out of an alley, he pedaled straight towards her while James was stopped at an intersection. His face was as handsome as ever, his cheeks turning pink from the cold air. An intense longing for him rolled over her like a boulder.

His attention was on the basket attached to his handlebars, which was filled with several packages wrapped in white paper. When he lifted his head, his eyes met Jess's and a shock of recognition came into them. He braked hard, skidding to a stop and some of the packages flew out, landing on the sidewalk between them. He remained still, staring at her with wide eyes. Jess held her breath, waiting. Was his heart pounding like hers? Was he filled with longing too – or regret, guilt, pain? Was he going to *do* something?

James pulled away and accelerated down the road. She wanted to cry out for him to stop, but she clamped her mouth shut. She twisted to look out the back window and saw Marty picking up his fallen packages with his back to her.

If that's what was most important to him after seeing her for the first time since he'd shattered her heart, then it was clear he no longer cared.

She faced forward as a tidal wave of grief consumed her. *It's really over.*

Chapter Fifty-Four
Town Without Pity

May 1962

JESS FANNED HERSELF with a notebook in the back of the black car after another sweltering May day in school. She couldn't wait to change into cooler clothing. Walking in the back door, she lifted her head with surprise. The air that surrounded her was filled with the delicious aroma of roasting chicken.

Could it be? Then someone stepped out of the butler's pantry.

"Annie!" Jess ran to her. "I've missed you," she said, hugging her tight.

"Oh, pumpkin. I've missed you too."

When Jess let go, Annie's smile dropped. "Why, pumpkin, you've lost weight."

"I guess I've been missing your good cooking," Jess said, keeping her smile going. "Why didn't you tell us you were coming back?"

The Boy in the Woods

"As soon as my sister was released from the hospital and settled in her apartment, she insisted I go home. The doctor said she could manage on her own, and I didn't want to wait. I called your uncle, and he got me a ticket on the very next train."

"Does Doug know you're back?"

"Yes, James took me to the office so I could see him and your uncle before he brought me here. So tell me everything that's happened since I've been gone."

"Uh, final exams are next week, and my friend Louise has a steady beau, and–" While she tried to think of more, all that came to her were things she couldn't tell Annie. Her devastating break up with Marty. That Doug was in love with her. Uncle Jonathon attacking her and accusing her of having an affair with James. "It's been real quiet," she said, but tears sprang to her eyes. She wiped them away and struggled to keep her smile going, but more came.

Annie put her hand on Jess's shoulder. "Pumpkin, what's happened?"

Jess sobbed, no longer able to hold back, "I missed you."

Annie held her. "I'm home now. I'm not going away again."

"I'm okay now," Jess said as she let go, and wiped her eyes with determination.

"Good girl. Why don't you change your clothes and I'll fix your basket with a good snack. We need to get you eating healthy again."

Annie turned to retrieve the basket from the butler's pantry and Jess opened her mouth to stop her, but hesitated as conflicting emotions swirled inside her. What if Marty had started using the cabin again? It had been his refuge for years, and it wasn't that farfetched he'd decide to come back. She hadn't been to the cabin once since Marty had broken her heart. He could have been going there for months.

Climbing the backstairs, butterflies filled her stomach. Did she and Marty have a chance after all? Or would he reject her again?

Minutes later, she was heading down the drive with her basket and school books. What would be his reaction when he saw her? Would he be angry she'd caught him? Or would he be full of regrets about breaking things off? If she was honest with herself, she was still in love with him even though he'd hurt her almost more than she could bear. They'd been too close and shared too much for her feelings for him to fade.

When she stepped inside the cabin, she sniffed the stuffy air scented with pine. While her eyes adjusted to the darkened room, she noticed a light coating of dust on the floor. In the fireplace there were old ashes, the same ashes from the night he'd left her. He hadn't been back at all.

Jess sank into the nearest chair, dark desolation enveloping her. Their love and friendship truly was gone forever. Wiping her tears away, anger swelled to take its place, and she embraced it. She'd been stupid to allow herself to get her hopes up. Marty had tossed her aside without a care, and it was time for her to move on. She stomped out of the cabin and slammed the door shut behind her. The minute she could, she was leaving this cruddy town and never coming back.

Not wanting to spend any more time around the cabin, or anywhere else that held painful memories, she took a circuitous route home, stopping every so often to unwrap the food Annie had packed for her and dropping it on the ground for the animals.

The Boy in the Woods

Back in the kitchen, Annie looked up with surprise from where she was seated at the table, peeling potatoes for dinner.

"You're back so soon," she said.

"I ate and then decided to come home." She turned her back to Annie while she set the basket on the counter, not wanting her to see she'd been crying. "I stopped going to the cabin while you were gone. I'm too old for it now. It's boring there."

"It was bound to happen, I suppose." Annie stood to take care of the basket. "It's probably for the best. Now we won't have to worry about your uncle finding out."

At the beginning of lunch period the next day, Jess joined Louise at her locker. "You go on without me. I have to go see the guidance counselor and then I'll join you."

"You know, you're not coming back next year," Louise said with a laugh. "You don't need to choose classes."

"I need to see her about something else."

"Okay, I'll save your seat."

When Jess found the counselor's office, she knocked on the door frame. "Mrs. Hayes?"

The older woman seated at a wooden desk covered with papers looked up. "Hello, Jess," she replied with a smile, taking off her reading glasses.

"Do you have a minute to talk?"

"Of course. I always have a minute for you. Come have a seat."

Jess entered, grateful for once of being a Blackwell.

"What can I do for you?" Mrs. Hayes said.

"I want to apply to college, but I don't know which ones I can apply to, and how to do it."

"There aren't a lot to choose from around here." Mrs. Hayes stood and went to a file cabinet piled high with more papers. She pulled the top drawer open. "But I think I can find you at least one or two good choices."

"I should have said, I want to go to a school on the east coast."

Mrs. Hayes stopped looking through file folders.

"I would like to attend college in New York City if I can."

Mrs. Hayes closed the drawer and returned to her seat. "Why would you want to go to a school so far from home?"

"Uh, I thought it would be – a good idea," Jess said, hesitating when Mrs. Hayes' expression became more sober.

"Most girls go to college close to home, Jess," Mrs. Hayes said in a serious tone, as if this was information Jess hadn't realized. "That's so their families are nearby in case they need help, or get homesick."

"I won't get homesick, Mrs. Hayes. I used to live in New York City."

"Most families prefer having their daughters nearby, so they know they're okay," she continued, as if Jess hadn't spoken. "It's for their peace of mind, you see."

"Yes, I understand, but I want to go to New York City."

There was silence while Mrs. Hayes studied her. "What were you planning on doing at college?"

"Um, I haven't decided yet." She'd been considering studying the sciences when Marty was still a part of her plans. She'd enjoyed those classes and that way they could spend more time together. But now that he wasn't going with her, she'd decided it would be too painful. Lacking any other obvious choices, she'd hoped once she took a few classes, something would attract her interest.

"Now, Jess," Mrs. Hayes said, resuming her lecturing tone. "The vast majority of girls only attend college until they find a husband and get married. It would be much better if you attend school close to home. That way—"

"I'm not going to college to find a husband." Jess tried to keep the frustration out of her voice. "I want to get a degree so I can have a career."

"Oh." Mrs. Hayes leaned back in her chair. "I didn't realize."

Wasn't that what they were talking about, Jess thought, her irritation surging.

"What classes are you taking now?"

"I'm taking Latin, law, calculus, earth science…" She trailed off as the furrow in Mrs. Hayes' brow deepened.

The woman leaned forward, clasping her hands on her desk. "I know your mother has been gone for a number of years."

Jess stared at her, shocked her mother would be brought into the conversation.

"Even though your uncle is a very good parent, and I'm sure doing the best he can, perhaps you haven't had the kind of upbringing most young ladies have, the ones who still have a mother to guide them."

Anger boiled through Jess. She *had* a mother. Annie had done every bit as good a job raising her as her real mother.

Mrs. Hayes shook her head. "It's a proven fact, Jess.

The Boy in the Woods

Men don't like to marry girls who are smarter than they are."

Jess opened her mouth to reply, but Mrs. Hayes lifted her hand to stop her.

"I know you said you're not looking for a husband at college, but by the time you're finished, you will be. You wouldn't want to do something that would make it impossible to ever get married, would you?"

While Mrs. Hayes waited, Jess struggled for a response, but the things that came to mind were too rude to say out loud. "Mrs. Hayes," she said, deciding it was pointless to argue. "This is what I've decided. Will you please help me apply to colleges in New York City?"

"Have you talked to your uncle about this?"

Jess's stomach sank. "No, I haven't talked to him."

"Then I'm afraid I can't help you. I would not be serving him, or you, by helping you do something he might not approve of. If he says it's all right for you to attend college that far from home, then I'll be happy to guide you towards some appropriate choices. But without his approval, it's out of the question."

Jess felt her hopes collapsing. If she needed his approval, her chance of going to college in New York had become much smaller. "Thank you, Mrs. Hayes," she mumbled as she stood.

"Not at all." Mrs. Hayes appeared relieved that Jess was leaving. "Have your uncle call me, and then we can go from there."

Jess didn't bother to answer as she left the office. On the way to the gym, she considered whether her uncle would agree. After years of battling with him over the smallest things, she feared he would refuse outright.

But they had been getting along a lot better over the

The Boy in the Woods

last few months. When she'd told him she needed a new spring jacket, he hadn't hesitated to say yes, even giving money to Doug so he could take her shopping. It gave her a small amount of hope that he might be agreeable about this too.

As she took her spot at the table next to Louise, her doubts mounted. Would Uncle Jonathon refuse when he realized he wouldn't be able to control her if she lived so far away.

"Are you ready for your tests?" Jess asked Louise the morning of their first final exam.

Louise sighed. "As ready as I'll ever be. I practiced my stenography all weekend while I took orders at the restaurant. Of course I had to translate everything so Dad could read them."

Jess laughed, imagining how confusing it would be if Louise handed orders written in shorthand to her dad.

"How about you?"

"I'm worried about them," Jess admitted.

"I'm sure you'll be fine. You always say you're worried, and then you do swell."

That's because she'd always studied with Marty. This was the first semester she'd been doing homework on her own. Even though Mr. Miller, her former math teacher, had been wrong about her only being able to do higher math because she'd been teaching it to someone else, she had to admit it was harder to learn now. "I guess I'm as ready as I'll ever be."

"Good luck," Louise said, over the loud ringing of the first bell.

"You too."

While Jess waited for the exam to start, the students around her had their notebooks open, attempting to cram in a few more facts. Jess didn't bother, knowing it was futile. She was already nervous enough without making it worse by rushing to gain last-minute knowledge.

Out of her peripheral vision, she saw a familiar shape, and when her head snapped up, her breath left her body. Marty crossed the threshold and when he saw her, he froze. With their eyes locked, she searched his face while the terrible ache of losing him returned. She longed to get up, run across the room and throw herself into his arms.

He hunched his shoulders and headed to the back of the classroom. She turned to watch him along with the other students who gave him curious stares. He chose a desk in the rear of the room, avoiding looking at anyone. Dark circles pooled under his eyes like the last day she saw him, and his face was thinner. Did he not get enough to eat now that she was no longer giving him extra food?

Realizing she was staring, she swung back in her chair. *I can't do this*, she thought with desperation. It would be torture to sit in the same room with him for the next hour and a half. And then it occurred to her that he would be in *all* her final exams since they'd started the school year with all the same classes. Every time she saw him, she'd feel this same wrenching pain.

Watching Mr. Larson handing out test papers, tears stung her eyes. How could she possibly concentrate on Latin verbs while she was in this much agony? She wanted to walk out, go hide in the girl's bathroom until the day was over, but then she would fail her exams.

She swallowed and straightened in her seat, a firm resolve taking hold. She had to pass her classes. If she didn't, she'd be stuck, locked inside the iron fence with her uncle controlling her for the rest of her life. Obviously Marty wasn't going to let the fact that she was there stop *him* from graduating high school, and she wouldn't let him crush her dreams either.

Bent over her paper with her pencil ready, she was determined to take her destiny in her own hands. She would pass this test and all the other ones, even if Marty was there. And that night at dinner, she'd ask Uncle Jonathon about going to school in New York. She'd put off asking him because she'd been afraid of how he would react, but she wasn't going to delay it any longer. If he wasn't willing to say yes, she'd find a way to convince him. She had to go somewhere far away, someplace where she would never run into Marty again.

Chapter Fifty-Five
You Don't Know Me

JESS HAD NERVOUS butterflies in her stomach all throughout breakfast. She'd intended to ask her uncle's permission to attend college in New York two days before, but he'd been in the best mood she'd ever seen him, smiling and gracious with Annie, joking with Doug, and kind towards her. With things going so well, she'd been reluctant to begin a discussion that would most likely turn into a fight.

But then she'd gone back to school the next day to take her last exams, and each time Marty had come into the classroom, he'd made a point of not looking at her. Pretending she didn't exist hurt far worse than his reaction the first day, and when she'd come home, she was filled with a renewed determination to get away from town.

Now that the time had arrived, her heart was racing and her palms were sweaty. Unable to eat, she'd decided she had to do it before her resolve crumbled again. "Uncle J-Jonathon?" she said, hating how shaky she already sounded.

He smiled at her. "Yes, Jessica?"

The Boy in the Woods

"I asked my guidance counselor, Mrs. Hayes, about going to college in New York City. She said if you call her and say it's okay, she can help me apply to some schools."

Uncle Jonathan's smile wavered and then fell as he stared at her.

She swallowed, and dared to continue. "Since it's my hometown, I want to go back."

"Who gave you this idea?" Uncle Jonathon said, his voice steely.

"No one. I've been thinking about it for a long time."

A muscle in his cheek twitched. "Well, I don't give my permission."

"Please let me go, Uncle Jonathon. I want to go to college so I can have a career and–"

"You have *got* to be joking. A Blackwell female out in the workforce?"

"A lot of women work now. Don't you have women working in your office?"

He scoffed. "Secretaries."

"What if I go to school here in the state?" she said, her panic rising. "I can go to the same one Doug–"

He hit the table with his fist, making her jump along with the dishes. "You've had enough education! You're not going and that's my final word."

"Dad," Doug said.

"Don't get involved in this, Douglas," he said, pointing his finger at Doug. His face was becoming redder by the second. "It's obvious she got this crazy idea because you insisted on going."

Doug slouched over his plate while Jess struggled to

get enough oxygen in her lungs. He had no intention of ever letting her go. She lifted her chin in an attempt to appear stronger. "I'll pay for college myself. I have my own money."

"No, you don't." Uncle Jonathon said.

"But, my *trust*. I *do* have money."

"You can't touch that until you're twenty-five." He leaned back in his chair with a satisfied expression.

Her mouth dropped open. "That can't be."

"But it is." He picked up his fork. "So, that's it."

Jess's mind raced, watching him cut into his fried egg. She was sure he was lying. Her parents loved her too much to leave her without a way to support herself once she was an adult. But if she challenged her uncle, it could get ugly. He might even lose his temper and attack her again. She looked at Doug, pushing the food around his plate. He would protect her if it came to that, wouldn't he?

"I want to ask the lawyer about it, the one who set up my trust," she said.

Uncle Jonathon's eyes narrowed. "What are you implying?"

She forced herself to meet his glare. "I have a hard time believing my dad would set it up that way."

"You want to talk to the lawyer?" he said, his face reddening again. "Let's call him now." He threw his napkin on the table. "Douglas, you might as well come too since she's turned this breakfast into a farce."

He pushed his chair back and stalked out. She looked to Doug for support, but he avoided her eyes as he stood.

She approached the phone in the foyer, and Uncle Jonathon thrust a business card at her. "There you go."

She took the card and dialed zero with a shaking hand.

"Operator. How may I help you?"

"I need to place a long distance call, to New York City, New York. The number is Fleetwood 8-5599."

"One moment please."

She heard several clicks. Uncle Jonathon was still glaring at her, his face red. Doug had gone pale, staring at the floor. His Then she heard ringing and turned her back to them.

"Shriver, Levin, and Lipton," a woman with a strong Brooklyn accent said.

"Hello. This is Jessica Blackwell. I would like to speak to Mr. Levin, please."

"Of course, Miss Blackwell. I'll have him on in a moment."

She didn't move while the line went silent, too nervous to face Uncle Jonathon. How angry would he get when she proved he'd lied? What if Doug wasn't able or willing to protect her? This could be the moment he'd take his dad's side instead of hers.

"Hello, Miss Blackwell," Mr. Levin said. "How can I help you today?"

"I had a question about my trust," she said, her breathing becoming short. "Do I have to wait until I'm twenty-five before I can access my money?"

"Yes, I'm afraid that's right."

Jess leaned against the wall. Her chest constricted, intensifying her feeling of being trapped.

"Your father was concerned about you having access to your estate at such a young age. He thought it best that you were older, so you'd be mature enough to handle it."

"I see."

"Your uncle is the trustee, however. If you need to draw on the funds, you can ask him."

She swallowed. "Thank you, Mr. Levin."

"Have a good day, Miss Blackwell. If you have more questions, don't hesitate to contact me."

"Yes, sir." She hung up the phone.

"Well?" Uncle Jonathon said.

Jess turned to face him. "You were right."

He straightened, smiling with triumph. In that smile, Jess saw her future – seven more years of living under his iron control. She couldn't do it.

"Uncle Jonathon, please give me some of my money so I can go to college."

His smile dropped. "No."

"Then I'll get a job and pay my own way."

"You will not."

"I'm not staying here!" Jess said, unwilling to back down. "As soon as I graduate, I'm moving out."

"You're still a minor and you're not going anywhere," Uncle Jonathon roared, spittle flying while his face turned an alarming purple color. He was a frightening sight, but Jess didn't care. Her life was at stake, and if she gave in now, she'd never be free.

"I'll leave when I turn eighteen. You can't stop me."

Annie appeared in the hallway, rushing from the dining room. "What's going on?"

"You're not going anywhere!"

"Dad, please," Doug said.

"You can't keep me locked up here. Not if I don't want to stay."

Uncle Jonathon sneered. "Is that so?"

"Just stop," Doug said.

"I'm leaving this house and I'm never coming back!"

"Jess, what are you saying?" Annie cried.

"How dare you speak to me like that?" Uncle Jonathon said, taking a step towards her.

"Leave her alone!" Doug said, tears coming to his eyes. "I can't do this anymore."

Uncle Jonathon rounded on his son. "Don't interfere, Douglas. You're the reason this whole mess has been kicked up."

"No, I'm not. Can't you see this isn't right? I can't be a part of it anymore."

Uncle Jonathon pointed at the stairs. "Go to your room."

"I won't! This is over."

Uncle Jonathon staggered backwards, dropping his arm and holding it as if Doug's refusal had injured him.

"Jess deserves to know the truth," Doug said.

"What truth?" Jess asked.

Uncle Jonathon let out hoarse gasps, his breathing becoming erratic. "Don't say anything," he croaked.

"Will someone tell me what's going on?" Annie said, ringing her hands.

"My father wants to keep you here so he can keep control over the business," Doug said to Jess.

The Boy in the Woods

"What?" Jess said.

Uncle Jonathon hugged himself. "Douglas, I'm – begging," he choked out.

"The mine, the house, all the property, it'll belong to you, Jess," Doug said. "You're the heir, not me."

"Is that true?" Annie asked Uncle Jonathon.

He staggered back against the wall, shaking his head.

"He wanted me to marry you," Doug said, his eyes filled with shame. "That way I could take charge after you inherited it."

Jess covered her mouth. Uncle Jonathon had made Doug lie about being in love with her?

"Johnny, tell me it isn't true," Annie said.

"He was afraid if you married someone else, they'd take the business away from us. I wouldn't blame you if you hated me. You never deserved this, Jess. I'm sorry."

Annie looked at Uncle Jonathon with horror. "Johnny, what have you done?"

"It's not... not like that," Uncle Jonathon gasped. "It was already agreed... with Billy. He said... Douglas could have it."

"They're your *children*," Annie said.

"But he didn't... He was supposed to..."

"I thought you *loved* Doug," Annie wiped her eyes, growing anger evident in her voice. "How could you hurt him, and Jess? How could you hurt them?"

Uncle Jonathon slid down the wall, and fell over on the floor, groaning as he clutched his arm.

Doug dropped to the floor next to him. "Dad! What's wrong?"

The Boy in the Woods

"Oh, God. It hurts," Uncle Jonathon said through gritted teeth.

Annie joined Doug on the floor as Uncle Jonathon roared in pain, his body stiffening.

"Johnny," she screamed.

"Tell me what's wrong," Doug begged.

"He's having a heart attack," Annie said as he writhed on the floor.

"No. Dad, please don't die."

Watching Doug and Annie struggling to help him, Jess knew it wasn't enough. If someone didn't act, he would die. Picking up the telephone receiver, she dialed zero again.

"Operator. How can I–"

"We need an ambulance at the Blackwell estate. My uncle – Jonathon Blackwell is having a heart attack."

"Johnny," Annie wailed.

"I'm passing on the information right now," the operator said.

Jess hung up the phone and went out the front door. "James," she shouted as she ran towards the open garage doors, and he appeared. "Open the gate! An ambulance is coming. Uncle Jonathon is having a heart attack."

His face fell, and he turned towards the black car. Jess ran back into the house to find Annie and Doug crying over Uncle Jonathon who was lying still, his eyes closed.

"Is he…" she asked, tears coming to her eyes.

"He's breathing, but I don't know," Doug said.

"An ambulance is coming," Jess said, joining them on the floor. "They'll help him."

The Boy in the Woods

"Dad, I need you," Doug cried while Annie wept next to him. "Please don't leave me."

It seemed like it took forever, but they finally heard the wail of a siren, and Jess ran outside. A long white Cadillac with a red stripe appeared from behind the trees, a flashing light on top of its low roof. James followed in the black car. Two men in white uniforms stepped out and once they'd retrieved their equipment, Jess waved them in. She and Doug helped Annie up, and they stood out of the way while the men worked on Uncle Jonathon.

He looked terrible, his face ashen and covered in a sheen of sweat. They strapped him to a gurney and took him outside to the ambulance. After they pushed it in, Doug climbed in after, ducking low to fit inside the back. Jess and Annie got in the black car.

Once seated, Annie sobbed and Jess put her arms around her, trying to comfort her. All the way to the hospital, Jess prayed her uncle would be okay. As angry as she was with him, she didn't want him to die. It would devastate Doug and Annie.

The arrival at the hospital was hectic. Uncle Jonathon was taken away and Doug attempted to follow, but was held back. A nurse asked for information from him, but he was too distracted to answer questions. With Annie still crying uncontrollably, Jess tried to help by answering for Doug or prodding him to reply. When the last of the paperwork was completed, all that was left to do was wait. Because of the prominence of the family, they were given a private room instead of having to sit in the crowded waiting room.

By now Annie had calmed, and the three of them sat in silence, each consumed with their own thoughts. It was then that Jess sifted through the staggering information she'd learned from Doug.

The Boy in the Woods

Uncle Jonathon had seemed angry from the moment he'd arrived to arrange her parents' funeral. Now she knew why. In his mind, she was standing in the way of Doug taking his rightful place at the head of the company. She believed what Uncle Jonathon had said, that her dad hadn't wanted her to be the heir. He had probably felt the same way she did, that Doug deserved it even though he was adopted.

She remembered Doug's reaction when he first met her, *"She's just a kid!"* Uncle Jonathon must have formed the plan to have Doug marry her from the beginning, even before he'd left for New York. Jess thought of all the times Doug had taken her to town, trying to get her to fall in love with him. How could her uncle have thought it was okay to force such a sick plan on both of them?

She should be mad at Doug for agreeing to take part in such an awful scheme. Instead she just felt sorry for him. His father had manipulated and used him, and Doug had gone along with it to prove his loyalty. If only the agreement between her dad and Uncle Jonathon had been finalized before he died, how different all of their lives might have been.

There was a knock on the door and a doctor walked in. All three of them stood.

"How is he?" Doug asked.

"It was touch and go for a while, but he's going to make it."

"Thank goodness," Annie said, as they all let out a sigh of relief.

"We have him stabilized and he's resting." The doctor pulled a pack of cigarettes out of his pocket. "There has been damage to his heart, but I believe he'll recover. However, he'll have to be careful from now on. He won't be able to work like he has, or maybe not at all."

"I can take over the business," Doug said. "He won't have to do anything."

While the doctor lit his cigarette, Jess looked at Doug's sober expression. At nineteen, he was now responsible for their family and all those men's jobs. Jess wondered if this was how it had been for Uncle Jonathon. As a young man, he'd carried the weight of it all, and lost his father from a heart attack on top of it.

The doctor blew out a lungful of smoke. "Good. Until we know how bad the damage is, we won't know how much he'll be able to do."

"Can we see him?" Annie said.

"Not yet. We don't want to overexert him right now. Later tonight you can visit him one at a time for a few minutes if he continues to improve."

"Thank you, doctor," Doug said, reaching out to shake his hand.

"I'll have a nurse come back in a while to update you." He stepped in the direction of the door. "But for now, you might as well grab a coffee and something to eat. It's going to be a long day."

When the door closed, Doug collapsed back into his chair and put his head in his hands.

"He's okay," Annie said with a wobbly smile, her eyes shiny.

"Yes, he is," Jess said.

"I think I'd like some coffee," Annie said. "How about you, Doug?"

"No, thanks," he said, sitting up.

"Do you want anything, Jess?"

"No, I'm fine."

"Okay. Hopefully I won't get lost," she said with a laugh, and headed out of the room.

"You must hate me," Doug said, once Annie had closed the door. He was leaning his head against the wall behind him, looking up at the ceiling.

"I don't hate you, Doug."

"You *should* hate me." His icy eyes met hers. "I hate myself. I knew what he was doing, what *I* was doing, was wrong. Not at first, but I knew it when I started to care about you."

"You loved your dad. You wanted to be a good son."

"You're such a sweet kid." Doug shook his head with a sad smile. "You're better than all of us. Well, maybe not Annie," he added with a grim laugh.

"I wish your dad had asked me about the business. I would've given everything to you. I'll give it to you now. I don't want to run the mine, or even own the house. This isn't the kind of life I want to live."

Doug's face filled sorrow.

"My plans are still the same," Jess continued. "I want to go to college in New York, but your dad is still in control of my money."

Doug studied her for a moment. "I'll talk to the lawyers about having him removed as the trustee of your estate. They'll have to agree since he's too ill to deal with it now. I'll make sure you have access to your money."

"Thanks." Jess blinked back tears as she realized he'd just given her freedom.

"I can't believe you don't hate me for what I did."

"Doug, it's really—"

"Please, Jess," he said, interrupting her. "I want you to know the truth. All the times we went out, I was supposed to be trying to get you to fall in love with me. But everything I said to you when we were together, it was all real. I wasn't making up any of that stuff. I did grow to love you, but like you did with me, like a sister."

"Thank you for telling me that."

He bowed his head with shame. "When you said you didn't love me, I knew it was never going to happen. I tried to convince Dad, but he wouldn't give up. He still thought there was a chance. I decided that was the end for me. I wasn't going along with it anymore, and I wouldn't let him hurt you either. That's why I quit college, because I didn't want to leave you alone with him. I shouldn't have waited to tell you. I should have told you the truth on Christmas Day. Then you wouldn't have felt like you had to fight to leave, and maybe he wouldn't have had a heart attack."

Jess felt sad for what he'd been going through. His father had done so much damage to all of them, including himself. If only he hadn't been so blinded by his determination to have everything his way, he could've seen how wrong it was. Perhaps one day he'd understand how much he'd hurt his family, but she wasn't sure his heart could take it when he did.

Chapter Fifty-Six
Do You Love Me?

June 1962

ANNIE TURNED FROM the delivery man at the front door with a tall vase filled with yellow gladiolus. "Jess, take these and find *somewhere* to put them," she said waving her hand. "I need to get the furniture moved out of the way in the living room before they deliver the hospital bed for your uncle."

"Yes, ma'am." Jess took the vase from her and went to the grand parlor.

So many flowers were being delivered to her uncle that the hospital had insisted they be sent to the house since his private room wasn't large enough to contain them all. While she looked around to see if there was a surface available to accept another arrangement, she found the one place that still had space.

Setting it on the closed bar cabinet, she turned around. The sweet smell of roses, chrysanthemums, daisies, and lilies was overwhelming. They were pretty, but their home resembled a funeral parlor. One good thing had come out of it, however. The gate was now left open all day for the delivery men.

If only that had happened when Marty was still coming over, she thought with a sigh. She returned to Annie to help her with the furniture.

Uncle Jonathon was arriving home later that day after a week in the hospital and Annie had been busy getting the house ready for him. It was decided he'd sleep in the living room so he wouldn't have to deal with the stairs until he was healthier, and Jess's father's old bedroom was prepared for a live-in nurse. Doug had moved into his father's room so she could have a private bath.

"How are you doing, pumpkin?" Annie asked once they'd cleared a space for the hospital bed.

Jess shrugged and looked away. "I'm okay."

"I know all of this can't be easy for you. I told your uncle I'm still angry at him for what he did to you and Doug."

"Do you think he understands?" Jess said, wondering if he'd come around while he'd been in the hospital. She hadn't visited him once, nor had anyone suggested she should. Annie and Doug were most likely worried it would be too stressful for his weakened heart. She thought it might be too, but she also wasn't ready to see him yet.

"I don't know," Annie said. "He doesn't say much when I bring it up. He doesn't say much of anything. But then he's never been one to talk about things. Maybe after he's been home for a while and had time to reflect, he'll start to open up."

"I suppose." He'd been so selfish, only thinking about himself for so long. Did he have the ability to change?

The Boy in the Woods

The ambulance arrived that afternoon with Doug following in his car. He climbed out, and hovered nearby while the ambulance crew opened the back. A nurse climbed out, allowing them to pull out the gurney with Uncle Jonathon strapped to it. When Jess saw him, her mouth dropped open. He looked older, with more gray in his hair and deep lines etched in his face.

Once they'd negotiated the gurney into the living room, they removed the straps holding him on the bed. He grunted when the nurse helped him sit up and swing his legs over the side. When he stood, his legs trembled. Wearing a robe over pajamas, he seemed smaller, as if the heart attack had diminished him. Even though it wasn't far to his bed, he struggled to walk to it. When he turned to sit on it, he lifted his head, and met Jess's eyes. He looked away with embarrassment. After a hesitating a moment, she left the room.

On the way to the kitchen, she was awash with conflicting emotions. She was still upset at what he'd done to her, but it was sad to see how damaged he'd been by the heart attack.

A few minutes later, Doug came into the kitchen. He took a pitcher of lemonade out of the icebox. After pouring a glass, he joined her at the table, where she was snapping green beans to help Annie get a start on dinner.

"The nurse and Annie are making sure he's comfortable." He slouched over his glass, the dark circles under his eyes evidence of his sleepless nights since he'd taken over the mine.

Jess didn't reply, not knowing what to say.

His sad blue eyes met hers. "He's so weak."

"He brought it on himself," she muttered, anger flaring up.

He bent forward, eyes on his glass. "I know he did."

Jess felt a stab of guilt. Uncle Jonathon was still Doug's dad in spite of everything.

He drained the last of his lemonade. "We can go to the lawyer's as soon as you're ready."

"I'm ready now." She stood to wash her hands.

Both of them had talked to Mr. Levin in New York, and the three of them decided that Doug should be made trustee of her estate. The law firm in town that worked for Blackwell Iron and Mining had called to say they'd received the paperwork that morning in the mail. As soon as it was signed, Jess would be free from her uncle's control.

As Doug drove them past the open iron gates, Jess said, "I want the gates kept open all the time, not just while your dad's getting flowers. I don't want to live behind locked gates anymore."

"We can do that."

"And I want to be allowed to go into town and see my friends."

"Of course, Jess. I don't want you to feel like you're stuck here. Things will be different from now on."

"I don't want to lie about my friends, or pretend I don't have the kinds of friends I have. I don't think you should either."

He sighed. "You're right. It's going to be a big adjustment for Dad."

"It's something we have to do, Doug. We shouldn't have to sneak around. Aren't you tired of the lies?"

He wouldn't meet her eyes, and there was shame in his expression. "I guess."

The Boy in the Woods

Jess looked out the passenger window. Maybe one day they could talk about the past without Doug feeling guilty for his part in his dad's plan.

Inside the law firm, they were ushered into an office, and after Jess was introduced to Mr. Anderson, one of the firms' partners, they sat in front of his desk. "You understand that this will transfer the role of trustee from your uncle, to Douglas," he said, setting the papers in front of them.

"Yes, sir. I understand," Jess said.

"And when you turn twenty-five, you'll have full access to your money and the estate; all the properties, including the house and Blackwell Iron and Mining."

"Yes, sir, but I want to give the mine and property to Doug. I think he should have it. It's not fair he didn't inherit it because–" She stopped, realizing she was about to say too much.

"It's okay, Jess," Doug said. "They know I'm adopted."

"That is commendable," Mr. Anderson said, nodding. "If that's what you wish, when the time comes I'm sure Mr. Levin will be happy to help with the transfer of ownership."

Jess smiled at Doug.

"Douglas, I need you to sign here, and here." Mr. Anderson pointed to two different lines, and turned to a second page. "And here."

He handed Doug a fountain pen and Doug leaned forward. "Should I sign my full name, or–"

"Yes, your full, legal name," Mr. Anderson said.

When he was done signing, he held the pen out to Mr. Anderson.

"Jessica will sign directly below your signature on the

The Boy in the Woods

second page."

Doug handed her the pen. Jess scooted forward in her seat, ready to sign, then straightened with surprise. She looked at Doug.

"What's wrong?" he said, concerned.

"Uh, nothing," she said, and leaned forward to sign her name under his.

"Thank you." The lawyer scooped up the papers. "We'll send these back to Mr. Levin in New York."

There were handshakes all around and then Jess and Doug left the building. Back in the car, Jess faced Doug as he turned the key in the ignition. "Your middle name," she said.

"What about it?" he asked, a muscle in his cheek twitching.

"It's *Dwyer*."

"Yeah." He put the car in reverse, avoiding looking at her.

"Are you... Is Mr. Dwyer your *grandfather*?"

"Yeah."

"That's why you didn't want to go to the drugstore on Louise's birthday," she said, remembering that long ago day.

Doug didn't respond. While he pulled onto the two-lane highway, more memories came to Jess. It all made sense now. Doug's mother, not Annie, had been in a relationship with Mr. Dwyer's son.

"Have you ever talked to Mr. Dwyer?" she said, wondering if the anger Mr. Dwyer felt towards the family was because he'd been cut off from his grandson.

"No," he said, keeping his eyes on the road ahead.

"Why not?"

"He wouldn't want anything to do with me."

"I can't believe that. Of course he would want to know you. You're his grandson."

In the silence that followed, she thought of Mr. Dwyer. He'd done so much to help Marty, not just giving him a job, but he'd encouraged him with his schooling, and offered him the drugstore. Marty's future was set because of the kindness and generosity of a man he thought of as a father figure. When Mr. Dwyer had reached out to help a teen boy in need, was he thinking of the grandson he'd lost, the one he couldn't help raise and love?

Then Jess remembered her first Christmas shopping trip at the drugstore, and something else clicked into place. "When I wanted to buy a Christmas present for a – a friend one year, he helped me even though he didn't have what I wanted. He sold me something he'd bought for himself, and it was because he thought I was buying it for you, Doug. He was sad when he did it, and I know it's because he couldn't give it to you himself."

Doug pressed his lips together.

"You should go see him. He cares about you." *Marty will be there*, a voice inside her said, and an intense ache came over her. Now that the papers were signed and she was free, they had a chance – if he still loved her.

Doug shook his head. "It's not a good idea."

"I'll go with you. I'll introduce you."

Doug pulled up to the gate and stopped even though it was open. "You don't understand." He turned towards her. "I can't go there."

"Doug, I *know* Mr. Dwyer. He's a kind and decent man, and he's your family."

Doug lowered his head. "He won't want to see me

because – because of what Dad did to him – and to that fellow who works for him."

Jess was suddenly finding it difficult to breathe. "What fellow who works for him?"

"That fellow you were in love with."

Chapter Fifty-Seven
My True Story

December 1961 (Five Months Earlier)

MARTY WALKED INTO the back room of the drugstore after kicking the door frame to dislodge as much snow from his boots as possible.

"How is it out there?" Mr. Dwyer said, bent over his work table, tying string around a wrapped package.

"Some of the sidewalks are cleared, but the roads are still a mess."

"After a blizzard this big, I reckon it will take at least another day for the crews to get to all the roads in town. The phone's been ringing off the hook." Mr. Dwyer straightened, stretching his back. "Why don't you have some coffee and a sandwich? Once you've had a bite to eat and warm up, you can run these new orders out."

Marty went to the electric percolator and poured himself a cup of coffee. After adding three teaspoons of sugar, he stirred it.

Mr. Dwyer joined him and picked up the percolator. "A girl called for you."

"Oh?"

Mr. Dwyer poured himself a cup of coffee. "She wouldn't give me her name. She said she wanted to be sure you were okay."

Jess. She'd called to make sure he'd made it to the drug store. Memories of the night before in the cabin filled Marty's mind, and he turned away to hide his grin from Mr. Dwyer. He was still astonished she'd kissed him, that he'd gotten to kiss her. It was the craziest thing that had ever happened to him. Her body had felt so good in his arms, her lips pressed against his, her fingers in his hair. She'd *wanted* him.

"Marty."

He composed his face before he turned around. "Yes?"

"Are you seeing girls, son?"

Marty dropped his eyes, suddenly uncomfortable. "Uh, not exactly."

"But you're seeing that girl." It was a statement rather than a question.

Marty didn't want to answer, worried how much Mr. Dwyer would want to know, but he didn't want to lie either. "I am, sir."

"You care about her?"

"Yes, sir."

Mr. Dwyer let out a breath, and Marty was surprised by the look of sadness in Mr. Dwyer's blue eyes. "Son, I don't want to meddle in your life. You're a man now and you have the right to make your own decisions, but..." He sighed. "I've seen a whole lot of heartache and trouble caused when fellows aren't careful with the girls they love."

Heat crept up Marty's cheeks, understanding what Mr. Dwyer meant.

"It's a man's responsibility to protect girls, and one of the things you need to protect her from is your urges."

Marty hung his head, unable to look at Mr. Dwyer while his face burned.

"It's not something that's easy to talk about, but I know when you love a girl, what it makes you want to do with her. If you really care about that girl, you'll do whatever it takes to protect her and keep her safe, you understand?"

"Yes, sir," Marty mumbled to the floor.

"Because if you don't, you're going to hurt her real bad, and I know you don't want to do that."

"No, sir," he said, meeting his eyes. Mr. Dwyer was right. He could never allow anything to happen to Jess.

"I'm proud of you, son." He gripped Marty's shoulder. "Real proud." He turned back to the work table and cleared his throat. "With the snow as bad as it is, I reckon you should stay the night again. The only way you'll manage to get home is walking on the highway, and I don't feel right about it. Better to have you safe here than risking your life in the dark."

"Yes, sir," Marty said, trying to mask his disappointment. He couldn't disagree, but he hated not being able to see Jess. On the other hand, she might not be able to make it to the cabin anyway. They'd struggled to walk the path to her home. Now that the storm was over, she'd have to take the long route through the woods.

After snagging a bologna sandwich from the plate next to the percolator, Marty took a seat on the cot Mr. Dwyer had set up for him. He hoped the roads would be plowed by the next day. Then he'd go to the cabin, and hopefully Jess would too. He couldn't wait to see her. He'd take her in his arms and kiss her again. *Beautiful Jess*, he thought, smiling as he chewed. *My girl.*

The next day, Mr. Dwyer came into the backroom where Marty was grinding crystals with a mortar and pestle.

"You'll have to watch the store," he said with a scowl. "Norm Kennedy called and his mother's medications have gotten all mixed up. They left her alone, and she took the labels off all the bottles." He retrieved his coat from a hook by the back door. "It should be slow since people are still digging out, so why don't you get some cleaning done while you're out there. The perfume boxes are getting dusty."

"Will do." Marty reached for a feather duster.

He went up front as Mr. Dwyer let himself out the back and headed for the perfume section. Dusting the boxes, he made his way to the colognes, and then he heard the bell on the door ring. He turned around and his heart leapt into his throat. Jonathon Blackwell had stepped inside the store.

What should I do? Blackwell looked around the shop as he walked to the soda fountain, and Marty's heart raced. He had the urge to run to the back room, and keep right on running, out the back door and down the alley. He took a deep breath, trying to calm himself. He had every right to be in the store.

Blackwell stood in front of the soda fountain counter, looking at the photo of Mr. Dwyer's son, and Marty waited. Since Blackwell hadn't noticed him, there was no point in showing himself if he didn't have to. Then Blackwell sat on a stool, and Marty slumped. He tucked the feather duster out of sight behind an Old Spice display, and approached the soda fountain.

"Can I help you?" He kept his back to Blackwell while he took the apron off the hook on the wall.

"Coffee."

"Uh, we don't have any made." Marty turned around. He searched the man's eyes, wondering if Blackwell would remember him.

Blackwell smiled. "I'll wait."

He didn't remember. Marty took the carafe from the coffee machine and went to the sink.

"You know, you look familiar," Blackwell said.

Marty tensed. "Do I?" He turned on the water and filled the carafe. His heart was racing again, but he tried to stay calm. Even if Blackwell recognized him, what was the big deal? He couldn't do anything to him now.

"I'm sure we've met before."

Marty stayed quiet while he poured water into the top of the coffee machine.

"Now I remember," Blackwell said, snapping his fingers. "You're the delinquent who trespassed on my property."

Marty grit his teeth while he opened the can of coffee grounds. He wouldn't give the man the satisfaction of getting a rise out of him.

"It's funny, though. Back then I didn't know what was really going on."

Fear gripped Marty. What had Blackwell figured out?

"I thought you were some punk looking to make trouble," Blackwell said, his voice lower and more menacing. "But instead you were sniffing around my niece."

Marty continued to measure out the coffee grounds,

The Boy in the Woods

but his hands had started shaking. How did he find out? And then he thought of Jess. If Blackwell knew, had he confronted her? Had he hurt her?

"Oh, yes," Blackwell continued, as if he'd heard Marty's thoughts. "I know *all* about it. How it's been going on for years now."

Marty turned on the machine.

"It's quite the plan you had going, preying on a naive, young girl."

Marty was familiar with this tactic. Blackwell was baiting him.

"Get your hooks into her so you'd be set for life, sucking off her trust fund."

Marty spun around. "That's not true!"

Blackwell leaned back with a smug smile, making Marty regret his outburst. "It's not true now, because you're not going to see her anymore. She's out of your league, boy, and you know it."

Looking in the man's hard brown eyes, Marty swallowed against the lump in his throat. It was a truth he'd carried deep inside him for years. The moment had come when he'd have to give her up, but it was like a knife in his chest.

"Here's how this is going to work," Blackwell said, his eyes cold. "You're going to break things off with her, and you're going to make her believe it's your decision."

"No," Marty choked out, the pain inside him now searing. "I won't see her again, but I won't hurt her."

Blackwell slammed his fist on the counter, his face turning red. "You *will* do it! I will not have her wasting her life away, mooning over you and imagining she's living out some modern-day Romeo and Juliet fantasy."

Marty lifted his chin. "I won't hurt her."

Blackwell straightened, his features smoothing out.

Marty knew what was coming. Blackwell was going to threaten him with arrest, but he didn't care. If Blackwell put him in jail, at least Jess would know he hadn't betrayed her.

"You know," Blackwell said as his eyes traveled around the store. "This old place has been around forever. I used to come here when I was a kid." His attention returned to Marty. "Dwyer's been running this business since before I was born. I suppose when you get that old, you're not as sharp as you used to be. You start making mistakes, not noticing the chemicals have expired, not storing them properly, not being as careful making medications as you should be. If the state board inspectors came here, I wonder what they'd find."

Marty's blood turned cold, understanding the choice Blackwell was forcing him to make.

"It would be a shame if Dwyer had to pay so many fines that he couldn't keep this place going, or even faced criminal charges for risking the lives of the citizens of this town. I imagine prison would be hard on a man his age."

He waited for Marty to reply, but Marty's throat had closed up.

Blackwell stood, reaching into his pocket. "Don't drag it out, boy." He tossed a few coins on the counter. "I don't have a lot of patience."

Marty remained where he was standing, looking at the coins. When the bell on the door rang, signaling that Blackwell had walked out, he put his hands on the soda fountain counter and bent over.

Jess. He squeezed his eyes shut against his tears and took deep breaths. How could he go to the cabin, look his sweet Jess in the eyes, and tell her he wouldn't see her anymore? He *loved* her.

Mr. Dwyer walked in from the back room and Marty straightened, quickly wiping his eyes as he turned in the opposite direction.

"It wasn't too difficult to get the bottles relabeled," Mr. Dwyer said. "I hope they keep an eye on Mrs. Kennedy from now on. The poor woman has no idea what's going on. Any calls for deliveries?"

Marty cleared his throat."No, sir." He went to the hook on the wall while untying the strings on his apron.

"Did you finish the dusting?"

"No, sir. I'll finish now," he said, keeping his back to Mr. Dwyer.

"Don't worry I'll take care of it. You go ahead and get back to your work."

"The feather duster is behind the Old Spice sign."

Mr. Dwyer headed for the display, and Marty went to the back room. At the long table, he took several more deep breaths, trying to keep his emotions under control.

He'd always known that one day he'd lose Jess. Maybe it was best to get it over with now. After they graduated from college, they'd be even more attached. He picked up the pestle, and ground it into the blue crystals harder than was necessary. He didn't want to do it, but he had to let her go, and the thought filled him with more pain than he'd ever felt before.

Two nights later, Marty slammed the cabin door shut,

The Boy in the Woods

and shoved his way through the deep snow. Rage boiled through him while his cheek stung. How could Jess have slapped him?

Halfway to the trees, he heard a sound that made him stop. Jess was wailing inside the cabin. He'd never heard her make a sound like that before, full of anguish. It punctured his anger. He'd broken her – his kind, loving Jess, who had never once done anything to hurt him.

He pressed on, fighting his way through the drifts. He had to get away before her crying made him run back to her. His breathing came in gasps as he struggled forward in the snow, and then the gasps turned into sobs, but he didn't stop. At the fence, he took a moment to collect himself. His time with Jess was over. All he could do now was to tough it out and move on.

While he climbed over the spikes for the last time, he shut down his emotions. Back on the ground on the other side, he headed across the two-lane highway to the dirt road, leaving his childhood behind.

When he walked through the front door of his house, his old man was sitting on the couch with a bottle of beer, watching a comedy show on the TV.

"Hey," he said when Marty passed him on the way to the kitchen, but Marty ignored him. "Hey! Where you been?"

Marty heard the squeak of springs while he opened the bread box. Taking out the bag, he swore. The loaf he'd bought before the storm was almost all gone.

His old man entered the kitchen. "I said, where you been, boy?"

"Did you eat my bread?" Marty shouted, holding up the bag.

"*Your* bread?"

"I'm the one who bought it."

"Why, you worthless bum, you're lucky I let you live here."

Marty forced himself to turn around and took two slices out of the bag.

"I asked where you been."

Marty slapped peanut butter on the bread. "I've been working."

"Don't think you don't owe me rent for the nights you didn't stay here."

Marty ground his teeth.

"I expect all the rent you owe me, and it better come on time."

That was the last straw. Marty spun around. "So I can watch you waste it, pouring it down your throat?"

The old man grabbed him by the neck of his shirt. "How dare you talk back to me!"

He threw a punch aimed at Marty's nose. Marty dodged sideways, but he wasn't quick enough and the fist slammed into his ear. A rage that came from years of weathering abuse at the hands of his father engulfed him, and he shoved his old man backwards. He staggered out of the kitchen and fell to the floor. "Don't you *ever* do that again," he roared, standing over him with his fists clenched.

"You ungrateful–" the old man sputtered, trying to get up. "When I get my belt off, I'm going to tear into your hide."

"Come and try it, old man, and I'll kill you."

His old man stilled, staring at Marty with shock. "Get out of my house! Get out of my house and don't you never

The Boy in the Woods

come back."

"Gladly," Marty snarled, heading for the door.

"When you're freezing to death, don't you come crawling back here, begging me to take you in."

Marty wrenched the door open and it banged against the wall. He stalked out, not stopping to close it.

"Cos I ain't gonna do it!"

He'd lost his wool cap in the fight, but the anger boiling inside him kept him warm. When he reached the end of the dirt road, he tried not to look at the iron fence. He only had one place left he could go now, and he turned towards town.

By the time he'd reached it, the sun had set and a bitter wind picked up. He hurried through the alleyways until he got to the back of the drugstore, where he stopped and reached into his pocket for the keys.

After letting himself in, he paused for a moment to let his eyes adjust to the darkness. Earlier that day, he'd put away the cot he'd been sleeping on, but it didn't take him long to locate it and set it up. Mr. Dwyer had taken the bedding upstairs, but he'd be warm enough in his coat.

The lights came on, blinding him.

"Who's there?"

"It's me, Mr. Dwyer."

"Marty?" Mr. Dwyer said, entering the room with a baseball bat in his hand.

"I'm sorry I woke you. I was trying to be quiet."

Mr. Dwyer went to him with concern. "What happened to your ear?"

Marty touched the ear his old man had punched and

felt something sticky. He didn't realize he'd been bleeding.

"Come here, son. Let me clean you up."

Marty followed him to the long table and sat while Mr. Dwyer collected first aid supplies.

"Did your father do this?" he asked, wiping the wound with a piece of gauze soaked with hydrogen peroxide.

"Yeah. I need to stay here tonight, if I can. Tomorrow I'm going to find a place to live. I'm not going back there."

Mr. Dwyer pursed his lips while he worked. "I've got my son's room upstairs," he said after a moment of silence.

Marty knew he shouldn't accept it, but the offer was too tempting. "I can pay you the rent I would've given my old man."

"The room's sat empty for nigh on twenty years now. I think you should put that money in the bank for when you're ready to go to college."

Marty's reflex was to refuse, but the emotions he'd kept bottled up since he'd left Jess wailing in the cabin came flooding back.

This was one of the worst days of his life. He'd lost the girl who'd been his whole life, his best friend, his love. He'd finally been driven from his home like his brothers, but Dwyer was there for him, taking care of him, offering him a future he never could have dreamed of when he was a kid. He ducked his head, hoping Mr. Dwyer didn't notice the wetness that had collected in his eyes.

Mr. Dwyer tossed the dirty gauze in the garbage and put away the first aid supplies. "It's alright, son. We can talk about it tomorrow after you've had a chance to sleep on the matter."

Marty nodded, not trusting himself to speak.

The Boy in the Woods

"Let's go upstairs and get you settled in."

Chapter Fifty-Eight
Don't Break the Heart That Loves You

June 1962

"WHAT DID UNCLE Jonathon do to Marty?" Jess shouted at Doug, and he winced.

"I'm sorry, Jess."

"What did he do?"

Doug hung his head. "When you told me you were in love with someone else, I told Dad. I thought he'd finally realize it was over and give up. But he put two and two together and figured out that kid who climbed the fence had to be the one. I said where he worked, and Dad went to confront him. I swear I didn't know he would do that, Jess. I never would have said anything if I'd known."

"We were in *love*, Doug," Jess said, tears stinging her eyes as the pain of losing Marty seared through her all over again. "What did he say to him?" she said, wiping her face. Whatever it was, it must have been bad for Marty to break things off the way he did.

The Boy in the Woods

Doug slouched further in his seat. "He had one of the fellows from the mine call over to Dwyer's to get Mr. Dwyer out of the store. That way Dad could talk to him alone. I don't know everything he said, but Dad threatened to go after Mr. Dwyer if he didn't break up with you."

Jess was speechless. Out of all the things Uncle Jonathon had done, this was the worst. *Marty*, she thought, covering her face He had to have been in agony, being forced to choose which of the two people he cared most about to hurt. It must have been torture for him to come to the cabin, knowing he'd have to say goodbye to her. And afterward, he'd have been grieving as much as she had.

She'd *slapped* him, she remembered with a moan, and more tears came. She'd hit him like his abusive dad and called him a coward. Did he hate her now?

"I wouldn't blame you if you never talked to me again," Doug said. "I hate myself for telling Dad, and for not coming clean with you. Now that it's over–"

"It's *not* over. I *still* love him, but he probably hates me. You don't know what you *took* from me, Doug. He was everything to me."

"I can't change what's happened, but I will take responsibility for it. I'll go to Dwyer's and apologize, to both of them. Maybe I can convince him to not hold it against you. If he wants to hate someone, I'll gladly have him hate me."

Searching his face, Jess wondered if there was any room left for hope. Would Marty want her back in his life after everything she and her family had done to him?

"You can come with me. I'll do my best for you, Jess. I'll support you in any way I can, that is, if you want me to."

Jess longed to see Marty, but what if he didn't love her anymore? Could she take the pain of rejection again? Still, it was her responsibility to face him and apologize for

The Boy in the Woods

hitting him. She couldn't live with herself if she didn't. "I'll go."

Doug put the car in reverse. While they rode back to town, that moment in the cabin kept replaying in her head, her slapping Marty so hard her hand hurt and screaming at him. The guilt was unbearable. Would he shout at her when he saw her? Would he throw her out? She'd deserve it if he did, but at least he'd know she no longer blamed him for hurting her.

Doug parked the car in front of Dwyer's Drugs. Now that she was close to seeing Marty, she couldn't stop clasping and unclasping her hands.

"Ready?" Doug said. His face was pale. He was nervous too.

She sucked in a deep breath and blew it out. "Yeah."

Doug held the door to the drugstore open, and she walked in on wobbly legs. Marty wasn't anywhere in sight, but she spotted Mr. Dwyer with his back to them straightening tins of shoe polish. He turned around. "Can I help–" He stopped mid-sentence, his blue eyes going wide.

Doug's hand slipped into hers. She gave it a reassuring squeeze and let go.

"Mr. Dwyer," he said.

"You look just like him," Mr. Dwyer said, and let out a sob. He pulled a handkerchief from his back pocket.

Jess glanced at the photograph of his son behind the soda fountain, and with a shock of recognition, she realized he was right. The resemblance had been there all along. Doug and his father shared the same straight nose, the same square chin softened by full lips, and even though the photo was black and white, it was clear they had the same blue eyes. How had she never noticed it before?

She tore her attention away from the photo, and her

heart skipped a beat. Marty was in the doorway to the back room, gaping at the photo of Mr. Dwyer's son.

"I came here to apologize to you, sir. I came to apologize for everything my – my – dad did," Doug said, stumbling over the word.

"Son, there's no need to apologize," Mr. Dwyer said with a rough voice. "What was done happened when you were a baby. You're not responsible for that."

Marty's eyes locked on Jess. She held her breath, waiting, but he scowled and disappeared into the back room. She blinked back tears as grief engulfed her. *He hates me.*

"That's not entirely true, sir," Doug said. "I'm afraid you may not know all of it."

With her heart aching, Jess decided it was time to face Marty. She'd apologize, and then it would be over. While Doug began a halting explanation to Mr. Dwyer, she went to the rear of the store, and stepped through the doorway. Marty was standing in front of a long table with shelves of medicines on the wall above it, his back to her.

"Marty, can I talk to you?"

"Did he come here to make a claim on the drugstore?" he said, without moving. His voice was laced with bitterness.

"No, he came to apologize."

Marty's head dropped, but he didn't say anything.

She stepped closer to him. "I came to apologize too. Doug told me what happened, that my uncle threatened Mr. Dwyer if you didn't stop seeing me. I'm sorry he did that to you, Marty. And I'm sorry I hit you." She wiped away tears while Marty remained still. "Even though I didn't know why you – I shouldn't have hit you. I know it must have hurt, because of your dad. If I could take it back, I would."

The Boy in the Woods

She waited for him to say something. His shoulders, though stooped, were broader now, and he was wearing his golden brown hair longer. His arms looked as tanned and strong as ever. She wanted to run to him, wanted those strong arms around her, but she couldn't. That would never happen again. "Anyway, I wanted to tell you how sorry I am about everything," she said in a choked voice, struggling not to break down as she backed away. "And I wish you all the best. You deserve it, Marty." She turned and headed for the door.

"*Jess.*"

She stopped.

Marty's eyes were brimming, and his face was etched with torment, but he was holding his hand out to her. She didn't hesitate to run to him, and he grabbed onto her.

"I still love you, Marty," she sobbed, clutching onto him. "I never stopped."

"I still love you too," he said gruffly into her hair. "But we have to let go."

"*No,*" she wailed, and he tightened his hold on her.

"Jess, it will never work. You know your uncle will never accept me."

Gasping, she lifted her head. *He didn't know.* "But – he had – I'm free," she said, her mind too jumbled to form a complete sentence.

Marty studied her with confusion. "What?"

"Everything has changed. My uncle had a–"

"A heart attack. I know."

"He's not in charge of my trust anymore, Doug is. He can't control me. I can do what I want now."

Marty shook his head. "I can't believe it."

"He can't stop me from seeing you, or you seeing me. We can be together." New tears came, but they were tears of happiness.

Marty put his hands on her cheeks, holding her face. "Jess," he said, searching her eyes with intensity. "Is this *real*?"

She nodded and pressed her lips on his. The delicate touch made her eager for more, and she slipped her fingers into his hair to deepen the kiss. His mouth was warm and insistent, and a fire burned through her, the flames taking away all the pain and sorrow of the last few months until all that was left was the two of them, together and complete.

When he let go, they were both breathless. "We're really together," he said as if he still couldn't believe it had happened.

She laughed. "Yes, we really are." She took his hand. "Come with me. There's something I have to do." While she led him in the direction of the doorway, a grin lit his face.

"Where are we going?"

"You'll see."

When they walked back into the store, Doug and Mr. Dwyer were still talking, but stopped when they noticed them approaching. Doug appeared wary, while Mr. Dwyer eyed them curiously.

"Doug, Mr. Dwyer," Jess said. "Marty and I are now going steady."

There was silence for a few seconds, then Doug stuck his hand out to Marty.

After a hesitation, Marty took it.

The Boy in the Woods

"I'm sorry for what my dad did to you," Doug said. "He was wrong to threaten you, but he won't cause you any more trouble."

"Uh, okay," Marty said, letting go after a short hand shake.

"*This* was the girl you were seeing?" Mr. Dwyer asked.

"Yes, sir."

Mr. Dwyer shook his head. "I never would have guessed."

"Marty was climbing the fence to our property for years," Jess said. This was the first chance she'd had to come clean about all her secrets, and she wasn't letting the opportunity pass. "He needed a place to go, to get away from his home, and that's where I met him. I met him at the cabin the first summer I lived here."

Doug's mouth dropped open.

"We've been spending time together almost every day since then."

"She's the one who helped me with my schooling," Marty said to Mr. Dwyer.

"And he kept me company so I wouldn't be lonely."

"You made it possible for Marty to graduate," Mr. Dwyer said to Jess.

"Well, I taught him my lessons."

"Your daddy would be real proud of what you did," Mr. Dwyer said.

She couldn't help smiling. "Thank you."

"We should go," Doug said. "I'm sure you have work to do, and we don't want to keep you."

The Boy in the Woods

"You'll stop by and visit again?" Mr. Dwyer said, his tone hopeful.

"I will, sir. Do you want to stay, Jess?"

She turned to Marty. She could tell he didn't want her to leave, and she didn't either, but there was one more thing she had to do. "I should go home. We have things to talk about with the family, but I'll see you when you get off work, won't I?"

His face lit up. "Yes."

"The gate is open so you don't have to climb the fence."

His expression changed, and he looked away.

"Is something wrong?"

"No," he said, shaking his head, but he wouldn't meet her eyes.

"You don't have to come to the house if you don't want to," Doug said. "My dad will be there, and I know you won't want to see him. You can see Jess at the cabin, or wherever."

Marty seemed relieved. "Okay, I'll see you later." He squeezed her hand.

She wanted to kiss him, but it wouldn't be proper with Doug and Mr. Dwyer there. "See you," she replied, giving him a squeeze back as Doug shook Mr. Dwyer's hand, saying his own goodbyes.

She followed Doug to the door, and as he held it open for her, she took one last look back. Marty was in the center of the store, smiling at her, happiness apparent in his warm brown eyes. She grinned and gave him a wave.

"Now it's time to talk to Dad," Doug said when he turned on the car. "The nurse should be there in case anything happens." He shook his head. "Poor Annie. When she finds out what he did to Mr. Dwyer and Marty, it'll be another blow."

"It's going to be a blow for her to hear I wasn't exactly truthful with her either," Jess said ruefully, realizing the confession she'd have to make.

Doug glanced at her.

"She figured out Marty had come to see me that day he got caught. She doesn't know I've been meeting him at the cabin since then. I don't know if she'll be very happy about it." Thinking about the uncomfortable conversation she was about to have, Jess felt terrible. "I never wanted to lie to you and Annie. It was because of Uncle Jonathon. I had to protect Marty so he could keep coming to the cabin. His dad beats him."

"I get it, Jess. I had my secrets too."

She guessed he meant Donna.

Doug let out a humorless laugh. "I guess we'll all have to get used to living with the truth from now on."

"Yes, we will," Jess said.

Later that evening, Jess heard Marty coming into the cabin, and she left the kitchen where she'd finished setting the table. He looked so handsome as he strode across the floor towards her, and her heart swelled. *He's mine.*

She ran the last few steps and threw her arms around him. Burying her face in his shirt, she breathed deeply, taking in his familiar smell. His face was in her hair and his warm breaths tickled her neck.

After a few minutes, he let go.

"Are you hungry?" She took his hand so she could lead him to the kitchen.

"Yes, but not for food," he growled, pulling her back into an embrace. In an instant, his mouth was on hers and she kissed him back eagerly, the fire consuming her once again. When they pulled apart, she had to catch her breath.

"I've been dreaming about doing that forever," he said, his eyes filled with joy.

"We should eat," Jess said, backing up. They might end up kissing all night if she didn't distract him.

"If you say so." He allowed her to pull him into the kitchen, then wrapped his arm around her waist while he surveyed the table. "This looks real nice."

"I'm glad you think so." She'd wanted to make their first night together as a couple special. Not only did she make sure Annie packed his favorite foods, she'd picked flowers on the way to the cabin and arranged them in a Mason jar on the table.

"How'd they take it at home when you told them about me?" he said, once they were settled on their stools. He'd tried to appear nonchalant, but Jess heard the concern in his voice.

"Once I explained everything, Annie was okay. She's still worried, but I did my best to convince her." Marty's head shot up, and she realized he'd misunderstood her meaning. "She's afraid if we spend time alone, something might – happen." Her face flushed with embarrassment and she dropped her head.

"You know I won't let that happen to you, Jess. I wouldn't ever do anything that would get you in trouble."

She looked up through her lashes, her face reddening more. "I know." She was still glad he'd said it. Both of them would make sure they were careful. "My uncle had a lot to answer for today. He said he was sorry, but..." She shrugged. "I don't know if he can fully understand the harm he's done, to all of us."

"So it's okay for us to be together?"

"Yes, Marty." She reached across the table to take his hand. "I make my own decisions now. Doug is the head of the family, and he won't stand in our way."

His shoulders relaxed. "Good," he said with a smile.

She grinned. "It is good."

His eyes held hers as he soaked in the knowledge that they were free.

"We should eat," Jess reminded him, "or we'll end up staring at each other all evening."

Marty laughed. "Would that be a bad thing?"

Jess handed Marty a sandwich. "It's our first evening together and I don't intend to spend it sitting at this table."

"Yes, ma'am," Marty said, giving her a salute.

After they'd finished eating, Jess suggested they go to the pond. Taking their time, they walked hand in hand, enjoying the cooler evening air. When they sat under the willow tree, Marty put his arms around her and she leaned against him. While he held her, Jess watched the sun set behind the trees, hearing the crickets and thinking that at that moment, she was happier than she'd ever been.

"This changes a lot of things," Marty murmured in her hair. "Mr. Dwyer still wants me to attend college, but I don't know what your plans are."

She pulled away so she could look at him. "I'm going too."

"He said I should go to State. He says they have the best program for pharmacologists."

"Then that's where we're going."

The Boy in the Woods

He hugged her close.

"After we graduate, I can come back with you and help you run the drugstore," Jess said.

He kissed the top of her head. "That would be swell, Jess."

As she snuggled closer to him, a gentle breeze blew through the woods, making the leaves on the trees flutter. The cattails rustled as the willow branches skimmed the top of the water. Marty ran his fingers through her hair, and she sighed with contentment.

Chapter Fifty-Nine
Epilogue: Baby, It's You

August 1962

JESS SURVEYED THE dining room table. "Do we have everything we need?"

"I think so," Annie said.

"I feel like we're missing something."

Annie looked at the place settings. "I'm sure it's all here."

"Do you think we made enough food?"

Annie laughed. "Yes, we made enough. We could feed an army today."

"I want this lunch to go well."

Annie went to her. "It's going to be fine. You don't need to worry about it."

"What about Uncle Jonathon?"

"He knows how important this is to you." She put her hand on Jess's shoulder. "Everything will be okay, pumpkin."

The Boy in the Woods

There was no use disagreeing with her. Annie remained determined to see the positive in Uncle Jonathon, but Jess wasn't sure. Since when did her uncle ever care about what was important to her?

Now that he'd lost control of the family and business, he'd become more insular. He spent most of his time reading in the library or taking walks in the yard with Annie. But what hadn't changed was that he showed no sign he was sorry for what he'd done. He acted as if none of it had ever happened. Still angry about how he'd treated her for the past four years, Jess had as little to do with him as possible.

"They're here," Annie said.

Jess watched through the bay window as a beat-up Buick approached the garage, her nerves increasing. It was too late to back out now. She just hoped her uncle wouldn't say or do something that would embarrass her.

"I'll get your uncle."

Annie left the dining room with Jess following. Annie disappeared into the library and Doug stepped out of the grand parlor. "I was coming for you. It looks like your friends are here."

"Will you come outside and greet them with me?" Jess said.

"They're your friends, Jess."

"I know, but, please?"

"Okay."

Harold, Louise's beau, was climbing out the driver's side door when they stepped outside, and behind him, Marty got out of the back seat. He looked handsome with his golden brown hair neatly styled, and wearing dark trousers and a short-sleeved shirt. Jess smiled, feeling better now that he was there. Then she noticed his dark expression as he walked around the back of the car. He was focused on James, who was scowling at him from inside the open garage.

She turned to Doug. "Look at James. It's like he doesn't think my friends should be allowed to visit."

Doug observed him with a frown. "I'll talk to him later."

"I don't know why he has to be so rude all the time. Can't he at least, just this once–"

"Donna," Doug gasped, his eyes widening. Jess turned back to the car.

Marty was holding the door open for her as she got out of the back seat. She was stunning in a pale yellow sheath dress and white pumps. Her blonde hair was shorter than the last time Jess had seen her and styled in a bouffant with a matching yellow bow pinned on one side. The only thing that marred her beauty was the way she clutched her handbag to her chest and the worry in her pale blue eyes as she examined the house.

"You invited her?" Doug said.

"I didn't think it was fair for me to get to be with the person I love, when you didn't. I hope it's okay that I asked her."

Doug shook his head. "She'd never want me back, not after all the times I hurt her."

"She's here, isn't she?" Jess took his hand. "She *wanted* to see you."

He didn't move, his face full of uncertainty.

"I know you still love her, and I want you to be happy, Doug. Come on, this is your chance." She pulled on his arm, and after a short hesitation, he let her lead him off the porch.

Harold helped Louise out, and she approached Jess.

The Boy in the Woods

Jess let go of Doug so she could give her a hug. "Thanks for coming."

"Gosh, Jess. Your home is so pretty." When Jess released her, Louise leaned close and whispered, "I hope I dressed okay."

"You look great, I love your dress," she said, admiring how her green sundress complimented her auburn shoulder-length curls.

"Thanks."

"Hello, Harold," Jess said, shaking his hand. "It's nice to see you again."

"Hi," he said, ducking his head.

Jess had to suppress the urge to laugh, it seemed impossible that he could still be so shy around her. She turned to Marty. "Hi, Marty," she said, trying not to smile too hard.

He grinned back at her. "Hey."

She felt the urge to hug him, but not knowing who could be watching from inside the house, she squeezed his hand instead. She went past him to greet Donna. "I'm awful glad you came." She took Donna's gloved hand. It was trembling so she gave Donna a reassuring smile.

"Thank you for inviting me," Donna said, and then looked over Jess's shoulder, her expression changing. It was the same uncertainty Jess had seen on Doug's face a moment earlier. Jess turned to Doug and held her hand out to him. When he took it, she placed Donna's hand in his. "Doug is glad you're here too, aren't you, Doug?"

"Yes. Yes, I am. You look beautiful."

He leaned forward to kiss her cheek. When he pulled back, Donna's face was glowing, and Jess felt hopeful. If they could work through everything that had happened in the past, they had a good chance of making it.

Turning to her friends, she realized she'd now reached the hardest part. "Should we go inside?" she said in a cheery tone to mask her nervousness.

"What about our things?" Louise asked. "Should we leave them in the car?"

"Why don't you bring them in?"

Harold opened the trunk and Louise and Donna pulled out canvas bags while Marty took a rolled-up towel. Doug led Donna inside the house, and Harold and Louise followed. Jess held her hand out to Marty, and he took it. Even though he smiled, she could sense he was as nervous as she was.

After leaving their bags in the foyer, they followed Doug through the hallway to the dining room, where Uncle Jonathon sat at the head of the table. As they entered, he stood and Annie stepped close to him. When Marty saw him, he stopped. His hold on Jess's hand tightened, shock registering in his expression. By now, Jess was used to how the heart attack had affected Uncle Jonathon, but this was Marty's first time seeing him.

Jess forced her nerves down and came forward to do the introductions. "Uncle Jonathon, Annie, this is Louise, my best friend."

"It's nice to finally meet you," Annie said, holding her hand out. "I've heard a lot about you over the years."

"It's nice to meet you too," Louise said.

"Louise," Uncle Jonathon said when it was his turn to shake her hand.

"And this is her steady beau, Harold."

Harold bobbed his head when he shook their hands, unable to speak.

The Boy in the Woods

"And Marty," Jess said, not knowing how else to introduce him.

"Marty, I'm glad you're here," Annie said, taking his hand.

"Thank you," he said, smiling at her, but then it dropped when he looked at Uncle Jonathon. Uncle Jonathon stuck out his hand, and they had the briefest of handshakes before letting go, neither saying a word.

Jess breathed a sigh of relief. The most important thing to her was that Marty be welcomed by her family, or at least the family she cared about. With Uncle Jonathon refusing to acknowledge he'd done anything wrong, it had left her in a terrible bind. Marty deserved an apology from him, and that was probably never going to come. It wasn't right, but in the end, Jess decided she wasn't about to let her uncle deprive her of what she'd wanted for so long.

"Dad, Annie, this is Donna," Doug said, bringing her forward.

"It's nice to meet you," Annie said, taking Donna's hand in both of hers.

"Thank you," she replied, almost in a whisper. "Sir," she said, bowing her head when she shook Uncle Jonathon's hand.

Jess felt for her, knowing how intimidated she must feel.

Annie put her arm around Donna's shoulders. "Why don't you sit next to me and Doug, you can sit on her other side."

Donna smiled at Annie. Then at Annie's direction, Louise and Harold took seats on Uncle Jonathon's other side, and Jess and Marty sat next to them. Jess was grateful. Annie had smoothly sat Donna in a sheltered position and put

Marty in the spot furthest from her uncle.

Once they were settled, they passed around dishes heaped with potato salad, buttered beans, fried chicken, jellied salad, and bread rolls. There was a tense silence when they began eating until Annie asked Louise how her family's restaurant was doing. Soon there was a steady stream of conversation and Jess could see her friends relax. Except for Uncle Jonathon and Harold, who remained silent, everyone seemed to have a good time, even Marty.

As they were finishing dessert, Annie looked around the table. "It's great to have all you young people here. This is like the old days, isn't it?" she said to Uncle Jonathon. "You and Billy used to have the best parties."

Jess glanced at Doug, and he seemed as startled as she was. It was hard to believe Uncle Jonathon and her dad had friends over for parties. Except for Doug's birthday and Uncle Jonathon's yearly office Christmas party, they never had visitors.

"Yes, we did," Uncle Jonathon said, and then he looked at his plate. "I miss them." His voice went gruff.

"I miss them too," Annie said, reaching for his hand. "Too many of the old gang are gone."

Uncle Jonathon continued to frown at his plate while Annie blinked hard. They seemed lost in memories, their sadness over long gone friends obvious. Then Jess noticed the intense way Doug was watching Annie holding his father's hand. When his eyes met hers, she knew he'd figured out what she'd known for almost two years – that Annie was in love with his father. Jess gave him a comforting smile, hoping the revelation wasn't as big of a blow to him as it had been for her. "Should we change into our bathing suits?" she said to cover the awkward silence.

Everyone stood, thanking Annie for the lunch.

The Boy in the Woods

"It was my pleasure," she said. "I'll pack some fruit and cookies for you to take to the pond."

Jess led the way to the foyer so they could collect their bags, and then the girls followed her upstairs to change.

"Your bedroom is huge," Louise said as soon as she'd walked through the doorway.

"You're so lucky," Donna said, taking in the room.

"When I first came here, it scared me to have such a large room," Jess said, remembering how unsettling it had been. "It was a big adjustment coming from a tiny apartment in New York City to all of this."

"I bet. And you'd lost your parents too," Louise said. "I could tell you were still sad about them when I met you."

Jess didn't want her friend to feel sorry for her. "It wasn't easy to adjust, but Annie did a lot to make me feel welcome. She took care of me like a mom almost right away, and there was Marty." Louise opened her mouth, but Jess spoke. "I'll tell you all about that later. We should change or the boys will be waiting."

As soon as they had their bathing suits and cover-ups on, Jess led them down the backstairs to the kitchen. Annie was washing dishes at the sink and on the counter was a picnic basket and folded blanket. "Have fun, girls," she said, while they headed to the butler's pantry.

The boys were waiting for them at the front door dressed in swim trunks and T-shirts.

"Took you long enough," Doug said with a smile.

He picked up Jess's portable record player and a stack of 45s, and then held his free hand out for Donna. She smiled as she took it and they went out the front door, followed by Louise and Harold. Marty threw his towel over his shoulder and took the picnic basket from Jess. She slipped her fingers through his and they stepped outside.

With Doug in the lead, they circled behind the garage to the path. They hadn't walked far before Marty's hold on her hand tightened and he stopped. She gave him a questioning look as he pulled her towards him, but he was peering over her shoulder to make sure Louise and Harold hadn't noticed. As they disappeared from view beyond the curve, he wrapped his free arm around her waist, pulling her close.

"I'm overdue for my first kiss of the day," he said. Before she could respond, his mouth was on hers, his tongue touching her lips. It was something he'd done with more frequency, and the effect was always instantaneous. She was consumed with a heat that burned through her entire body. She leaned into him, all thoughts of what they were supposed to be doing driven from her mind. Swept up in the intensity of the moment, he tightened his arm, pulling her against him. When he let go, the corners of his mouth were twitching. "I sure hated having to wait for that."

"Me too," she said, breathless. "But we better go." She headed down the path, but he pulled her back.

"Not so fast. I'm overdue for my second kiss of the day too." Before she could protest, his mouth was on hers again, taking her breath away, but after a moment, she struggled out of his embrace.

"They're going to wonder what happened to us," she said. He kissed her neck and her eyes fluttered closed while he tasted her skin.

"No – they – won't," he said between kisses.

"But what if they come looking for us?" she said, and he lifted his head.

"Okay," he said, letting her go with a rueful smile. "I

can see I'm going to have to get used to sharing you."

She took his hand. "Yes, you are."

They rounded the corner, where to Jess's embarrassment, the other two couples were waiting for them. "We thought we'd lost you," Louise said with a glint in her eye.

"You two lovebirds need to save it for the pond," Doug said, and Jess's face flushed. "You're holding up the show."

"Sorry." Jess turned to Marty. *"I told you,"* she mouthed, and he barked out a laugh, enjoying her embarrassment.

When they entered the clearing, Jess heard an audible gasp from Donna. "What a cute little cabin. Can we go inside?"

"Uh." Doug put his arm around her waist to keep her walking. "It's just a shack. There's nothing to see in there."

Marty and Jess exchanged looks.

"Okay," Donna said, sounding disappointed.

Doug drew her closer. "I can't wait for you to see the pond."

She smiled up at him.

"I know you're going to love it."

Marty whispered in Jess's ear, "Did you ever find out what the deal is with the cabin?"

"No," Jess replied, keeping an eye on the others to make sure they couldn't hear. "Whatever happened there must have been pretty bad, the way everyone acts when the subject comes up. When I'm alone with Annie, I'm going to see if I can get her to tell me the story."

They reached the pond and stashed their things under the willow tree, then waded into the water. Marty and Jess splashed each other and soon a water war erupted between all of them. When they tired of swimming, Jess started up the record player. With song after song playing, they danced the twist while the sun dried them.

Thirsty and hot, Jess went to the picnic basket and passed around bottles of Coca Cola to everyone. When she handed Doug and Donna theirs, Doug led Donna away from the willow tree to sit under another tree by themselves.

"I'm ready to swim again," Marty declared after draining his bottle.

"Not me, I'm tired," Jess said.

"Me too. I want to rest," Louise said.

"Want to swim?" Marty asked Harold.

"Sure," Harold said with a shrug, and they left the girls.

"I didn't know Doug and Donna were back together," Louise said.

"This is the first time they've seen each other in a while." Jess lay back on the blanket. "I'm hoping things will work out for them."

"So... you and Marty. Were you really seeing each other all these years?"

Jess sat up and took a sip from her bottle to hide her sudden guilt. She knew this question was coming. "Yes, we were. I'm sorry I didn't tell you the truth from the beginning."

Louise shook her head. "I *knew* there was something going on between you two."

"I wanted to be honest with you, but it had to be a

The Boy in the Woods

secret. He was trespassing on our property and if my uncle found out, both of us would have gotten in a lot of trouble."

"It's okay, Jess. I understand. How are things with your uncle now? I mean, if Marty and me are coming to your house, it must be a lot better between the two of you."

Jess shrugged. "It's better because he's no longer in charge of my life, but I wouldn't say things are okay between us. He did a lot of things he shouldn't have to me and Doug, and to Marty. Until he's apologized, and I know he means it, I won't be able to forgive him."

"I'm sorry."

"Enough about me," Jess said, wanting to change the subject. "Tell me about you and Harold. It looks like things are going well between you."

Louise's face lit up at the mention of his name. "They're going *very* well." She leaned closer. "You won't believe it. When he picked me up, he asked if he could talk to my dad tonight."

Jess's mouth dropped open. "*No.*"

"Yes. I was so shocked, I couldn't speak. I think he thought I was going to say no."

Jess laughed.

"We've been talking about getting married for a while, but I wasn't sure he'd have the courage to ask my dad for permission."

"Good for him. I'm so happy for you." Jess hugged her friend, and Louise let out an excited squeal.

"Someday, it'll be you and Marty, and then we'll be two old married ladies."

"College first." She looked out at the pond where Harold and Marty were talking while they floated. "Marty

The Boy in the Woods

doesn't want to get married until we've graduated and he can support me."

"Do you think you can wait that long?"

Jess's face flushed, remembering the heat from Marty's kisses earlier. "It won't be easy, but I think we're strong enough." She looked over at Doug, thinking of how much trouble had been caused because Doug's mother wasn't married when she got pregnant. She and Marty wouldn't make that mistake.

"What are you two talking about?" Marty said, appearing through the willow branches with Harold behind him.

"Nothing," Louise said, giving Jess a knowing smile.

Marty flopped on the blanket next to Jess. "Then why is Jess blushing?"

"I'm not blushing." Jess covered her cheeks while her face became hotter.

Marty smirked.

She tried to grab his arm to give him a shake, but he dodged backwards, laughing. "You're incorrigible!"

"What did I do?" he said, his eyes feigning innocence.

Louise and Harold laughed, and even though Jess tried to hold it in, she burst out laughing as well.

Later, when the sun sank below the tree line, Louise stood. "We should get going."

Jess wanted her friends to stay longer since they were having such a good time, but she understood why Louise wanted to go home.

After they packed up their towels, empty Coca Cola bottles, and the 45s, Doug took Donna's hand. "I'm going to

The Boy in the Woods

take Donna for a walk, to, uh, show her around the property. I'll take her home later."

"Oh, okay." Jess had tried to sound casual, but inside she was leaping with joy. Her plan to get them back together was working.

While Doug shook hands with Marty and Harold, Donna came up to Jess and gave her a hug.

"Thank you for inviting me," she said in Jess's ear.

"I'm glad you came, and I look forward to seeing lots more of you in the future."

Doug stepped forward and surprised Jess by giving her a hug too. "Thanks, Jess. Thanks for everything."

"I'm happy to see you two together."

Doug and Donna set off across the grassy field, hand in hand while the remaining four retraced the route back to the house. When they reached Harold's car, Jess and Louise hugged.

"Call me tomorrow," Jess whispered. "I want to hear *everything*."

"I will."

Marty put his arm around Jess's waist while they watched them drive away, and Louise stuck her head out the window. "Bye," she yelled, waving, and Jess waved back until the car disappeared behind the trees.

"What now?" Marty said.

Jess balanced the record player and 45s on the folded blanket so she could take the picnic basket from him. "I'll take these inside, and once I'm changed, I'll meet you at the cabin."

"Don't take too long," he growled, pulling her

closer. "I'm overdue for a few more kisses."

Jess giggled, extricating herself from his arms. "I won't."

Once inside, she set the 45s on the table with the telephone, then went to the kitchen to drop off the picnic basket and blanket. She didn't waste any time changing in her bedroom, excited for some time alone with Marty. The records were still on the table when she came down the stairs, and she decided to put them away instead of leaving them for Annie to deal with. After scooping them up, she went into the grand parlor to deposit them in the stereo cabinet.

"Jessica."

The sound of her uncle's voice startled her. He stood from a high-backed chair in front of the fireplace with a book in his hand.

"I'm going out again, but you can tell Annie I'll be back later." Jess turned her back to him, not wanting him to see how unnerved she was. Sliding open the lid of the stereo cabinet, she hurried to put the 45s away.

"Have your friends left?"

"Not all of them," she said through a clenched jaw. She slid the lid closed and headed for the doorway.

"You understand why I did it, don't you?"

She stopped.

Uncle Jonathon spread his hands out. "It was for Douglas. Everything I did was for him."

"How can you say that? You didn't do it for Doug. You did it for yourself!"

He took a step forward. "That's not true. When Billy died, I could see it was happening all over again. So many

The Boy in the Woods

times, everything would be going as it should, and then it would all be taken from me. Only this time it was Douglas who was losing everything. I didn't want him to be hurt."

"But *you* hurt Doug. Don't you see that?"

"No, Douglas loved the mine. That's what he wanted."

"Doug loved *Donna*."

He waved his hand. "That wasn't serious."

Jess took a step closer to him, her body shaking with anger. He still didn't care that he'd hurt her, but she would make sure he knew what he'd done to Doug.

"That was just a–"

"Donna was here today because he's *still* in love with her. He's been in love with her for years, and you made him break up with her."

"But he would lose everything if I–"

"Would you have given up all of this if it meant you could spend the rest of your life with your wife?"

He opened his mouth to respond, but nothing came out. With a gasp, understanding came into his eyes and he collapsed on the arm of his chair. He put his head in his hands, and Jess left the room.

When she closed the front door behind her, she took in a deep breath. She didn't know if her uncle would be able to come to terms with the rest of what he'd done, but she'd been able to get him this far and she was glad, for Doug's sake.

The puffy clouds in the sky were tinged with orange from the setting sun. It was promising to be a beautiful summer evening, and she hurried to the cabin.

"What took you so long?" Marty said, when she

stepped inside.

"My uncle."

Marty's expression became stony. "What happened?"

"He tried to make excuses for why he did what he did, but I think now he at least knows how much he hurt Doug."

Marty pulled her close. "What did he say?"

"I'll tell you another time." She wrapped her arms around his neck. "Today was the best day of my life. I was able to have you and my friends in my home for the first time, and now I want to spend the rest of the evening with you."

"It *was* a pretty good day."

She leaned against him. "We'll have to do it again soon. Before long, we'll be away at college."

"I don't know," Marty said, stroking her hair. "I reckon we'll be coming home for a few weddings."

"A few?"

"Doug and Donna look like they're pretty tight, and Harold and Louise–"

"How do you know about that?"

"Harold told me." He grinned. "In a few years, it'll be our turn."

The depth of happiness in his brown eyes, almost took her breath away. The two of them had shared so much growing up together. After thinking all that time she would have to let him go, the impossible had happened. They were going to get married and spend the rest of their lives together. "I can't wait," she said, rising on her toes.

"Neither can I," he said, just before she kissed him.

Thank you so much for reading my story! If you enjoyed it, please leave a review on Amazon and Goodreads.

Thank you!

Katherine A. Ganzel

The Boy in the Woods

Acknowledgments

I would first like to thank my husband, Blaise and daughters, Laura, Grace, and Hye-Jin, and my extended family for being so supportive of my writing. I couldn't ask for more.

I would like to thank my thousands of readers who were so kind to share their feedback and give encouragement during the crafting of this story. I owe you more than I can ever say.

I would like to thank my editor, Monica, and my beta readers, Camille Funk, Helen Graul, Emily Nord, Jeff Nevins, Brenda Davis, Aparna Lakkaraju, Mikayla Brown, Elaha Hamidy, Jennifer L Mickle, Josie Cavaliere, Wardah Aziz, Joe Rover, Chantel Bongiovanni, E. Ibara, Yesenia, Jenni Clarke, and Nash Lantey.

And finally, I would like to thank Emmett for his invaluable insights. Without you, there would be no Marty.

About the Author

Katherine A. Ganzel began writing late in life, starting her first novel when her children were nearly grown. She has published The Stolen Hearts Trilogy on Wattpad.com where the first two books were finalists in the 2012 and 2013 Watty's. Her next story, The Boy in the Woods, was a Talk of the Town winner in the 2014 Watty's. The prequel to The Boy in the Woods, The Man Behind the Iron Fence: Jonathon's Story is completed and can be found on Wattpad.

In addition to The Boy in the Woods, he has one published short story, Finding Marty, which was included in the anthology, Library of Dreams.

Currently residing in Ann Arbor, Michigan, she shares her home with her husband and many pets.

You can find the author at www.wattpad.com as KatherineArlene and at Smashwords

Made in the USA
Middletown, DE
24 September 2020